W9-BDY-006

Long, hot summer days…

It's the start of the polo season in the Hamptons,
playground of the rich and famous.

Handsome polo players, celebrities, adored
beauties—no wonder there's a veritable
feast of love, sex and scandal…

Summer
of
Scandals

Summer
of
Scandals

Katherine Garbera
Yvonne Lindsay
Brenda Jackson
Olivia Gates
Catherine Mann
Emily McKay

MILLS
BOON

DID YOU PURCHASE THIS BOOK WITHOUT A COVER?

If you did, you should be aware it is **stolen property** as it was reported *unsold and destroyed* by a retailer. Neither the author nor the publisher has received any payment for this book.

All the characters in this book have no existence outside the imagination of the author, and have no relation whatsoever to anyone bearing the same name or names. They are not even distantly inspired by any individual known or unknown to the author, and all the incidents are pure invention.

All Rights Reserved including the right of reproduction in whole or in part in any form. This edition is published by arrangement with Harlequin Enterprises II B.V./S.à.r.l. The text of this publication or any part thereof may not be reproduced or transmitted in any form or by any means, electronic or mechanical, including photocopying, recording, storage in an information retrieval system, or otherwise, without the written permission of the publisher.

This book is sold subject to the condition that it shall not, by way of trade or otherwise, be lent, resold, hired out or otherwise circulated without the prior consent of the publisher in any form of binding or cover other than that in which it is published and without a similar condition including this condition being imposed on the subsequent purchaser.

® and ™ are trademarks owned and used by the trademark owner and/or its licensee. Trademarks marked with ® are registered with the United Kingdom Patent Office and/or the Office for Harmonisation in the Internal Market and in other countries.

Mills & Boon, an imprint of Harlequin (UK) Limited,
Eton House, 18-24 Paradise Road, Richmond, Surrey TW9 1SR

SUMMER OF SCANDALS © Harlequin Books S.A. 2011

The publisher acknowledges the copyright holders of the individual works as follows:

CEO's Summer Seduction © Harlequin Books S.A. 2010
Katherine Garbera is acknowledged as the author of *CEO's Summer Seduction*

Magnate's Mistress-for-a-Month © Harlequin Books S.A. 2010
Yvonne Lindsay is acknowledged as the author of *Magnate's Mistress-for-a-Month*

Husband Material © Harlequin Books S.A. 2010
Brenda Jackson is acknowledged as the author of *Husband Material*

The Sheikh's Bargained Bride © 2010 by Harlequin Books S.A.
Olivia Gates is acknowledged as the author of *The Sheikh's Bargained Bride*.

Pregnant with the Playboy's Baby © Harlequin Books S.A. 2010
Catherine Mann is acknowledged as the author of *Pregnant with the Playboy's Baby*

His Accidental Fiancée © Harlequin Books S.A. 2010
Emily McKay is acknowledged as the author of *His Accidental Fiancée*

ISBN: 978 0 263 88762 4

025-0711

Printed in the UK
by CPI Mackays, Chatham, ME5 8TD

CONTENTS

Katherine Garbera is a strong believer in happily-ever-after. She's written more than thirty-five books and has been nominated for career achievement awards in series fantasy and series adventure from *RT Book Reviews*. Her books have appeared on the bestseller list for series romance and on the *USA TODAY* extended bestseller list. Visit Katherine on the web at www.katherinegarbera.com.

CEO'S SUMMER SEDUCTION

Katherine Garbera

To my new Soma friends for making me feel so welcome
in their store and being a heck of a lot of fun!

One

Julia Fitzgerald glanced at the Cartier diamond-encrusted watch on her wrist and then back at her notepad. Her boss would be here in exactly thirty seconds. Sebastian Hughes was prompt—he'd said more than once that time was money, and even though he had more of the green stuff than Midas, he still didn't like to waste it.

The Cartier was a constant reminder of why she skipped family celebrations and nights out with the girls—why she put up with such a demanding boss. Sebastian paid her very well to be his girl Friday.

The Seven Oaks Farm was a sprawling green farm with large horse paddocks and barns spread out. Right now it was quiet, but starting tonight it would become the epicenter of high society for the polo season.

"Julia, walk with me," Sebastian said as he strode

toward her. "I need to go down to the stables and check on the horses."

She nodded. She wore a pair of brown pumps with a nice square heel, ideal for traipsing all over the grounds—something that she knew Sebastian would want to do, since they only had two days before the opening of this year's polo season. And the Hugheses were the founders of the Bridgehampton Polo Club.

The polo club was actually an "in residence" club at the farm. Sebastian's family owned the farm with its two large houses and an apartment house that the sheikh had leased for the season for his grooms. She and Seb used his home office as their base of operations.

"This is where I want the tailgating tents set up. Bobby Flay is going to come down here to do one of his throwdowns with Marc Ambrose, our head chef. That will get us some great publicity for the opening. Please make sure that you have every detail of that ironed out."

"No problem," she said, tucking a strand of her long brown hair behind her ear.

Sebastian stopped and looked out over the grounds. He was tall and lanky and had a bit of five o'clock shadow on his jaw. He had a thick head of stylishly rumpled hair, which made him look like he'd just come from the arms of his latest lover.

"That's one thing I like about you, Jules."

"What? That I never say no?"

She spoke in a teasing tone because she knew that was what he expected. But to be honest she was a little annoyed. He called her Jules, even though she preferred to go by Julia. It sounded like a little thing, but she'd spent the first year she'd worked for Sebastian reminding him time and again that she went by Julia.

But it didn't matter. He was Sebastian Hughes, used to getting his own way in all things and intent on calling her Jules. And she was used to her salary.

"Exactly. You never say no," he said with that wide, sexy grin of his.

She hated that she found him attractive. Of course she'd have to be dead not to. He was tall, dark and rakishly handsome—a potent combination.

"Have you touched base with the gossip sites and the papers?"

"Yes. I've been working the phone night and day, making sure we have enough celebrities for them to cover. And rumor has it that Carmen Akins is coming this year. Since her divorce from Matthew Birmingham she is the paps' favorite target. That should guarantee us some extra coverage."

"Stay on it. Coverage is money, as far as this set is concerned. If no one knows they're here, they don't have a reason to come."

"I know," she said.

"After we check out the stables, I need you to run by the rehab home and update my father on our plans."

"Not a problem," Julia said. She actually liked visiting Sebastian's father at the rehab facility for people who were still recovering from chemo and cancer. Christian Hughes was a ladies' man who knew how to pour on the charm. She knew that Sebastian had the same skills, but they had never been directed at her since she worked for him.

Her BlackBerry twittered, and she glanced down at the screen. "Richard is driving up from the city. I've made sure the guesthouse is ready for him, stocked with all his favorite foods and drinks."

"Good. It's important that you see to Richard's

every need. I want him to have a carefree summer. He's stressed out due to that divorce of his."

"You're concerned about Richard's stress level?" she asked.

"It impacts our business. He needs to relax so he can start being engaged at work again."

Richard Wells was not only Sebastian's good friend but also his business partner—they had established the very successful Clearwater Media together. Julia knew Richard's divorce had more than shaken him. It had made him into someone different.

"I will do my best to make sure he enjoys his time here."

"That's all I ask," Sebastian said. "Have you heard from Sheikh Adham Aal Ferjani?"

"His flight is en route. I have confirmed he will be arriving at the heliport. I know you wanted to meet him, but he'll be landing about the same time as Richard."

Sebastian pulled out his BlackBerry and glanced at the screen. "I'll have drinks with Richard later. I will meet the sheikh. Or maybe I can send Vanessa."

"I'll be happy to call her," Julia said.

"Not necessary. I don't know if she can handle the sheikh, actually. What else do I have tonight?"

"Dinner with Cici."

Cici O'Neal was the heiress to the Morton Mansions luxury hotel chain and Sebastian's latest arm candy. She was actually a first-class pain. She called Julia almost every day with a new list of must-haves for her attendance at the polo season.

"I have one more thing I need you to do for me, Jules."

She glanced up from her big, leather-bound day planner into those crystal-blue eyes of his and wondered if he realized that she was on the edge of losing it. Maybe it was because he kept calling her Jules or maybe it was the fact that she was going to have to deal with Cici once again—she couldn't say for certain. She only knew that she was about to go ballistic, and that wasn't like her. She took a deep breath, but yoga breathing wasn't going to help. She was tired of being paid well to be invisible. She doubted Sebastian noticed that she kept her emotions carefully buttoned up. And he didn't pay her much attention anyway.

"Anything," she said with a forced smile.

Out of the corner of her eye she saw the sexy Argentine polo player Nicolas Valera riding out with the team. He was a ridiculously skilled polo player. Rumor had it that when he stopped playing he was going to model for Polo by Ralph Lauren.

"I need you to call Cici and tell her that things are over between us."

"What?" she asked, certain she'd misunderstood him because she'd let Nicholas distract her.

"Call Cici. After you speak to her, send her this," Sebastian said, removing a blue Tiffany's box from his pocket and handing it to her.

Julia automatically took the box before realizing what she was agreeing to do. She wasn't about to call his latest fling and break up with the woman for him. No matter how big a pain Cici was, she deserved to get the news from Sebastian himself.

Julia pushed the Tiffany's box back into his hands. She shook her head. "Absolutely not, Sebastian. You're going to have to take care of that yourself."

Sebastian blinked at his assistant. Jules never said no. At least not to him. He wasn't used to being denied anything. Ever. From anyone. He had learned early that if he acted like a man who always got his way then he did.

"I said no. I'm not going to break up with her for you. A private discussion between the two of you is what is needed."

"I'll decide what is needed. Cici knows we're not serious. This gift will ease any discomfort she might have."

Jules shook her head. "Cici has been calling every day with requests for the entire season here. That sounds serious to me. I'm not doing it. It's the most personal thing you've ever asked me to do—too personal."

"Visiting my father is personal. You have no problem with that," he said. "I don't have time for this, Jules."

"How many times have I asked you to call me Julia? You never listen to me."

"Hey, hold on here. I'm not sure where this is coming from. I thought we settled the nickname thing."

She gave him a sardonic smile. "No, *we* didn't. I just stopped mentioning it when it became clear you were never going to hear me."

Sebastian looked closely at Julia, possibly for the first time since he'd hired her two years ago. She was very attractive with long, silky brown hair hanging around her shoulders and deep chocolate eyes. He had realized when he interviewed her that he was attracted to her. But he knew he would never act on it. Men who slept with their assistants ended up looking like asses in business. And Sebastian was no one's fool. So he put the feelings aside.

But today, with the summer sun shining down on her, he was struck again by how pretty she was wearing a slinky sundress that left her muscled arms bare. With her sunglasses pushed to the top of her head and her eyes glaring up at him, however, she was more than just pretty—she was mad. He knew he was in trouble.

It wasn't anything he couldn't handle or easily rectify. Perhaps if he offered her a big enough bonus, she'd cave and do his dirty work.

"Let's talk, Jules—Julia," he said. He'd thought the nickname was fine, but he saw now that it really got to her. Or maybe it was the fact that he hadn't listened to her. Perhaps he should have.

"You can call Cici. I will make arrangements to deliver her gift," she said.

"I will make it worth your time to talk to Cici for me," he said. He didn't want to have to deal with Cici today. If they'd had a deeper relationship he would never have asked Julia to do this. But Cici was going out with him only because of his connections and standing. He liked the way she looked on his arm, but he had too many details to take care of this season. He'd expected—hell, they'd all expected—his dad to be back at the helm this year. But pancreatic cancer was taking longer to battle than Sebastian and his father had anticipated. His younger sister, Vanessa, said it was because Dad was used to getting his way in all things. So when Christian had told the doctors he needed to be back in his office by May, they'd all expected it would happen.

"Sebastian, are you listening to me? You can't make it worth my while. You're just going to have to talk to her yourself."

Underneath her tough-as-nails exterior, Julia had a soft heart. She was always trying to tell him what the women in his life wanted from him, like little romantic gestures that he imagined his assistant wanted from the men in her life.

"I will give you and your family an all-expenses paid vacation to Capri if you do this." He didn't know her family; he just assumed she had some and she'd like to spend time with them.

"Liar."

"What?"

"You won't let me have that vacation. My parents will be there enjoying Capri, and I'll be on my BlackBerry doing things for you."

"Fair enough," he said. "But how can I function without you, Jules, I mean, Julia. You are my right-hand gal."

"I know that. And you know I'll do just about anything you ask. But I'm not breaking up with Cici for you, Sebby."

"Sebby?"

"Why not? You keep calling me Jules."

He sighed, noting the gleam of amusement in her eyes. "I'm willing to give you fifty thousand dollars to do this."

The gleam of amusement changed to a look of pure anger, which took him aback.

"I thought we were negotiating," he said.

"No, we're not. I refuse to break up with a woman for you. That's a line I won't cross. Visiting your sick father, holding the hand of your divorced partner, keeping tabs on your wild sister—these things fit into my very broad job description. But breaking up with a woman? I won't do it."

"I'll double my offer," he said.

Julia looked stunned for a second. "You know what? I quit. I should have a long time ago. I keep telling myself that hard work will get me what I want, but I just can't do this anymore."

"Julia, you can't quit right as the polo season is starting. You know I need you, and you have me at your mercy."

"Do I? Or is this just another one of your games to get me to do what you want?"

"I do need you," he said sincerely. There was no way he could replace her and get the new person up to speed before the games started. He needed Jules by his side, taking care of the details he couldn't attend to.

"I want to believe that, but you'd say anything to keep me here now."

"Of course I would. I'll take care of Cici, and then we can go back to the way things were," he said.

She shook her head. "We can't. You think I'd do anything for money."

"You've just proven you won't," he said. "If you stay with me through the polo season, I will double your last month's salary and make sure you get a job at Clearwater where you are the boss. You can call the shots from now on. How does that sound?" he asked.

She tipped her head to the side and the breeze blew across the polo field, stirring her hair as they stood near the stables. He saw on her face that she wanted to believe him.

"I'm a man of my word. You know that."

She nodded. "It's a deal. But you have to break up with Cici."

"I already said I would," he reminded her.

She stuck her hand out. "Shake on it."

He did, feeling a little tingle go up his arm. Dammit, he didn't need to be reminded of his attraction to her right now. Her spark of temper and the way she'd stuck to her guns had kicked things up a notch.

"We have a deal, Julia," he said, holding on to her hand longer than he should have.

Julia didn't know what to make of Sebastian's latest offer. But he smiled smugly at her, making her feel like he'd gotten the better of her once again. She glanced at the Cartier watch on her wrist. Apparently she had a price after all. But then she'd grown up in a world far removed from the Hamptons and organizations like the Bridgehampton Polo Club. In fact, she'd never even realized what a big event polo could be until she'd taken this job with Sebastian.

He'd introduced her to a world that was beyond what she'd come to expect during her small-town Texas upbringing. And that world was one she'd always dreamed of.

"I'm going to visit Christian now," she said, pulling her hand out of his strong grasp, trying to ignore the little shiver that ran through her at his touch.

"Sounds good. I need to talk to Vanessa, and then I'll take care of Cici," Sebastian said.

"Later, I'm sampling the menu for our Black and White pre-opening night dinner. I want to make sure we don't have any hiccups." She turned to walk away.

"Jules."

"Yes?"

"Thank you for staying," he said.

He reached out and touched her shoulder, gazing at her with gorgeous blue eyes.

She could hardly think. After two years of being nothing but his girl Friday, she was suddenly very aware of him as a man—and that was dangerous. She didn't want to be attracted to Sebastian Hughes. He wasn't the kind of man who would give her what she needed in a boyfriend. He was more of a wild, hot fling.

Hadn't she seen enough of his dating roadkill to know that?

She nodded. "It was the professional thing to do."

"And you are always very professional."

"I try." This entire day was backfiring on her, and she was losing control of the situation. She stepped back from Sebastian, and his hand slid down her arm.

She almost gasped at the feel of his big, warm hand on her bare skin. He'd never really touched her before. Now she was glad of that—she would have been a mess in the office if he'd been like this when she'd first started.

"I don't think you should…" She struggled to finish the sentence.

"You have very soft skin," he said, stroking her arm.

"I use a moisturizer every day," she said, realizing how inane that sounded.

"I know. Peaches, right?"

"Yes," she said, heat rising to her face. How did he know that?

He rubbed his forefinger at the juncture inside her elbow, and she shivered with awareness. The ripple of his touch spread up her arm and down her chest to her breasts. She felt herself swell—her nipples tingled. She wanted to know what his touch would feel like on other parts of her body.

She shook her head, trying to force herself to stop feeling this attraction to him. To Sebastian Hughes. Her boss.

"I'm your assistant," she said, stepping back from him and pulling her arm from his hand. She wrapped it around her waist, then realized she was broadcasting vulnerability and dropped it to her side.

"For one more season. But I think my rule about no office romances is going to be bent."

"I have no intention of helping you bend that rule, Sebastian."

He leaned in closer, and the scent of his aftershave assailed her. He was taller than she was, and he blocked out the midafternoon sun that shone down on them. "Your eyes tell a different story when they linger on my face and my lips."

She felt her eyes widen. He knew she had lusted after him. So? She was human, and he was a very good-looking man. But he was her boss. And girls that slept with their bosses had notoriously short careers. "No."

He smiled. "We aren't going to be working together for much longer, Julia."

She shook her head. "Sebastian, I'm not an acquisition. You can't just insist that I do whatever you say. And I'm not going to change my mind simply because you won't take no for an answer," she said.

"Yes, you will."

Why was he so confident that he could have her? She thought she'd done a very good job of burying her attraction to him, but apparently it had not escaped his notice. Had he just been waiting for the right moment to take advantage of it?

No. It was too easy to accept Sebastian's public persona as his real personality. Underneath the born-with-a-silver-spoon exterior was the heart of a man who was a good friend, a loving son and brother and a good boss, no matter how demanding he was.

But what exactly was he demanding now?

"Mr. Hughes?"

Sebastian turned to greet the man who was coming across the field, and Julia took the opportunity to disappear. She wasn't sure what had just happened, but she knew she needed to get away from Sebastian Hughes. Quickly.

She made her way back to the office and sat down at her desk. In front of her computer, she regained her equilibrium. At least here she was in control and knew what was expected of her.

She confirmed with Chef Ambrose that he would have the sample menu ready for her to evaluate tonight at 7:00 p.m. Then she took care of a few last-minute details before getting ready to visit Christian.

She pushed the conversation with Sebastian to the back of her mind, shoving her response to his touch deep down into a box and locking it away. She was close to having what she wanted—Sebastian had promised to help her get a position in which she called the shots. She wanted to be in charge. She'd had enough of taking orders and was ready to be the boss.

She wasn't about to mess that up now.

She walked to her Volkswagen Bug convertible and got behind the wheel. It was a nice July day, and though it was hot, the heat wasn't as bad here as it was in her native Texas. She put the top down, tied a brightly colored scarf around her hair and put on her sunglasses.

With a new job, she might be able to afford that Audi A3 convertible that she'd had her eye on. She wouldn't be working with Sebastian, and that was for the best. He was a complicated man and made her life more complicated just by being in it. Should she have walked away?

It would have been hard, because she cared about the

Hughes family. Sebastian; his father, Christian; and his little sister, Vanessa, had all become a big part of her life and walking away…well, she wasn't ready to do that just yet. She had started over once, and doing so again now wasn't in her plans. Her plans, she thought. It would be best if she just remembered that she'd stayed because she wanted to.

She wasn't about to start over again, not now that she was close to having everything she'd always said she wanted. More money, a chance to be her own boss and Sebastian Hughes.

Whoa! She didn't want Sebastian!

She shook her head.

Yes, she did. And knowing she was here for only one more season was going to make him hard to resist.

Two

Christian Hughes was a smooth talker. Julia could hear the sound of his deep voice as she walked down the hall to his room. His private nurse, Lola, smiled at Julia as they passed each other in the hall.

"How is he today?" Julia asked.

"Full of himself," Lola said.

She'd tried to visit Christian yesterday but when she'd arrived, he'd already gone to sleep. So she'd come bright and early this morning with his favorite pastry—a chocolate-chip brioche—by way of apology.

She walked around the corner with a smile on her face. "Good morning, Christian."

"Ah, Julia, always a reason to have a good morning when you are visiting."

She smiled down at him. Christian waved the attendant from the room as Julia came to sit in the chair next to the bed. His head was shaved and he wore a dressing gown of deep navy blue, which made his own blue eyes seem brighter. In his lapel he had tucked a small rose, and he looked dapper and gentlemanly.

He had a breakfast tray next to his bed, and she shifted it into place. The rehab center where Christian was convalescing as he recovered from his latest round of chemo catered to a very wealthy crowd, so his private room scarcely resembled a hospital room. It had marble floors and à Moroccan rug that, according to Christian, Vanessa had purchased for him. There were photos on the wall of Vanessa and Sebastian, plus a few framed prints of past polo champion teams.

Seven Oaks Farm and the polo club were Christian's pride and joy, just as his children were.

"Sorry I didn't get to visit with you yesterday," she said. She took the bouquet she'd picked up at the grocery store out of her large Coach bag and changed the flowers next to his bedside table.

"I understand. Did the sheikh arrive yesterday?"

"He did. Sebastian made sure he was welcomed. His prized ponies are in the stables."

"Have you seen them yet?" Christian asked.

"No, not yet. I'm hoping to get down there today."

"If they are anything like their sire, I think you will be impressed. I'll look forward to hearing about them," Christian said.

Julia made a mental note to bring pictures of the horses when she came back. Everyone had expected Christian to have recovered in time for this season but it was just not going to happen.

"I'll give you a full report," Julia assured him. Then she launched into the specifics of the Black and White event that they were hosting as a preopening party. The details were coming together. Christian asked lots of questions, as she'd expected him to, and he made a few suggestions. When she glanced at her watch, she realized that more than an hour had passed.

He saw her check the time and sighed. "I suppose you have to be going."

"I do. Your son is a very demanding boss."

"I guess that's trying," he said.

"Not at all. He reminds me a lot of you," she said. "I know it takes determination and drive to be successful in life."

"That's true. I tried to raise him right."

"I think you did. Was your wife as driven as you are?" she asked. Julia knew little of Sebastian's mother, Lynette, other than that she'd died in a car accident five years earlier.

"Lynette was a very good wife for me and understood the importance of position," Christian said.

Julia sensed there was more to Lynette than Christian was saying but she appreciated the fact that he wasn't going to gossip about his deceased wife.

"I'll stop by tomorrow," Julia said, standing. She made a note to see when Vanessa would be visiting her father. Julia always tried to time her visits when she knew Christian would be alone. Though she had no close family, she knew it was important that she not intrude on his children's time with him.

"I will look forward to it."

"What will you look forward to, Dad?" Sebastian said, entering the room. He smiled at her and went to give his dad a hug. Julia stood back to give him room. Her gaze lingered on Sebastian, and she had to force herself to look away.

Seeing this side of her boss always unnerved her. In the office he was demanding and could even be ruthless.

But here his guard was down, and she saw the man as a loving, devoted son.

"Seeing Julia," Christian said.

"We all look forward to that," Sebastian said. "Did she tell you that she almost quit on me?"

"No. What did you do?" Christian asked.

"Why do you assume I did something?" Sebastian asked with an easy grin. He winked at her, and she felt a twinge of sexual awareness. It didn't help that she'd dreamed of him last night.

"I *am* your father, Seb."

"True enough. Did Julia catch you up on all of the details for the Black and White event?"

"She did. But I want to hear about Sheikh Adham Aal Ferjani's ponies. Did you see them?"

"I'm going to let you two chat," Julia said.

"Dad, I'll be right back. I need to speak to Julia alone for a minute."

"Take your time," Christian said.

Julia walked out of the room with Sebastian at her side. He led the way down the hall to the sitting room for the visiting families. She took her notepad from her bag so she could take notes, but Sebastian put his hand on hers and shook his head.

"Thank you."

"For what?"

"For not letting yesterday affect the way you deal with my dad."

"I like him."

"Good. He likes you, too. So we're okay now?"

"Yes," she said. "I'm not holding on to any anger from yesterday."

"You were angry?" he asked.

She playfully punched him in the arm, trying to

maintain the relationship they'd always had, but things were changing between them. Sebastian had never thanked her for doing this type of thing before and she couldn't help but think that he was starting to see her in a different way.

"I think you know I was," she said.

"I do," he said, leaning closer to her. The scent of his aftershave made her very aware of him as a man. He was ratcheting up the charm, she thought. She'd seen him act this way before with other women, but somehow this felt different.

"Julia, we didn't get to finish our conversation," he said.

"Which one?"

"About breaking the rules of office romances."

Julia took a deep breath. "I've got work to do and we are done with that conversation."

He stared deep into her eyes and she caught her breath. "Do you really mean that?"

"Yes, I do," she said, but she knew it was a lie. *Oh, my God,* she thought, *Sebastian Hughes has turned me into a liar.* She turned on her heel and fled down the hall before she decided to confess all and give Sebastian carte blanche to her heart.

Sebastian stayed with his father until Vanessa arrived. Christian was much healthier now than he had been two months earlier, but he and Vanessa were still worried about him. They'd never been close to their mother, who had cared more about her position in Hamptons society than about her children. Their father had been their rock.

When he got back to Bridgehampton and Seven Oaks Farm, he found a neatly written note from Julia on his desk in the main house. The scent of her lingered in his office. He was going to miss working with her every day. But if he had his way, he would be getting to know her much better before she left at the end of the season. And who knew what that might lead to?

He suddenly realized he needed to be very careful. Emotional connections could be the downfall of a successful man. Richard was a perfect example of that. His friend's divorce had shaken him and left him devastated. He no longer functioned the way he used to. Sebastian couldn't afford to let something like that happen to him. Maybe he should back off a bit.

He heard footsteps on the Italian marble floor outside his office, and then Julia walked in. "Oh, you're back."

"Indeed, I am."

"I'm going to talk to Chef Ambrose. He is doing a caviar and white truffle hors d'oeuvre for the Black and White event. And last night's didn't taste right. I wanted your opinion on it," she said, sounding completely businesslike.

"I'll come with you," he said, standing. "I only have a few minutes before I head over to the training field. I know that the sheikh's horses will be worked out this morning, and I want to see them in action."

"Me, too," she admitted. "I've heard so much about them. Your father is jealous he can't be here for the event."

"I'm working on that," Sebastian said as they walked. "I'd like to try to get him here for the opening match."

"I will talk to Lola when I get back to the office and see what she thinks about that."

"Good. Please call Dr. Gold and get his opinion."

"I will do that."

They'd reached the main kitchens. Even though it was midmorning, they were already busy. The Seven Oaks Farm had a first-class chef, and the kitchens were always available for their guests and club members.

"Chef Ambrose asked that you wait for him in the kitchen," Jeff said. Jeff was Ambrose's saucier and was a valuable asset.

"Thank you, Jeff." Sebastian led the way.

Julia stood off to one side making notes in her leather-bound planner. The sun shone through the small window, making her dark hair shine. She tipped her head to the side, and he realized again what a beautiful woman she was. Not because she was an asset to his office but because she was a woman. He saw beyond his ultraefficient, never-says-no assistant to…Julia.

"Why are you staring at me?" she asked.

"You're very pretty," he said. Then he realized he sounded like an idiot.

She laughed. "Thanks. Are you just now noticing?"

"I guess I am. I've always thought you were pleasing to look at. But this is different."

She arched one eyebrow. "How so?"

He shrugged. "I'm not sure. But—"

"Sebastian…I don't think—"

He figured she'd say that. "Listen, I want you to know—"

"Sorry to keep you waiting, Seb," Marc Ambrose said. "I had to talk to the Food Network people for tomorrow's cooking event."

"It's not a problem. We didn't mind the wait. Now what do you have for us?" Sebastian asked.

Julia had moved away from him and set down her

clipboard next to the plate that Marc indicated she should taste first.

He knew it was a bad idea to be attracted to his assistant. But he had promised to help her move on, and in his mind, that meant they weren't working together for that much longer. She was no longer off-limits to him.

And knowing that had changed the way he saw her. But he knew she might not feel the same way. He was a demanding boss, and he often saw the telltale signs of her irritation with him. But she always held her tongue and did what he asked.

That had been enough for him before, but now…now he wanted more. He wanted to see those pretty eyes of hers watching him with desire. He wanted her to want him.

He had never been a man to accept no for an answer, and he wasn't going to start with Julia now. But perhaps he was going about this all wrong. Clearly Julia knew him very well—better than most—and wouldn't be swayed by his usual tactics. He was going to have to get real with her. And stop ordering her around like a regular employee. It was time to step up his game.

She glanced at him and mouthed the word *what?* He waited until Marc left the room to get the next plate and walked over to her.

"We are having dinner together tonight," he said.

"At the VIP Black and White event, yes, I know."

"I want you by my side tonight." Apparently it wasn't as easy to stop issuing her orders as he'd thought.

"Why?" she asked. "I think we should cover different sides of the room."

He shook his head. "Not this year. This year you will be with me. I'd like you by my side."

Surprise registered in her dark eyes, and she gave a quick nod as the chef brought them another plate.

Julia's day was very busy, which was good—it kept her from feeling nervous about the dinner. What had gotten into Sebastian? Why had he asked her to join him tonight in such a...formal way? She tried to shake off the anxiety and focus. She looked at her to-do list as she sat in her office. She still had to get down to the stables and take pictures of the sheikh's horses to show Christian tomorrow.

It was almost four-thirty, and she had to go to the house she was staying in to get changed before tonight's dinner. She grabbed her digital camera and headed down to the stables, where she ran into Richard walking back toward the guesthouse. He was a good-looking man, but the events of the last few months weighed on him.

She knew Sebastian was hoping that this month spent at Seven Oaks would relax Richard and help him find his way back to the man he used to be.

"Julia," Richard said.

"Are you enjoying yourself, Richard?" she asked. Though Richard and Sebastian were partners, she didn't work closely enough with Richard to feel comfortable asking him anything more personal than that.

"I am. I spent the morning watching the grooms practice with the polo ponics."

"Are the sheikh's horses as impressive as I've heard?" she asked.

"They are," Richard said. She noticed that he had a far-off look in his eyes, and she wondered if perhaps there was more going on with him than just recovering from his recent divorce.

"Good. I promised Christian a full report on them," she said, holding up her camera.

"I bet you could ask the trainer to talk to Christian via videoconference," Richard said.

"What a great idea. That way he'll feel like he's here even though he can't leave his room. Thanks, Richard."

"No problem. Christian is a great guy. The kind of father I wish I had."

"Don't we all. Sebastian is one lucky man."

"Yes," Richard said, "he is."

Richard left, walking back toward the main building, and Julia continued down toward the stables. Why hadn't she thought of the videoconference idea? It was fantastic. She quickly called Lola and asked if they could set up a computer monitor in Christian's room.

When she arrived in the stables, she saw Catherine Lawson, the sheikh's head groom. "Ms. Lawson?"

"Yes?"

"I'm Julia Fitzgerald, Sebastian Hughes's assistant."

"Nice to meet you. Are you here to see the ponies?"

"I am. I'd also like to ask a favor."

"I can't let you ride them," she said with a grin.

Julia laughed. "Thank God. I'd probably fall off and break my neck."

Catherine laughed, too. "What can I do for you?"

"Sebastian's dad started the Bridgehampton Polo Club and is a huge polo fan, but he can't come to the matches. I was wondering if you'd mind letting me take some photos and maybe a video of you with the horses so he could see them."

"I don't mind at all," Catherine said.

"Great." Julia talked to Catherine for the next hour, spending longer than she'd meant to at the stables. She got the photos and video she wanted, and set up a time for the videoconference.

She got back to the office with no time to spare and found Sebastian waiting for her. "I'm meeting Richard for a game of tennis in the morning. Would you please add that to my schedule?"

"I will."

"Tonight, Carmen Akins is coming to the Star Room. If you could be there when she arrives and make sure that every detail is taken care of, that would be great. We want to make the most of having her here."

"I'm on it. I need thirty minutes to run home and change, and then I'll be back here."

"I'll pick you up," Sebastian said. "We have a date tonight."

"A work function," she replied, trying to not make it seem so intimate. But she knew it was too late. She was going out with Sebastian tonight and she wanted to make sure she looked her best.

"It's a date," Sebastian said. "And later on we will stop by the Star Room and check out the local scene."

"I'm not sure—"

"I am."

She sighed. Sebastian was making it very hard for her to keep up the wall she wanted between them.

"Vanessa mentioned you had Dad talk to Catherine Lawson via a videoconference. That was brilliant."

She blushed at his praise. "It was Richard's suggestion."

"He's a good friend, but you pulled it together."

"Richard seems to be enjoying his time out here," Julia said, not wanting the praise that Sebastian was giving her.

"He is. If you can find time on the calendar for next week, let's see if the three of us can sit down and talk about your new role within our organization."

She nodded. She had made a note to bring up that very topic but hadn't had a chance to. She'd never doubted that Sebastian would follow through on what he'd said. She was glad that he was moving forward with it, but a part of her was going to miss this job and Sebastian.

"Anything else?" she asked.

"Yes. My dad really enjoyed the videoconference. Thank you, Julia."

She shook her head. "I was just doing my job."

"You did a lot more than that."

She needed to change the conversation—he was making her wish that she could keep working for him. But she knew that would never happen. He wouldn't be treating her the way he was now if she wasn't leaving. *Remember that,* she thought.

She left his office without a backward glance, before he could say anything else. Her mind should have been full of all the tasks she still had to accomplish before the end of the evening, but instead she could think only of Sebastian, of the new way he was speaking to her and looking at her. Just yesterday he'd been hitting on her mercilessly. Now he was behaving like a gentleman—almost.

Was he trying to convince her he could be serious about her?

Could she handle it if he was?

Sebastian Hughes was so far out of her league that

she hardly even knew how to process the thought. He was so shockingly wealthy, and she was…not. How would people respond if they were a couple? Would the relationship last?

Or would she just end up with a phone call from his new assistant and a blue box from Tiffany's?

Three

It was almost eleven o'clock, and the Star Room was busy and noisy—exactly the kind of atmosphere they needed. The local jet set was in attendance, as well as celebrities who'd either come up from the city for the weekend or flown out from the West coast.

All in all Sebastian was pleased by what he saw. The Bridgehampton Polo Club was still a draw and he was glad to know that the VIPs would still turn up, even if he was at the helm and not his father.

He spotted Julia standing near the bar talking to Catherine Lawson. Both women seemed out of place in the nightclub but for different reasons. Despite the martini in her hand, Julia looked like she was still working, and Catherine looked like she wanted to be back out in the stables.

Sebastian made his way through the room, taking the time to talk to everyone he saw. Working the room was important not just because it was the start of the season but because the Hughes family had always tried to make everyone who came for the opening feel at home.

When he was finally at Julia's side, she had finished her martini and was chatting with two young women he didn't recognize.

"Hello, Sebastian," Julia said as he approached.

"Evening, Julia, ladies." The women said their goodbyes to Julia and walked off. They were as alone as they could be in the crowded club.

Julia smiled at him. "Do you want a drink?"

"No. Just a word with you—in private."

"Good. I'm ready for my evening to be over," she said.

"I bet you are," he said. "Long day?"

"Yes, it has been. Shall we debrief?" she asked.

"Let's go outside."

"It's closed tonight," she said.

"Not for me."

"I forgot who I was with."

"Did you?"

"Only for a minute," she said. "I'm going to miss this next year."

"You'll still be invited next year," he said. "You are a valuable part of the Clearwater family."

She nodded. She meant she'd miss being with him. And that was the truth, she thought. It didn't matter that she'd tried to pretend she was working tonight—she'd enjoyed herself at dinner. Had liked being at Sebastian's side as his hostess, and that was the job she really wanted. But Sebastian was dangerous. She had to be careful not to let him seduce her into falling for him. He was a player and he would move on.

Sebastian led the way out of the Star Room. He didn't

want to think about Julia not being here with him next year. Even though he'd given his word to help her find another job—a position where she could be in charge and not have to answer directly to him—he wanted her by his side.

"I've been thinking about your new job."

"What about it?" she asked. "Did you change your mind?"

"Not at all. You know I'm a man of my word."

"I do know that. I'm just afraid that…well, that something will come up and I won't get a good position within Clearwater."

Sebastian shook his head. "Not if I have anything to do with it. I want you to have what you've worked so hard for. That's important to me, Julia."

She glanced up at him. Her hair was pulled back in a loose chignon, making her features seem even more delicate than usual. In the moonlight, with the warm summer breeze stirring the air, she seemed ethereal. Like she didn't belong here with him. In fact, he knew she didn't. Julia Fitzgerald wasn't his kind of woman. Or rather, he wasn't her kind of man.

He knew she was too solid, too real for the come-and-go relationships he usually engaged in. She wasn't the kind of woman who would accept a piece of jewelry when things ended. And they would end. Because he couldn't be the man she deserved. But for some reason that wasn't enough to deter him. He still wanted her.

He closed the distance between them and caught a tendril of hair that had escaped from her updo. He twirled the long, silky length around his finger.

"Sebastian, as I tried to say earlier, this isn't a good time for this," she said. "I have thought of nothing else but my career since I came here. I don't want to lose my focus now."

"I know that, Julia, but I'm afraid that I can't ignore this any longer. There is something about you...."

"Are you saying I've mesmerized you?" she asked in that sardonic way she had.

"No. I'm saying that now that I've allowed myself to see you as a sexy woman, I can't get you out of my head."

"A sexy woman? I'm not that. Not at all."

"Yes, you are," he said. There was something innately sensual about Julia. He'd noticed from the very beginning, from the first time he'd interviewed her. She was simply someone who moved with a very feminine awareness of her body. She was at home with herself, and that made men appreciate her looks.

"I'm not prepared to be your latest fling," she said.

"I'm not asking you to be," he said.

"Then what is it you want, Sebastian?" she asked, looking up at him with confusion in her eyes.

She licked her lips, and he realized he knew exactly what he wanted. Her mouth under his and her curvy body pressed against him. He pulled her to him and lowered his head to take her mouth in a kiss that would change everything.

Julia hadn't meant to kiss Sebastian, or even let him kiss her, but once his mouth touched hers all bets were off. He tasted of the martini and something that was uniquely Sebastian. His mouth felt right against hers— exactly right.

Even his hands on her shoulders, drawing her closer into the curve of his body, felt right. He skimmed his hands down her bare arms and tangled his fingers with hers as his mouth roamed and his tongue plunged deeper, making her forget about everything except this balcony and this moment.

The summer wind stirred the hair at the nape of her neck, wrapping around them both. She let go of his hands and slipped her arms around Sebastian's lean waist, holding on to him as he deepened their embrace. His free hand roamed up and down her back, urging her closer to his body. She liked the feel of his muscled chest pressed against her.

He pulled back and dropped a couple of nibbling kisses against her lips. Then he opened his mouth over hers, and she felt the brush of his lips and the humid warmth of his breath. She shivered in response to his touch.

She felt wicked kissing him out here where the world could see. She'd never done anything the least bit untoward—and now she wanted to. With Sebastian, she wanted to be the woman she'd never had the courage to be.

She put a hand on the back of his neck and felt the smoothness and coolness of his hair against her fingers. She traced a line over his neck and down to his shoulder and then pulled back to look up at him. His eyes were half-closed, and in the moonlight she'd never seen anything sexier than this man.

She'd never felt as feminine and womanly as she did in his arms. It had never felt this intense with other lovers. The fire in her veins overpowered her and scared her. Suddenly, she didn't want to feel it anymore.

She jerked back from Sebastian, stumbling a little until she found her balance.

"That was interesting," Sebastian said.

"That was wrong. I work for you."

"Not for much longer."

"I'll still be working for you, even if not so directly. I can't do this, Seb...."

"Why not?"

"This is too intense for me. Our relationship works because I do my job and keep my head down. I don't want to start this."

"I don't think I can stop now that we've started, Julia."

She stared at him in the moonlight. His features were stark, and she saw the signs of desire in his eyes. He wanted her. Heck, she wanted him, too, but how was she going to work with him when she knew what it felt like to be in his arms?

This was a mistake. She should have quit when he'd asked her to break up with his girlfriend.

"Please stop overthinking this, Julia. We'll figure it out."

"How?"

"By not worrying about it. We're both adults. I know we can handle this."

"I don't want people to think of me as your latest fling." Not that she cared what other people thought, but what she felt right now was too intense to share with anyone.

"No one needs to know," he said. "It will be our business. I want it to develop naturally. I like kissing you and having you in my arms."

"I like it, too," she admitted. "But something doesn't feel right."

"What is it?" he asked.

"We're from two different worlds. Yours has money, mine doesn't. I can't exist in your world unless I'm working for you. And I don't think you'd know how to put a woman first if you tried."

Sebastian didn't say anything. She wondered for a moment if she'd said too much, but to be honest, she didn't care. She had to tell the truth, and if he walked away now, that was better than if she slept with him and fell for him and he walked away later.

She'd express-mailed enough Tiffany's boxes for Sebastian to have a very clear picture of just how often he changed women in his life.

"You deserve to come first, Julia. Every woman does," he said. "I'm not in a position to make you any promises about anything except that I want you and will make you a very happy woman while we are together."

Was that enough for her? Could she give in to her desire and just deal with the consequences later?

"I'm not sure—"

"Why not have a little fun?" he asked with that roguish grin of his. "We aren't going to be boss/assistant for much longer. You could use some fun, Julia—you work too hard."

He had a point. And she'd always wondered what it would be like to have a summer fling. She'd always been too serious to accept an offer like this before. And she'd certainly never received such an offer from a man like Sebastian Hughes.

"Okay," she said. "But please, Sebastian, remember who I am. I'm not Cici. I'm not a girl who wants to end up on the society page."

"I know what kind of girl you are." He pulled her into his arms again. "This is the kind of deal that needs to be sealed with a kiss."

He lowered his head, and this time she thought she was ready for the intensity of his kiss but she wasn't.

His touch was electric and made everything feminine in her react.

It was going to be one heck of a summer.

Sebastian wanted to take Julia home with him tonight. But he wasn't sure she was ready, so he glanced around the room.

"Do you mind staying a little longer?"

"No! I mean, that's fine with me."

He knew he'd read Julia right.

He watched Julia as she talked to Scott Markim, a professional basketball player, and his latest girlfriend. She handled herself with great ease for someone who claimed to feel out of place. Julia was the first woman he'd been with at an event like this who didn't constantly demand his attention. Julia did her own thing.

It was as if they were equals.

Of course they were equals. She'd probably smack him if she realized he'd thought something like that. But what he'd meant was she didn't need him to tell her where she belonged. Though this wasn't her social set, she blended in well here. During the last two years that she had worked for him, she'd picked up all the skills she needed to fit right in.

They had a deejay tonight but tomorrow night after the opening day polo match, they were going to have Brit pop sensation Steph Cordo performing live. Steph was the U.K.'s answer to Kelly Clarkson. She was young and had a voice that could wring emotion out of any lyric. And it had been a coup for them to get her to perform here. In their favor was that Steph was a Brit and she liked polo.

He spotted Vanessa working her way through the crowd with Nicolas Valera, and he watched her. Last year she'd had an affair with him, and it had ended badly with Vanessa acting out and giving the gossipmongers a lot to talk about.

Sebastian kept an eye on her because he didn't want a repeat of last year. He felt partially responsible for her behavior because their father had been sick, and Sebastian had taken on more duties, leaving Vanessa at loose ends.

She'd been easy prey for a playboy like Nicolas. Most of the polo players were treated like rock stars and had groupies. He never wanted Vanessa to be thought of as being in that crowd, though she had always been a wild child. He imagined that came from being the much-loved, very indulged younger sister.

When it was clear that their mother was not at all interested in her children, Sebastian had stepped in to make sure that Vanessa felt loved and never suffered from the cold shoulder that their mother offered. He knew it wasn't the same—a brother could never take the place of a mother—but he had tried.

"Enjoying the night?" he asked Vanessa as he dropped a kiss on her cheek.

"I am. Lots of fun people here tonight. You did a great job of getting exactly the right mix."

"Thank you," Sebastian said. "I think most of the credit should go to Julia. She worked the phone like nobody's business."

"She is an asset. I know Dad thinks she's part of the reason you've made the club even more successful."

"Part of the reason? He doesn't think it's just my charming way?" he teased her.

"You're the only one who thinks you are charming."

"I'm wounded."

"As if," she said. "What do you know about Nicolas Valera?"

"Nessa, you're not getting involved with him again."

Vanessa's face went white for a second. Then she groaned. "Stop being overprotective, Seb. I want to know if he's involved with anyone right now. Just curiosity."

"He hurt you," Sebastian said, wrapping his arm around her. "Stay away from him. You know he's not the man for you."

"I don't need your protection any longer," she said.

"I'll decide that."

"You are impossible," she said, and turned and walked away.

Sebastian took a sip of his soda water and watched his little sister walk away. He just wanted what was best for her. He didn't want to see her hurt again by Valera. And if she was talking about Valera, then that meant she was still interested in him.

"Still bossing your sister around?" Richard asked behind him.

"Always. I was going to come by your place for a drink in a little while."

"I needed some air, so I decided to put in an appearance after all."

"Are you doing okay?" Sebastian asked, leading the way to one of the banquettes at the edge of the room.

"I'm fine. I just don't want to spend too much time thinking, you know?"

Sebastian did know. After his mother's death, he'd analyzed that relationship up one side and down the other trying to figure out what he could have done differently. Could he have been a better son to her? Would that have changed the way she'd treated him?

In the end, he'd come to no conclusion except that he needed to stop thinking about it.

"I do. Have you been relaxing at all?"

"Had an early morning walk around the grounds and checked out the stables."

"There are lots of women here that can help you forget your troubles, Rich."

"I'm not ready for lots of women," his friend said.

"Fair enough. But don't let too much time pass."

"I'm not like you are, Seb, always moving on. I liked being married."

That was true, from what he'd observed. A part of Sebastian had always envied Richard's marriage and the fact that he had someone to go home to every night. But seeing the pain his friend had been in…that had convinced Sebastian the short-term affairs he was best suited to were better in the long run anyway.

He glanced up and saw Julia was looking at him. He wondered how he was going to say goodbye to her. He wanted her more than he had any of the other women he'd had in his life. But he knew he wasn't marriage material.

He knew he shouldn't be thinking of goodbye when they were just starting their affair, but remembering that this would end was important—he didn't want to end up like Richard.

Not that she'd even want him. She was a career-focused woman. Still, he wanted her. And he didn't want to have to think about why he did.

Four

Julia went to work the next day expecting things to be different, but in the office Sebastian was the same. He'd kissed her, talked her into an affair, and then backed off. She felt unsure and hated that.

He was hosting Geoff Devonshire, a schoolmate of his who was the son of Malcolm Devonshire, the billionaire entrepreneur, as well as a minor royal. So he was out of her hair for the day. She spent the bulk of the morning checking gossip Web sites and making sure that the polo club and Seven Oaks Farm were mentioned. It was important that the people who wanted to be talked about were, and the ones who wanted to keep their presence a secret did.

And Sebastian and Christian before him had prided themselves on giving their guests what they wanted.

Her phone rang, and she answered it without looking

at the caller ID. "Bridgehampton Polo Club, Sebastian Hughes's office, this is Julia."

"Jules, baby, how's it shaking?" Sebastian said.

She rolled her eyes. "I thought I said don't call me 'Jules.'"

"Now that we've kissed, I thought a nickname would be appropriate."

She shivered, remembering his mouth on hers. And the steamy dreams it had inspired last night. She hated to admit it, but "Jules" was growing on her. Perhaps it was because his voice softened the slightest bit when he called her by that nickname. "Fine. You can call me that when no one else is around."

He laughed. "You do remember I'm the boss, right?"

"Not in our off-hours."

"Are you going to order me around?" he asked. His voice dropped down to a low, husky tone that made her stomach flutter.

"Do you want me to?" she asked.

"Maybe. I prefer to be in charge, but if you need to be then we can talk about it," he replied. She could hear the grin in his voice.

"Did you call simply to give me a hard time?" she asked.

"Not at all. Listen, Geoff's wife is arriving at the heliport, and we can't break away from our round of golf. Would you pick her up?" Sebastian asked.

"What did I say about personal errands?" She was already putting her computer to sleep and getting her keys out.

"Believe it or not, this is polo club business. She's the heiress Amelia Munroe."

"Okay, I'll fetch her for you. Is she here low-key or should I let the media know?" Julia asked.

"I think low-key for right now. I'll give you the go-ahead when they want people to know she's here. They're staying in the guesthouse."

"Should I take her there?"

"No, bring her out to the stables. Geoff is going to take her riding."

"Anything else, boss?"

"Yes."

She waited, pen in hand so she could take notes.

"Thank you for taking that video over to Dad. He called me to tell me how great you are and warned me not to let you slip away. Did you set up another videoconference?"

"Yes, with Nicolas."

"Do you think that's wise?" Sebastian asked. But she ignored that. His affair with Vanessa had left tension between the two men.

She was touched that Christian had called to praise her. But she knew that no matter what his father said, Sebastian wasn't going to hold on to her. Not professionally—and not personally, either.

Suddenly she wanted to ask him some questions. She needed to figure out why Sebastian was always going through life—and women—at breakneck speed. Why didn't he want to put down roots the way his father had? What was it that made Sebastian the way he was? Of course, those were the very questions that would send a man like him running in the opposite direction.

"I didn't mind talking to your dad," she said, changing the topic from Nicolas. "I like your dad. He's funny and charming. How did that skip you?"

Sebastian laughed. "Thanks for agreeing to get

Amelia. Geoff is actually doing business on the golf course, and he didn't want her to be alone."

"I don't mind. I'll text you when we're on our way back."

"Thanks. You know, I've thought of nothing but our kiss last night and taking it further."

"Me, too," she confessed.

"Good."

She hung up and tidied her office area, which was really a sitting room attached to Sebastian's office. Her little Louis XIV desk was beautiful and she loved the large glass windows that looked out over the Seven Oaks Farm. From here she could see the paddocks where the horses were roaming. She could get used to this life.

She had to sign for a FedEx package, which she put on Sebastian's desk before leaving. She drove to the heliport to pick up the heiress and found that the paparazzi were already alerted to her presence.

Amelia smiled as she walked over to her, waving at the media. "Are you Jules?"

Julia nodded, knowing that Sebastian was having a bit of fun with her. "I am. And you're Amelia Munroe-Devonshire, right?"

"Too right," she said crisply. "Geoff's doing a deal right now?"

"That's what I heard, but he and Sebastian are on the golf course so it's anyone's guess what's going on."

"I know my husband. If he's not here, it must be business."

She smiled at Amelia's confidence. She was a woman very secure in her relationship, and Julia envied her that. She wished that she could be that confident in her relationship with Sebastian. But she knew when she'd agreed to date him what she was getting into. Had she made a mistake?

"I'm to take you to the farm. I think you attended our season two years ago, is that right?" Julia said as they got into her car and pulled away from the heliport. Julia had looked up Amelia and made sure she knew everything there was on the heiress.

"I did. It was a lot of fun. Christian Hughes is such a darling man. I didn't know that Geoff and Sebastian had been school chums until we were married."

Amelia kept Julia's mind off the fact that she was becoming more and more insecure about her decision by the minute. No matter what Sebastian said, she knew she didn't belong to the world of people like Amelia and Geoff Devonshire. Wouldn't Sebastian just get bored with her and go looking for someone who did belong? As she dropped Amelia off, she hesitated for a moment, wanting to join them. But in the end, she still felt like Sebastian's girl Friday, not his lover. And there was a good chance that would never change.

Sebastian watched Julia drive away, wishing she had stayed. But it would have been awkward to explain why he'd had his assistant come to dinner with them. And though Geoff was one of the most discreet men he knew, he sensed that he couldn't push things with Julia.

She seemed skittish about making their relationship public. And given his track record with women, he supposed he didn't blame her. But he wanted her around—he wanted to look at her, hear her laugh, touch her flawless skin. He missed her while he spent the evening with his friend and new wife. They were obviously in love and enjoyed being married.

He made an excuse to Geoff and Amelia and cut out

early. Not that the lovebirds would miss him. He drove to the guesthouse where Richard was staying, but his friend wasn't home. He didn't relish going back to an empty house. He wanted to see Julia. He couldn't deny it any longer. He needed to taste those lips again, to feel her perfect body pressed against his. He didn't want to wait.

He dialed her cell, and she answered on the first ring.

"Sebby, what's up?"

"Nothing, Jules. I was calling to see if you were free," he said.

"I am not."

"Got a date?" he asked. He didn't think she had time in her life to date anyone, and he knew Julia well enough to know that if there was a man in her life, she would have told him to shove off when he'd kissed her last night. Damn, was that only last night? It seemed like a lifetime had passed since he'd held her. He needed more—a lot more.

"I do have a date. With my DVR. I've been recording that new detective show with the crime writer and policewoman, and I'm dying to catch up."

"You'd rather watch TV than come out with me?"

"Sebastian, it's bad enough that I let you make me a workaholic. I need a night where I sit and stare at the wall to recover."

"Can I come help you recover?" he asked.

He turned his car around and headed toward Julia's place as she gave him a bunch of reasons why he shouldn't come over. She was just finishing as he pulled into the long driveway and drove up to the front of the house.

"Are you outside my door?" she asked.

"Yes, ma'am. Are you going to let me in?" he asked.

"Why aren't you partying with the Devonshires?" The front porch light came on and then her door opened.

"Because they're newlyweds and it was too…"

He hung up his phone without finishing his thought, pocketing it as he got out of the car. He walked toward her front door and took in the sight of her. She was gorgeous, and he couldn't wait to be with her. He didn't want to feel this way—not about Julia and not right now. But that didn't change the fact that he did.

"I suppose you think I'm going to let you in," she said.

They both knew she was going to. "I do indeed. And I'm hoping you have more of whatever it is you are drinking."

"I have an entire case. It's from the Grant Vineyards."

"Sabrina's family?"

"Yes. She sent a case to you, as well. It's at the office."

"I see you took the pinot noir," he said, knowing from past experience it was her favorite.

"I did," she said. They were quiet for a moment. She didn't step back and welcome him inside her house. "Sebastian, if I let you in, you have to promise not to make me just another speed bump on the Sebastian Hughes girlfriend superhighway."

He stared down at her. Her thick, dark hair hung in long waves past her shoulders. She had on a figure-hugging camisole, a pair of skintight jeans and no shoes. Her pretty little feet had delicately painted red nails. And she looked small and feminine. And he knew that he couldn't just move ahead the way he usually did with his damn-the-consequences attitude, no matter how much he wanted her.

Julia needed more from him. For once, he wanted to deliver. But he didn't know if he had anything to give. Could he keep a promise not to break her heart?

Did he want to?

Hell, yes, he did want to. He'd never felt for anyone what he felt for Julia. She was the last person in the world he'd want to hurt.

"Julia, give me a chance," he said, his voice husky with desire.

She stood back and held open the door. He stepped over the threshold and took in her house. Though she'd only been here for a few months, she'd taken the time to decorate. In the hallway sat a small framed photo of Julia in her cap and gown at college graduation, with two older people he guessed were her parents. He picked the frame up and looked at it as she closed the door behind him.

"You don't talk about your parents much," he said. "Would you like to invite them to visit?"

"I wish I could, but they died five years ago."

"Oh. Julia, I'm sorry."

"They died shortly after that photo was taken. I guess it was time for me to grow up," she said.

"But that doesn't mean you were ready to."

"No, I wasn't," she admitted. "Come into the living room. I'll get you a glass of wine."

She left him standing there. He looked down at the photo, feeling like an ass for having worked with her for two years without once asking about her family. What kind of person would do that?

He vowed to himself that he would start making up for lost time.

* * *

Julia opened the cabinet and found a second wine-glass. The last thing she wanted to do was be with Sebastian while she was in this kind of mood. She'd been feeling lonely and melancholy—and like she was in the wrong place in her life. And then he'd shown up.

He looked good—better than she wanted him to. She kept hoping that the lust she felt for him would simply fade away, but no. No chance. Every time she saw him, she felt a fierce desire for him that wasn't going away.

"You okay in there?" he called from the living room.

"Yes," she said. She pulled out the breakfast tray she used every morning and put the wine bottle, their glasses and some snacks on it. She didn't have a sophisticated palate, as she was sure Sebastian did. She just ate cheddar-flavored popcorn with her wine and some fresh fruit. It would have to do.

She hefted the tray and carried it out to the living room. Sebastian had taken off his suit jacket and tie, and he'd rolled up his shirtsleeves. His sock-clad feet were propped up on the glass coffee table, and there was an NBA game on the TV.

"Uh-uh. We're not watching sports tonight."

"I just wanted to catch the score," he said, getting to his feet and taking the tray from her. "I wouldn't dare get in between you and your DVR." He winked at her, and she felt heat rise to her face. He was sexy as hell—and he knew it.

She scooped up the remote, hit the button for the DVR selections and found the show she wanted to watch.

Though now that he was here, she doubted she'd be able to concentrate and enjoy it. Instead she'd probably just sit next to him wishing he'd unbutton his shirt buttons so she could see more of his chest.

She was pathetic. She'd turned into a sex-crazed woman because Sebastian had kissed her. One kiss, she thought. That was all it had taken to make her rethink everything she thought she knew about herself.

It was a spectacular kiss, though.

She handed him a wineglass and took one for herself. She almost apologized for not having the right cheese and crackers to go with the wine, but she stopped herself. If he wanted to be with a nice, regular girl from Texas, he would just have to get used to her ways. Right? Right.

"To new relationships," Sebastian said, toasting her.

"Cheers," she said, clinking her glass against his before taking a sip. She maintained eye contact while she sipped, as her father had taught her to do when she'd first gotten old enough to drink.

She noticed that Sebastian did it, too. But maybe he was just flirting with her. When he looked at her like that, she could understand why women fell for him… hell, she was doing it right now.

"I might not be the best company tonight."

"I'm not either. I just needed to see you," he said.

His words caught her off guard and touched her as nothing else could have, but she didn't want him to know that. "I'm glad."

"You're not giving an inch, are you?" he asked.

"What do you mean?"

"You can't let down your guard," he said.

"I'm afraid to. I'm worried that I'm just letting you take advantage of me."

"Julia, I don't think you're the kind of woman who lets anyone take advantage of you."

"It's tough with you, Sebastian. You're very… persuasive."

He gave her a half smile. "I'm used to having my way."

"Duh," she said.

He grabbed a handful of popcorn. "I like this."

"Sorry, I don't have cheese."

He looked confused for a second. "No, I mean *this*. Us."

She blushed. "Sorry," she said again.

He watched her for a second. "Julia, I'm sorry I never asked about your parents."

"My…? Oh. Well, why would you have?" she asked.

"You know everything about my family. You visit my father for me, and I never once wondered about your family."

She took a sip of her wine and grinned at him. "You're you-centric."

"I am, aren't I? That's my dad's fault."

"How is Christian to blame for that?" she asked.

"He told me I was the center of the universe. And I believed him."

That startled a laugh out of her. Sebastian could be alarmingly charming when he wanted to be.

"Is there any amount of money I can offer you to put the game back on?"

She shook her head. "It's time to be Julia-centric."

"Jules, baby—"

"Stop it. You're making me like a nickname that I hate."

"Why do you hate it?" he asked.

She took another sip of her wine. "In middle school, some kids used to call me Jules Verne. I liked to read sci-fi and I guess they thought it was funny."

"Julia, I never meant to make you feel bad. I was just teasing," he said.

"I know. Which is why I never made a big deal about it."

"Until I asked you to break up with Cici and you blew up at me."

"You had that one coming," she said. "You should have known better than to ask me to do that."

"I should have. But I'm glad I did because now I get the chance to know the real Julia Fitzgerald. And I wouldn't trade that for the world."

She could hardly believe her ears. There was something about Sebastian tonight that was very sincere and sweet—something she'd never seen before. The combination of his charm, sincerity and sexy good looks was deadly. Especially when he was saying things she'd always wanted to hear from a man.

She didn't stand a chance—and she knew it.

Five

Sebastian enjoyed being with Julia much more than he would have enjoyed being in the hustle and bustle of the polo club, which surprised him. Normally an evening on a woman's couch had him faking an emergency text from the office—something Julia would see right through. But the point was that he didn't want to leave.

He liked sitting next to her and listening to her rant about commercials that demeaned the intelligence of the average viewer. He liked her laugh, too. He rarely heard it in the office. The show they were watching had a lot of zingers between the male and female leads, and Julia laughed a full-bodied, sensual laugh at each one.

When they finished the episodes she'd recorded they'd almost finished a bottle of wine. Julia was looking very relaxed—and very sexy. She turned off the DVR and clicked another button to turn on some music.

"I can't stand silence," she said.

"Why not?" he asked as she stood to clean up the snacks.

"I had to live in my parents' house for six months after they died. I didn't have a job or money or anything, and the house was so quiet," she said. She glanced over at him. "Do you know what I mean? Was it like that after your mom died?"

"No. It wasn't the same for me. I still had my dad, so I was focused on keeping him healthy."

"You have a great dad," she said.

Sebastian knew that. He'd heard it his whole life. But to be honest, he'd taken his dad for granted until the cancer scare. He'd always just assumed that Christian Hughes would live forever because he was such a force to be reckoned with. Seeing him sick and almost losing him had shaken Sebastian to the core.

"I'm glad Dad is doing better now."

"Me, too. I'm glad I'm getting to know him. He's a charmer, like you," Julia said as she carried the tray into the kitchen.

"Like me?"

"Stop it. You know you can be charming when you put your mind to it."

He put his wineglass down and walked up behind Julia. He put one arm around her waist and drew her back against his chest, lowering his head so his chin rested on her shoulder.

"Can I?" he asked.

She turned her head, and her big eyes captivated him instantly. "I don't want to like you, but I can't help myself."

He hugged her tight. "Lucky for me," he said.

"I wanted to dance with you last night," she admitted.

"In the Star Room?"

"Yes."

"Why didn't you say something?" he asked.

She shrugged. "It didn't seem right."

"Let's dance now. No one can see us but the moon," he whispered in her ear, turning her around and taking her hand.

"Really?"

"Yes," he said. He led her into the living room and opened the doors to the large patio that overlooked the ocean. Sea grass and dunes protected their privacy. He found a music channel on the television that played love songs and then drew Julia into his arms.

He danced her around the living room, using all the knowledge he could remember from his seventh-grade group dance classes. "I'm afraid the best I can manage is a turning box step."

"I can't even do that. Maybe an electric slide."

"Not really a romance dance," he said.

"Are you romancing me?" she asked.

"I am," he said. He put his hands on her hips and they swayed together to Michael Bublé singing "Call Me Irresponsible." He found that ironic, wondering if he was being irresponsible right now. Was letting this relationship develop a mistake? He was making unspoken promises he wasn't sure he could keep, but walking away was no longer an option.

He wanted to share that bond he'd seen between Geoff and Amelia tonight. He now understood why Richard had been so devastated when his marriage ended. His friend had seen a glimpse of what life between a man and a woman could really be like, and then he'd had it snatched away.

Had Richard chosen the wrong woman, or were all relationships simply destined to end?

The next song was Percy Sledge singing "When a Man Loves a Woman." Julia closed her eyes and started moving her hips to the music, rubbing her body against his. The tips of her breasts brushed against his chest, and it took him only a second to realize she wasn't wearing a bra beneath her camisole. He put his hands on her hips and pulled her even closer.

Holding her this way made him believe this was where he was meant to be. It didn't matter that he wasn't thinking with his brain. It felt like everything in his life had narrowed down to this woman. He felt so lucky to be here with her.

She'd given him more than he'd expected, and he wanted everything she had to offer him—every last bit of Julia. He needed to claim her for his own, and nothing was going to stop him.

Except maybe Julia. But she wrapped her arms around his neck and stood up on her tiptoes to kiss him; he knew she wasn't going to send him home.

It was now or never. And he was choosing now.

Julia had never taken much time for personal relationships. Losing her parents had scared her, and she'd reacted by deciding to take care of her financial future first, always figuring that the rest of her life would sort itself out sometime. But it hadn't.

When she'd started working for Sebastian, she'd gotten even further away from finding a person to share her life with. But with Sebastian's arms around her, she felt like she was finally letting herself have…love? Could it be? Or was she confusing lust and love? If she was, she could be in serious danger.

She soon lost track of her thoughts as he slipped his hands under her camisole and slid them across her back. His hands were big and warm as he rubbed them up her spine and cupped her shoulder blades. His movements caused the fabric of her top to rub over her bare nipples, making them harden even more than the feel of Sebastian's arms around her had. She wanted more.

She really hadn't had that many lovers. Two guys in college, but that was it. Tony had taken her virginity in the back of his Mercedes-Benz. They'd had sex two more times before he had moved on to another girl, and then she'd dated a guy her senior year—Michael. They'd actually lived together. She'd thought…who knew what she'd thought.

She shifted, trying to get closer to him, but the fabric between them frustrated her. She reached for his shirt and drew it out of the waistband of his pants so she could tunnel her fingers underneath it and feel the warm skin of his back. She wanted to see his chest.

She fumbled with the buttons of his shirt. He unbuttoned it smoothly and quickly and took it off. His chest was smooth and nearly hairless, with just a small dusting between his nipples and a thin line that disappeared into his waistband. Before she knew what she was doing, she was tracing that line.

Circling his belly button, she saw his penis jump in reaction to her touch. She scraped her nail around the edge of his belly button, and his breath sawed in. She could tell he liked that.

She bent down and licked his stomach, using her teeth to tease him with little bites. His hands tightened in her hair, and she slowly nibbled her way down toward his belt. Then she worked her way back up until she was standing again. She brought her hand up between his legs and stroked his erection through his pants.

She reached lower and cupped him, and he let out a groan. He reached between them and undid his pants, and she slid her hand inside to find his hot, hard length. He found the hem of her shirt and drew it up her body until her breasts were revealed to his gaze.

"You are very pretty, Julia," he said.

She flushed as he stared at her breasts. He touched her softly, using only the tips of his fingers on the full globes of her breasts, and then rubbed his thumb back and forth over her nipple until she was almost crazy from his touch.

She felt a pulse between her legs—and wetness. She wanted him. She needed him right now. She reached for the button on her jeans and unfastened it, desperate to feel his hand between her legs.

He stopped her. "Let me do that," he growled.

The feel of his hands reaching between their bodies and unzipping her pants nearly undid her. She felt his fingers dip beneath the fabric of her bikini panties, and then his finger brushed her. She shivered and went up on her tiptoes as she continued to stroke his erection.

He lowered his head to hers and kissed her as he had last night. Desire was raging through her. She rubbed the tips of her nipples against his chest and moaned. He plunged his hand into her hair and held her as he plundered her mouth. His other hand reached lower until he could slip the tip of his finger inside her body.

She shuddered as she felt his finger start to enter her. It had been a long time since a man had touched her, and she knew she was going to come. But she didn't want to—not yet. She wanted him right there with her when she went over the edge.

She tried to bring him along, but he took her hand from his erection and held it loosely. "I want you to come for me."

"I don't think I could stop if I tried," she said breathlessly.

He pushed his finger farther into her, and his thumb found the center of her passion again. Rubbing lightly up and down, he brought her so close to the edge she could hardly stand it.

He lowered his head and took the tip of her breast in his mouth, suckling her deep and hard. The next thing she knew, stars exploded between her legs as every nerve ending in her body started to pulse. The explosion rocked her and sent waves radiating out from where he touched her.

She couldn't stop rubbing against his hand, and the sensations continued to build. He switched his attention to her other breast as he took his hand from between her legs, leaving her weak in the knees.

He lifted her into his arms and carried her to the couch, where he laid her down and gazed at her for a moment.

"Take your pants off, Julia."

She pushed her tight jeans down her legs as he watched. Sebastian kneeled beside her and reached out to touch her hip, drawing his fingers down her thigh toward her knee and then back up again to the junction between her legs. He skimmed her neatly trimmed hair and brought his fingers to his face. "I love the smell of you."

No man had ever loved anything about her. Not the way Sebastian did. She wanted to be his completely.

"Are you... I'm not on the pill," she said.

"I don't have a condom," he said.

She bit her lower lip. "I bought a box this afternoon."

"You did?"

"Yes. I... You... Let's just say I was hopeful that we'd be able to use them sometime soon."

"That seems..."

"Not me, I know. But once I agreed to be with you, I wanted to be prepared. I don't want to look back and say you seduced me into this."

He kissed her deeply. "Me either. Where are they?" he asked.

"In the bathroom."

Now that they were talking and he wasn't touching her, she was starting to feel very exposed. But he stood up and pulled her up with him. "Show me your bedroom. And then let me make love to you all night long."

Sebastian was glad they had to slow down and come into her bedroom. As desperate as he was to get inside her beautiful body, he wanted their lovemaking to be perfect.

"Get undressed and get in bed. I'll be right back," he said.

He went into her bathroom and saw the box of condoms on the counter. Julia had invested herself in him and he was touched. He took off his pants and his socks. And then he took the box and went back into the bedroom. She'd turned off all the lights except for a small nightstand lamp that cast the room in a soft glow.

She lay in the center of the bed under the sheets, the pillows piled high behind her head and her thick hair fanning out around her. She was so sexy and captivating; he paused at the end of the bed just to look at her.

"Will you move the covers aside so I can see all of you?"

She hesitated. He knew he was asking for a lot. Despite being bold and brassy in the office, Julia was shy about her body. She slowly pushed the sheet down her body. Each curve that was revealed made him harder.

Her breasts were full, with large pinkish-brown nipples, which were hard. He remembered the velvet smoothness of them in his mouth. Her waist was small, and there was a slight curve to her belly. His eyes traveled to the dark hair that guarded her secrets and down long, toned legs, which were pressed close together as if she were afraid to reveal too much. He took the covers and flipped them back toward the foot of the bed. Then he took her ankles in his hands and drew her legs apart. She turned a bright red as he stared at her most feminine part.

He knelt on the bed and crawled up toward her, pausing to drop a kiss on her secrets and letting his tongue tease the bud that was the center of her pleasure. Then he moved up over her body.

He braced himself on his elbows and lowered his hips until he rested in the cradle of her thighs, shifting until he felt the humid warmth of her against him.

Then he pulled back, cursing. "I forgot the condom."

She laughed, and he reached for the box that he held crushed in one hand. He opened it and pulled out the packet.

He put it on as quickly as he could and then moved back over her. The wall of his chest brushed over those hard nipples of hers, and he rotated his shoulders so his chest hair abraded them.

Then he let his hips fall against hers. He moved his

hips until his tip was at the entrance of her body. He leaned in to her and bent his head so he could whisper directly into her ear.

"You are so sexy."

"You make me feel that way," she said.

"I want you."

"Me, too, Sebastian."

She tried to lift her hips and force him to take her, but he made her wait until she was moving frantically against him. Then he slipped inside her just slightly, so that she could feel him but still not have him as deep as she wanted.

She moaned and begged him for more, which got him harder than he'd ever been in his life. And slowly he gave her what she wanted. He kept her with him the entire time, wanting her to come when he did. He soon felt the telltale tightening at the base of his spine and was surprised by how quickly he was going to come.

But this was Julia, and nothing was normal with her. All of his reactions were off the scale with this woman. He clasped her hands and stretched her right arm over her head as he slid all the way home, making her gasp. He plunged deep into her body, and his hips pistoned in and out until he heard a roaring in his ears. He felt the tightening of her body around his and then he could hold it no longer—he exploded.

He called her name and thrust into her three more times as his body emptied itself of everything. Then he collapsed against her breasts.

She wrapped her arms around his shoulders and held him to her. Her fingers toyed with the hair at the nape of his neck as her breathing slowed. He knew he couldn't fall asleep on top of her, but he wanted to sleep right there in her arms, wanted to let the solace he felt continue to wrap around him.

He pushed himself up on his elbows and looked down at her. She smiled up at him.

"I want to spend the night," he said. "Can I?"

She nodded. "I want you to, as well."

He moved the pillows around until he was comfortable and then pulled her into his arms.

She shifted, her breasts brushing against the side of his body and her hand drifting low on his stomach to rest against his hip bone. He held her close and knew that even though only the moon had witnessed their becoming lovers, the world was going to know about it soon. Julia had changed something inside of him that he'd never realized could be changed—and nothing would ever be the same.

Six

Julia spent her days working like crazy—and her nights in Sebastian's arms. The month of June was flying by, and she still hadn't figured out exactly what the future held for her, but for the first time since her parents' death it didn't matter. She wasn't planning carefully for her next step. Instead she was simply living her life in the warm embrace of the sexy man who was stealing her heart.

She made sure that every detail of the season's polo matches went off without a hitch. She visited Christian, whose health improved a little more each day. She suspected his days in rehab were almost over and had no problem imagining him sitting next to Sebastian in the owner's box by the end of the season.

Tonight was a low-key weeknight, and there were no big events. She hadn't seen Sebastian all day, but he had left her a message telling her to meet him on the beach behind her house. Her skin tingled at the very thought of it.

She went home, changed into a sundress and made it down to the beach just as the sun was beginning to set. Sebastian was nowhere to be seen, but two Adirondack chairs sat side by side facing the ocean. In front of them was a fire pit with some low coals burning.

There was a note tacked to the cooler that informed her he would be right back.

She sat down in one of the chairs and closed her eyes, enjoying the summer breeze and the evening. She wanted nothing more than to figure out how to make this relationship last. And it *was* a relationship—not an affair.

They spent most nights in her bed, and they ate breakfast together almost every day. When they were at the office, he sometimes pulled her into his arms behind closed doors simply because he had to kiss her—his words.

She had no idea where this was going, and despite his reassurances that he was crazy about her, she was nervous. She needed a plan. She needed to know what the next step was going to be so she could believe that she wasn't going to end up with a broken heart.

Sebastian had arranged an interview for her with the VP of PR for Clearwater, John Martin.

The interview was promising, and she was flattered that Sebastian's recommendation had led to it. She was excited about it, mainly because she knew the moment she took that job she'd be saying goodbye to Sebastian, the boss. And then she could focus on Sebastian, the man.

"Hello, Julia."

She stood up at the sound of his voice and saw that

he was loaded down with a picnic basket. He wore a pair of faded, low-slung jeans and a lightweight summer sweater. His feet were bare.

"What can I do to help?"

"You can sit back and talk to me. I've got dinner under control."

She sat back down.

"Do you want a drink?"

"Yes, please," she said.

He opened the cooler, took out a chilled wineglass and poured her some pinot grigio. He handed her a glass and then poured one for himself. She held hers up to his and said, "To dinners on the beach."

He clinked her glass and then went back to the cooler. "What happened at the office after I left?"

"Not much. That Broadway producer canceled his event for next week. I did a little scrambling but found another sponsor for it."

"Good."

"I e-mailed you the details."

He nodded. "Did John get back to you with a job offer? I know June is the end of our agreement. We'll be right in the thick of polo here."

She took a sip of her wine. "Yes, he did."

"Are you going to take it?"

She didn't know yet, but she knew she couldn't say that to Sebastian. He'd done his part, getting her an interview for a job where she could run the show and advance her career. But now she wasn't sure she wanted it.

"I haven't decided yet. But either way, you're off the hook."

"No, I'm not," he said, handing her a plate with grilled salmon, sautéed new potatoes and steamed asparagus.

He made his own plate and sat down next to her.

She was impressed he went to all this trouble for her. She picked at the food, not ready to have this conversation with him. She wanted Sebastian to be the self-involved boss she'd always known him to be instead of the kind, caring man she'd come to know. It would make accepting the job so much easier. It would make leaving him so much simpler.

In the past few weeks, she'd started to fall for him. Okay, she'd fallen for him completely—and that was probably the dumbest thing she'd ever done. She wasn't the kind of person who fell in love easily, she thought, but somehow, with Sebastian, she had.

"If that job isn't what you had in mind, don't take it. There's no hurry for you to leave. I have other colleagues I can get you an interview with," he said.

That made her care even more for him. He wasn't just using money to ease his way out of his obligation. He was making sure she had everything she needed to be happy, and that meant more to her than she could say.

"Sebastian, you've done your best by me, and I can't ask for anything more."

He looked at her with a smile that took her breath away. "I wish you would," he said.

Sebastian loved the way Julia looked tonight. She was simply dressed, but she looked amazing sitting on the beach by the small fire. Sharing the end of the day with her was something he'd gotten used to, and he didn't want to give it up.

He was coming to depend on her personally as well as professionally, and that should have worried him, but it didn't. There wasn't a relationship in his life he didn't know how to control and keep on track, and he couldn't see why this one would be any different.

He noticed that she was shivering, and he pulled a cashmere shawl out of the picnic basket that he'd purchased for her earlier in the day.

"Lean forward," he said.

She did, and he draped it over her shoulders.

"This is really nice," she said.

"I'm glad you like it. It's for you."

"You picked this out for me? Without any help?"

"I have my ways, and I can't reveal them," he said.

She laughed. "Who did you scheme with?"

"My *dad*. He told me that I worked you too hard and that you needed a nice night of relaxing and a present. And he wanted me to thank you for your brilliant inspiration that allows him to see what's going on at the Seven Oaks."

Thanks to Julia, Sebastian had put in a direct satellite link to the polo matches that beamed a private broadcast to Christian's room. His father hadn't missed a match all season. Julia was one of the most thoughtful people Sebastian had ever met.

"Can you believe how well Nicolas played today? I think he really is the best player of our time," she said.

"I agree. He is a dynamo on the field," Sebastian said. And off it, as well. The man never stopped moving. He was very popular in the VIP tents and more and more women were trickling in as the days progressed. Every one of them wanted a piece of the star player. "I'm concerned about Vanessa. She was asking about him the other night, and Nicolas already broke her heart once."

"Your sister is a smart woman. She won't let him hurt her again."

"You think so?" Sebastian asked her.

"Yes," she said, but she wasn't sure. She was falling for Sebastian and she knew that it wasn't smart, yet here she was having this romantic picnic with him.

She finished her meal and he tucked the plates back into the basket. He stoked the fire and drew their chairs closer together.

"Why did you invite me here tonight?" she asked.

"To say thank you."

"But I haven't done anything this week that I wouldn't have done before, and you never even bought me dinner," she said.

He loved that she didn't let him get away with anything. Many of the women he'd dated just let him have his way—but not Julia.

"I totally took you for granted before, and I'm trying to make it up to you. You are coming to mean more to me, Julia, than I ever expected."

She tipped her head to the side and stared at him in the flickering glow of the fire's light. "You, too."

"Me, too?"

"I didn't want to fall for you, Sebastian. I've seen how long most of your relationships last. But this time it feels different. I guess that's because I think I'm different."

"You are," he said. She cared about the people around her, and because of that, he was slowly coming to see the world through her eyes. His priorities were changing. For the first time, he was living his life and not worrying about moving ahead and conquering the next big thing.

"I'm glad you feel that way. I think that's part of the reason I'm reluctant to take John's offer."

"Why?"

"I was thinking that I could stay in your office but take on more of a managerial role instead of being your girl Friday. We make a really good team."

"We do," he said. But he didn't know if working together would be a good idea now that they were sleeping together. He was distracted by her. He wanted to pull her into his arms and make love to her at the oddest moments during the day, and that wouldn't be very appropriate in their office back in Manhattan.

He had given her his word about the job, doing his best to find her a good one. But seeing her every day had become important to him, and he knew he didn't want to let her slip away now.

He couldn't.

Damn. When had she slipped past his guard?

"Sebastian?"

"Huh?"

"What do you think about that?" she asked.

She wanted to talk about it, but he didn't have the words. He could smooth talk anyone into anything, but not Julia. She was different. Being with her had changed his life.

And that scared him.

Sebastian Hughes, who'd never let anything frighten him, was suddenly afraid of losing this woman.

"Let's go for a walk. I want to show you something." He stood up and offered her his hand, but she just stared at it.

"I guess that's an answer."

She rose and started to walk away, but he stopped her.

"I don't have an answer for you. I'm not sure how to put my emotions into words. I only know that you are important to me, and I'm not sure working together will be what either of us needs."

"Will you consider it?"

He nodded. "I don't want to lose you."

She turned and put her arms around his waist, hugging him close. "I feel the same way. I'm falling for you, Sebastian."

He had no response. He only knew that having her in his arms made him feel like everything was right in his world. But try as he might, he couldn't tell her that.

Julia dressed for work the next morning with care. She had a jam-packed day with lots of VIPs to attend to. Sebastian had been gone when she woke up, but there had been a note on her table saying he wanted to see her for dinner that night.

She thought last night had changed the dynamic in their relationship, and she felt like they might have a chance of making it last for more than the summer. But she had to wait for Sebastian to tell her what he thought.

As she drove to work, she saw the polo ponies being exercised and realized how much she loved this place and the life she had here. She didn't want to risk losing any part of it. In fact, she wanted to build on it.

And the nights in Sebastian's arms were part of that. It was only once she knew that she was leaving this that she'd realized how much she wanted to stay.

She would miss talking to Christian every day and hearing his stories about starting the polo club. She'd miss talking to celebrities and their handlers and making sure that all details of their visits were taken care of.

She stopped and looked around her, realizing if Sebastian didn't agree to her idea she was going to have to leave. She didn't think she could stand to keep working at Clearwater and not work closely with Sebastian, especially if their affair ended. She'd miss him too much.

She knew more about the inner workings of the celebrity media machine than most people did—and she liked it.

She entered her office, gathered the faxes and went over the itineraries and menus for the day's events.

Grant Vineyards and Wines was sponsoring a pre-polo match event and of course the sheikh would be attending. Despite his new bride, women were still flocking to see him and hoping to catch his eye. Julia didn't envy the sheikh's young bride. She knew she'd be extremely jealous.

Though rumor had it that the sheikh was very much in love with his new wife, and that made Julia a bit envious. She wanted Sebastian to be in love with her.

Wait a minute, she thought. Was that really what she wanted?

She sat down in her office chair. Of course it was. She had fallen in love with her boss…soon to be ex-boss. She didn't have to think hard to figure out why.

Once he'd known she was leaving, he'd relaxed his guard and their working relationship had changed. He'd changed. And so had she.

She bit her lower lip. Things had only changed once he realized she was leaving. Was that some kind of omen?

The phone rang. It was him. She reached for it but stopped before she answered. She needed a minute to figure this out.

She didn't want to end up like all of Sebastian's other women, sitting alone at a table with a box from Tiffany's.

She imagined her cell phone ringing with a call from his assistant.

She'd seen how he'd walked away when things got too intense for him. Why did she think she'd be any different? Had she scared him with her request to step things up professionally?

She was a simple girl from Texas, not a sophisticated woman used to wheeling and dealing—and handling a man like Sebastian.

She was scared—really scared that she might have finally let Sebastian get the better of her. And that was the one thing she'd promised herself she'd never let happen. But it had happened, and now she was between a rock and a hard place.

The phone rang again. She answered it.

"This is Julia."

"You okay? I called just a minute ago and got voice mail," he said.

"I'm fine. Sorry about that. What's up?"

"I need you to go down to the stables and see if you can find Richard. He's been spending a lot of time there. I need to talk to him right away about the Henderson deal."

"I'm on it."

"Great. I'll be in the office in an hour. I'm visiting Dad, and then I have to stop by the heliport and pick up the senator. Is that right?"

"Yes. I'll text you the details. Should Richard call your cell?"

"Definitely."

"I'll take care of it," she said.

"Thank you, Julia. And don't forget about our dinner tonight. We need to talk."

"I haven't forgotten," she said, a sick feeling in the pit

of her stomach. He hung up and she sat there, staring at her desk. Their conversation was like a million they'd had before—all business and to the point, until the end. Something was up. What did he need to tell her?

She shook her head. She was turning into some kind of desperate woman, and she hated it. Whatever he had to say, she would be fine.

She put her phones to voice mail and went outside the polo club office and got on her golf cart. Getting around Seven Oaks was easier with the aid of a golf cart. She drove through the early morning mist toward the stables in search of Richard.

Though Sebastian had mentioned not being able to get through to Richard's cell, Julia tried anyway and left him a message. She pulled up outside the stables but when she went inside she didn't find anyone but a couple of grooms.

One of the sheikh's ponies poked his head over the stable door. She walked close to the glossy black horse, knowing that no one but the sheikh and his trainer ever rode the horse.

She stood there, seeing the power in those black eyes. Power didn't necessarily come from money. Sebastian would have it no matter how much he had in the bank. She wanted to reach out but stopped when she heard the sound of hooves behind her.

She turned around to find Catherine returning from working out a horse.

"Hi, Julia. What's up?" Catherine asked.

"I'm looking for Richard. Have you seen him this morning?"

She quickly shook her head. "Why?"

"I thought he spent a lot of time down here. If he does show up will you ask him to call Sebastian?"

"Sure," said Catherine, dismounting and walking the horse away.

Julia left the stables feeling more distracted than ever. Today should be one of the happiest days of her life—she'd just realized she was in love. Instead, those emotions just made her realize that she was more vulnerable than ever.

She didn't want to lose everything she'd worked for, but losing Sebastian would be worse. She didn't realize love could feel this intense. She needed Sebastian Hughes, and he wasn't known for being there for her.

Seven

Sebastian had avoided his office all day. Last night on the beach, he'd felt fear for the first time, and he knew that meant one thing. He couldn't keep seeing Julia.

She was becoming his Achilles' heel. And he'd always been careful to make sure he had no weaknesses. The thought of building a life with her personally and professionally was too much for him. It felt too dangerous.

So he'd spoken to the chef about arranging an intimate meal at the house and ordered a nice piece of jewelry from Tiffany's. He felt like a bastard as he made his plans for the evening, but he knew that the only way they were both going to survive was if he did this.

He had no idea how to be in a long-term relationship. And if he didn't promote her, Julia was leaving him anyway. She had to. How could she stay with a man who didn't respect her enough to see just how valuable her skills were?

He shook his head. It was pride that was motivating him. But when hadn't it been? He understood pride, which was why he had done a good job of running the polo club and keeping his own business going at the same time.

He needed someone to talk to, but Richard was dealing with his own crap and Geoff was back in London. He was on his own. And he could only handle this the best way he knew how.

He walked into the dining room to await a chat with the chef.

The last few weeks had been more than he'd ever expected to have with any woman. He loved the hot nights making love in her bed, but he also enjoyed the quiet moments watching TV with her, or glancing over at her during a polo match and seeing her smile at him.

If he were a different man maybe he'd be able to figure out how to make this work, figure out a way to make her stay with him. But he wasn't a different man.

He heard the door open behind him and turned around to see Marc there. "I wanted to double-check the timing for your dinner, sir."

"Drinks and appetizers when Julia arrives, and then I'll signal the waiter when we're ready for dinner."

Marc nodded and left.

Sebastian walked nervously around the room, staring at the box. It was the same gift he gave every woman he broke up with, and he didn't know if he could do it. He didn't know if he was going to be able to treat Julia like every other woman in his life, though he tried to convince himself he could.

He walked around the walnut-paneled room and stopped under the portrait of his father. The painting had been done by a prominent American portrait artist and portrayed his father in the year he'd founded the club. The same year that Christian had met Lynette and started courting her.

His father had a full head of hair and looked down at Sebastian with that young face. It was hard to picture his dad as a young man because most of his life, well, Christian had simply seemed older and wiser.

He'd married Lynette because of her family connections, and that marriage had been a cold one. Sebastian and Vanessa had lived that firsthand.

He didn't want to repeat the mistakes his father had made. He didn't want to spend his life in a cold marriage—or in no marriage at all. And he didn't want to let the right woman slip through his fingers now.

Was he being too hasty by ending things with Julia tonight?

He heard the door open behind him. The waiter came in to place the wine bucket and a tray of crudités on the table. Sebastian's nerves were frayed.

Julia was just a woman, he thought. She was like every other woman he'd ever dated. Tonight he would end things with her once and for all. He might find another woman in his life to marry or he might not. But he knew that he couldn't be with Julia. He couldn't be with her until he figured out a way to manage the emotions she brought so easily to the surface in him.

The door opened again, and he turned around.

She was here.

Julia wore a lovely gray cocktail dress that enhanced her smooth white skin. Her long hair was down, and her lips were glossy and luscious. For a minute, he couldn't breathe as he stared at her.

He took a step forward, and then two, and then he had her in his arms. He tunneled his fingers through her hair as he kissed her, crushing her to him.

The thought of not being able to do this made his hands shake. He pulled back and looked down at her. She stared up at him.

"Are you okay?" she asked.

He nodded. "I am now."

He held her in his arms, knowing that he couldn't end things with her. He couldn't let her walk away from him, whatever it was that she made him feel. He was afraid to admit it might be love.

"Come sit down. I have a lot to say to you tonight," he said.

He led the way to the table. Julia stopped dead in her tracks as she got close enough to see the Tiffany's box placed on her plate.

"Really, Sebastian? You can't be serious."

Julia could only shake her head. She was furious—and devastated. But anger was the thing she wanted to hold on to. He'd just kissed her like she was the missing half of his soul and then she'd turned around and seen this.

"I can't believe you."

"It's not what you are thinking. Please sit down so we can talk."

"Talk? I don't want to talk. I thought you'd changed, Sebastian. But this…well, this shows me you are still the man who wanted his assistant to break up with his girlfriend."

"This has nothing to do with Cici," he said. He

walked back to her. "You don't know anything about what I'm feeling right now."

"You're right, I don't," she said, feeling the first sting of tears at the back of her eyes. "I thought…I thought I had been getting to know the real man these last few weeks."

"You have been," he assured her. He put his hand out as if to touch her arm, and she backed away.

"Please don't touch me."

"It's not what you think," he said.

For a minute she started to listen, but she knew what that box meant. "Stop. I'm not content to take scraps of caring you throw my way. And I think I deserve better than that."

Sebastian rubbed the back of his neck. "I want better than that for you, too."

She thought he cared about her. Was he doing this because she wanted to work with him as his equal? "I don't get this. Are you afraid that I'll get too close? That you won't be able to keep me at arm's length if we work together?"

"You thought we'd just keep on this way?" he asked her.

"Yes, I did. I'm starting to care for you. Hell, why hedge my bets? I want to stay here. I don't want to leave you, Sebastian."

"I don't think we can work together anymore."

Those words just confirmed what she already knew. He needed her to go quietly out of his life. She wasn't going to take a job working for John Martin. Maybe she'd just go back to Texas where she could resume a quiet life far away from the glitz and glitter of the Bridgehampton Polo Club.

But before she left she wanted him to understand that. "I guess we can't," she said.

"Julia, it's not that I don't want you in the office with me, but I can't look at you the same way. You are a distraction. Once I see you in the office, all I want to do is pull you into my arms. And that's not what either of us wants."

Speak for yourself, she thought. She wanted to feel his arms around her whenever she laid eyes on him. She'd liked working with him publicly and then seeing him at night when it was only the two of them.

Sharing every second of the day together was exactly what she wanted, but that wasn't going to happen. "I think you are scared."

"I am," he admitted. "No woman has ever affected me the way you do, and I don't want to make a mistake that I will regret the rest of my life. You asked me once about my mother, and I hedged because I didn't want to tell you that my father married Lynette because she was beautiful and then he found himself stuck in a loveless marriage. She married him for his money."

"I'm sorry your father made the choice to stay with someone he didn't love. But you don't have to repeat his mistakes," she said.

"I know. I'm just trying to figure it out. I made a promise to myself that I'd stay unencumbered and free. I don't want to be trapped, or trap anyone. Until I met you, that worked for me, Julia."

"And now?"

"I don't know. I told you that I'm scared, and that is the truth. I don't know if I should keep you by my side or send you away. I brought you here tonight to end things, but the longer I waited for you, the harder it was for me to believe that I could really say goodbye."

She stared at him, afraid to believe what she was hearing. But she knew he wouldn't lie to her. Sebastian didn't lie to anyone. He was a straight shooter.

"What are you trying to say?"

He took her hand in his. "I love you, Julia Fitzgerald."

She started to speak, to confess her love for him, but he put his finger over her lips. "Let me finish. Loving you is the scariest thing I've ever experienced, and I don't know which way to turn or what decision to make."

"I think we should be making decisions together," she said.

"Why?"

"Because I love you, too, Sebastian. I have been trying to figure out how to say those words to you. I've been trying to figure out how to make you see that I don't want to live without you."

Sebastian pulled her into his arms and held her close. He whispered his love to her again, and she held him tightly to her. She was afraid to believe what he'd told her, afraid that this might all be a dream. But the next morning, when she woke up in his arms, she was able to start believing that it might be true.

And then after the trip to Bridgehampton Jewelers for an engagement ring, she knew it was starting to feel real not just to her but to Sebastian, as well.

"Let's go tell my dad."

"Really?" she asked. "Once you do, he'll tell the world."

"I'm ready for the world to know," Sebastian said. He pulled her into his arms and kissed her deeply.

Christian was watching the video monitor of the horses when they walked into his room. Sebastian had his arm around her and Julia knew she had the biggest smile of her life on her face.

Christian arched one eyebrow at them. "I see that Sebastian has made you a happy woman."

"He has," Julia said.

"I'll make her even happier once she becomes my wife. We're getting married, Dad."

"About damned time," Christian said.

* * * * *

New Zealand-born to Dutch immigrant parents, **Yvonne Lindsay** became an avid romance reader at the age of thirteen. Now married to her "blind date" and with two surprisingly amenable teenagers, she remains a firm believer in the power of romance. Yvonne feels privileged to be able to bring to her readers the stories of her heart. In her spare time, when not writing, she can be found with her nose firmly in a book, reliving the power of love in all walks of life. She can be contacted via her website, www.yvonnelindsay.com.

MAGNATE'S MISTRESS-FOR-A-MONTH

Yvonne Lindsay

With special acknowledgement to the lovely, generous and knowledgeable Genevie Hogg. Thanks so much for your time and for opening up the fascinating world of polo to me.

One

Sebastian was right. He seriously needed to get laid.

Richard Wells rolled off his stomach—and off the early morning discomfort that painfully reminded him of his newly permanent single state. Funny how that hadn't been an issue in the whole year it had taken for his divorce to be finalized. Now his heart and mind were free, the rest of his body had decided to rapidly follow suit.

Birdsong penetrated his sleep-fogged mind—the sound was a welcome difference from the low hum of traffic and muted sirens he usually heard through his double-glazed high-rise windows—reminding him of his current location and the fact that this was his first vacation in far too long.

He lay there for a moment, relishing the sensation of the Seven Oaks Farm guesthouse's fine Egyptian cotton sheets against his bare skin. Yeah, he liked this feeling.

Freedom. It was a feeling he hadn't enjoyed in far too long.

Richard kicked away his covers. Vacation or not, he didn't want to stay in bed a moment longer. Always an early riser—in more ways than one, he smiled ruefully as he adjusted himself on his way to the bathroom—it would be sacrilege to waste even one second of the beautiful June morning that had begun to shine through the gauzy curtains on the window. Seb had been at him for months now to take some time out for R & R. The lure of polo, ponies and a plethora of beautiful people looking for a good time, not a long time, was just the medicine he needed.

Divorcing Daniella had taken more out of him than he'd wanted to admit—fiscally and personally. It still rankled that he'd allowed himself to be swayed by a beautiful face and an even more beautiful body. How could he not have seen past her facade to the avaricious creature beneath? Still, he'd finally broken free of her, and now it was time for new beginnings. New beginnings of a more casual nature. There was no way he was ready to embark on anything more permanent again.

Richard padded into the bathroom and turned on the shower, letting the cool stream of water refresh his body and his mind. He'd left the office so late last night he'd almost decided not to drive out to Seven Oaks. But the second he'd hit the Montauk Highway, he knew he'd done the right thing in giving in to the lure of fresh air and a peace he never quite managed to attain in the city.

He stepped out of the shower and grabbed a luxuriously thick, fluffy towel to dry off. Now that he was finally here, he was eager to get down to the stables and check out the ponies. It had been far too long since he'd allowed himself the downtime to indulge in the things he loved, riding being one of them. Seb had told him yesterday that Sheikh Adham Aal Ferjani's string of ponies for the polo season were exceptional. Now was probably a good time to find that out for himself. He dragged on a pair of jeans and a well-washed designer T-shirt before sliding his feet into a pair of butter-soft leather loafers.

The sun was an encroaching halo of light on the horizon as Richard let himself out of the guesthouse. He'd been too tired last night, and it had been too late for him to really appreciate his surroundings but now, in the dawn air, he could fully admire the beauty around him. He felt a sense of energy and promise that had been lacking from his world for too long.

Seven Oaks boasted several buildings, including a small apartment house for the grooms who cared for the horses as well as three barns and world-class polo fields. With the huge amount of sponsorship and money being thrown around in the coming months, the farm was most definitely the central pulse for what promised to be a high-stakes season. The Clearwater Media Cup, sponsored by the company he and Seb ran together, would start this coming weekend.

Several horses lifted their heads in interest as he passed their paddocks, one whickering softly. Richard felt his lips relax into a smile at the sound. Yeah, it had been far too long since he'd put aside the rigors of work and simply enjoyed life.

He leaned his arms across the top rail of the fence, hitched one foot on the lower rail and took a moment to watch the horses. Bit by bit the tension accumulated over the past few months—work pressure with the demands of his drawn-out divorce proceedings—started to drain from his shoulders.

Seb had been right about the ponies, if the handful in this field were anything to go by. Richard let his eyes roam over their forms, taking pleasure in the perfection of their powerful bodies and the graceful bow of their strong necks. Thoroughbred bloodlines showed clearly in each and every one.

The rhythmic thud of hooves on the hard-packed ground echoed a short distance away. Curious, Richard followed the noise.

Silhouetted by the rising sun, horse and rider appeared in one majestic silhouette as they cantered around another paddock. Despite the animal's obvious spirited nature, the rider left the reins loosely knotted on the pony's neck. The pony could stop and turn on a dime, guided by little more than the rider's thighs and subtle shifts of his supple, lightly muscled body as he gracefully wielded a polo stick, striking a white ball up and down the paddock.

Her body, Richard realized as the rider moved side on, revealing very feminine curves and the flick of a long, braided mass of hair down her back. Every nerve in his body knotted as he watched her, his eyes eagerly roaming the lean length of her legs clad in snug-fitting riding breeches, the way her gently rounded backside skimmed the saddle, her perfectly aligned spine and the straight set of her shoulders.

It was as if she and the horse had been carved from the same malleable substance, moving as one incredibly graceful, cohesive unit.

She appeared impervious to the slight chill in the early morning air. Impervious, too, to the man watching her. Richard found himself mesmerized and acknowledged the unbidden fire of need that began smoldering deep down, low in his groin. He wondered if she was one of Seb's staff and racked his memory for any mention of a particularly attractive groom or polo player, but he came up blank.

While the farm and the polo club had traditionally been Seb's father's domain, Seb had become very hands-on in the past couple of years as Christian Hughes waged war on the cancer that attacked him. No, if Seb had hired someone who looked like this, Richard would have heard about it, even if only in passing. Which only left the sheikh's team and staff, who were staying at the farm for the duration of the season.

Richard rubbed his chin reflectively. That could prove more difficult, depending on exactly what her role was in the sheikh's employ—if she even was on his payroll. The soft murmur of the rider's voice as she picked up the reins and encouraged the animal in the direction of the nearest barn galvanized Richard into action.

How hard could it be to find out who she was—and just how well he'd be able to get to know her? After all, it wasn't as if he was looking for forever.

Catherine Lawson slid from the saddle and handed the polo stick she'd been training the pony to become used to, to one of the junior grooms. The pony was a recent addition to her boss's string, and she'd been eager to try her out.

"How'd Ambrosia go?" the freckle-faced teen asked.

"Pretty good, but it'll be a while before she's up to the standards of those guys." Catherine nodded in the direction of the ponies that had been turned out into the fields last night after the afternoon practice.

"You want me to take care of her for you?"

"No, it's okay. I'll do it." Catherine smiled at the girl's eagerness.

Had she ever been that young and eager to work with the horses? She supposed she had, but it seemed like a long, long time ago. While she loved her work—loved horses above all else—she still held on to her dream of setting up her own riding stables one day. And, she reminded herself, if she slacked off in her current role, that day would be a great deal further away than it already was.

Catherine lifted off the saddle and stacked it on its peg before untacking the pony and sliding on a halter in place of the bridle. The pony butted her shoulder gently as she did so, raising a smile on Catherine's lips.

"Impatient, are we?" she crooned softly, rubbing her hand gently across Ambrosia's soft nose.

"You looked amazing out there. Are you a player?"

Catherine wheeled around to find the source of the deep male voice that stroked through the air. Ambrosia startled, jerking her head and Catherine's hand up high. Catherine took a minute to settle the pony, then felt her heart rate accelerate as she studied the man opposite.

A slow, languorous heat suffused her body. She knew this guy—she had seen his pictures in the business pages of the *Times* as well as featured in the glossy tabloids she was hopelessly addicted to. Richard Wells—business developer extraordinaire, business partner to Sebastian Hughes in Clearwater Media and totally out of her league.

Taller than her own five feet nine inches, she found herself having to look slightly up to meet clear gray eyes edged with sooty dark lashes. His nose was a straight blade of male perfection bisecting a face that photographed well but was even more handsome in person. Rich sable-brown hair was expertly cut but had been tousled by the morning breeze, leaving his forehead bare, and a smudge of whiskers shadowed his jaw.

She quelled the urgent burn of longing that simmered deep inside her. Last she'd heard, he was in the middle of a very messy divorce. If he was making a play for her now, which she fully suspected was the case given the light of interest burning in those beautiful eyes, then he wasn't her type at all. She wasn't prepared to potentially put herself in the limelight that was his world.

No doubt he'd lose interest soon enough when she made it clear she wasn't that kind of girl.

"No, I'm head groom to Sheikh Adham ben Khaleel ben Haamed Aal Ferjani," she replied, using her boss's name to full effect.

Usually, it had just the outcome she wanted. Most people, impressed or intimidated, would withdraw. Unfortunately, it looked as if Richard Wells wasn't "most people."

"Head groom, huh? You must be good for the sheikh to have a woman in that role."

She fought back the urge to bristle. His was a natural reaction and one she'd come across often in the twelve years she'd been in Sheikh Adham Aal Ferjani's employ. But there was a subtle double entendre in his words that rankled. The same entendre she'd sensed in his initial overture to her with his use of the word *player*.

"I earned my position with him, as does everyone in his employ. Now, if you'll excuse me, I have work to do."

"You have an accent. Where are you from?"

Catherine drew in a short breath. Didn't he get it? She

wasn't interested. Ambrosia shifted nervously, picking up on her tension. She laid a soothing hand on the mare's neck and murmured gently to her before answering.

"New Zealand. Although I haven't been back for a long time."

"A pity. It's a beautiful country."

"You can find beauty wherever you are. If you want to, that is."

"Good point," Richard replied, and again there was that hint of innuendo that unsettled her.

Catherine led Ambrosia into a stall and clipped cross ties to her halter to discourage the pony from her irritating habit of reaching around to nip the backside of whoever groomed her. She quickly checked the pony's hooves, then reached for a brush and started working with firm, brisk strokes. Maybe he'd take the hint and leave her alone if she just kept about her business.

"When do you have time off?" he asked.

"Time off?" She shrugged, continuing to work. "There's always something to do, especially during tournament time."

"Meet me for dinner tonight. You can tell me more about yourself."

Was he so sure of himself that he didn't even couch his invitation as a question? She should have been irritated by his assurance but, perversely, she felt a sudden tingle of excitement ripple through her. A thoroughly unwelcome tingle.

"Sorry, I can't. I'm too busy."

She felt the air between them move, solidify. Then the warm pressure of his hand over hers, his fingers tangling with her own over the brush she held against the pony's flank. An electric sizzle of awareness tracked up her arm and through her body. The heat of him behind her suffused the too-thin fabric of her polo shirt, making her all too aware of his nearness—his very maleness. She held herself rigid to prevent herself from leaning back against that all too enticing wall of confidence and strength he projected.

"People don't usually refuse me," he said, his lips suddenly altogether too close to her ear.

She slid her hand out from beneath his and ducked under Ambrosia's neck to start brushing her other side while she fought to control a heartbeat that was too rapid. She knew her cheeks would be flushed, a curse of her fair skin, and she swallowed before replying.

"Sounds like it's past time you got used to that, then."

Catherine bit the inside of her cheek, forcing herself not to respond any further. She was not normally this blunt, nor was she usually averse to dinner with a handsome man. But Richard Wells was off-limits, no matter how much he pinged every sensor in her body. Wealthy, entitled and, above all, totally out of her league. No. She did not want to go down that path.

His sudden burst of laughter made her startle, causing Ambrosia to shift again, this time landing one well-shod hoof firmly on top of Catherine's boot. She bit back a curse and pushed against the pony, extricating her foot.

"C'mon," Richard cajoled, "it's only dinner."

"Why on earth would you want to have dinner with me? You don't even know me."

He looked at her. Catherine felt her breasts tighten as his gaze flicked over her body before settling on her face.

"We could change that."

Her mouth dried, and the words she knew she should

utter to stop him once and for all hovered, for the moment, unsaid on her lips. His clear, gray eyes bored into hers, mesmerizing her with the intent mirrored there.

"No."

She was adamant. She simply wasn't going there.

"At least tell me your name," he coaxed.

"Catherine," she replied, her voice a little husky. "Catherine Lawson."

"Well, Catherine Lawson, I'm Richard Wells, and I'm *very* pleased to meet you."

"I know who you are," she answered, ignoring the hand he'd thrust out over Ambrosia's back in a parody of a formal introduction.

She wasn't letting him touch her again—no way. He affected her too darn much for her to risk that. The last thing she wanted was to be linked to him this season. She knew full well how the taint of scandal clung to a person and how damaging the fallout was for the weaker parties involved.

No. No matter how enticing, Richard Wells would remain firmly out of bounds.

Two

"Your admirer is here again."

Catherine stifled a groan and fought the urge to scan the fence around the field where they were doing stick and ball practice with the sheikh's top string of ponies for the major tournament starting in six weeks. But she couldn't help herself—she looked. Dressed in a silky black shirt and designer jeans, Richard leaned casually against the fence, his eyes shaded by a ball cap. They might be shaded, she thought, but his eyes were very firmly upon her, if the prickle between her shoulder blades was anything to go by.

Didn't he have better things to do than to shadow her on a daily basis? Every day for a week he'd either turned up at the stables, helping out as if he were a groom and not some gold-edged, white-collared multibillionaire, or had come to watch her on the fields during practice.

Every day he asked her to dinner again, and every day she turned him down.

She would not turn and look at him. She. Would. Not.

She looked.

Her heart skipped a beat. It was bad enough that he invaded her waking thoughts, but now he filled her sleeping ones, as well, and last night had been a doozy. She'd woken before dawn, drenched in sweat, her sheets in a tangle and her body humming with a longing that just wouldn't go away. A longing that never got the chance to go away with him standing there, watching her, day after day. Clearly the word "no" simply meant "try harder" for men like Richard Wells.

Her grooms bore the brunt of her frustration. Each day's chores were more meticulously supervised than they had been the day before. Each time a pony's legs were bandaged in preparation for practice, they were more carefully examined and checked before being deemed to be okay. Tack had to be in pristine condition before being returned to the tack room.

She knew she was being a pain, but she couldn't help it. Richard Wells had her so wound up she could barely think straight. She was doing her best to hold firm, but somehow her best simply wasn't quite enough to ensure a good night's sleep anymore.

On top of everything, this afternoon, instead of working the pony lines and supervising her grooms, she'd been summoned to make an appearance in the sheikh's VIP tent. It seemed that the ponies had garnered the attention of some overseas interest, and the people involved wanted to meet her, as well. Why, she had no idea. Sheikh Adham Aal Ferjani was as hands-on as his work allowed. It was one of the things that she most respected about him. He wasn't a figurehead, but an integral part of the process of bringing his polo ponies up to the standards he demanded in play. He expected the same level of commitment from all his team members, no matter their worldwide ranking. The sheikh was more than capable of fielding any and all enquiries about his horses.

Catherine loathed the idea of having to wear a dress, heels and makeup and make polite conversation with the kind of people who usually set her teeth on edge. The social side of polo had never been her scene. Which was another reason why she and a man like Richard Wells could never amount to anything together.

No, his type would be more like the sycophantic designer-clad hordes who deluged the Hamptons with their perfect hair and their perfect smiles and their perfect clothes. Catherine gave herself a mental shake. She wasn't being entirely fair. Sure, as with any endeavor steeped in tradition and money, there were those who were only there to see and be seen, but there were just as many with a genuine interest and love of the sport.

She'd let Richard Wells get too far under her skin, she decided as she called a halt to the practice session and led her team back to the barn. Or maybe, a sneaky little voice inside her suggested, she hadn't allowed him under her skin quite deep enough.

As soon as she'd thought it, a sharply edged visual image painted itself in her mind, and her inner muscles clenched tight. A tiny moan escaped from her lips as a surge of longing swelled deep within her.

"Are you okay?" one of her grooms asked as he drew alongside her.

Catherine felt her cheeks flame at the prospect of his having heard her.

"I'm fine. Just not looking forward to this afternoon, is all."

"Hey, you'll be in the shade, drinking champagne and rubbing shoulders with the powers that be. What's not to like?"

"All of the above?" she managed, with a wry smile.

The other groom laughed and dismounted his horse, leading it into the barn ahead of her. Catherine reached up to unclip her helmet and remove it. Sometimes she wished she could be more like some of her grooms. Most of them were much younger than her twenty-eight years and, for them, relationships came and went and were purely to be enjoyed. Many were working solely for the experience and to have a chance to increase their rankings, hopefully with a view of catching the eye of a wealthy patron who would boost their polo playing career into the stratosphere.

But Catherine's dreams lay in other areas. A natural left-hander, she'd trained herself as competently as any right-handed player—doing so had been vital to her being able to do her job well. But even so, her heart wasn't in the game itself. No, her heart lay firmly and squarely with the horses, and she wanted nothing more than to establish her own riding stables. A pipe dream at the best of times, unless she could secure some serious sponsorship to get her ideas off the ground. But she hoped to one day be able to provide riding lessons to kids from underprivileged backgrounds as well as those who could afford to pay for the pleasure.

"Penny for them?"

Richard's voice dragged her attention firmly back to where it belonged.

"Not even worth that, unfortunately," she replied,

swinging her leg over and dropping from her saddle to the yard floor.

"So, about dinner…"

She'd had enough. Catherine handed her pony off to one of the other grooms with a short command and turned to give Richard her full attention.

"I thought I made it perfectly clear. I'm not interested in having dinner with you."

"If I gave up every time I heard the word *no,* I wouldn't be where I am today."

He smiled at her, the action softening the sharp planes of his face and lending a lighter, more boyish, cast to his features. She fought the natural instinct to smile in return, instead focusing on a point just past his ear.

"It's not going to happen."

"Why not?"

"Because I'm not interested in you."

"So, then, you have nothing to lose, do you?"

"I also have nothing to gain, either."

"Good point. Okay, so back to the not interested thing. I've learned to be a pretty good judge of a person's character and to read visual cues that most people don't realize they're sending out."

He crossed his arms and took his time to peruse her from the soles of her boots to the top of her helmet.

"Frankly," he said, "I don't believe you."

Catherine huffed out a breath in frustration. "I really don't care if you believe me or not. Look, let me put it this way. There's no way I'm going to be your summer fling. We're from completely different backgrounds, completely different worlds. All I care about is horses, not people, so please stop wasting your time and go ask someone who might actually say yes."

"I don't recall asking you to be my summer fling, although the idea has merit."

He let his gaze drift over her face, his eyes fixing on her lips and making her think twice about her sudden urge to run her tongue across them.

"Catherine, it's just a meal. Shared between two adults."

His subtle emphasis on the word *adults* sent a pull through her body as visceral as if he'd reached out and stroked the full length of her. She gathered her scattered wits and juggled the words in her mind.

"The answer is still, and will continue to be, no. Now, please, I have work to do."

Richard watched Catherine as she straightened her shoulders and walked away, every step of her booted feet resonating on the yard surface and echoing her displeasure. Why was he being so persistent? It wasn't as if he was hard-pressed for female company. Ah, but not company who challenged him. And not company who wouldn't expect more than he was prepared to give.

He'd kept the news of the final dissolution of his marriage quiet for a darn good reason and thanked the perspicacity of his lawyer for insisting on a gag clause to prevent Daniella from leaking the information. He wasn't being narcissistic when he said he knew he was fair game on the marriage market. He was passably good-looking, fit, still young and financially healthy— very healthy. He had no desire to suddenly be the object of several hundred single—and some not-so-single— women looking for their next alimony check. No. He'd made that mistake once, and he wasn't about to do it again.

When he sought female company from now on it

would be entirely on his terms, which was why he was so determined to win Catherine over. Physically, she was as different from Daniella as night from day. Her lean, lightly muscled limbs were a far cry from his ex-wife's voluptuous curves and shorter frame. He clenched his hands into fists as he imagined how Catherine's body would feel beneath him, how her lithe limbs would entangle with his, how her slim hips would cradle his own, how her pert small breasts would feel in his hands, beneath his tongue….

Fire licked through his body, starting at the soles of his feet and roaring through him, setting every nerve into full aching arousal. If just thinking about making love with her did this to him, what would the real thing be like? He genuinely looked forward to finding out. That it would take relentless chipping at the hard granite of her determination to refuse him just sweetened the deal.

Damn, she was stubborn. And he liked stubborn. Richard hadn't yet met a challenge he couldn't coerce into submission, and Catherine's submission was something he was very much looking forward to. In fact, the harder she worked to dissuade him, the more certain he became he'd succeed. And he'd ensure it was totally worth her while to capitulate. Totally.

Richard turned and headed back to the guesthouse. He needed a long, cold shower before he got ready for watching the matches this afternoon. A very long, very cold shower.

Three

Richard strolled among the crowds as people bustled and gossiped around the VIP tents at the polo field. Hard to believe some were even here to watch the games, he thought with a touch of cynicism. To his eye, it appeared that most spectators were interested in being seen by the right people. But then that was all part and parcel of the sport, he conceded as he greeted one of his colleagues from the city.

Seb had introduced him today to Catherine's boss, Sheikh Adham Aal Ferjani. Richard had liked the man instantly and had been intrigued by the fact that his dark eyes had never strayed far from his beautiful, but somewhat quiet, wife. He knew she'd suffered a family bereavement recently. Perhaps that explained her husband's ever-watchful gaze.

Over near the entrance to the tents, paparazzi were scrambling for the best shot of newly arrived Carmen

Akins. The award-winning actress was even more beautiful in the flesh than on screen, although there was a tense set to her mouth. Security was quick to step in and prevent the mob from following her any farther, however.

And there was Vanessa Hughes, wearing her trade-mark white designer gear and black-rimmed sun-glasses that almost obscured her face, and carrying the voluminous bag he knew contained the flat-heeled shoes she preferred to wear to stomp the divots at half-time despite the fact they reduced her to her very petite five foot two. He'd always loved her for her practicality in this if nothing else. She smiled and waved before her attention was caught by a mutual friend.

He wondered how Catherine was faring. The busyness of the pony lines was a far cry from the circus of people and behaviors in the tents, he was certain. No doubt it was vastly preferable, too.

Richard took a sip of his champagne and scanned the assembly, his gaze flitting over his companions before halting in surprise on one particular face.

Catherine. A very dressed up and elegant Catherine at that. Her hair had been pulled back from her face, and instead of the usual wisps slipping from the loose braid that usually hung down her back, every strand was firmly secured into an elegant knot at her nape. A deliciously exposed nape. A nape made for nuzzling, he thought with a smile.

The severe style suited her, revealing her smooth forehead and high cheekbones to perfection. A small silver ring pierced the top of her right ear, her only jewelry. She wore barely any makeup, but he could tell she'd applied some mascara and probably some foundation, as the faint freckles that so intrigued him each day were smoothly obscured. A slick shiny tint on her lips was just about his undoing, however. If she'd been here as his partner there was no way she'd still have that on. It would've been kissed off quite thoroughly by now.

He saw the exact moment she registered his perusal of her, her eyes flicking across him, her body stiffening, her smile becoming forced. And beneath the filmy fabric of the dress she wore he could swear he saw her nipples tighten and bud against the teal-green cloth that gave her eyes a hint of the sea. A stormy sea, if that tense jaw was anything to go by.

This was the first time he'd seen her in anything other than riding breeches, boots and a polo shirt. He liked this side of her—a lot. Always graceful and regal on horseback, she was even more so clad in the simple but elegant dress that clung lovingly to her body. The knee-length dress showcased her lower legs and a very slender, fine turn of ankle. Even her feet looked beautiful in stylish heeled sandals. Nothing ostentatious—just simple, quiet chic.

She'd painted her toenails a soft, peachy pink that went well with her skin tone. He had to admit surprise that she'd even bother with such frippery when she spent most of her time in boots anyway. It only served to remind him how little he really knew about Catherine Lawson—and how very much he wanted to know more.

He smiled to himself again and turned slightly away from her. She knew he was here. It would be interesting to see whether or not she'd come talk to him. He'd wager not.

The next game was due to commence, and people had begun to filter out of the tent. Richard decided to follow Catherine, perhaps even take a place next to her as they watched the game, but the sound of her name made him pause.

"Isn't that Catherine Lawson, Del Lawson's girl?" asked a tall slender blonde of her equally slender and glamorously attired companion.

"Del Lawson? Wasn't he linked to that doping scandal in New Zealand years ago?"

Just ahead of him, Richard noticed Catherine's shoulders stiffen and her step falter.

"The sheikh had better look after his ponies if she's working for him," the first blonde commented.

"They do say the apple never falls far from the tree," her cohort said and laughed snidely as they continued with their champagne glasses out to the main spectator area.

Richard edged his way through the exiting crowd, suddenly desperate to get to Catherine's side. There was no way she hadn't heard the two women discussing her. He'd seen the way she'd reacted. He scanned the crowd for the kingfisher flash of teal fabric, but he couldn't see her anywhere.

Then he caught sight of her, past the VIP tents and heading in the direction of the pony lines. Every inch of her body was held taut and straight, and he could almost see the waves of distress pouring off her. He followed, suddenly filled with the overwhelming desire to protect her. He knew he couldn't undo what she'd heard, but he could get to the root of what had upset her—and then maybe he could make things right for her again.

Richard didn't question the unexpected and un-characteristic urge to shield and defend a woman who was still essentially a stranger to him. All he knew was that she was upset and, come hell or high water, he was going to fix that.

Catherine blinked back the burn of tears that ached at the back of her eyes. She would not cry. She refused to let the cattiness of a couple of strangers break through the wall she'd spent the last twelve years shoring up around her. Who'd have believed that a handful of words, carelessly spoken, could still have the capacity to reach into her heart and claw it open like this?

She tripped, one of her high heels catching on the uneven ground, but she steadied herself and kept going, desperate to create some distance between herself and the aching pain of the past.

"Catherine. Catherine. Stop."

Warm hands caught her arms, forcing her to a halt. Even as Richard's voice registered, she struggled to pull free.

"Let me go."

"No. I won't let you go."

His hands slid up her arms to her shoulders and turned her around before pulling her into the warm heat of his body. She knew she ought to push him away, that she shouldn't find instant, gratifying comfort against the hard plane of his chest. That the feel of his arms, looped across her back and holding her fast, shouldn't make her feel as if she wasn't totally and completely alone in the world.

She couldn't help it. The tears she'd been fighting so hard to hold back began to slide inexorably down her cheeks. She sniffed, then felt Richard shift slightly before he pressed a clean, white handkerchief into her hands. He only let her go long enough to blow her nose and dab futilely at the moisture on her face before gathering her close again.

Slowly she felt the tension begin to ease from her back and shoulders. Her body sank into his as if he were the only thing holding her upright. Wiping at her face one more time, Catherine pulled away.

"Thank you, I think," she said shakily. "I'll, um, get this back to you once it's been laundered." She gestured to the wadded fist of cotton in her hand.

"Don't worry about it. Are you okay now?"

"Yeah."

She turned her face away, hardly able to bear his scrutiny. She never, never let go like this in front of anyone. Since she was sixteen, she'd essentially been on her own. Estranged from her mother. Her father dead. She'd learned to stand on her own two feet. Losing control like this, especially with someone like Richard Wells, was anathema to her. She dredged up the steel mantle under which she usually maintained control.

It was stupid to have reacted that way to those women's throwaway remarks. She'd heard worse over the years, words that had far more capacity to hurt than any aspersion on her own character.

Richard stood a mere foot away from her, watching her, poised as if to shelter her from harm. The sensation that someone else was looking out for her was foreign but strangely alluring. And dangerous—way too dangerous.

"You want to talk about it?" he asked.

"No," she responded flatly. Run, hide, escape—yes. Talking about it was the last thing she wanted to do.

"Do you have to go back?" he asked, his eyes not leaving her face.

"Go back?" she answered, momentarily confused.

"To the tents."

"No. No, I did my thing. The sheikh has some potential buyers for some of the ponies. They wanted to meet me, too."

"Can I walk you? Or would you rather we drove?"

Catherine shook her head. "No, I'll be fine. I was going to go to the pony lines, check that everything's okay and then head back to my apartment."

"I'll come with you."

"That's not necessary. I don't need you to hold my hand."

"I know. You're tough and brave—you don't need anybody, do you?"

Richard studied her carefully. Catherine felt her eyes widen as the shock of his words hit home. Was that what he really thought about her? That she didn't need anybody?

He couldn't be more wrong. She ached to belong to someone, someone who wouldn't judge her for who she was or where she'd come from. Someone who wouldn't look down their nose at her because she didn't have a university degree. Someone who would understand that while horses were her life, she still needed that special person in her world to make her complete. A man who could help her reach for the stars yet keep her grounded in the security of his love.

"I bet you don't know what it feels like to be constantly rejected," he said. A twinkle of amusement in his slate-colored eyes gave the lie to the implied hurt in his words.

She couldn't help it. She laughed, the sound bubbling up in her throat to chase away the lingering sorrow and bitterness left by the comments she'd overhead in the VIP tent.

"Are you talking about yourself now?" she teased lightly.

"Of course I am."

"I doubt you've ever been soundly rejected in your whole life."

"You've rejected me. It's left me wounded."

She laughed again. "You're kidding me. Men like you—you're so tough. You just move on to the next conquest, don't you?"

He didn't respond immediately, but his expression changed a little.

"Is that how you see me?"

Catherine's breath caught in her throat. Had she offended him? So close on the heels of the kindness he'd just shown her, that was the last thing she'd wanted to do.

"I…" Words dried on her tongue.

"Go on. Ask me on a date and I'll show you what it feels like."

"What? You want me to ask *you* on a date?"

"That's the idea."

"And you'll say no, so I know how it feels to be rejected? No, thanks. I know. Trust me on this."

"I'd never have figured you for a coward," he goaded with a smile on his face that went all the way to his eyes, crinkling the corners with devilish mirth.

"Oh, all right, then." Catherine gave a long-suffering sigh. "Would you like to go out with me sometime?"

"Love to. Where and when?"

Her heart slammed into her chest. The sneak! He'd tricked her into asking him out, and she'd fallen for it. Hook, line and sinker. Now she felt as if she'd just reined in a half-broken stallion but had no idea what to do next.

"That's not fair. I didn't mean it. You made me ask you under false pretences," she backpedaled.

"Catherine, you need to learn something about me. When I want something, I will get it eventually. Even if it means going a different, or less conventional, route."

He smiled at her again, but this time there was no guile in his expression. This was the determined, hardheaded businessman who'd co-founded an internationally successful media company with Sebastian Hughes, without a single ounce of assistance from anyone else.

She should be annoyed—very annoyed. Yet deep down there was a piece of her that was glad he'd said yes, despite their very obvious differences. But what on earth could she do with a man like Richard Wells who was used to the best of everything—restaurants, cars, people?

How could she, a groom, expect to compete with the dates he was used to? Every penny she made she tried to save for her own stables. She was lucky that in the course of her work she was provided with accommodation and Sheik Adham was generous with allowances for riding gear, but she still had a ways to go to reach her goal.

Would Richard be satisfied with something simple? And why did she even care? He'd tricked her into this date. It would serve him right if it was something he didn't expect or enjoy.

Something her father used to say to her when she was young echoed from the back of her mind. *You can tell a lot about a man by the way he treats a horse.* Perfect. Suddenly she knew exactly what they'd be doing.

"Fine." Catherine nodded. "Meet me at the barn tomorrow morning at sunup. Wear riding gear, if you have any."

"That's it? We're going for a ride?"

"Hey, you asked me where and when. Consider yourself told. If you stand me up, I won't come looking for you."

"Don't worry, I'll be there. You can count on it."

Richard turned and walked back toward the polo field. As she watched him go, Catherine wondered if perhaps she hadn't bitten off more than she could chew. Richard Wells outclassed her, outmaneuvered her and, quite simply, took her breath away.

Four

It was a morning just like any other morning, Catherine reminded herself. Chores to do, horses to attend to, notes to make for the vet who'd be calling in a few hours to check the ponies already under his care after the hardships of yesterday's games.

And yet, it was a morning unlike any other, too. Bubbles of anticipation popped and fizzed in her stomach. Anticipation tinged with a healthy dose of nerves. She'd barely been able to sleep last night and had fully intended to leave a message with the Hugheses' housekeeping staff to tell Richard she couldn't make it today. But despite the fact she knew he wouldn't let her off so lightly, there was a part of her that looked forward to this time alone with him, as well.

"Pathetic," she growled at herself as she tacked up two of her favorite horses for the early morning ride. Both were gentle in nature because she had no idea how comfortable Richard would be on horseback, and she didn't want to put him in a position where he might be embarrassed. Although she doubted that embarrassment occurred very often in his world.

Even though she'd braided her hair back in its customary single rope, tendrils already escaped to kiss the sides of her neck and face. A shiver rippled down her spine. It was more than the sensation of a drift of hair across bare skin. He was here. She knew it as surely as she knew her own face in the mirror each morning. Catherine didn't hasten in checking the girth strap and adjusting the stirrup leathers of the mount she'd chosen for herself. Eventually, though, she knew she'd have to face him.

She gave her horse a final pat and turned around. The instant she did, the sensation she'd felt only seconds ago sharpened and honed in on her chest, squeezing the air out of her lungs. She'd suspected he wasn't unfamiliar with horses, but you could never assume anything in the privileged world in which she worked.

He looked the part, from the polo shirt he'd topped with a sleeveless jacket to the well-worn boots on his feet. That his gear was anything but for show was obvious. The fitted leather boots hugged his calves, and his breeches followed the taut line of his thighs and hips with near-sinful intimacy. A riding helmet dangled from his fingers—again, well used and more for function than for show.

She could only imagine how good he'd look in the saddle, those powerful thighs nudging his horse on, reins comfortably held between his long fingers. Catherine swallowed against the sudden dryness in her throat.

"Good morning," he said. "I take it you were serious about going for a ride?"

Even his smile was enough to set her nerves skittering throughout her body.

"You gather correctly," she managed to reply far more evenly than she'd expected. She gestured to his gear. "I take it you can ride. Maybe you'd like a mount a bit more spirited than old Gryphon here," she said, patting the tall but docile gray gelding on the rump.

"Not today. Today I want to concentrate on you. In fact," he said as he opened one side of his jacket to show his cell phone tucked in a purpose-made pocket, "my phone is even on silent."

His eyes met and dueled with hers, making it impossible to look away. As he smiled again, she noted the way the corners of his eyes fanned softly, as if smiling were a natural thing for him. She supposed he had little to worry about. Raised on money, making his own money—what was there to concern him on a daily basis besides stock values and who his next escort would be?

Richard broke the contact himself and stepped over to Gryphon, taking a moment to say hello to the horse.

"I think Gryphon and I will get along just fine. Besides, it's been a while since I've had the time to ride. It'll be good to relax and enjoy the scenery."

He flashed her another look that left her in no doubt as to what "scenery" he referred to. For a second—a split second, no more—she allowed herself to preen just a little under his regard. To believe that she was the kind of woman who attracted a man like Richard Wells for real, not just for some passing fancy, which was all this could ever be.

"Well, then. We'd better head out and enjoy some of that scenery," she said, sliding her foot into a stirrup and pulling herself up onto her saddle. "There's rain forecast for later today. I'm hoping it'll hold off for now."

Richard quickly checked his stirrup leathers then followed suit. Together they rode out of the yard and down the lane that led away from the main farm buildings.

Catherine found herself enjoying the companionable silence between them although she kept wondering what it really was that made Richard tick. He hadn't let up on her for a second since he'd been at Seven Oaks. Even the days he'd been at the games he'd sought her out, and if he hadn't caught her at the pony lines, he'd found her later in the evening exercising the horses that hadn't been played.

She hated to admit it to herself, but she'd come to look forward to seeing him every day. Every day but yesterday, she reminded herself. She certainly hadn't needed him to witness either the shaming remarks those women had so casually thrown out like a discarded handbag or her reaction to them. Over the years she'd taught herself to cope so much better than that, but knowing Richard had heard them had lent an even more bitter tang to the encounter. She wondered if he'd made it his business to find out about the scandal that had ultimately led to her father's death.

She was such a fool for letting him trick her into this date. She'd chosen to take him riding thinking, wrongly, that it would give her the upper hand. But if the way he sat Gryphon was any indicator, he was probably as at home in a saddle as he was at the head of a boardroom table in the city.

The sun was a little higher in the sky now, filtering through gathering clouds, and the birdsong around them grew louder as they approached a tall stand of trees.

"Want to stretch him out a bit?" she asked as she bent to unlatch the gate they'd ridden up to.

"I thought you'd never ask," Richard replied, guiding his horse through the open gate and waiting for her on the other side. As she pulled up alongside him, he nodded to a solitary tree silhouetted against the rising sun. "Race you."

"You're on," Catherine answered after relatching the gate.

Without a second thought, she urged her mount forward. Gryphon was fast, but he wasn't quite as fleet of foot as her own horse, which required very little urging to stretch out into a full gallop. The sound of two sets of hooves thundering across the ground rang in her ears as they raced toward their goal.

If only life could always be this simple, she thought briefly before reminding herself to just relish the moment instead. Laughter began to bubble from her throat as she edged ahead of Richard and his horse, pulling up in the lead and reaching the tree a few seconds ahead of him.

"You're good," she acknowledged. "Not everyone can get that much speed out of him."

Richard patted Gryphon's strong neck before replying. "We reached an understanding."

"That's quite an understanding." Catherine smiled in return.

"Oh, I'm pretty amenable to most things. Clearly Gryphon and I are similar in that regard."

They resumed their trek side by side across the field in silence. Surprisingly for Catherine it was very comfortable just being with Richard. If anything, perhaps it was a bit too comfortable. She could get used to this kind of companionable closeness all too easily. But she knew this was only a short-lived stint in the countryside for him. His world was the city and its teeming busyness of life and work there. Her world, such as it was, was quite different.

Richard sensed Catherine's mood had changed. Somehow she'd slipped from carefree to quiet intro- spection and was withdrawing from him emotionally. He knew he'd surprised her by coming down in his riding gear. No doubt she'd expected him to be more like the rest of the guests staying at Seven Oaks and in neighboring compounds—only there for the society and the games and whatever peripheral activities they entailed.

He drew in a deep breath. Man, he'd give up working in the city if every day could be like this. He knew Seb's time here was bittersweet with the worry about his father's illness and the additional responsibilities he'd had to take on, but to be able to live this life— complementary to their usual world—would be the perfect marriage of ideals.

Catherine pulled up ahead of him, beside one of several ponds on the property. Her eyes fixed on the serene smoothness of the water. She was a lot like that herself, he realized. Calm on the surface, yet who knew what hidden depths she veiled from view? Suddenly, he was sick of playing the game he'd played with her for days now. He wasn't the kind of man to wait for someone else to make the first move. And he knew Catherine would run a mile before admitting she found him even moderately attractive.

He let his eyes drift over her as she sat so perfectly in her saddle. Her figure was lithe and strong, and he woke each morning consumed with the desire to know how she'd feel beneath his touch. Would she be shy, or reserved? Or would she take control and ride him as effortlessly as she became a part of the horses that were her charge?

He drew his mount alongside hers. They were so close that their legs brushed against one another. She turned to him, distracted from her reveries, and he knew exactly what he had to do next. Leaning over, he reached for her and cupped the back of her neck with one hand to draw her closer.

He absorbed the scent of her, fresh and clean, with a hint of lemon and mint—none of the cloying sweetness or spice of so many of the fragrances women wore. Nothing but the essence of her. He'd never smelled anything more enticing.

Her lips parted to protest, but he pressed his mouth to hers. She froze, rigid beside him, as his lips teased hers, as he supped and tasted their softness—a softness in direct contrast with the strength of her body and the steel will he sensed drove her to be who she was.

Fire leaped in his veins, licking at his insides, burning him up with a heat he knew could only be quenched by one thing, one woman. He slid his tongue along her lower lip and felt a thrill of triumph as it trembled at his touch. He'd half expected her to pull away, but instead she leaned in closer, appearing to want to absorb him as much as he wanted her.

He couldn't get enough. He deepened the kiss, letting his tongue slide between her lips to claim hers. The fire inside him turned molten, his thoughts and awareness flowing with the inexorable slow heat of a river of lava.

Sound retreated, leaving only sensation—and what sensation. All he was doing was kissing her. But no, this was so much more. This was a total communion of spirit.

He sucked gently on her full lower lip one more time before releasing her.

"You're beautiful, you know that?" he said, his voice low and steady.

Catherine shook her head. "You don't have to lie to me."

He lifted his hand and took her chin with strong fingers, making her look him directly in the eye. How could she not know how stunning she was, how she affected him on every level?

"I don't make a habit of lying, Catherine. You are beautiful. Always remember that."

She opened her mouth as if to protest, but the gathering clouds chose that moment to open and let the full weight of the moisture they carried fall pell-mell to the ground.

"Oh, no, I was hoping that would hold off until we got back," Catherine said, gathering her reins and turning her horse away from the pond. "There's an old barn not too far away. It'll be closer than heading back to the main farm. We can shelter there until the rain stops."

Without waiting for him to reply, she urged her horse forward, leaving him with nothing to do but follow her. Gryphon appeared equally motivated to get out of the weather as quickly as he could, Richard noticed. He wondered whether the downpour would be at all effective in cooling his ardor.

Catherine had dismounted and was wrestling two large doors open, the rain plastering her lightweight shirt to her skin, outlining her bra in intimate detail. He shouldn't feel so aroused—it wasn't as if the practical cotton garment had been designed to entice and titillate—but the sight of it only served to increase his growing hunger for its wearer.

The rain grew even heavier. Richard slid from his saddle and splashed through the rapidly growing puddles to help Catherine maneuver the doors open. Together they swung the massive doors wide and led their horses into the barn before pulling the doors closed behind them. While Richard secured them from the inside, Catherine led the horses to a couple of empty stalls and tethered them inside before loosening their girth straps and giving them each a bucket of water.

Richard took off his helmet and looked around the barn. It was old but seemed to be kept in very good condition, and he said as much to Catherine.

"I believe Mr. Hughes uses it as an overflow barn from time to time during tournaments. Saves other teams from having to transport their horses in. This time, though, the sheikh requested exclusive use of the farm." She shivered slightly. "There must be blankets or towels around here somewhere."

Richard followed her as she went to what looked like a small tack room off to one side of the barn. The room was pretty bare—a sagging sofa along one wall, a small wooden table pushed against another and one small window set high up, beneath which was an array of empty pegs and hooks for holding the various saddlery and tack for the horses. Dust motes spun in the sparse, watery light cast through the window.

He shucked off his jacket and tossed it across the table while Catherine riffled through a cupboard. If he was any kind of gentleman he'd avert his eyes from her almost completely transparent shirt, but right now manners were the furthest thing from his mind.

Outside, the rain battered the curved roof of the

barn with increasing ferocity, and the light inside the tack room dimmed even more. They were cocooned in here, safe from the elements, but not at all safe from the elemental need that coursed through his veins.

"Here, use this to dry yourself off a bit," Catherine said, passing him a towel.

"What about you?"

"I'll dry off after you."

She shivered again, a delicate ripple of muscle over bone.

"Here, let me help you. You look as though you need it more than me."

Truth be told, he should be steaming he felt so warm right now. Without waiting for Catherine's response, he unclipped her helmet, his fingers grazing the soft skin at her throat. He tossed the helmet onto the tabletop and gently wiped the moisture from her face and, turning her away from him, wrapped her braid in the thin towel to squeeze the water from her hair.

"The towel's going to be useless after that," she commented, her voice a little unsteady.

"Yeah," he agreed, his fingers already sliding the band off the end of her braid and rapidly loosening her hair.

"What are you doing?"

"It'll dry faster like this. Besides, I've always wanted to see your hair out."

"I'll look like a hairy drowned rat."

A smile pulled at his lips. "You look beautiful, remember?"

He turned her to face him and traced the shape of one brow with a finger.

"Beautiful," he said, his voice suddenly thick with need.

He bent his head and kissed her again, pulling her to

him, letting her slight frame nestle damply against his. Another tremor rocked her, but this time he doubted it was from the cold. Her lips burned against his, and he could feel the points of her nipples harden against his chest as they pressed through the thin fabric of her bra.

"I want to see you. All of you," he whispered against her lips.

He thought for a moment she'd refuse. Felt her denial building in the air between them. But then she nodded. Just the slightest inclination of her head.

He ran his hands down her back to the hem of her shirt and lightly tugged it upward, relinquishing her lips for long enough to pull the sodden garment over her head and let it drop to the floor. A flick of his wrist and her bra was undone. Slowly, almost reverently, he peeled the straps off her shoulders and down her arms, exposing her small, high breasts to his touch. He brushed her pale pink nipples lightly with his fingertips, feeling them tighten even more beneath his touch, before tracing her ribs and the gentle curve of her waist.

Carefully he backed her against the table before bending to remove her boots and socks and finally her riding breeches and panties. As he straightened, so did she, standing there before him, slender and proud. His for the taking. He felt as if he'd been waiting for this moment all his life. And he sure as hell wasn't about to let it pass him by.

Five

Catherine had never felt as bold as she did right now standing naked before Richard. There was a look of awe on his face as his eyes roamed her body, and she felt his gaze as if it were a physical flame warming her from the inside out.

He made her feel beautiful. Strong. Female.

She watched as he seemed to come to his senses, bending to remove his boots, followed quickly by the rest of his clothing. And there he stood opposite her. Completely naked but for a smattering of dark hair at the center of his chest. A smattering that narrowed into a fine line and arrowed down past his belly button. Her fingers itched to trace it, to touch him—taste him.

He'd said she was beautiful, but she could just as easily have said the same of him. There wasn't a visible ounce of fat on his body. He was lean, sculpted muscle from the breadth of his shoulders all the way to his calves. She reached out to touch him and felt his skin shiver slightly beneath her fingertips as she did so. She trailed her fingers lightly across his shoulders and down over his pectoral muscles before circling his small dark brown nipples.

Obeying her body's demands, she bent her head to flick her tongue over one taut disk and was rewarded with a barely suppressed groan. Richard's hands reached out and tangled in the long, loose strands of her hair as he pulled her closer to him, aligning her body against his.

He was so hard and hot—everywhere. His erection was trapped between them and feeling his solid length made her move against him, eager to assuage the ache that gathered from deep inside. She lifted one leg, hooked it across his hip and angled her pelvis so his hardness sent tiny shock waves spiraling out from her center.

One moment she'd been cold and chilled, the next she was an inferno of need. For a split second, she hesitated. She couldn't believe she was here. With him. Doing this. But then his warmth enveloped her as her body burned against his and his arms closed around her back, his hands spread against her skin. Any thought of hesitation, of stopping and recovering her sanity, was utterly lost. There was time enough later to worry about the self-recriminations that would come, but now, right now, she wanted Richard with a need that went bone deep.

His hands coasted down her back and over her buttocks, pulling her even closer against him. She tilted her hips again, back and forth, desperate to relieve some of the demanding pressure at her core that begged to be assuaged. It wasn't enough but it would do for now, and she both heard and felt the purr of satisfaction that rippled uncontrollably from her throat.

"So you like that, do you?" Richard nuzzled against her neck.

She flexed again and nodded, words completely failing her as sharp points of pleasure zapped through her. Richard stifled a groan, the vibration of the sound against the tender skin at her throat initiating its own drumbeat of want. His hands gripped her buttocks tighter, lifting her higher.

"Put your other leg around me," he instructed, his voice little more than a growl.

Catherine did as he bade and, holding her with one hand, he quickly spread out his jacket across the table's surface and lowered her onto the dry, quilted lining. She hissed in a breath as the cool skin of her buttocks settled against the lingering warmth of his body that remained in the silky fabric beneath her. She locked her ankles behind him, loath to lose the delicious sensations that cascaded through her at their point of contact.

"Lean back a little," he said.

Catherine transferred her weight to her hands, spreading her fingers against the tabletop. A tiny mew of protest fled her throat as he unhooked her feet and let them dangle down, her legs splayed.

He took his time, watching her carefully as he ran his hands up her legs, softly massaging her calves, gently tracing behind her knees and stroking firmly over her thighs toward the small nest of curls at their apex. Catherine sucked her lower lip in between her teeth and caught it fast as his fingers teased—circling ever closer, yet not touching the point that burned for him.

Richard leaned forward and flicked one nipple, then

the other, with his tongue. A groan ripped from her throat as he simultaneously palmed her heated entrance. She thrust against him and groaned again as he took one nipple in his mouth, suckling hard, rasping the tender flesh with the edge of his teeth, then laving it gently with his tongue once more.

He was driving her crazy.

Crazy with need.

Crazy for him.

She felt his fingers stroke the folds of skin at the entrance to her body, felt him part them, then slide one finger inside her. Her hips took up a slow undulating rhythm of their own as she strived to reach the ephemeral peak his touch promised.

"Ah, you taste so sweet," he said, transferring his attention to her other nipple. "You have no idea how many times I've imagined doing this to you."

Words failed her as he slid his thumb over her, stroking and pressing against the hooded pearl in time with the rise and fall of her hips. She was so close. So very close. Any second now and she'd fracture apart.

Her arms began to shake, and she felt him withdraw his hand from her body.

"Don't stop. Please, don't stop now," she all but begged, her voice a foreign sound to her ears.

"Don't worry, I have no intention of stopping."

Through the glaze of desire in her eyes she watched him dig his hand into an interior pocket of his jacket and extract a condom.

"Don't tell me," she said, laughing, "you were a Boy Scout in another life."

"In this one, actually." He smiled as he ripped open the packet and sheathed himself. "Now, where were we?"

The guttural sound that escaped her throat as he

slowly entered her body was as raw and heartfelt as the delicious sensation of him stretching and filling her. Sex had never felt so good or so right. She pushed back with her hips, meeting his every thrust, at first slow and gentle and driving her mad, then faster and faster until with a scream she gave over to her orgasm and pleasure ripped through her in ever-increasing waves. As if her climax had been his trigger, she felt him plunge even deeper and shudder against her, over and over until she lost track.

Catherine collapsed back against the tabletop, the cool wood against her shoulders a direct contrast to the perspiration-drenched heat of her body. Richard followed, and she pulled him to her, cushioning his weight with her body, wrapping her arms around him as if to let go would mean she'd float away forever.

Richard lifted his head and met her gaze.

"That was…intense," he said, still fighting to regain his breath.

"Yeah, that's one word for it," she agreed.

"I knew we'd be good together, but that? That surpassed all my expectations."

Catherine traced tiny circles on his back with a feather-light touch. She'd never felt comfortable with sex talk, especially after the act.

"Do you always conduct a postmortem after sex?" she teased.

"After making love," he corrected. "Not one for words, huh?"

"No," she admitted, letting her fingers continue tracing shapes down his spine and over the curve of his buttocks. She loved the feel of him, every glorious inch.

"Prefer action?"

"Always."

"Then I suggest we adjourn to the sofa and continue this in a little more comfort," he said, flexing his hips, causing a swell of pleasure to surge through her again in one powerful wave.

"You brought more than one condom?"

He winked at her as he straightened and slowly withdrew from her body, one hand reaching to cup her breast and caress her gently.

"As I said, I've been thinking about you a lot," he replied.

He dispensed with the used condom, wrapping it in a large cotton handkerchief before taking her hand and helping her off the table.

"So, I've had this fantasy," he started before leaning down to nip at her lips softly.

"Is that right?" she answered before giving back more of the same. "What kind of fantasy?"

He whispered into her ear, his breath sending shivers down her neck that made her skin suddenly feel more sensitive than it ever had before.

"I think we can arrange that," she answered, gently pushing his shoulders until he lay on his back on the sofa.

She extracted another packet from his pocket, then lifted one leg over his hips, straddling him and settling herself on his thighs.

"My turn," she said, her voice husky with intent.

The rain had stopped and the silence in the aftermath of the maelstrom of sensation she'd just experienced was a stark contrast to the sighs and moans, the slap of flesh, the cries of completion. A sense of time hit her with the subtlety of a cold, wet slap. It was getting late in the morning—people would be wondering where the heck she was.

She wriggled free of Richard's light clasp and grabbed her panties from the floor where she'd dropped them.

"What are you doing?"

"What does it look like I'm doing? I'm getting dressed."

"Come back here, surely we can—"

"Look—" she gestured with her hand "—this was all very nice—great, in fact—but I'm not here on holiday. I have work to do, staff to organize."

She reached over and grabbed his left arm, turning it slightly so she could read the face of his Rolex.

"And I'm running very late."

She searched around for the rest of her clothing, grimacing at the damp clinginess as she wriggled back into her riding breeches and tried to pull on her socks. Without a word, Richard rose from the sofa. In the brightening light, he looked gorgeous and she clenched her hands to prevent herself from reaching for him again.

On the table, his cell phone buzzed in its pocket. She reached over and grabbed it, catching sight of a name on the screen—Daniella—before she handed it to him.

"Maybe it's important," Catherine said as she nudged her way past him and out into the barn, desperate for some distance. While she readied their horses, she scolded herself silently.

So his ex was calling him. That wasn't so unusual, was it? Even so, she was racked with guilt. She knew she should never have given in to him. Now that she had, she only wanted him more, and he wasn't hers to have.

Richard was a city dweller. A high-flying businessman with high-flying demands on his time and his mind. Demands like the woman he was supposedly divorcing.

She didn't have time for this kind of dalliance. She wasn't that kind of girl. Of course she wasn't totally innocent, but emotionally, when it came to trust and building a relationship with someone, she was probably about as stunted as you could get. And, she told herself as she ignored the gnawing ache in the pit of her belly, she was quite happy to keep things that way. What was she even thinking allowing herself this slice of time with him?

Catherine's gut clenched tight. She knew what she'd been thinking. She'd tried to ignore the growing feelings she'd developed for him. Avoided confronting just how very much she'd looked forward to seeing him every single day. Refused to admit how much she'd craved his comfort yesterday after that awful moment in the VIP tent.

As stupid as it was, she was starting to fall for Richard Wells—fall very hard indeed—and that was the last thing she could afford to do. She couldn't love him. It was destined to fail. This interlude with Richard could never be anything more than just that, and the sooner she got her head around that the better.

But why couldn't she just take what she could for now, a little voice asked deep inside her. Compartmentalize. Wasn't that what high-flyers like Richard did in their everyday world? If she could train herself to do that, there was no reason to stop herself from enjoying him for as long as she could. And as often as she could.

Six

Richard pulled on his damp clothes with distaste. Nothing like coming back down to earth in a hurry. For a short while there, he'd thought he'd had her, had finally broken the barriers she kept so firmly between herself and the rest of the world. But then she'd gone and bolted from the tack room before he could begin to assimilate what had happened between them. Damn Daniella for choosing that moment to call him again. He'd have to see about blocking her calls.

He groaned in the silence of the tack room. He'd gone about this all wrong. He'd treated Catherine as if she were worth no more than a furtive roll in the hay, so to speak. And he knew on a gut level that she was worth so much more. Sure, the sex had been great. Better than great. But there'd been more than that. A communion of spirit. A give-and-take that he'd never felt on such a deep level before.

He should have taken her out. Wooed her slowly. Appealed to the very sensual side of her that lingered beneath the surface. Made love to her in more luxurious surroundings than those of a disused tack room, at the very least.

And yet, he couldn't regret today. Not by any definition of the word.

Out in the barn, he heard her talking to the horses. He suppressed an ironic laugh. She'd probably spoken more words to those horses today than she had to him in the whole time since they'd met. But that was going to change, he decided. And Ms. Catherine Lawson was going to let him into her life—one way or another.

Catherine still had her back to him as he approached her. He saw the exact second she sensed his presence, saw the brief stiffening of her spine, the set of her shoulders, as if she were shoring up her defenses the way she always seemed to do around him. And then, miracle of miracles, he saw her relax. He closed the short distance between them and put his arms around her waist.

She leaned back against him, and he felt a keen sense of relief. Things were going to be okay.

"I want to keep seeing you, starting tonight. Let me take you out. Dinner and dancing," he murmured against her hair, which was still loose.

"I'd like that," she answered, placing her hands over his and pressing them tightly to her.

"I'll meet you at your apartment at seven-thirty, okay?"

Catherine turned in his arms and kissed him lightly on the lips. "Are you sure you want to go out? We could stay at my place."

He knew what she was offering. In fact, every cell in

his body understood her subtext and responded in kind. But he had other plans.

"Catherine, I don't want to hide you away or make you think that this is just about sex. You're more than that."

Her blue eyes darkened and never wavered from his for what felt like a full minute. Then she slowly blinked, and a small smile curved her beautiful, lush lips.

"Thank you. That means more to me than you probably realize. Now, we'd better get going."

There was a heck of a crush in the Star Room by the time they made their way there. It was certainly the place to see people and be seen. Catherine felt as if the champagne she'd consumed at dinner was fizzing in her veins as Richard guided her through the crowd toward a slightly less frenetic spot on one side of the bar.

She was glad she'd worn high heels and a dress. She'd have felt so out of place if she'd chosen anything else. But she knew the midnight-blue satin suited her, and the way the fabric hugged her body and swayed with her every step made her feel a million times more feminine than she usually did in her customary riding breeches or jeans. Richard's expression when he'd arrived at her apartment this evening had been a testament to her hard work to transform into the kind of woman he deserved to have at his side, and he'd barely taken his eyes off her the entire time they'd dined at a nearby restaurant.

She couldn't even remember what they'd eaten, to be honest. She'd been just as rapt with his attention as he'd apparently been with hers. Now, he seemed to need constant contact with her. Tiny electric pulses ran down her arm as he gently stroked it with his hand.

"More champagne?" he asked, bending his head close to her ear.

She nodded. "I'll come with you to the bar."

"It's okay. I won't be a minute. Don't move from here or I'll never find you."

He smiled and kissed her cheek before turning and making the short distance to the bar. Catherine watched him, admiring the way he moved. Oh yes, the man could move. Another bolt of electricity hit her deep and low, making her lower muscles clench involuntarily.

"Nice to see you out socializing."

Catherine turned with a start to the source of the male voice that had come from her side. She recognized one of the visiting Argentinean team members, Alejandro Dallorso. Usually knee-deep in adoring women, he was surprisingly alone tonight.

"Nice to be out for a change."

"You work too hard." He smiled his hundred-watt smile at her.

"You play too hard," she replied with a raised eyebrow so he'd know she wasn't exactly referring to his on-field activity.

Alejandro shrugged expressively. "You're only young once, right?"

"Maybe if you played less, you'd have edged your six-goal handicap up to nine or even a ten."

The guy was loaded with talent and made playing polo look effortless, but he was definitely as interested in scoring off the field as on it.

"What? And miss all this fun? Why bother? I'm satisfied with my six, for now. It gets me what I want. Come, dance with me."

"I don't think so. Catherine is with me tonight," Richard interrupted before Catherine could respond.

Alejandro put both his hands up in mock surrender. "No problem. Maybe some other time."

Richard fought the urge to tell the other man that there would be no other time. It was ridiculous to feel so jealous, so possessive, this early—especially in a relationship that in all likelihood would end when he returned to the city. But something feral had awoken deep inside him when he'd seen the attractive Argentinean sidle up to Catherine.

He forced his lips into an approximation of a smile and nodded farewell as the man melted back into the crowd.

"Here," he said, passing a champagne flute to Catherine and clinking his against hers. "To a great night."

She smiled in response and tipped the glass up to her lips. Watching her throat move as she swallowed the sip of golden liquid sent a spear of desire straight through him. Now he'd had a taste of her, he was hungry for more. He forced his empty hand into his pocket to prevent himself from reaching out and touching her. If he did that, he'd likely lose control and want to take her from the Star Room and take her home in double quick time. He'd promised her a night out, to show her he was capable of treating her as a gentleman treated a woman.

"Richard?"

"Yeah?"

"Did you want to dance?" Catherine eyed him over the rim of her champagne glass.

He looked out over the dance floor at the bodies writhing to the beat and knew he had to be honest with her.

"No."

"Me either," she answered softly before putting a hand on his arm. "Take me to bed."

He didn't hesitate. He took her glass from her and placed it on a nearby table with his own, then took her by the hand and headed for the door. They covered the distance between the club and his guesthouse in minutes. Minutes punctuated by stolen kisses in the moonlight. By the time he thrust the door open to his suite of rooms, his heart was pounding so hard he could hear it beat inside his head.

Without even bothering to switch on the lights, he led her to his bedroom. This time he planned to take it slow.

Silver strands of moonlight strafed the wide expanse of his bed. Catherine appeared to be transfixed by the way the bed was lit, the only obvious piece of furniture in the room. Richard leaned forward to place a gentle kiss at the nape of her neck. She'd worn her hair up tonight in a casual knot high on her head that had exposed the slender line of her throat and the graceful curve of her neck. All night he'd wanted to do this.

As soon as his lips touched her skin, he was afire. His hands trembled as he placed them on her shoulders and gently eased the straps of her gown over the gentle curves. He peppered tiny kisses along the line of her shoulder, a smile curving his lips as he felt her skin tighten into tiny goose bumps and heard her breathing hitch infinitesimally. He reached for the zipper and slowly lowered it, relishing the unveiling of her beautiful back, inch by inch.

She wasn't wearing a bra, and the smooth line of her spine was unmarred as he pushed the dress away, letting the satin slide with a soft whisper all the way down her body. She wore only the tiniest of G-strings and high heels, and standing there with her back presented to him, the smooth globes of her taut buttocks bisected by only a scrap of dark fabric, he knew he'd never seen anything more beautiful.

Richard placed his hands on her shoulders again and ran them down the length of her arms before stroking back up and sliding his fingers down her spine. He felt the tremor that rippled through her as his fingers teased the outline of her panties, heard her catch and hold her breath before releasing it in a whoosh of air. He continued to trace the outline of her panties, following the line of her hips and around to her lower belly.

Touching her like this was sweet torment, but he forced himself to keep it slow. He trailed his fingertips across her flat belly and upward to the lower curve of her rib cage, following the line of each rib, one by one, until he skimmed the lower edges of her breasts. A barely suppressed groan sounded from her throat, breaking the cocoon of silence that surrounded them, and he pushed his hands higher, cupping her breasts and stroking the pads of his thumbs over her tautly budded nipples.

Catherine let her head drop back against his shoulder and pressed her buttocks back against him, against his engorged flesh. She lifted her hands to cover his, holding them tight against her, showing him what she wanted, how she needed to be touched.

Richard turned his head slightly and pressed his mouth against the exposed column of her throat, letting his teeth rasp against her skin, feeling the beat of her pulse beneath his lips, a pulse that skipped to a frantic beat. He pulled one hand from beneath hers and placed it over her own, silently encouraging her to continue to touch and stroke herself, mirroring the action with his other hand. Then, he skimmed his hand firmly down over her body, hesitating only briefly at the edge of her panties, tracing that edge across the top of her thigh and lower, until he could feel the heat of her through the dampened fabric.

He slid his hand beneath the flimsy material and let his fingers tangle briefly in her curls before dipping his middle finger in her honeyed warmth. She squirmed against him, pressing into his arousal again, forcing a groan from him that was as guttural as it was a mark of his pleasure. If she kept that up, he'd come in his pants, and he had far, far better plans for them than that.

Richard intensified his assault on her senses, sliding his moistened finger up a little, grazing her now prominent nub, at first gentle, fleeting, then with increasing pressure until he knew she was on the edge of her climax. He eased off incrementally, dragging time out, dragging the pleasure out for her. With each touch, promising her more—promising her the world.

Her entire body trembled against his as she uttered tiny, incoherent sounds, her head rolling against his shoulder, and he zoned back in on her most sensitive tissue, circling with increasing pressure until she gave herself over to the waves that now pulsed through her body. He felt all-powerful, as though he'd bestowed upon her the greatest gift, the knowledge that she, and she alone, was his entire focus. That her pleasure was paramount to him.

He scooped her into his arms and walked the short distance to the bed, laying her with exquisite care on the deliciously smooth cotton sheeting. He slipped off her high-heeled pumps, placing a kiss on the instep of each foot as he dropped her shoes to the ground, then stood and ripped his shirt over his head, unheedful of the buttons that pulled from the silk and fell to the floor. As he toed off his shoes, he undid his trousers and carefully eased them and his briefs over his straining erection, sliding them off together until he was gloriously naked.

Catherine pushed herself upright and onto her knees. She could only see Richard's silhouette in the soft, silver light streaming through his bedroom window, but she could sense him looking at her. Feel his eyes as they coasted over her body. He'd just brought her to what was probably one of the strongest climaxes she'd ever enjoyed, and yet here she was, aching for him again already. Wanting him to fill her, stretch her and become a part of her once more.

He swiftly pulled open a bedside drawer and rolled on a condom. She regretted she wouldn't have the chance to play with him a little longer, but the fact that he'd reached for protection now spoke volumes about how close he was to losing control with her altogether. The knowledge made her feel heady with power and a secret feminine awareness that she had the capacity to bring this powerful and intelligent man into such a state.

She reached out. Touching him was such a joy. He was so smooth and powerful, his muscles clearly delineated. A testament to his own personal disciplines. She lifted her face to him and he kissed her—his mouth possessive, his tongue entangling with hers in a dance more sensual than anything they could have achieved at the Star Room tonight.

She hooked her arms around his neck and dragged him closer, fusing their skin together. She felt his fingers loosen the few pins that held her hair up until it slid in its mass down her back.

The warmth of his hands followed the path of her hair, and tiny trickles of electricity passed through her skin. She'd never felt such an awareness of any man before, never wanted to be as much a part of him as he was rapidly becoming a part of her. Self-preservation, reason, distance—all three fled from her consciousness as they lay down on the bed together, as his body covered hers. And when he entwined his fingers with hers, lifting her arms up over her head to rest on the voluminous feather pillows, and slid his hard flesh slowly inside her, she knew that no matter how hard she tried, a piece of her heart would always belong to Richard Wells.

Seven

It was her day off. She was surprised the sheikh had insisted so vehemently on her taking the time, especially with it being a tournament day. Realistically, given that the day was supposedly her own, she should be down at the beach—catching a few waves, relaxing in the sun—instead of sipping champagne and balancing on high heels on the grassy field. But she'd discovered over the past two weeks that it was anatomically impossible for her to be away from Richard. The ache that lived inside her was monumental. He consumed every waking thought and a huge percentage of her sleeping ones, too.

When he'd insisted she accompany him to the VIP tents today and enjoy the polo purely as a spectator, she'd demurred. As much as she wanted to be with him, she also recognized that from time to time she had to create the illusion of independence. At least make him think that, for some of the time, she wasn't living minute by minute until they could be together again.

The past few days had been intense as they'd given in to their powerful attraction to one another to the exclusion of all others and any other activity. While her days had been busy with the horses and her usual duties, her nights had been full of the wonder of learning every amazing inch of Richard's body. And in their quiet times together—over a picnic in his bed, a shared dinner at her apartment, or even just a drive around Suffolk County—she learned a little more about what made Richard Wells tick.

When she'd tried to raise objections to accompanying him today, he'd simply brushed them aside. When she brought up the issue of her boss, he'd told her he'd already discussed her being there as his companion and had received no objections.

Companion. It was such an innocuous word and could mean so much—or so little.

She knew he was only in the Hamptons for a month and yes, realistically, she could expect to see a bit more of him even after he'd returned to the city, especially for the finals of the Clearwater Media Cup. Deep down, though, she knew her allure would fade and that he'd eventually find activities closer to home that would keep him in the city. It hurt but, she told herself over and over, it was worth it to have had this incredible time with him.

Catherine looked at the spectators who mingled and drank and brushed against one another. The tent seethed with people from all walks of life, but there was one thing they all had in common—money—and that was something Catherine would never be able to compete with. So, she'd have fun while she was here with Richard, and then somehow she'd find the strength to say goodbye when it was time for this idyll to end.

Her eye was suddenly caught by an older gentleman making a beeline toward her. There was something familiar about him that she couldn't quite put her finger on.

"A beautiful woman like yourself should never be left alone." The man smiled warmly.

Despite herself, Catherine smiled in return. As a pickup line it left a lot to be desired, but she had the feeling his interest in her wasn't sexual, which was a relief. Within the heady and glamorous world of polo, it wasn't unusual for liaisons to be formed and unformed between people who were virtual strangers.

"How could anyone be alone in a crush like this?" she answered, taking a sip of her champagne.

"You'd be surprised how lonely a person can be in company," the man replied. "I detect a bit of an accent there. Australian?"

"No, I'm a New Zealander. Although it's been a long time since I was home."

"Hmm," he nodded. "Trouble at home?"

"Not my trouble, but I still wanted to remove myself from it. Besides, working with horses is all I've ever really wanted to do. I would have been foolish not to have taken the opportunity to work with the sheikh and his horses when it presented itself."

"It always pays to follow your dream," he said sagely. "Although it can come at a great personal cost at times."

Through the throng, Catherine saw Richard making his way toward her, his dark brows drawn in a straight line. Surely he wasn't jealous, she thought. He had no right to be. After she'd seen and heard his proprietary manner at the Star Room that night, she realized he didn't want to share her with anyone, but seriously, to be annoyed with her for talking to an older man? It was ridiculous.

"Catherine." Richard nodded in her direction. "Is everything all right?"

"And why shouldn't it be?" the older man beside her said, his tone challenging.

Richard didn't take his eyes off her. "Is this man bothering you?"

"No, of course not," she sputtered. What the heck was going on?

"Come on, then, let's find our places in the stands."

Without so much as acknowledging the man who'd been talking to her, Richard took her arm and guided her toward the stands. Irritation rose within her. Perhaps it was time they established some ground rules. Starting with him not dictating who she talked to.

"I don't think I want to be with you right now," she finally managed through her anger and yanked her arm free of his hold.

"Trust me. You didn't want to talk to him anyway."

"How would I know? I never really got the opportunity. And while I'm on the subject, who appointed you my keeper? You have no right to say who I can and can't speak to."

Catherine bent down, slipped off her high heels and began to walk toward the road that led to the grooms' apartments.

"Catherine! Stop, please."

Richard's voice came from close behind her, encouraging her to step up her pace. The warmth of his fingers soon closed over her shoulders. She should have known he'd follow.

"Leave me alone. I'm too angry to talk to you right now."

"I'm sorry. I was wrong. I shouldn't have behaved like that."

Catherine stopped in her tracks. An apology. She hadn't expected that. Men like him didn't make a habit of saying they were sorry. At least not in her experience.

"Apology accepted," she said grudgingly. "But I'm still mad."

"Look, why don't I take you for an early dinner to explain. We'll get away from here for a bit."

She looked at him closely.

"Sure," she said, sliding her feet back into her shoes. "Promise me one thing, though."

"What's that?"

"That you won't piss me off again until after I've eaten."

His laughter warmed her heart. She really didn't want any conflict between them—not during the short time they'd have together. She allowed him to tug her close, accepted the pressure of his lips against hers and answered back with a passion that would leave him in no doubt of her forgiveness.

They headed out in Richard's car—some top-of-the-line thing, judging by the plush leather upholstery and the dashboard that looked as though it wouldn't be amiss on a fighter plane.

"Where are we going?" she asked as they drove along Millstone Road.

"Noyack Bay. There's a good seafood place there. You do like seafood, don't you?"

"Love it," she reassured him.

He wasn't kidding when he said the place was good. It

was better than good. The food was delicious, the decor luxurious and comfortable, and the company—well, the company was one hundred percent focused on ensuring she had a great time. Given his attentive behavior right now, if Catherine hadn't seen the way he'd snubbed that other man back at the polo grounds, she'd never have thought him capable of such a thing.

The contrast was a little disconcerting, and as much as she hated to burst the intimate bubble of attention she was receiving she had to know why he'd been so incredibly impolite. Catherine leaned back in the deep cushioned rattan chair and looked out over the Bay. She took a deep breath before looking back at Richard.

"Tell me, why were you so rude to that man back at the tent? You acted like—"

"Like I couldn't stand the sight of him?" Richard interrupted drily.

"Well, yeah. He was only chatting to me. So what's the story? Why did you behave like that?"

"He's my father."

The glass in her hand slid from her fingers, falling to the tiled floor with a resounding smash and shattering glass around the tables and chairs. Like a well-oiled machine, staff materialized from nowhere, sweeping away the debris, mopping up the champagne she'd been drinking and bringing a fresh glass filled with the delicious French vintage Richard had ordered for her with her dinner.

She knew she'd never drink it. Not now. Not with the shock of Richard's revelation still reverberating through her body with an echoing chill. *His father!* And he treated him like that?

The cold shock was rapidly followed by an ache in her chest. She'd give anything to be able to speak to her father again—to feel his big, strong arms around her one more time, to ask his advice on a difficult pony. Anything.

"But why?" Her voice came out in croak. "What happened to make you so angry at him?"

She knew he'd been angry. She had seen firsthand the blaze of fury that shone from Richard's gray eyes, turning them to steel. But worse, she'd seen faint hope in his father's eyes and then seen that hope dashed as effectively as the crystal champagne flute she'd just dropped to the floor.

Her shock must have shown on her face. Richard's eyes narrowed, and he reached across the table to hold her hand.

"You'd have to understand what happened to understand why."

"So tell me. What on earth was so bad that you can't even be civil to him anymore?"

That Richard was the angry one was clear to her now as she replayed the short scene back in her head. His father had spoken directly to him. It was Richard who'd acted as if he didn't exist, hadn't so much as spoken. It was Richard who'd cut him out of her sphere and led her away.

"It's complicated," he hedged.

"We have time. I'm listening," she encouraged.

Richard sighed and leaned back in his chair, looking at her across the table as if he were weighing what he had to say. Catherine found herself holding her breath. The man in front of her was nothing like the passionate and generous lover she'd spent her nights with this past week. Nothing like the playful, teasing suitor who'd shadowed her until she'd finally agreed to a date with him. No, this was the corporate Richard. The man she didn't know. The man who was as far removed from her as the earth from the sun. And she knew—by getting this close, by probing into something so deep and so personal—she risked getting badly burned.

"You have to understand a bit about my father before we go any further." Richard sighed and gestured to the waiter. "Coffee, please, and keep it coming. We may be a while."

Catherine waited patiently for the waiter to return with their coffee and smiled her thanks as he added milk and the two sugars that were her only sweet vice. Once he'd gone again, she lifted her cup to her lips, watching Richard carefully over the rim as she sipped.

"My father's family came over from Ireland. My great-grandfather was a typesetter by trade but was suspected of printing and distributing seditious material. I understand the family got out of the country and onto a boat so fast that they didn't have time to pack more than a few sets of clothes and loaves of bread. When they arrived here they had next to nothing, and he didn't find it easy to find work right away.

"Over time, though, he got back into printing and eventually had his own small press. When my grandfather took it over, he turned it into a series of papers being distributed not just citywide but statewide. By the time my father joined the family business, it had expanded even farther. Their interests are now global."

"That's quite an achievement over just three generations," Catherine commented.

Richard nodded in agreement. "Pretty phenomenal, especially when you know how many other businesses thrived then failed due to economic crises, wars, even something as simple as poor circulation."

"So why didn't you follow in your father's footsteps?" It was clear to her that that was the crux of the problem.

"Why? Because he's a stubborn old coot who wouldn't listen to new ideas for expansion or growth. I was nearly done with my degree when we started talking about my future with the family firm. I had ideas I couldn't wait to implement. It was way past time we hopped on the digital express that was pulling out of the station, but he wouldn't listen to me. Said I lacked the experience to pull off the expansion I wanted to head. Said I'd have to prove my worth and bide my time before developing my ideas any further.

"I told him he could stick his job, that he was entrenched in the dark ages. I'd grown up with ink running through my veins, had spent every holiday working with him or in different departments of the business. I knew what was involved, I knew what was at stake and I knew that if I didn't act soon for him, Wells & Son would eventually hit the wall."

And has it? The question echoed silently in her head. She could understand Richard's frustration, but by the same token, she could see his father's point of view. Sure, Richard had had some experience in the industry—probably more than most other interns—but she could imagine that his enthusiasm for change had to be tempered with the experience of living and working the industry for years.

She carefully put her cup down on its saucer and leaned forward, resting her elbows on the table, propping her chin in her hands.

"How did he take it? You telling him to stick his job."

Richard shook his head slowly before answering. "I

have to hand it to the old man. He's got balls. He actually laughed at me. Told me the door was always open but that I needed to grow up some more before I could work for him. He actually let me go."

"So what did you do next?"

"Finished my degree. Graduated summa cum laude. Set up Clearwater Media with Seb and showed my father how it was supposed to be done."

"And you haven't spoken to him since?"

"No."

"You must miss him."

"Hey, it's water under the bridge now. I've made my own future from the ground up. Clearwater has turned into one of the fastest-growing media companies worldwide. It has solid foundations, and we still have a long way to go. We will be around for generations."

It struck Catherine that Richard's future generations would never get to know his father if the men didn't mend their differences. She gathered up her courage to ask out loud the question she'd silently posed.

"Has your father's firm gone to the wall like you said?"

Richard's laugh lacked any humor. "No, of course not. The old man was far too canny for that. Seems he'd been intending to expand digitally for years but was handpicking his team to implement it. Clearly he never considered me good enough for that."

The hurt in that statement cut to Catherine's heart. The two men must have been very close. To have severed all ties must have been immeasurably painful to them both for different reasons. And both were obviously too proud to reach out and rebuild.

She didn't condone what Richard had done. Not by any means. He must have come across as brash and arrogant to his more experienced father. She'd seen it so often herself with younger grooms pitting their limited skills against those with a lifetime of experience working with horses. But his father hadn't done the right thing by Richard either. No wonder he'd strived so hard to succeed. And no wonder he took so many opportunities to laud his success in the news. She supposed, under normal circumstances, that she would have been unlikely to have heard as much about Richard Wells if he hadn't been so hell-bent on shoving his prowess in his father's face.

His hurt, his determination and drive, even his upbringing—all of those things combined to make Richard who he was today. And as much as she failed to fit into his world, she couldn't help but love the man in it.

"So, there you have it. What would you like to do for the rest of the evening?" Richard broke into her thoughts.

That was it? Subject now closed? Judging by the look on his face, the topic was most definitely no longer open to further discussion. But a part of her burned to help Richard make things right with his father—before it was too late for both of them.

Eight

Richard lay back against the pillows, his heart still thudding in his chest, thunderbolts of pleasure still pounding through his body. It didn't matter how they made love, how fast or how often, the result was always the same as the first time. An unending sense of completion—of rightness. He so wasn't ready for this. The ink on the papers to his divorce from Daniella was barely dry and here he was, imagining that Catherine was "the one"?

Man, if his friends knew what he was thinking, they'd call him certifiable. But there were no other words for how he felt—for how Catherine made him feel.

She lay sprawled over his body, her legs entangled with his, her hair a curtain across his chest, her head just over his heart. Did she know that it beat for her? Did she understand that she was becoming more and more important to him with every day that passed? Even though he wasn't ready for anything permanent—maybe never would be again—he couldn't deny that she brought out the best in him and he liked that. He'd forgotten what the best was.

In return, he wanted to be that man who brought the smile to her face, the quiet humor to her eyes, the cries of pleasure to her lips. She hadn't looked so happy today, though. There'd been a reserve in her eyes that had appeared when he'd caught his father talking to her in the VIP tent and, despite his explanation for their estrangement, that reserve had remained. It wasn't until they'd come back to his place after stopping at the beach to walk along the white sand and watch the waves roll in off the Atlantic that she'd lost that slightly haunted look in her eyes.

Richard let his fingers draw lazy shapes over Catherine's back, relishing the softness of her skin, the hidden strength in her long, lean form. She'd said nothing about him and his dad not being on speaking terms. Aside from her original anger at his behavior, there hadn't been so much as a hint of disapproval.

Playing their conversation over in his head, he started to feel uncomfortable, wondering how she'd really felt hearing about the rift for the first time. The person he'd been, the man he'd described to her, had been very young and hotheaded—totally passionate about his cause, as he saw it. His anger toward his father had driven him to succeed, to refuse to accept failure as an option. He supposed he should thank the old man for that, if nothing else.

Suddenly his churlishness left a bitter taste in his mouth. His father had never actually held him back or cut ties. That had been Richard's choice. There were hundreds of things his father could have done—financially and socially—to completely shut him down if he had really wanted to retaliate, but he'd done none of them. He'd let his only son make his own path.

Looking back now, Richard seriously doubted he would consider hiring someone so young and inexperienced to implement a major policy change within Clearwater Media. Sebastian would have him declared insane, and invoke the power of attorney they each held for one another in extenuating circumstances, if he were ever so foolish as to entertain the idea. As much as it galled him to admit it, his father had been right to do what he did. To step away. To let him sink or swim.

The distance that had grown between them over the issue had been more Richard's doing than his dad's, but how could he even begin to rectify the issue after so many years, and so much anger and bitterness? They were equally pigheaded and stubborn. It had sadly become easier to be apart than to try and mend the gaping hole in what had once been a strong bond between them.

Catherine stirred from her languor and lifted her head, distracting him from his thoughts.

"You okay?" she asked.

"Yeah, just doing some thinking."

"Oh? Good things, I hope."

"Good and bad."

She shifted and nestled into his side, snuggling up against him and drifting her hand across his chest. He loved her touch. It did the most incredible things to him. For now, though, he was happy to simply lie here.

"Want to talk about it?"

"No, I'm okay. Besides, I'd rather talk about you.

We've spent all this time together and you've hardly told me anything about yourself."

"There's not much to know."

"Try me. Start with what you want."

"That's simple. You."

She pressed a kiss against his skin and followed it up with a tiny nip that sent a spear of longing straight to his groin.

"Aside from me—" he laughed "—what do you want long-term? What's the big picture for Ms. Catherine Lawson?"

"Ah, that's easy. I want my own stables. Initially to teach those who can afford it, but one day I'd like to be able to teach kids who have it tough—whether financially or emotionally—to learn to ride and care for horses. It's what I've always wanted to do. There are so many kids out there desperate for something to do, for someone to spend time with them, for the chance to love something. So, yeah. That's the long-term plan. How I'm going to get there—" she shrugged "—is the hard part."

"Why not start with finding sponsorship? Your idea is bound to resonate with enough of the money men needing an outlet for charitable funds or positive publicity associated with community projects. Then you'd have your start-up costs taken care of, and you wouldn't have to wait to expand the second stage of your dream."

She shook her head. "It's not that easy."

"Why not? Have you tried?"

"No," she hedged.

"What's stopping you?"

"You wouldn't understand."

"Try me," he encouraged her gently. "You might be surprised. I have contacts, you know."

"You remember what happened last week, when those women said those things?"

"Yes," he said. "Something to do with your dad, right?"

"Yeah," she sighed. "He worked with horses on the polo circuit, too. He was a good player, but he lacked the competitive spirit to ever go up the ranks. But he was damn good at making polo ponies."

"Like you."

"I'm not even half as good as he was."

"If you really only have half his talent, he must have been quite a man."

Richard rubbed his hand down Catherine's back and pulled her in closer.

"He was. His reputation was huge no matter where we went, and he was the center of my universe. Mum was always quite happy being on the social edges of polo. She loved the hype of being Del Lawson's wife."

Catherine fell quiet for a moment, and Richard waited patiently for her to continue. From the tension he could feel in her body, he knew what was coming wouldn't be pleasant, and he sensed it was already exacting a toll from her.

"I was about fifteen when it happened. A patron had seen the ponies Dad had worked with during a tournament at Palm Beach. He approached Dad with an offer to work with a low-goal team and a string of ponies through the New Zealand season with a view to putting them in tournaments in the U.K. later on.

"He was so excited. The chance of working with a talented group of international riders, bringing them up to a higher level of play and improving their ponies, was more than he could resist. Of course it wasn't as good as it seemed. Nothing ever is."

"The guy was rigging the team?"

"He was doping the horses. He had brought with him a vet who gave the ponies doctored supplements. Something went wrong with the cocktail he was giving them. Dad had no idea—he'd believed it was the usual supplement, one commonly used pretty much everywhere. The ponies went on the field for a tournament and things started going wrong. The officials ordered an investigation."

"Going wrong?"

"One of the horses collapsed and died on the field. The others began showing signs of extreme distress. Dad did what he could, but it was too late. Of course the fingers all started pointing at him. He could never prove that he'd had nothing to do with the incident, and it destroyed his reputation. No one would hire him."

"Did he fight back? Didn't your polo association order an investigation?"

"Yes, but Dad was head groom. He and he alone had the final say on how the ponies were fed, supplemented and trained. No one believed he'd had no idea about what the vet had been doing—or that the patron was complicit. Dad took the rap and eventually it killed him."

Richard felt hot tears begin to fall upon his chest. He was filled with a helplessness that was foreign to him. He wanted to make everything right in Catherine's world, but he knew he could no more turn back the clock and fix the problem than he could spin glass from moonbeams.

"Mum was horrified. Her world, as she knew it, was destroyed. She distanced herself from him as soon as she could and ended up going to Australia and finding herself a new partner before she and Dad were even divorced. I stayed with Dad. I couldn't leave him. He had nothing else. He'd worshipped Mum. When she left, it was as if she believed he'd been capable of doing those things he'd been accused of. That hurt him more than anything.

"He started drinking—heavily. He got a job when I was sixteen, breaking horses on a farm where his reputation hadn't quite caught up with him. But then one day a buyer recognized him and brought it to his boss's attention. No one looked at him the same after that, and one night, after a few drinks, he took one of the horses and rode out into the bush. The horse came back, but it was two days before rescue workers found Dad. The coroner's report said he'd died of exposure and the rumors said suicide. But I know he died of a broken heart."

"And you're saying what happened in the tent the other day, that's what you have to deal with? People talking about your father's reputation?"

"Who on earth would sponsor the child of the man who created world headlines with what happened? It's been twelve years, but memories are long—you saw that. When I was younger, all I wanted to do was to clear Dad's name. But the more years that pass, the more I realize how impossible that is."

Richard swallowed back the anger that welled within him and forced himself to speak calmly.

"Clearly Sheikh Adham didn't feel that way or you wouldn't be working for him."

"No. I was very lucky there. Soon after Dad died, I was helping out at the grounds in Clevedon, and he was there. One of his horses got spooked by a stray dog that wandered onto the field. I caught her and calmed her down before she could hurt herself. He offered me a job, so, with nothing left for me in New Zealand, I took it."

"What happened to the guy who let your dad take the fall for him?"

"He's around. Not in the league the sheikh competes in, so it's some comfort I haven't bumped into him yet."

"And is he still up to the same tricks?"

"I don't know."

"I bet it wouldn't be too hard to find out."

Catherine sighed. "Probably not, but that's not my fight anymore. If I thought I could, I'd move heaven and earth to clear my dad's name—for his sake, not for mine. I reconciled myself a couple years ago to the fact that that kind of thing is totally out of my reach. The only thing I can do now is keep doing what I do, as well as I can do it. The sheikh's a generous employer. I'm paid very well. I already have a deposit saved for a small farm. In time I'll have the balance of what I need to be able to set up, and once I've proved myself—hopefully before I'm too old to get up on a horse—" she laughed quietly "—then I'll have my own reputation to stand on when I start applying for loans for the rest. As for sponsorship—that's still just a dream."

Catherine started drawing little circles on his belly, her light touch making his skin tingle and sending more demanding sensations through his body. But her next words dashed his ardor more effectively than a bucket of ice water.

"I'd do anything to have my dad back, Richard. I know you've had your differences with yours, but you only get one father in your life. You and your father used to be close—I could hear that in your voice even as you told me how the two of you fell out. You miss that closeness. You miss him. Don't waste any more time, because when he's gone you will never have that opportunity to make things right again. Never."

Richard's instinctive reaction to his father, to her words, rushed through him. Miss his dad? She had to be kidding. But as much as he didn't want to acknowledge that truth, he knew she was right.

After walking her home, Richard thought long and hard about what she'd said. Especially, what she'd told him about her father and how intensely loyal she remained to his memory weighed on his mind. He was surprised to feel a pang of envy that she had a far stronger relationship with her dead father than he had with his father who was still living.

She'd opened his eyes earlier in the evening to how idiotic his behavior appeared to anyone not aware of the situation that had led to the rift between father and son. At the time, though, it had been so real—the hurt, the distrust, the lack of confidence. It occurred to him now that he wouldn't have worked under his father's umbrella forever. It had been an introduction to the industry he loved, but he'd have wanted to branch out, to pursue his own ambitions.

Richard thrived on the cut and thrust of taking something new and expanding it to its fullest potential. Developing ideas with Seb had given them a powerful edge over their competition. The way they worked was tailor-made to his intensity.

If anything, his father had probably done him a favor by not agreeing to his demands. He shoved a hand through his hair and leaned against one of the moonlit fence railings. Why did life have to be so damn complicated?

Here was Catherine, who would probably give anything to have five more minutes with her father, and Seb, whose father was battling cancer, the threat of losing that battle hanging like Damocles's sword over his best friend's head every day. And then there was him. Letting pride and an unhealthy dose of ego stand in the way of reaching out to the only father he'd ever have.

Richard pushed off the railings with a muttered curse and stalked back to the guesthouse. There were no easy answers anymore, but he was certain of one thing. Whatever had passed between him and his father had well and truly passed. He was his own man now, and part of being that man was owning up to his mistakes.

He'd been happy to take everything his father had ever given him, but he'd done nothing in return. The thought of losing him, without ever having made the time to mend the prideful fences between them, sliced through him like a knife.

With each step he took back to the house, he firmed his resolve that he would not let that happen. He would talk to his father at the game this coming weekend, starting with an apology and hopefully ending with a new basis for them to move forward.

His eyes had been opened. And he had Catherine to thank for that.

Nine

It had been a busy week. The struggle to balance the demands of her job and her nights with Richard had hit Catherine full force this morning, leaving her feeling out of sorts when she awoke.

There was a match later today, and she busied herself with her usual chores, making time pass quickly. By the time the ponies were prepared, she was about ready to fall into bed. That was a faint hope, she conceded grimly, with a game due to start at four o'clock. She looked around at the field, anxious for the sight of Richard.

Things had been different between them this week. *He'd* been different. She'd seen his ex-wife's name on his caller ID several times, and despite his attentions to Catherine, the other woman's constant contact with Richard made her feel unsettled. On top of that was her concern that maybe she'd overstepped the mark when she'd urged Richard to make up with his father. It really wasn't her place to have said anything, but in the face of what she'd learned about their estrangement, she couldn't stop herself.

In the distance, a dark head caught her attention, and her heart did that strange flip-flop it always did whenever she saw him. She waved but Richard, despite looking straight in her direction, didn't appear to notice her. Or if he did, he was avoiding her. Catherine tried not to feel hurt but she knew she was in too deep for the snub, real or imagined, not to sting a little. If he wasn't on the lookout for her, it clearly spelled out something else—he was definitely cooling things off.

Would it be better to make a clean break and be done with it? She knew he only had a few more days before he had to go back to the city. Instantly, her heart rebelled. No, she was in this for however long she could take it—and for however much of him she could have. The memories would give her something to cling to as she refocused on her dream. Maybe it was even time to have a chat with a bank manager and see just how much she could borrow to start things moving with her riding school. She had a strong feeling that she would need to be very busy to keep her mind off Richard Wells, and what he'd come to mean to her, once he left.

Her eyes tracked Richard's every move. He was looking for someone—someone who wasn't her, that much was obvious. When she saw him stiffen, she knew he'd found who he was looking for. She watched as he strode purposefully toward a group and singled someone out, drawing him away from the throng of spectators.

His father! Richard was talking to his father. Catherine's hand flew to her mouth, and her weariness was forgotten as she watched the two men face one another.

She was too far away to catch the expression on the older man's face, but she saw him reach out to clasp his son's hand in his, and then Richard drew his father close, closing the older man in an embrace that brought tears to her eyes.

The two men stayed that way for some time, and Catherine forced herself to look away before she became a blubbering mess. Richard had taken the first monumental step. Slowly it began to sink in that what she'd said to him last week had actually meant something to him.

No wonder he'd been quiet. She'd learned from watching him that he was single-minded in his purpose—his pursuit of her was a prime example. He'd been weighing up what she'd said, how he felt and whether he was prepared to do something about it.

She dashed away the tears from her cheeks and turned back to the pony lines. He'd done the right thing. Her step was a great deal lighter as she rejoined her grooms and double-checked the ponies and players were all ready to go for the first chukka that was due to start shortly.

It wasn't until the stomping of the divots at halftime that she caught sight of him again. He was still with his father, their heads close together as they spoke, not even looking at the field. Again, she felt that flutter deep in her chest. She had it bad, she admitted to herself. Real bad.

A couple of the local girls she'd taken on for the season came up and stood alongside Catherine by the railings.

"That's Richard Wells, isn't it?" said one to the other.

"Yeah, I heard he was back on the market. It's a shame he's too old for us. I wonder if he could be persuaded to look at a younger model next time around," the other said and laughed. "He's totally hot and filthy rich."

"He's not on the market, from what I've heard around the tents."

Catherine's ears pricked up. While they hadn't deliberately kept their time together a big secret, they hadn't exactly showcased their relationship in the public eye, either. Were the two girls talking about her without even realizing it?

"What? He's got someone new?"

"No, I heard he's still married and that there's a reunion on the cards."

The contents of Catherine's stomach solidified and shifted sharply, lodging at the base of her throat. An icy chill drenched her body from head to foot.

He was still married?

Murmuring something about checking equipment, she stumbled away. No wonder he'd had so many calls from his ex. Catherine felt as if she were being torn apart in every way. She loved him but he was forever forbidden to her. She didn't do married men. It was one of her absolute irrevocable rules about life. She'd seen how it had destroyed her father when her mother had drifted away from him and started a new relationship before they'd even divorced. Catherine had sworn she would never be party to anything like that in her life.

She was such a fool. She should have known, should have followed her instincts and stayed away from him. Should have stayed out of his arms and out of his bed. Should never—ever—have fallen in love with him.

Catherine threw herself into work for the rest of the afternoon, and when Richard texted her later that evening, she put him off, telling him she was extremely tired and wanted nothing more than a soak in a hot bath and an early night. When he easily accepted her excuse, she didn't know whether to be pleased or disappointed. Was he relieved that she wasn't available tonight? Did it mean he was already preparing to let her go?

She reminded herself that she'd gone into their relationship with her eyes wide open. That she'd known there could never be a future for them together because their worlds were so far apart that she could never dream of bridging the gap. She deserved this sense of loss—it was punishment for daring to reach out and take what was not hers to own. But knowing all that didn't make any of it any easier.

Richard threw his cell phone on his bed in frustration. Something was wrong. This was the fourth day in a row that Catherine had refused to see him, and he still had no logical reason why. He missed her with an ache that drew from the soles of his feet all the way up through his body—an ache he was desperate to relieve. He hadn't wanted to admit just how much she'd gotten under his skin, how important she'd become to him. This was supposed to have been a fling, a summer affair to get him back in the single man's swing of things, but it was turning out to be so very much more.

The distance in her tone the past few days puzzled him. Friendly yet remote. And while she'd sounded happy for him when he'd told her about how he and his father had agreed to put the past behind them, that had been it. There'd been no further enquiries, no gentle encouragement. None of what he'd come to expect in her company. The loss of her companionship struck him harder than he could have imagined.

He tried to rationalize it. Maybe she'd decided to back off a bit and let him spend time with his father while he was in the Hamptons, but even that rang empty as an excuse. There was no reason why she couldn't still be a part of it. He'd hoped she might have wanted to share his joy, to talk it over with him because it wasn't going to be an easy relationship to rebuild. He and his father were too similar on many levels—but they were both committed to making it work this time.

Richard paced his bedroom floor. It was as if Catherine had reverted back to how she'd been the day he first saw her. Reserved and aloof. Rejecting him. Something had happened to make her withdraw like this; he just knew it. But what?

His phone buzzed from among the expensive bed linens, and he snatched it up. Maybe she'd changed her mind. The number on the caller ID taunted him for his hopes. Sebastian.

"Yeah, Seb, how are you?"

"Haven't seen much of you this vacation, my friend, what with the club and keeping that sister of mine in line. Everything okay?"

"I've been—" he hesitated a moment before continuing "—preoccupied. But I'm free tonight. How about we meet for a drink?"

Later that evening, the two men reclined in plush seats in Sebastian's den at the main house, comfortable in one another's company.

"So, did you take my advice?" Sebastian asked, taking a sip of his drink.

"To get laid?" Richard snorted a laugh. "That would be telling, and a gentleman never tells."

Sebastian smiled in return and raised his glass in a toast. "Good for you. Has it helped?"

Had it helped, Richard wondered? Sure, it had taken his mind off his divorce from Daniella, but *helped?* He twirled his brandy in his glass, seemingly absorbed by the amber liquid, but his mind was focused very much on just one person, Catherine. On how she looked astride a horse, so in command, so lithe and strong. How she looked first thing in the morning, her long hair tousled and spread across his pillow. The expression in her eyes as he entered her body, giving herself to him with utter abandon.

Every muscle in his body tautened, and his fingers clenched against the tumbler holding his drink.

"Richard?" Sebastian prompted.

"I believe I've fallen in love."

Saying the words out loud sent a shudder of fear through him. How could he be saying it or even be thinking it? He'd just come out of a nasty, bitter divorce—the by-product of a marriage entered into in haste, with a partner with whom he'd had little in common.

"Are you sure about this?" Seb looked at him seriously across the coffee table.

"Yeah, I know. I've taken this route before. But this is different, you know? *She's* different."

"Does she feel the same way about you?"

"I don't know. Right now she's avoiding me."

"A ploy, maybe?"

Both men knew all too well how Daniella had behaved. How she'd sulk like a child one minute and then vamp herself up the next.

"No. I'm sure of that. Catherine wouldn't be bothered with that kind of thing. She's not into games."

"Catherine? You mean the sheikh's head groom?"

Richard nodded.

"Wow, she's different from Daniella, all right. In fact, I'd say she's her polar opposite."

"I know. I thought it would just be some mutual fun, you know? But she's come to mean so much more. She's even got me talking to my dad again."

"Hey, Richard, that's great. She must be pretty amazing to get you to cross that bridge. I mean, I know Daniella wanted you and your dad to reconcile, but that was more from the point of view of what you'd stand to inherit than anything else."

"I know. And yeah, Catherine is amazing. She made me see things—*me,* more precisely—from a different perspective."

"Well," Sebastian said, getting up to refresh their drinks, "that kills the rumors flying around the tents at the moment."

"Rumors?"

"Yeah, that your divorce isn't final and that a reconciliation is in the works."

Richard laughed out loud. "Where the hell did that come from?"

Sebastian shrugged. "You know how these things start. Someone gets the wrong end of the stick, and before you know it, it's gospel."

Richard accepted his refill from Sebastian and considered his best friend's words. Was it possible that Catherine had heard those rumors and, rather than asking him if they were true, had believed them? Choosing to withdraw rather than confront? That would be her style, especially given her history.

"Just when did these rumors start? Do you know?" he asked.

"Couple of days ago. Vanessa asked me if it was

true and offered to pay to get your head examined if it was."

The timing made sense. If Catherine *had* heard the rumor about him and Daniella, then she'd definitely have withdrawn from their relationship. She was old-fashioned like that—her sense of right and wrong was as indelibly marked on her as her fingerprints. In some ways, her old-fashioned demeanor was at odds with the lifestyle the polo set was famed for, but he'd found it both refreshing and challenging. No less challenging now would be convincing her that what she might have overheard was completely and utterly wrong. There was only one woman he wanted in his life—he knew that now with complete and utter certainty. And that woman was Catherine Lawson.

Ten

Catherine was bone weary—pretty much "situation normal" these days, she thought ironically. Her feet dragged on the stairs that led to her second-floor apartment in the groom's quarters. It had been a difficult day all around. One of the sheikh's favorite horses had come up lame and he wasn't happy, and to cap things off, a couple of the female grooms had gotten into a snit over some British player and she'd had to intervene before the girls did some serious damage to each other.

The prospect of falling into bed and managing to sleep until the morning was strongly alluring right now. The reality, she knew, would be something different. Since she'd made the decision not to see Richard again, she'd felt heartsick. No matter how hard she pushed herself, she couldn't get him out of her mind. Nor could she ignore the deep sense of loss at her decision.

She'd endured worse, she told herself, and she'd

survived. She'd known Richard, what, nearly a month? It was ridiculous to think she had fallen in love with him so completely. Simply and utterly ridiculous.

A shadow stepped out from the alcove by her front door, and her heart leaped in her chest when she recognized Richard's tall frame. In the dim light offered by the overhead lamp, he looked mighty fine to her eyes.

"We need to talk," he said, his voice deep and pitched low.

"Sure," she said, summoning every ounce of false bravado in her arsenal.

She could do this. She could let him go. Obviously that was why he was here—to tell her the truth about him and his wife. To say "Thanks for the memories, but I'm getting on with my life now." Her hand shook as she tried to put her key into the lock. Richard's hand closed over hers, taking the key.

"Here, let me. You look exhausted." He opened the door and ushered her in before him. "Tough day?"

Tough life, she answered silently but gave a short nod as she eased her boots off and headed to the kitchen.

"Coffee? Sorry, I can't offer you anything alcoholic," she said stiffly.

After observing firsthand her father's slide into the bottle, she reserved her drinking for social occasions only.

"No, I'm okay, thanks."

"Do you want to sit down?" she asked, keen to get off her feet herself, but more than that, she wanted him to be still and in one place. Right now she felt as if he were looming over her.

"No. I won't."

Despite all her pep talks to herself about ending their relationship, the knowledge that he didn't plan to be here long sent her heart plummeting to the soles of her feet. He had to be here to say goodbye. She wished to heck he'd just say it and get it over with—so she could start kidding herself that she was getting over him.

"Why haven't you seen me?"

His question startled her. She'd thought he'd have been glad of being given the distance—at least that way there'd be no messy goodbyes. He could have done this with a phone call.

"I've been busy and so have you. How are things going with your father? I thought I saw you together again the other day."

"Nice parry, Catherine, but you won't distract me. Tell me the truth." He stepped closer, took both her hands in his and locked gazes with her. "You owe me that much at least."

"I…I'm not into goodbyes. I just thought it would be easier, that's all."

"Easier? Goodbyes? What makes you think I want to say goodbye to you?"

"Well, it's coming up to the end of your vacation. You'll be leaving. Going back to work, your other life."

Your wife.

"And you think I don't want to see you anymore? That I can just walk away from you like that?"

His fingers curled around hers, tight, making it impossible to pull away.

"Look, I knew the score right from the start. It was only supposed to be a fling, and it has been. A great one. But we both knew all along it had to end."

"It doesn't have to end, Catherine," he said, his voice calm and deep.

Shock tore through her. He wanted to keep their affair

going even while he was considering reuniting with his wife?

"Yes, it does." She shook her head and yanked free of his hold, wrapping her arms around herself to stop him from taking her hands again. "It has to. I can't stand in the way of your happiness."

"What makes you think that being without you would make me happy? I don't see why this couldn't work. You're here until the end of summer. I can commute back here on weekends. Sure, I know we won't see as much of one another as we have but we can handle that, can't we?"

"And your wife? What will she have to say about that?"

"I have paid very handsomely to ensure that my *ex*-wife has nothing to say about my life at all." He crossed the short distance between them and cupped her face in his hands, tilting her head so she looked directly at him. "It was just a stupid rumor, Catherine. Don't you think that I would have treated you better than that? At least have had the courtesy to tell you if I wasn't divorced? Surely you must have understood that about me, if nothing else."

"I didn't know what to think. I couldn't help but notice she's always calling you. Besides, you know what it's like in the world I live in. People come and go. Love affairs are exactly that—affairs, with nothing more to them but a need to be together for however long before moving on to the next tournament or the next lover."

"I'm not like that. I love you. I couldn't walk away from you now, not for anything or anyone else." They were just words, she told herself, even as hope began to swell in her heart. She shook her head—she didn't dare to hope.

"I came here to have a vacation and maybe, yeah, sow some wild oats while I was here. I never expected to find you, to find love. I fought how I feel about you because I've just finalized an ugly and bitter divorce, which ended an equally ugly and bitter marriage. The last thing I was looking for was the person I want to spend the rest of my life with."

"It's a rebound thing, Richard. Be serious for a minute. What we have, it can't be real."

"Why not? It feels damn real to me. More real than anything I've ever felt or hoped for. I admit I rushed into my first marriage and regretted it deeply—still do, in fact. It wasn't fair to either of us, and it took well over a year to extricate myself from it. But this—" he pressed a kiss against her lips "—is so much more."

"How can you be sure?" Catherine asked, her voice quavering. "You admit yourself that you rushed into things the first time around. We've barely known each other four weeks! I spent the first week you were here trying to avoid you, for goodness' sake. People just don't fall in love that fast. Not forever."

"I did—once, with you. We haven't had much time together, but we have the rest of our lives to find out how well we fit."

"But don't you see? We're so different. Once you leave this, *my* world, we have nothing left in common but our physical attraction to one another. And that's not enough. It's never enough. I want more than that if I ever settle with someone. I *need* more than that. I lost everything once—my father, my home, my mother when she went away. I'm not prepared to take that risk again."

"Catherine, do you really think we're so very different? You want a home, a happier future—maybe even a family. What makes you think I don't want those things, too? I never looked past the moment with Daniella, but with you I want to look forward, and I see you there at my side."

Catherine shook her head again, trying to deny his words, but she couldn't deny how much she wanted them to be true. How much she wanted *him*.

"Listen to me, please," he implored her. "Let us at least give it a try. I know you need security. Let me prove to you that I can be the man to give it to you. That I will always be there for you. We can take this easy, keep seeing each other on weekends and whenever I can get away. Hell, I'll do whatever it takes to keep you, Catherine, even if it means signing over my share of Clearwater to Seb."

"No! Don't even think about that. You love your work. You love what the two of you have built together."

"Sure I do, but don't you see? I love you more. I worked hard at establishing Clearwater to spite my father, to prove him wrong. But it turns out I proved him right. He never doubted me—he just thought it was too soon. And maybe it's too soon for us, but I cannot walk away and think for one moment that we could never be together again. I want you in my life, Catherine. Forever."

She was shocked to see tears in his eyes.

"We'll take this as fast or as slow as you want to, but please, don't cut me out of your life. Even if it takes you the next year to be sure that you love me enough to marry me and spend the rest of your life with me. Even if it takes the next ten years."

She smiled a watery smile. "I think ten years might be a bit excessive. But Richard, I couldn't live in the city. I need my horses. I need to fulfill my dreams and my goals in life, too. You've done so much already in such a short time. Surely you can understand why this is important to me, too."

"I wouldn't expect you to live in the city. I can commute. There's a heliport right near my office. I want more than anything to see you attain your dreams. You wouldn't be you without them. But you can have your own stables and be my wife at the same time."

"My stables?" She gave a wry grin. "Like that's going to happen anytime soon. Maybe ten years isn't so much of a stretch after all. Scandal still hangs over my family name, Richard. You don't want that scandal attached to your name, as well."

"Scandal? Catherine, every part of my marriage was paraded through the media. I think I can handle it."

"But this is different. It's more than 'he said, she said.' It's the kind of thing that people don't forget."

"Which is why we're going to deal with it. We're going to clear your father's name once and for all—for *you*."

Catherine looked at him in shock. "But how?"

"I've already put an investigator on it. It's unlikely the people involved have changed all that much. Once we have proof, I'm sure with sufficient persuasion they can be induced to make a statement regarding your father's lack of involvement."

"You'd do that for me?" She was incredulous. No one had ever stood up for her like this. No one had looked after her in so very long.

"You gave me back my father. It's only fair I give you back yours."

All shreds of weariness fell away from her. He loved her. He truly loved her. And, more importantly, he was free to do so. Catherine threw her arms around him, burying her face in his neck.

"I love you so much. It was killing me to have to let you go. I didn't want to believe you were still married or that you could be married and still make love with me."

"So you're prepared to give us a try? To take things slow?"

She pulled back and looked him square in the eyes.

"No. I don't want to take things slow. I've waited this long for someone special in my life. I don't want to waste another minute. Is that okay?"

Richard's lips curved into a beautiful smile that was all the answer she needed.

Forever.

* * * * *

HUSBAND MATERIAL

Brenda Jackson

Brenda Jackson is a die "heart" romantic who married her childhood sweetheart and still proudly wears the "going steady" ring he gave her when she was fifteen. Because she's always believed in the power of love, Brenda's stories always have happy endings. In her real-life love story, Brenda and her husband of thirty-eight years live in Jacksonville, Florida, and have two sons.

A *New York Times* and *USA TODAY* bestselling author of more than seventy-five romance titles, Brenda is a recent retiree who now divides her time between family, writing and travelling with Gerald. You may write to Brenda at PO Box 28267, Jacksonville, Florida 32226, by e-mail at WriterBJackson@aol.com or visit her website at www.brendajackson.net.

To the love of my life, Gerald Jackson, Sr.
Happy 38th anniversary!

She is more precious than rubies: and all the things
thou canst desire are not to be compared to her.
—*Proverbs 3:15*

One

Carmen Akins made her way around the huge white tent, smiling at those she recognized as neighbors, knowing most had heard about the demise of her marriage. And to make matters worse, she figured the article in last week's tabloid had probably fueled their curiosity about the man rumored to be her current lover.

They would definitely be disappointed to know her alleged affair with Bruno Casey was nothing more than a publicity stunt cooked up by their agents. Her divorce from renowned Hollywood producer and director Matthew Birmingham had made headlines, especially since they had been thought of as one of Hollywood's happiest couples. Many had followed their storybook courtship, wedding and subsequent marriage, and all had been convinced it was the perfect romance. It had come as a shock when it had all ended after three years.

Carmen had hoped she and Matthew could separate

both peacefully and quietly, but thanks to the media that had not been the case. Rumors began flying, many put into bold print in various tabloids: Oscar-winning Actress Leaves Husband for Another Man, which was followed by Renowned Producer Dumps Oscar-winning Wife for His Mistress.

Those had been two of the most widespread, although neither was true. Yes, she had been the one who'd filed for a divorce but there was no "other man" involved. And the only mistress her ex-husband had ever had while they'd been married was his work.

The first year of their marriage was everything she'd ever dreamed about. They were madly in love and couldn't stand to spend a single minute away from each other. But that second year, things began to change. Matthew's career took precedence over their relationship. She had tried talking to him but had no luck. And to keep their marriage solid, she had even turned down a couple of major movies to spend time with him. But it was no use.

The breaking point had come after she'd shot the movie *Honor.* Although Matthew had flown to France a few times to see her while she was filming, she'd wanted more private time with him without being interrupted by others on the set.

After filming had ended, she had arranged their schedules so they could spend time together in Barcelona at a secluded villa. It was there that she had planned to share with him the news that he was to become a father. She had been so happy about it—she couldn't wait for him to arrive.

But he never did.

Instead he'd called to let her know something had come up, something of vital importance, and suggested that she arrange another excursion for them at a later date. That same night, she began having severe stomach pains and heavy bleeding, and she lost their baby, a baby who, to this day, Matthew knew nothing about. Nor did he know about the time she had spent at the villa under the care of a private doctor and nurse. It was a blessing none of it had gotten to the media. The only thing Matthew knew about was the divorce papers he'd gotten a few weeks later.

She glanced around as she kept moving, not bothering to stop and strike up a conversation with anyone. There was a crowd but luckily the media was being kept off the grounds so as not to harass any celebrities in attendance. She appreciated that. It was certainly comforting since a slew of cameras had been following her around lately, especially after the rumor about Bruno had been leaked.

Her plans were to spend the entire summer in the Hamptons, watching the Bridgehampton Club polo matches at the Seven Oaks Farm. She needed some unwind time. However, she had to be careful—there were gossips everywhere and the Hamptons were no exception, especially since Ardella Rowe had purchased a home in the area. The woman was considered Joan Rivers's twin when it came to having loose lips. The secrets of more than a few celebrities who owned summer homes here had made it to the media thanks to Ardella.

"Carmen, darling."

Carmen inwardly cringed. It was as if her thoughts had conjured up the woman. She considered not answering, but several had heard Ardella call out to her and it would be rude not to respond. And while Ardella was someone you wouldn't want as a friend, you definitely wouldn't want her as an enemy, either.

Taking a deep breath, she pasted a smile on her face and turned around. The woman was right there, as if she had no intention of letting Carmen get away. Evidently she figured Carmen had some juicy news to share.

"Ardella, you're looking well," Carmen said.

"Carmen, darling, forget about me. How are *you?*" Ardella asked with fake concern, leaning over and giving her a quick kiss on her cheek. "I heard about all those horrid things Matthew Birmingham is doing to you."

Carmen lifted a brow. She could only imagine the lies being spread now. The truth of the matter was that her ex-husband wasn't doing anything to her. In fact, as far as Matthew was concerned, it was as if she had never existed. She hadn't heard from him since the day their divorce had become final a year ago. However, she had seen him in March at the Academy Awards. Like her, he'd come alone, but that had just fueled the media frenzy as they walked down the red carpet separately.

When she'd accepted her best-supporting-actress Oscar for the blockbuster hit *Honor,* it had been natural to thank him for the support and encouragement he'd given her during shooting. The media had had a field day with her speech, sparking rumors of a reconciliation between them. He had refused to comment and so had she—there was no point when both of them knew there would not be a reconciliation of any kind. Their marriage was over and they were trying to move on, namely in different directions.

Moving on had taken her a little longer than Matthew. He hadn't wasted time after their divorce was final. Seeing those photos with him and his flavor of the month had hurt, but she hadn't gotten involved with anyone to get back at him. Instead, she'd concentrated on keeping her career on top.

With a practiced smile, she said, "Why, Ardella, sweetie, you must be mistaken. Matthew isn't doing anything to me.

In fact, regardless of what you've heard, we've decided to remain friends," she proclaimed, lying through her teeth.

Matthew couldn't stand the ground she walked on. She'd heard from mutual friends that he'd said he would never forgive her for leaving him. Well, she had news for him. She would never forgive him for not being there when she'd needed him most.

"So you can't believe everything you read in those tabloids," Carmen added.

The woman gave her a shrewd look while sipping her wine. "What is this I'm hearing about you and Bruno? And I understand Matthew is seeing that lingerie model, Candy Sumlar."

Blood rushed to Carmen's head at the mention of the woman's name, but she managed to keep her cool. "Like I said, you can't believe everything you hear or read."

Ardella sharpened her gaze. "And what about what I've seen with my own eyes, Carmen? I was in L.A. a few weeks ago and I saw Matthew at a party with Candy. How do you explain that?"

Carmen gave a dignified laugh. "I don't have to explain it. Matthew and I have been divorced now for a year. He has his life and I have mine."

"But the two of you have remained friends?"

If they weren't friends this woman would be the last to know, Carmen thought, remembering the column that had appeared about her a few years back, claiming the only reason Matthew had cast her in one of his movies when she'd first started out was because they'd slept together. Sources had revealed Ardella as the person who'd spread that lie.

Thinking that one lie deserved another, Carmen acknowledged, "Yes, Matthew and I are friends. It will take more than a divorce to make us enemies." She hoped the woman never got the chance to question Matthew regarding his feelings on the matter.

Ardella gazed over Carmen's shoulder and smiled. Carmen could only hope the woman had spotted her next victim. "Well, look who's here," Ardella said, glancing back at her with a full grin on her face.

The hair on the back of Carmen's neck stood up as the tent went silent. Everyone was staring at her. Her body had begun tingling. That could only mean...

She pulled in a deep breath, hoping she was wrong but knowing from the smirk on Ardella's face that she wasn't. Matthew had entered the tent. Ardella confirmed her guess when she commented, "Looks like your ex just showed up. Imagine that. Both of you here in the Hamptons. But then, you did say the two of you *are* friends."

Carmen could tell from Ardella's tone that she was mocking Carmen's earlier claim. And from the way the tent had gotten quiet, it was clear that the spectators who'd come to see the polo game were finding the drama unfolding under the tent more interesting than what was on the field.

"He's spotted you and is headed this way. I think this is where I say farewell and skedaddle," Ardella said with a wide grin on her face.

The woman's words had Carmen wanting to run, but she stood her ground and made a quick decision. She had to believe that the man she once loved and whom she believed had once loved her would not do anything to embarrass her. She and Matthew would be civil to each other, even if it killed them. And then she would find out just why he was here. He owned the Hampton compound, but the divorce settlement gave her the right to stay there whenever she liked, as long as he remained in L.A. So why wasn't he in California? He seldom found time to come to New York.

"Carmen."

She felt his heat at the same moment she heard her name issue from his lips. Both affected her greatly. He was standing directly behind her and as much as Carmen didn't want to, she slowly turned around and feasted her gaze on her ex-husband.

Feasting was definitely the right word to use. No matter when or where she saw him, he looked as enticing as any man could. Dressed casually in a pair of tan slacks and a designer navy blue polo shirt, he was the epitome of success. And with a clean shaven head, skin the color of rich cocoa, a strong jaw line, dark piercing eyes and full lips, he had stopped more than one woman in her tracks.

Before branching out to become a director and producer, he had starred in a few movies. And when he'd been an actor, Matthew Birmingham had been considered a heart-throb. To many he still was.

Knowing they were the center of attention, she knew what she had to do, and so she did. "Matthew," she said, rising on tiptoe to plant a kiss on his cheek. "It's good seeing you."

"Same here, sweetheart."

From the tone of his voice she knew her kiss had caught him off guard, and now he was only playing along for her benefit. She felt anger beginning to boil within her at seeing him here, on her turf. This was a place he knew she enjoyed coming during the summer months, a place he conveniently stayed away from since work usually kept him on the west coast.

"I'm sure we can do better than that," he whispered.

He reached out and pulled her into his arms, claiming her mouth. His tongue slid between her parted lips and immediately began a thorough exploration. She heard the click of a cell-phone camera and figured Ardella was at work. Carmen was tempted to pull her mouth away and break off the kiss but she didn't have the willpower to do so.

It was Matthew who finally retreated, leaving her in a daze, unable to think clearly. When she saw they'd caused a scene and people were staring, she figured she had to do something before things got out of hand.

"We need to talk privately," she stated, hearing the tremble in her voice and trying to ignore the sensations in her stomach. She moved to leave the tent. As expected, he fell in step beside her.

As soon as they were away from prying eyes and extended ears, she turned to him. The smile she'd fabricated earlier was wiped clean from her face. "Why did you kiss me like that?"

He smiled and a dimple appeared in his cheek, causing a swell of longing to flow through her entire body. "Because I wanted to. And need I remind you that you kissed me first," he said in an arrogant tone.

"That was my way of saying hello."

He chuckled. "And the way I kissed you was mine."

She pulled in an irritated breath. He was being difficult and she had no time for it—or for him. "What are you doing here, Matthew? You heard the judge. I get to come here and stay—"

"As long as I remain in California," he interrupted. "Well, I'm embarking on a new business venture in New York. It was finalized today. That means I'll be relocating here for a while." His smile widened as he added, "Which means you and I are going to be housemates."

Matthew was tempted to kiss that shocked frown right off his ex-wife's face. Just knowing his words had agitated the hell out of her was the satisfaction he needed. If looks could kill, he would be a dead man.

Trying to ignore the tumultuous emotions that always overtook him whenever he saw her, he added, "Of course, you can always pack up and leave. I would certainly understand."

He knew for certain that that suggestion would rattle her even more. He was well aware of just how much she enjoyed coming here every summer to hit the beach and hang out at the polo matches. That was one of the reasons he'd purchased the compound in the first place. And if she assumed for one minute that he would allow her to sleep with her lover under the roof of a house he'd paid for, then she had another thing coming.

"How dare you, Matthew."

He couldn't help but smile at that. There was a time she had loved his outrageous dares—especially the ones he'd carried out in the bedroom. "Careful, Carmen, people are still watching. You might want to continue to play the role you created for Ardella Rowe moments ago. I rather liked it."

She looked up at him with what everyone else assumed was a warm, friendly smile, but he could see the bared teeth. His gaze flicked over her features. She was still the most beautiful woman to walk the face of the earth. He'd come into contact with numerous glamorous women, but he'd known the first time he had set eyes on Carmen five years ago, when she'd read for a part in one of his movies, that her looks would stop men dead in their tracks. And on camera or off, she gave new meaning to the word *radiant*.

"We need to talk, Matthew."

He looked away, well aware that his demeanor was distant. She had wrapped him around her finger once but she wouldn't be doing it again. He would be the first to admit he was still having problems with the fact that she'd walked out on their marriage. That said, he was only human, and if he continued to look into the depths of her dark eyes, he would remember things he didn't want to. Like how her eyes would darken when her body exploded beneath him in a climax.

He pulled in a deep breath and met her gaze again when he felt his heart harden. "No, we don't need to talk, Carmen. When you left me, you said it all. Now if you will excuse me, the first match is about to begin."

And he walked off and left her standing there.

Two

Every nerve in Carmen's body tingled in anger as she drove off the grounds of the Seven Oaks Farm. After Matthew's kiss, no doubt rumors of a possible reconciliation would begin circulating again. Feigning a headache to several people, she had gotten into her car and left.

It was a beautiful July day and as she drove past the stables in her convertible sports car, she doubted if Matthew even cared that he'd ruined what would have been a perfect afternoon for her. He'd probably known when he'd shown up what would happen, which only proved once again what a selfish person he was.

Somehow he had lost sight of what she'd told him about her parents' marriage—how her father's need to be a successful financial adviser and her mother's drive to become the most prominent real-estate agent in Memphis had isolated them from each other, which eventually led to their divorce. She had wanted more from her marriage to Matthew, but in the end, he had somehow given her even less.

Glancing around, she admired the countryside and regretted she would have to leave though she'd just gotten here yesterday. Her summer vacation had been spoiled. She pulled in a frustrated breath, wondering just what kind of business deal he'd made that would take him from California. As her hair blew in the wind she decided she really didn't care. What he did was no concern of hers.

Moments later she turned down the narrow street that led to their estate and within seconds, the sprawling beachfront home loomed before her. She could remember the first time Matthew had brought her here, months after they'd married, promising this would be the place where they would spend all of their summers. She had come every summer after that, but he'd been too busy to get away. His work had taken precedence over spending time together.

As she parked in the driveway and got out of the car, she couldn't help wondering if Matthew had plans to bring Candy Sumlar here. Would he spend more time with his girlfriend than he had his wife?

The thought that he probably would annoyed the hell out of her. She fumed all the way to the front door and slammed it shut behind her before glancing around. When she'd walked through the doors yesterday evening upon arriving, she had felt warm and welcomed. Now she felt cold and unwanted.

She quickly went upstairs, determined to pack and be miles away by the time the polo match was over and Matthew returned. There was no way he would do the gentlemanly thing and go somewhere else. It didn't matter one iota that she had been here first.

Entering the bedroom, she stopped. He had placed his luggage in here, open, on the bed. Had he been surprised to find she was already in residence? He'd wasted no time finding her to let her know he was here. And he had kissed her, of all things. She placed her fingers on her mouth, still able to feel the impression of his lips there.

Shaking off the feeling, she went to the closet and flung it open. She sucked in a deep breath. His clothes were already hanging in there, right next to hers. Seeing their clothes together reminded her of how things used to be, and her heart felt heavy and threatened to break all over again.

She pushed his clothing out the way and grabbed an armful of hers, tossing it on the bed. She was glancing around for her luggage when she suddenly felt stupid for letting Matthew ruin the summer she had been looking forward to for months. Why should she be the one to leave?

She was tired of running. For a full year following her divorce, she had avoided going to places where she thought he would be, and had stayed out of the limelight as much as she could. She had practically become a workaholic just like him, and now she wanted to have some fun. Why was she allowing him to rain on her parade, to make her life miserable when really she should be making *his* miserable?

Suddenly, she knew just the way to do it.

She hung her clothes back in the closet. It was time to give Matthew Birmingham a taste of his own medicine, Carmen style. She would work him over, do everything in her power to make it impossible for him to resist her, and then when he thought he had her just where he wanted—on her back, beneath him in bed—she would call it a wrap and leave him high and dry…and hopefully hard as a rock.

She smiled. The taste of revenge had never been sweeter.

* * *

Matthew walked into the house, closed the door behind him and glanced around. He'd been surprised to see Carmen's car parked in the driveway. He'd expected her to be long gone by now.

Ardella Rowe had sought him out during divot stomping to let him know of Carmen's headache. Of course, to keep his ex-wife's charade going he'd had to show his concern and leave immediately, though he knew she had used the headache as an excuse to slip away.

He heard her moving around upstairs and from the sounds of things she was packing. Now that she knew he was here, she wasn't wasting any time hightailing it back to wherever she'd been hiding the last few months. She was good at disappearing when she didn't want to be found.

Moving toward the stairs, he decided to wish her well before returning to the polo fields, hoping to catch the last match if he was lucky. His footsteps echoed on the hardwood floor as he walked toward the master suite. Her scent met him the moment he stepped onto the landing. It was an alluring fragrance that he knew all too well, and it was so much a part of her that he couldn't imagine her wearing any other perfume.

Jamming his hands into his pockets, he continued his stroll. This would be the first time he'd be here without her. He shook off the dreary feeling that realization had brought on. He was a big boy and could handle it. Besides, Carmen had done enough damage to mess up his life. He doubted he would ever forgive her for breaking his heart, for making him believe there was such a thing as true love and then showing him there really wasn't.

He'd stopped trying to figure out at what point they'd begun drifting apart. He would be the first to admit he'd spent a lot of hours working, but all those hours he'd spent away from her were meant to build a nice nest egg so they wouldn't have to work forever.

And although she was paid well for her movies, as her husband, he'd still felt it was his duty to make sure she got anything and everything she wanted in life. They had talked about having a family, but she hadn't understood that knowing he could provide for her and any child they had was important to him.

Her parents had had money and unlike him, she hadn't grown up poor. More than anything, he'd wanted to keep her in the lifestyle she'd been accustomed to. What in the world could be so terribly wrong about wanting to do that? To this day he just couldn't figure it out, and the more he thought about it, the angrier he got.

He had built his world around her. She had been the only thing that truly mattered and everything he'd done had been for her. But she hadn't appreciated that. So now, because of a decision she'd made without him, he was a man whose life was still in turmoil, although he fought like hell to keep that a secret. And he placed the blame for his shattered life at her feet.

He reached the bedroom's double doors and without bothering to knock, he pushed opened the door.

And stopped dead in his tracks.

Three

Carmen swung around at the sound of the bedroom door opening and tightened her bathrobe around her. She threw her head back, sending hair cascading around her shoulders. "What are you doing in here, Matthew?"

For a moment he simply stood there staring at her, no doubt taking in the fact that she had just taken a shower and was probably stark naked beneath her short robe.

When he didn't answer, she said in a sharp tone, "Matthew, I asked you a question."

His attention shifted from her body and slid up to her face. "What do you think you're doing, Carmen?"

His voice sounded strained and his breathing shallow. "What does it look like I'm doing? I just finished taking a shower and now I'm putting on clothes. You should have knocked."

Carmen watched as something flickered in the depths of his dark eyes and a muscle clenched in his jaw. He took his hands out of his pockets, causing the material of his pants to stretch across the huge bulge at his center. It was quite obvious he'd gotten aroused from seeing her half-naked. She inwardly smiled. He'd taken the bait just the way she'd planned.

"I own this place. I don't have to knock, Carmen. And why are you still here? Why aren't you gone or at least packing?"

She crossed her arms over her chest and followed the movement of his eyes from her face to her breasts. She was very much aware that her curves were outlined through the silky material of her robe. It seemed he was very much aware of it, as well.

"I decided that I won't be leaving."

He pulled his gaze away from her chest. "Excuse me?"

"I said I won't be leaving. I'd assumed you would be in L.A. all summer, which is why I made plans to spend my vacation here. I don't intend to change that just because you've shown up."

A muscle clenched in his jaw again, making it obvious her statement hadn't gone over well with him. She wasn't surprised when he said, with an icy gaze, "You should have checked my plans for the summer. If you had, I would have told you this place was off-limits. I regret that you didn't. I also regret that you have to leave."

She inched her chin a little higher and declared, "I'm not going anywhere, Matthew. I deserve some peace and quiet. I've worked hard this year."

"And you don't think that I have?"

The sharpness of his tone had her gearing up for a fight. But she had to be careful what she said or he would toss her out and halt her plan. "I know you work hard, Matthew.

In fact, you carry working hard to the extreme," she said bluntly.

His gaze narrowed and she wondered if perhaps she'd pushed him too far. But she couldn't help saying how she felt. The amount of time he'd spent away from her would always be a wound that wouldn't heal.

He began moving toward her in that slow, precise walk that could make women drool. She wished she didn't notice his sex appeal or just how potently masculine he was. She had to get a grip. Her objective was to make him regret ever taking her for granted, to give him a taste of his own medicine, so to speak. She intended to turn her back on him like he'd done to her.

Carmen swallowed when he came to a stop in front of her but she refused to back up—or down.

"You," he said with deep emphasis, "are not staying here. I think things were pretty clear in the divorce settlement. You wanted to end our marriage and so you did. Under no circumstances will we stay under the same roof."

Carmen saw the hardness in his features. This face that once looked at her with so much love was staring at her with a degree of animosity that tore at her heart.

"Then nothing is different, Matthew, since we seldom stayed under the same roof anyway. I'm not leaving. I was almost mobbed by the paparazzi getting here and they are probably hanging around like vultures waiting for me to leave. Your recent love life has caused quite a stir and they are trying to bait me into giving my opinion."

"The media isn't giving me any more slack than they're giving you. And your affair with Bruno Casey isn't helping matters, either. I'm sure if you return to California, he'll be able to put you up for the summer in that place he owns off the bay."

It was on the tip of her tongue to tell him nothing was

going on with Bruno, but she decided it was none of his business, especially in light of his ongoing affair with Candy. She refused to bring the other woman up since the last thing she wanted was for him to think that she cared. Which she didn't.

"Bruno is shooting in Rome and this is where I want to be. I love it here. I've always loved it here and the only reason you didn't agree to let me have this place during the divorce was because you knew how much I wanted it. For spite, you were intentionally difficult."

"Think whatever you like. I'm leaving to catch the last of the polo matches. I want you gone when I return."

"I'm not leaving, Matthew."

His expression turned from stony to inexplicably weary. "I'm not going to waste my time arguing with you, Carmen."

"Then don't."

They stood there staring at each other, anger bouncing off both of them. Then, without saying another word, Matthew turned and walked out. Carmen held her breath until she heard the front door slam shut behind him.

Matthew decided not to return to the Seven Oaks Farm for the match. Instead, he went for a drive to clear his head and cool his anger. Carmen was being difficult—she hadn't behaved that way since the early days of their courtship.

He had pursued her with a single-minded determination he hadn't known he was capable of, and she had put up a brick wall, refusing to let him get close. But he'd known the first moment he'd laid eyes on her that he not only wanted her to star in his movie but he wanted her in his bed and wouldn't be satisfied until he got both.

She'd gotten the part in the movie, earning it fair and square. Getting her into his bed had proven to be difficult and before he got her there, he'd realized he had fallen in love with her. He wasn't certain how it had happened, but it had. He'd loved her so deeply, he knew he wasn't capable of ever loving another woman that way.

She'd stood before him in that church and promised to love him forever. So what if he worked long hours—didn't "till death do us part" mean anything to her? And if he hadn't worked so hard, he would not have earned the reputation of being one of the country's up-and-coming film producers.

A throbbing warmth flowed through his chest, which was immediately followed by a rush of anger that was trying to consume him. He had wanted so much for them and she had done something so unforgivable it hurt him to think about it. He had been absolutely certain she was the one person who understood his drive to build something of his own, the one person who would never let him down. His father had let him down by not marrying his mother when she'd gotten pregnant, and then his mother had let him down when she married Charles Murray, the stepfather from hell. Carmen had restored his faith that there was someone out there who wouldn't disappoint him. So much for that.

Matthew parked the car on the side of the road and just sat there, gazing at the beach. Walking into the bedroom and seeing her barely clothed had been too much. For a moment, lust had overshadowed his common sense and he could only think of how her breasts felt in his hands, how they tasted in his mouth.

With the sunlight streaming through the window, her nearly transparent robe had revealed the darkened triangle between her legs. It had taken all his strength not to cross the room, toss her on the bed and bury himself deep inside her body the way he used to after they'd argued and made up.

And they'd had to make up a lot since the amount of time he'd spent away from home had always been a bone of contention between them. But they'd always worked through it. What he'd tried so hard to figure out was, what had made the last time different? Why had she felt like throwing in the towel? She'd known his profession when she married him. As an actress, she of all people should have understood how things were on a set. Her filing for divorce had confused the hell out of him.

He remembered the night he hadn't shown up in Spain as planned. It had been a week from hell on the set. Wayne Reddick, the main investor for the movie he'd been producing at the time, had unexpectedly shown up on location. He and Wayne had butted heads several times and the man's impromptu visit had prompted him to cancel his plans to meet Carmen in Barcelona. The fate of his production, which had been behind schedule, was at stake and it had taken some serious talking for the man to agree to extend funds for the movie's completion. He had tried calling Carmen to explain things, but she hadn't answered the phone. The next thing he knew he was receiving divorce papers.

He tightened his hand on the steering wheel thinking that maybe he was handling the situation with his ex-wife all wrong. Since she was hell-bent on staying in the Hamptons, maybe he should just let her. It would give him the chance to extract some kind of revenge for the hell she'd put him through.

He glanced at his watch. A smile touched his lips when he pulled back onto the road and headed home, determined to return before she left. He needed to convince her that it was fine with him if she stayed, without making her suspicious of his motives.

He'd been an actor before becoming a director and producer. He would seduce her back into his bed and then make her leave. And he would go so far as to change the locks on the doors if he had to.

The more he thought about it, the more he liked the idea and knew just how he could pull it off. When it came to seduction, he was at the top of his game.

Four

"You're still here, Carmen."

Carmen drew in a quick breath before turning around where she stood in the kitchen. Matthew had said he was returning to the polo matches—she hadn't expected him back so soon. At least she'd had time to put on some clothes and start dinner.

"I told you that I'm not leaving, Matthew. I deserve my time here so I figure you can do one of two things."

"Which are?"

She was surprised he asked. "You can call the cops and have me arrested for trespassing, which should make interesting news this week. Or you can leave me be and ignore the fact that I'm here. This house is big enough for you to do that."

She studied his features for some clue as to which option he fancied. And then he said impassively as he leaned against the kitchen counter, "The latter will cause just as much ruckus as the former."

He was right about that. Ever since she had publicly thanked him when receiving her Oscar, the tabloids had claimed a reconciliation between them was in the works. The paparazzi had shadowed their every move, determined to find out if the rumors were true and the Hollywood darlings were ready to kiss and make up. And then her agent had come up with this idea to make things even more interesting by introducing Bruno into the mix. Plus there was the matter of his lingerie model.

"I'm sure when you explain things to Candy, she'll understand," she said with warm humor in her voice. Of course Candy wouldn't understand, but then Carmen really didn't give a royal flip. Candy had had her eyes on Matthew for years and hadn't wasted any time latching on to him after their divorce had become final.

He stared straight into her eyes when he asked, "And what about Bruno? Is he an understanding sort of guy?"

The heat of his gaze touched her in a way that she couldn't ignore. She knew he meant to be intimidating and not sexual, but that look was as sexual as anything could get and she wasn't happy about the surge of desire flowing through her. The memories of what usually followed such a look swirled all around her and touched her intimately. Bottom line, Matthew Birmingham could make her feel like no other man could.

"Must be pretty serious if you have to think about it."

She blinked upon realizing he'd been waiting for her response while she was thinking that he could still take her breath away. "Yes, he's an understanding sort of guy." She would let him ponder exactly what that said about the seriousness of their relationship.

Carmen turned to check the rolls she had put in the oven

earlier. She was wearing a pair of jeans and a tank top. He'd always liked how jeans hugged her backside, and she was giving him an eyeful now as she bent over. She heard the change in his breathing and inwardly smiled. Poor baby, he hadn't seen anything yet.

"If I decide to let you stay," he was saying behind her, "there have to be rules."

She turned around and lifted a brow. "What kind of rules?"

"Bruno isn't welcome here."

She could live with that, since she hadn't intended to invite him anyway. "And what about *your* Miss Candy? Will you respect me as your former wife and keep her away while I'm here?"

It annoyed her that he actually had to think about his answer. Then he said, "I guess our plans can be rearranged."

A coldness settled in her heart. His response meant two things. He *had* intended to bring Candy here, and the two of them were sleeping together. The latter shouldn't surprise her since she of all people knew how much Matthew enjoyed making love. That was the one thing the two of them had in common.

"Does that mean you're okay with me staying, Matthew?"

"Seems you're hell-bent on doing that anyway. And like you said, the less the media knows about our business, the better."

She laughed. "You're concerned with the media? You? The same person who kissed me in front of a tent filled with people, including Ardella Rowe?"

"Like I said, you kissed me first." He looked over her shoulder at the stove. "So, what are you cooking?"

"Something simple."

"I didn't know you could cook at all." The amused glint in the dark depths of his eyes made her smile, as well. Matthew didn't smile often but when he did, it was contagious—and sexy.

"I started cooking after Rachael Ray had me on her show." And then, because she couldn't help it, she added, "I'd prepared a couple of meals for you when I thought you would be coming home. When you never showed up, I fed everything to the garbage disposal."

He looked at her as if he wasn't sure she was serious. "Here's another rule, if we're going to be here together. No talk of the past. You bailed out on our marriage and I'd rather not get into it—"

"I wasn't the one who bailed out, Matthew," she countered, lifting her chin. "You replaced me."

A fierce frown covered his face. "What the hell are you talking about, Carmen? I was never unfaithful to you."

"Not in the way you're thinking," she said, truly believing it. "But there *was* a mistress, Matthew. Your work. And she was as alluring to you as any woman could be. I couldn't compete and eventually stopped trying."

His frown deepened. "I don't want to hear it. I've heard it all before."

He'd heard, but he hadn't listened. "Fine," she said, "then don't hear it because personally, I'm tired of saying it. "

"You don't have to say it. We're divorced now."

"Thanks for reminding me."

There was a moment of awkward silence between them, although the chemistry they shared was keeping things sizzling. She knew he felt it as much as she did, and wasn't surprised when he tried easing the tension by asking in a civil yet curious tone, "What are you making?"

She glanced over at him. "I've smothered pork chops

with gravy and got some rice going along with homemade rolls and field peas."

"You prepared all that?"

"Yes. I made more than enough—you're welcome to dig in, too. Later we can toss for the bedroom."

He raised a brow. "Toss for the bedroom?"

"Yes, toss a coin to see which one of us will get the master suite, and who will have to settle for one of the guest rooms."

He shrugged. "Save your coin, I don't mind using the guest room. I'm going to wash up."

Carmen watched him walk out the kitchen, thinking that while revenge might be sweet, she needed to watch her step where he was concerned, especially since all she had to do was look at him to remember how things used to be between them—both in and out of bed. But for some reason she was reminded more of how things were in bed than out. It didn't take much for sensuous chills to flow through her body whenever he was near, even during those times she found him infuriating.

A wave of uneasiness washed over her. It was too late to question whatever had possessed her to take him on since it was too late to back off now. And the one thing she did know was that she would not go down in defeat.

"I never got the chance to thank you for mentioning me at the Academy Awards during your acceptance speech," Matthew said, glancing across the table at Carmen as they ate. "You didn't have to do that."

He hadn't expected her to give him any kind of acknowledgment when she'd accepted her award. He'd figured, considering how things had been during the divorce, that his name would be the last one off her lips that night. It had been quite a surprise. But then, she was always surprising him, like when he'd returned from washing up to find she'd set the table for two.

"Of course I did, Matthew," she claimed. "Regardless of how and why our marriage ended, I would not have taken that role if it hadn't been for you. You made me believe I could do it."

He didn't say a word as he thought back over that time. He'd known she could do it and along with Bella Hudson-Garrison, who was cast as the lead, Carmen had given a stellar performance. Bella had walked away with an Oscar for best actress, and Carmen won best-supporting actress.

He had arrived at the Kodak Theater and walked the red carpet alone, surprising many by not having a woman on his arm. His manager, Stan, had tried convincing him to bring a date, since chances were Carmen would be bringing one. But he hadn't taken Stan's advice. And when he saw Carmen had also come alone, he'd been happy, although he'd tried convincing himself he didn't give a damn.

He'd felt bitter that night, knowing she should have strolled down the red carpet on his arm. And she'd looked absolutely radiant; her gown had been stunning. On that night for a brief moment, he had placed his anger aside and had rooted for her getting the award she truly deserved. And when she had unselfishly acknowledged him as the driving force behind her taking the part, the cameras of course had switched to him, to gauge his reaction. His features had remained emotionless but on the inside, he had been humbled by what she'd done.

"So, Matthew, what's this new business venture you're involved with here in New York?"

He blinked, and realized he'd been staring at her like a fool. He quickly glanced down at his wineglass to get his bearings and recoup his common sense. When he felt pretty sure he had done both, he responded, "You know that although I enjoy doing features, it's always been my dream to make a documentary."

Carmen had known that. While married, they had talked about his dream many times.

"Well, earlier this year I learned that New York is gearing up to celebrate the one hundred and twenty-fifth anniversary of the Statue of Liberty's dedication, and that the city is looking for someone to film a documentary highlighting the event. The last big documentary was directed by Ken Burns back in 1986, and it was nominated for Best Documentary Feature."

She nodded. "That was a while ago."

"My name was given to the committee, and I've met with them several times over the past year. I learned yesterday that I was selected. They've requested that I use a New York–based film crew, and I don't have a problem with that. It only means I need to be here for preproduction, not in L.A. It's important that I get to know the people I'll be working with and they get to know me and my style."

She knew just what he was talking about. Matthew was an outstanding director, dedicated to his work and he expected those who worked with him to be dedicated, as well. She'd been in two of his movies and both times had been in awe of his extraordinary skills.

A sincere smile touched her lips. She was happy for him. In fact, she was ecstatic. God knows he'd worked hard to prove himself in the industry, which was one of the reasons why they were sitting across the table from each other not as husband and wife but as exes. Still, she would put the bitterness aside and give him his due.

"Congratulations, Matthew, that's wonderful. I am truly happy for you," she admitted, standing and carrying their plates to the sink.

"Thank you," Matthew said, leaning back in his chair, steepling his fingers together as he watched Carmen move across the room with more grace than any woman he knew. There was a jaw-dropping sexiness to her walk that had the ability to turn on any man, big time—especially him.

It hit him just how much he missed seeing her and spending time with her. The last time they'd been together had been in the judge's chambers, ending their marriage with their attorneys battling it out to the end.

"So, you're committed to being here all summer then?" she asked, turning around, leaning against the counter and meeting his gaze.

He smiled, wondering what she would do if she knew he was practically stripping her naked with his eyes while thinking of all the naughty things he wanted to do to her body. "Yes."

"Working?"

"Basically."

"Which means I'll rarely see you."

Matthew flinched. She knew how to say things that could make him grit his teeth. She made it seem as if he'd never given her any attention while he worked. Well, that was about to change. He was on a mission to seduce her and then kick her out on that hot little behind of hers.

"Maybe you will and maybe you won't. There will be days when I'll be working from here."

She shrugged. "It doesn't matter, Matthew. Work drives you no matter when and where you're doing it. That's all you ever think about."

He could tell her that wasn't true since at that very moment, he was thinking about how he wanted to make love to her once he got her back in his bed. "If that's what you want to believe."

She laughed shortly. "That's what I know. Now, if you don't mind, I intend to go to bed."

He shot her a confused look. "Bed? Don't you think it's kind of early? The sun's still up," he pointed out.

She lifted a brow. "And your point?"

My point is that I can't very well seduce you if you are making yourself scarce. "There's still time to do things tonight."

"I agree, which is why, after putting on my pj's, I plan to sit out on my bedroom balcony with a good book and watch the sun set over the ocean. I might go for a swim in the pool later tonight, but you shouldn't be concerned that I'll be underfoot. Like I said, this house is big enough for both of us. See you later."

She turned and left the kitchen. He watched her go, admiring her body, remembering her touch, more determined than ever to get her in his bed.

Five

Carmen curled up on the chaise longue on the private balcony off the master suite. If she were going to seduce Matthew, the last thing she needed to do was appear too accessible, too anxious to be in his presence. That was the reason she'd decided to go to her room first rather than straight to the pool.

A cool breeze was coming in off the ocean. She recalled making love with Matthew on this very balcony one night that first year he had brought her to the Hamptons. She had been concerned that their neighbors would see them, but Matthew had assured her that they had total privacy. The house had even been built in a no-fly zone, which kept the overzealous paparazzi from taking to the skies.

She glanced at the book she'd placed on the table, a romance novel she had been trying to get through for the last couple of days. It's not that it wasn't a good book—it was—but it was hard to read about someone else's fantastic love life when hers had gone so badly.

Instead of resuming the book, she decided to close her eyes and conjure up her own love story with her and Matthew in the leading roles. Things between them had been romantic during the early days of their marriage, especially that first year when he hadn't wanted her out of his sight. They had been in bed more than they had been out. Matthew was something else in the bedroom—he'd been able to reach her on a level that went deeper than any man ever had—and a part of her knew that no other man ever would.

From the moment they'd met, something had passed between them that was instinctive, and primitive. She was surprised she'd been able to read her lines during the audition session. That day, for the first time in her life, she'd discovered how it felt to truly desire a man.

She had gotten the role because Matthew had seen something in her. He thought she was good, and was going places. Although the temptation to become his lover during filming had been great, she had been determined to keep things professional between them.

After they'd wrapped the movie, they had their first date. He had taken her someplace simple—his favorite bar and grill for hamburgers, fries and what he'd claimed was the best milk shake she would ever taste. He'd been right. That night had practically sealed her fate. They'd dated exclusively for six months and then that Christmas, he'd asked her to marry him and she'd said yes.

The media had kept tabs on their budding relationship, referring to them as Hollywood's Darlings—Matthew, the staunch bachelor who claimed he would never marry, and she, the woman who'd stolen his heart. Their courtship had been as private as they could make it, but that hadn't stopped the paparazzi from stalking their every move and painting them as the couple whose marriage was most likely to succeed in Hollywood. Boy, had they been wrong.

Nearly five years later and here they were, no different than most other Hollywood couples—divorced and blaming the other for what had gone wrong. She drew in a deep breath, not wanting to think of how she'd felt being replaced by his career. The loneliness and pain had nearly swallowed her whole. Although by that time she'd had success as an actress, as a wife she felt like a total failure—a woman who couldn't compete against her husband's workaholic nature, who couldn't entice him away for a smoldering-hot rendezvous.

More pain settled around her heart as she remembered she'd lost more than her husband's attention in Barcelona. She'd also lost the child they had made together. Had she gone full-term, their little girl or boy would have been almost four months old by now.

She felt her lip trembling and fought back tears. She wanted to recall the good things about their marriage. She wanted to remember how well they'd gotten along in the beginning, how she would respond to just about anything when it came to him. His soft laugh, his touch, the sound of his breathing…that look he would give her when he wanted to make love.

She had seen that same look in his eyes today in the kitchen. She didn't know what racy thoughts had been going through his mind, but her body had responded and a rush of sensations had flowed through her. Her hormones had surged to gigantic proportions and it would have been so easy to cross the room, slide onto his lap, curl into his arms and bury her face in the warmth of his chest. Then she would have kissed him the way she used to. Kissing him had the ability to make her all but moan out an orgasm. In fact, a few times she had done that very thing.

She had the satisfaction of knowing he wanted her. Although she was woman enough to admit she'd desired him, too. What she had to do was keep her desires at bay while continuing to stir up his. That was her game plan and she intended to stick to it. She would not get caught in her own trap.

But there was nothing wrong with getting wrapped up in memories while lying stretched out on a chaise longue with the breeze from the ocean caressing her skin. Memories were a lot safer than the real thing. With her eyes still closed, she vividly recalled the night when she and Matthew had come out here, naked and aroused, with only one thing on their minds.

They had gone to a polo match and returned home, barely making it up to their bedroom to strip off their clothes. And then he had swept her off her feet and carried her to the balcony. Even now she could recall how fast her heart had been beating and how her pulse had throbbed. Pretty similar to how she was feeling now, just thinking about it.

He'd reached out to touch her breasts and her stomach had automatically clenched in response. Then she had watched in heated lust as he'd leaned forward and used his tongue to capture a nipple between his lips and—

"Carmen? Why didn't you answer when I knocked?"

She found herself staring into a pair of dark, sensuous eyes. His lips were so close to hers that it wouldn't have taken much for him to lean in just a little closer and taste her. And then there was his scent—aftershave mingled with man—that began manipulating her senses in a way that could be deemed lethal.

Her eyes narrowed as she felt a warming sensation

between her thighs. Matthew was crouched down over her. She fought to ignore the sensual currents that were rippling through her.

"What are you doing here?" she asked, her voice sounding strained to her own ears.

His gaze continued to hold hers. "I knocked several times and you didn't answer."

The heat of his breath was like a warming balm to her lips. She was tempted to lick the fullness of his mouth from corner to corner. It didn't exactly surprise her that she was thinking of doing such a thing, considering what she'd been thinking about just moments ago.

She slowly pulled herself up in a sitting position, causing him to move back, for which she was grateful. The last thing she needed right now was to be in close proximity to him. The temptation was too great. "And why were you knocking on the bedroom door when I told you I would be out here on the balcony reading?" she asked.

"I need to get my things moved to the guest room." He paused a moment and said, "I noticed you were sleeping, but figured I could get my things without disturbing you. But then…"

She lifted a brow. "But then what?"

A sensual smile touched the corners of his lips when he said, "But then I heard you say my name in your sleep."

She faltered for a minute, then quickly fought not to show any emotions as she swung her legs to the side to get up, causing him to back up a little more. She stared at him, exasperated, not sure what she should say. She decided not to say anything at all. What was the use in denying such a thing? It probably hadn't been the first time she'd said his name in her sleep and more than likely it wouldn't be the last. After all, he'd once had the ability to make her come just by breathing on her. In fact, he probably still could.

"Go ahead and get your things, Matthew. I'm awake now," she said, breaking eye contact with him to stand and gaze toward the ocean. He could think whatever he liked about hearing her say his name. She figured all kinds of thoughts were running through his mind—he was probably trying to figure out the best way to get into her panties right now.

She glanced back at him and her nipples immediately hardened when she noticed how he was staring at her outfit. She had changed into a strapless terry-cloth romper and it fit real tight over her backside. She knew just how much he enjoyed looking at that part of her anatomy.

He also used to compliment her on what he said was a gorgeous pair of legs. And now he was scanning her from head to toe, and concentrating on the areas in between. He wasn't trying to hide his interest.

"Is there a problem, Matthew?" she asked, watching his gaze shift from her legs to her mouth. Seeing his eyes linger there ignited a burning sensation low and deep in her belly.

His survey then slowly moved up to her eyes. A flash of panic ripped through her when she recognized the *let me make you come* look in his eyes. She felt her body succumbing without her consent.

"There's no problem, if you don't think there's one, Carmen," he said throatily, her name rolling sensuously off his tongue.

"I don't," she replied, easing back down on the chaise longue, knowing he was watching her every move. She stretched in a way that caused his attention to be drawn to her backside and legs once again. "I'm sure you don't need my help packing up your things."

Too late she realized she'd said the wrong thing. His expression went from hot to furious. She knew he was recalling the last time she'd said those very words to him, when he was moving out of their home in Malibu.

"You're right, Carmen. I didn't need your help then and I don't need it now."

Six

As Matthew began opening drawers to collect his clothes, he had to keep reminding himself there was a reason he hadn't yet tossed his ex-wife out on her rear end.

When she hadn't opened the bedroom door, he'd figured she had fallen asleep on the balcony. He thought he could be in and out without waking her. But when he'd heard her moan his name, not just once but several times, nothing could have stopped him from going on that balcony.

He had found her stretched on the chaise with her eyes closed, wearing a hot, enticing outfit that barely covered her. Seeing her resting peacefully had tugged at his heart, while her clothing and her words had tugged on another part of his anatomy. He'd stood there, thinking about all the things he'd love to do to her while getting harder as the seconds ticked by.

And he had been tempted to kiss her, to make love to her mouth in a way that would not only leave her breathless but tottering on the brink of a climax. When she had awakened and looked into his eyes, he had seen a need as keen as any he'd ever known from her. And then she had ruined the moment by reminding him that they were no longer husband and wife, and wouldn't be sharing the same bedroom or bed.

But not for long.

He was looking forward to reminding her just what she'd been missing this past year. And the way he saw it, she was definitely missing something if she was moaning his name in her sleep.

As he pulled the briefs and socks out the drawer and tossed them into the bag on the bed, he glanced to the balcony where Carmen now stood with her back to him, leaning against the rail and gazing out at the ocean again. At that moment, intense emotion touched him and nearly swelled his heart while at the same time slicing it in two.

He had loved her and he had lost her. The latter should not have happened. She should have stuck by him and kept the vows they'd made to each other. But when the going got tough, she got going.

He pushed the drawer closed, deciding to put his plan into action. She had pushed a few of his buttons—now it was time for him to push a couple of hers.

Carmen felt Matthew's presence before he'd even made a sound. She felt a unique stimulation of her senses whenever he was near. She had felt it earlier today when he'd entered the tent at the polo match. She'd known he was there. Just like she knew he was here now.

Biting her bottom lip, her fingers gripped tight on the rail as her breathing quickened, her pulse escalated and heat flowed through her. He didn't say anything. She couldn't stand another second of silence and slowly turned around.

The sun had gone down and dusk had settled in. Behind him she saw the light from the lamp shining in the bedroom but her focus was on him. She studied him, not caring that it was obvious she was doing so. His eyes darkened and she felt his desire. And as she stood there, she couldn't help but relive all the times he had held her in his arms and made love to her.

He had been the most giving of lovers, making sure she enjoyed every sexual moment they'd shared to the fullest. Her body was tingling inside, remembering how it felt to have his mouth to her breasts, or how his lips could trail kisses all over her body, heating her passion to the highest degree. It had been her plan to get him to the boiling point, but she was ashamed to admit he had her there already.

She pulled in a deep breath. "Are you done?"

"Not quite."

And then he slowly crossed the distance separating them. "I came to say good-night."

The husky sound of his deep voice sent sensuous shudders running all through her. Total awareness of him slid down her spine. She forced her gaze away from his to look out at the ocean to say something, anything to keep her mind off having her way with him.

"I love it here, Matthew. Thanks for agreeing to let me stay." She glanced back at him and saw he'd come to stand directly beside her. "You didn't have to, considering the terms of our divorce," she decided to add.

He stared at her for a moment and then said, "It was the right thing to do. At the very least, we can be friends. I don't want to be your enemy, Carmen."

His words nearly melted her, but she had to remember that she wanted him to regret the day he began taking her for granted, to realize that when she'd needed him the most, he hadn't been there for her. She had been alone while grieving their loss.

"What are you thinking about, Carmen?"

She glanced up at him. "Nothing."

"Maybe I should give you something to think about," he said softly, in a deep, rich voice. And then he wrapped his arms around her waist and lowered his mouth to hers.

She saw it coming and should have done a number of things to resist, but it would have been a waste of time and effort. Every part of her turned to mush the moment his lips touched hers. When his tongue began mingling with hers, she moaned deep in her throat.

Carmen hadn't known how much she'd missed this until now. She had tried burying herself in her work so she wouldn't think about the loneliness, the lost passion, the feel of being in the arms of the one man who could evoke sensations in her that kept her wet for days.

I miss being with the one man who can make me feel like a woman.

He deepened the kiss and she felt the rush of sexual charge. And when he lowered his arms from her waist to cup her backside, bringing her closer to him, she felt the hardness of his huge erection pressing into her. On its own accord, her body eased in for a closer connection.

Their mouths continued to mate in the only way they knew how, a way they were used to. But regardless of the number of kisses they had shared in the past, she was totally unprepared for this one. She hadn't expected the degree of desire or the depth of longing it evoked, not only within her but within him, as well. She could feel it in the way his tongue dominated her mouth as if trying to reclaim what it once had, and was entitled to. He was not only taking what she was giving but going beyond and seizing everything else he could.

Then he began slowly grinding his body against her. She felt the hot throb of his erection between her legs as if the fabric of their clothing wasn't a barrier between them. His body rubbing against hers electrified her senses in a way that felt illegal. And how he fit so perfectly between her legs reminded her of just how things had been with them, whether they were standing up or lying down, in a bed or stretched out on top of a table. They'd always made love with an intensity that left them with tremors of pleasure that wouldn't subside for hours.

Everything around her began to swirl wildly, and as his large hands continued to palm the cheeks of her backside, pressing her even closer to him, an ache took over in the pit of her stomach and began spreading through every part of her.

He slowly released her mouth but didn't stop the movement of his body as he brushed kisses across her cheekbones and chin. She pulled in a deep breath and then released a whimpered sound of pleasure from deep in her throat as he licked a path from one corner of her mouth to the other.

Blood rushed through her veins and it took everything within her to keep from begging for more. But nothing could stop the waves of pleasure and the tremors that began to shake her. She closed her eyes and reveled in the sensations rushing through her, bit by glorious bit. And when he began nibbling on her lips and then proceeded to suck those lips into his mouth, she was literally thrown over the edge. She pulled her mouth from his and cried out as intense pleasure shook her to the very core while he continued to grind his body against hers with a rhythm that had her rocking in sensuous satisfaction.

"That's it, sweetheart, let go," he murmured against her moist lips. "You are totally beautiful when you come for me. So totally beautiful. I miss seeing that."

And she missed feeling it, she thought, as the orgasm that had ripped into her slowly began receding and returning her to earth after a shuddering release. And when she felt the heat of his tongue lap the perspiration from her brow, she slowly opened her eyes.

"Matthew."

His name was a breathless whisper from her lips. As if he understood, he leaned down and kissed her, tenderly but still with a hunger she could feel as well as a taste she could absorb.

He slowly pulled his mouth away and with a sated mind, she met his eyes. The gaze staring back at her was just as intense and desirous as earlier, making it obvious that although she'd easily managed a climax fully clothed, he'd maintained more control over his aroused state.

"Matthew, let me—"

He placed a finger to her lips to halt whatever she'd been about to say. "Good night, Carmen. Sweet dreams."

She watched him leave, thinking that thanks to him, her dreams tonight would be the sweetest she'd had in a long time. She had to admit that this was not how she had planned for things to go with Matthew. He had deliberately tapped into one of her weak spots, which was something she hadn't wanted to happen. Was he gloating that he'd gotten the upper hand?

Carmen drew in a deep breath as her body hummed with a satisfied sensation. A flush heated her cheeks when she remembered how he had kissed her into an orgasm; she was feeling completely sated. The chemistry between them was just as it had always been, explosive.

She leaned back against the rail and knew, even though

the sexual release had been just what she needed, she had to regroup her priorities and continue with her plans. Everyone was entitled to get off the track at least once, but the important thing was to get back on. And she was confident that after a good night's sleep, she would be back in control of her senses once again.

Seven

Pulling off his shirt, Matthew headed for the bathroom, needing a shower. A cold one. Just the thought that he had brought Carmen pleasure had nearly pushed him over the edge. While kissing her, he had been overtaken with a raw and urgent hunger. The sensation had been relentless, unyielding, and for him, nearly unbearable.

As soon as his lips had touched hers, the familiarity of being inside her mouth had driven him to deepen the kiss with a frenzy that had astounded him. And each time she had moaned his name, something deep inside him had stirred, threatening to make him lose all control.

It didn't take long after she'd bailed out of their marriage to realize that she was the only woman for him. Any time he held her in his arms, kissed her, made love to her, he'd felt like a man on top of the world, a man who could achieve and succeed in just about anything. He had worked so damn hard to make her happy and in the end all of his hard work had only made her sad.

He stripped off his clothes, filled with a frustration he was becoming accustomed to and a need he was fighting to ignore. He stepped in the shower and the moment the cold water hit, shocking his body, he knew he was getting what he deserved for letting a golden opportunity go by. But no matter the torment his body was going through, he was determined to stick to his plan, and at the moment he was right on target.

His goal was to build up a need within her, force her to remember how things were between them, and how easily they could stroke each other into one hell of a feverish pitch. And then when she couldn't handle any more, when she was ready to take things to another level, instead of sweeping her off her feet and taking her to the nearest bed like she would expect, he would show her the door.

He stepped out of the shower and was toweling himself dry when he heard his cell phone ring. Wrapping the towel around his middle, he made his way over to the nightstand to pick it up. Caller ID indicated it was his manager, Ryan Manning.

"Yes, Ryan?"

"It would have been nice if you'd given me a heads-up that you and Carmen were back together."

Matthew frowned. "We're not back together."

"Then how do you explain the photograph the *Wagging Tongue* plans to run of the two of you kissing? Luckily I have a contact over there who thought I'd be interested in seeing it before it went to press. They plan to make it front page news that the two of you have reconciled your differences and are remarrying. The papers hit the stands tomorrow."

Matthew rolled his eyes. The *Wagging Tongue* was one

of the worst tabloids around. "Carmen and I are divorced, nothing has changed."

"Then what was that kiss about?"

"It was just a kiss, Ryan, no big deal. People can read into it whatever they want."

"And what about Candy?"

"What about her?"

"What will she think?"

Matthew drew in a deep breath and said, "Candy and I don't have that kind of relationship, you know that."

"But the public doesn't know that, and this article will make her look like a jilted lover."

He had no desire to discuss Candy or their nonexistent bedroom activities. Ryan knew the real deal. Candy was trying to build a certain image in Hollywood, and Matthew had agreed to be Candy's escort to several social functions, but only because he had gotten sick and tired of hanging around the house moping when he wasn't working. Ryan and Candy's agent felt it would be good PR. He'd known the media would make more out of it than there was, but at the time he hadn't given a damn.

"And where is Carmen now?" Ryan asked.

"In bed." He smiled, imagining the erroneous vision going through his manager's mind.

"Dammit, Matthew, I hope you know what you're doing. Her leaving almost destroyed you."

A painful silence surrounded him. No one had to remind him of what he'd gone through. "Look, Ryan, I know you mean well, but this is between me and Carmen."

"And what am I supposed to tell the media when they can't contact you and then call me?"

"Tell them there's no comment. Good night, Ryan."

Matthew breathed a sigh of relief as he ended the call. Ryan could be a pain in the ass at times, especially when it came to the images of his clients. But then he could definitely understand the man's concerns. His separation and subsequent divorce from Carmen had left him in a bad way for a while. But that was then and this was now. He could handle things. He could handle her. Pride and the need for self-preservation would keep him from falling under her spell ever again. He felt good knowing that although he'd given her some sexual release, she would still go to bed tonight needing even more. There was no doubt in his mind she would be aching for his touch.

He smiled. This sort of revenge was pretty damn sweet.

The next morning Carmen was easing out of bed when her cell phone rang. She reached over and picked it up. The sunlight pouring through the window was promising a beautiful day.

"Hello?"

"Girl, I am so happy for you. When I saw that article and picture, I almost cried."

Carmen recognized the voice of her good friend Rachel Wellesley. Rachel was a makeup artist she'd met on the set of her first movie. The close friendship she and Rachel had developed still existed to this day.

She knew what Rachel was referring to and decided to stop the conversation before her friend went any further. Carmen was well aware that Rachel probably said a special prayer each night before she went to bed that Carmen and Matthew would reunite. Rachel liked taking credit for playing matchmaker and initially getting them together.

"Chill, Rachel, and hold back the tears. No matter what you've heard, seen or read, Matthew and I aren't getting back together."

There was silence on the other end of the line.

"But what about the kiss that's plastered all over the front page of the *Wagging Tongue* this morning?" Rachel asked, sounding disappointed. "And don't you dare try to convince me it's a photo that's been doctored."

Carmen didn't say anything as she remembered the kiss and the effect it had on her. "No, it's not a photo that's been doctored, although a part of me wishes that it were. It started when I ran into Ardella Rowe at the polo match yesterday and she mentioned something about Matthew and me being enemies. I firmly denied it and went further, painting a picture of the two of us as friends, regardless of what the tabloids were saying. Well, before I could get the words out of my mouth, Matthew walked into the tent and all eyes were on us. To save face, I greeted him with a kiss on the cheek. Of course he decided to take advantage of the situation by turning a casual kiss into something more."

"From the photo, it looked pretty damn hot, if you ask me."

It was. But it was nothing compared to the one they'd shared last night on the balcony. She felt heat rise to her face as she imagined what he'd thought of the fact that she'd climaxed from his kiss.

"You should talk to him, Carmen, and tell him the truth. You know what I think about you not telling him about losing the baby."

Carmen pulled in a deep breath. Rachel was one of the few people who knew about what had happened that night. When she'd found out about her pregnancy, she'd been so excited she had wanted to share it with someone. Rachel had actually been the one who'd come up with the idea of making a surprise video telling Matthew of her pregnancy.

While curling up in his arms on the sofa in the villa, she

had planned to suggest that they watch a few video pitches for possible projects that directors had sent her. Instead, unbeknownst to him, she would play the video of her first ultrasound, even though the baby was just a tiny speck in a sea of black.

But things hadn't worked out that way.

"Yes, I know how you feel and you know how I feel, as well. Matthew should have been there with me." He'd always had legitimate excuses why he was late arriving someplace or not able to show up at all because of some last-minute emergency on the set. But for once he should have placed her above everything else, and he hadn't.

Knowing that Rachel would try to make her see Matthew's side of things, reminding her that he had no idea what was going on, she quickly said, "Look, Rachel, let me call you back later. I'm just getting up."

"Sure. And where's Matthew?"

"I have no idea. We spent the night under the same roof but in different bedrooms, of course. Knowing him, he's probably gone by now. He has this new project here in New York, so I'm sure he's left already to go into the city."

"The two of you will be living there together all summer?" Rachel asked.

Carmen could hear the excitement in Rachel's voice. She knew it would be a waste of time telling her not to get her hopes up because it wasn't that kind of party. The guest room Matthew was using was on the other side of the house, and considering his schedule, their paths would probably only cross once or twice while they were there.

"Yes, for the most part, but this house is so big I doubt I'll even see him."

After ending her conversation with Rachel, Carmen got up and went into the bathroom. She planned to go swimming in the pool and then head down to the beach after breakfast.

Even though things had started off pretty rocky between her and Matthew yesterday, thanks to him she'd slept like a baby last night. An orgasm brought on by Matthew Birmingham never failed her. Whenever she'd had a tension-filled day on the set, he would make love to her to calm her frazzled nerves.

But upon waking her greedy body wanted more. It was as if she'd suddenly developed an addiction to Matthew's touch, a touch she had managed to do without for more than a year but was craving like crazy now.

An intense yearning and longing was rolling around in the pit of her stomach and although she was trying to ignore it, doing such a thing wasn't working. Now that her body recognized the familiarity of his touch, it seemed to have a mind of its own.

She frowned while stripping off her nightgown. She wondered if Matt had deliberately set her up for this—she wouldn't be surprised to discover that he had. He of all people knew how her body could react to him. So, okay, she would admit that he had bested her this round, but she was determined not to lower her guard with him again.

Eight

"I thought you had left to go into the city." Matthew glanced up and nearly swallowed his tongue. Carmen was standing in the kitchen doorway dressed in a two-piece bathing suit with a sheer, short sarong wrapped firmly around her small waist that placed emphasis on her curvaceous hips and beautiful long legs. Her hair was pulled up into a knot displaying the gracefulness of her neck, and even from across the room he could smell her luscious scent.

He felt a flash of anger with himself that she could still have this kind of effect on him. But last night had proven just how things were between them. Of course sex had never been the issue—her inability to believe she was the most important thing in his life had been. What he resented most was her not giving them time to work anything out. And once the media had gotten wind of their problems, they had made a field day of it, printing and stating things that hadn't been true.

But seeing her now almost made it impossible to recall why there were problems between them. She was the most beautiful, desirable woman he had ever laid eyes on.

He lowered his head and resumed eating. It was either that or do something real stupid like get up from the table, cross the room and pull her into his arms.

"I figured since you have business to take care of in Manhattan, you would have left already," she explained, looking genuinely surprised to see him.

He wondered if she'd actually been hoping their paths would not cross today, and he knew that was a pretty good assumption to make. Sighing, he picked up his coffee cup. "Sorry to disappoint you, but I'll be doing most of my work from here."

"Oh," she said. He continued to watch her as she crossed the room to the stove.

"I take it you're spending the day on the beach?" he asked, wondering why she had to look so ultra-feminine and much-too-sexy this morning. But then she always looked good, even when she'd just woken up in the morning. He'd so enjoyed making love to her then, stroking the sleepiness from her eyes as he stroked inside her body.

"Yes, that's my plan, after taking a dip in the pool first," she said, pouring a cup of coffee. She took a sip and smiled. "You still make good coffee."

He chuckled as he leaned back in his chair. "That's not the only thing I'm still good at, Carmen."

Carmen swallowed hard, thinking that he didn't have to remind her of that.

Her heart began pounding in her chest and she felt breathless when he stood. All six feet three inches of him was well built and dangerously male. And she thought now what she thought the first day she'd laid eyes on him: Matthew Birmingham had the ability to ignite passion in any woman.

Focus, Carmen, focus. Don't get off track here. You need to win back the upper hand. Remembering her call from Rachel, she asked, "Has Candy Sumlar called you yet?"

He pushed his chair under the table and went to the sink, pausing for a moment to glance at her. "Is she supposed to?"

Carmen shrugged. "Don't be surprised if she does. Someone took a picture of us yesterday and it made the front page of the *Wagging Tongue*."

He turned toward her after placing his cup in the sink. "I know. It could cause a problem or two, I suppose."

He took a few steps toward her until Carmen had to tilt her head back to look up into his face. "Then why did you kiss me?" she asked.

"Because I wanted to."

His words, precise and definitely unapologetic, gave her a funny feeling in the pit of her stomach. Sexual tension filled the room and for a moment, she was mesmerized by his gaze—those extraordinary dark eyes could render a woman breathless if she stared into them for too long.

So she broke eye contact and moved away. "Doing things that you want to do without thinking about the possible outcome can get you in trouble."

"And who said I didn't think about it?"

Carmen fell silent. Was Matthew insinuating that he'd kissed her knowing full well what he was doing? That he would have done so anyway, even if she hadn't made a move first with that kiss on the cheek? She ignored the tingle in her stomach at the mere thought that this was more than a game to him. That perhaps he had wanted her and initiating that kiss had been just the thing to push him over the edge.

Umm. The thought of that had her nipples feeling hard and pressing tight against the bikini top. She drew in a deep breath and as her lungs filled with the potent air they were both breathing she felt her nipples grow even more sensitive. He was leaning against the counter, his eyes roaming up and down her body. She wanted him to check her out good and assume that he could get more from her than just the hot-and-heavy kiss they'd shared last night. Then she would gladly show him how wrong that assumption was. If he was playing a game, she would show him that two could play.

She moved toward the table to sit down, intentionally swaying her hips as she did so. She took a sip of her coffee as she felt heat emitting from his gaze.

"There are some muffins in the refrigerator if you want something else to go with your coffee," he said.

"Thanks, I'm fine."

"There's another polo match tomorrow. Do you plan on going?" he asked.

"I do," she replied.

She knew why he was asking. By tomorrow, a number of people would have read the article and all sorts of speculations would be made. The main question was, how would they handle it?

The room got quiet. He finally broke the silence by asking, "What about Bruno? Will he get upset when he hears about the article?"

Carmen looked over at him and plastered a smile on her lips. "No, because he knows he has nothing to worry about." She knew that comment irked him. Back in the day when he'd been a movie star, Matthew and Bruno had been rivals as Hollywood heartbreakers. The two never developed a close friendship and even now merely tolerated each other for appearance's sake.

"Good. I wouldn't want to cause friction between the two of you."

"You won't." Seeing she would not be able to drink her coffee in peace while he was around, she stood and announced, "I'm going to the pool."

Matthew watched her leave, irritated by what she'd said about Bruno knowing he had nothing to worry about. The very thought that the man was that confident about their relationship didn't sit well with him. A sudden picture of her in Bruno's arms flashed through his mind and he felt anger gathering in his body, all the way to his fingertips.

He drew in a deep breath and then let it out slowly, wondering what Bruno would think if he knew his girl had gotten pleasured by her ex last night. Although they hadn't made love, Matthew knew her well enough to know that that orgasm had been real and potent. In fact, if he didn't know any better, he'd think it was the first she'd had in a while, which meant Bruno wasn't taking care of business like he should.

But the thought of that man taking care of business at all where Carmen was concerned had steam coming out of his ears and a tic working in his jaw. Deciding it was time to rev up his plans of seduction a notch, he left the kitchen to go upstairs to change.

Carmen opened her eyes when she heard footsteps on the brick pavers. She took one look at Matthew and wished she'd kept them closed. He was walking toward her wearing a pair of swim trunks that would probably be outlawed if worn in public.

Her gaze settled on his face and the intense expression she saw there, before lowering her eyes to the sculpted muscles of his bare chest and then sliding down to his midsection. The waistband of his trunks hung low and fully outlined a purely masculine male.

She stiffened slightly when she felt a deep stirring in the middle of her stomach and fought to keep perspective. She sat up on the chaise longue and held his stare, wishing her heart would stop beating so rapidly.

And wishing she still didn't love him like she knew she still did.

That stark realization had her moving quickly, jumping out her seat, nearly knocking over a small table in her haste. "What are you doing here, Matthew?"

He came to a stop in front of her. "Why do you always ask me that like I'm out of place or something?"

Silence hung heavy between them. Then she lifted her chin and said, "Probably because I feel like you are. I'm not exactly used to having you around." She then moved toward the pool.

Matthew didn't say anything, mainly because he was focused on the pain in her voice—as well as the realization that she was right. This *was* the longest they had been together in the same place in a long time—including when they were married.

Suddenly, he couldn't even fortify himself with the excuse that all those hours he'd been away working had been for her. Because in the end, he'd still failed to give her the one thing she'd wanted and needed the most: his time.

He had missed this—her presence, the connection they'd shared in the beginning but had somehow lost in the end. How could he have been so wrong about what he thought she truly wanted and needed? He had wanted them both to find happiness, but they sure as hell weren't happy now. At least, he wasn't. His stomach clenched at the thought of just how unhappy he was. His plan for revenge didn't taste as sweet as it had yesterday, and he had no idea what to do.

He watched as she stood by the pool, untying the sarong from around her waist and dropping it to the ground. And then she dove in, hitting the water with a splash. He stood watching her, remembering when all he'd wanted was to make her his wife and to have children together one day. He had loved and wanted her so much.

And I still love her and want her.

The admission was like a sharp punch to his gut. Nothing mattered at that moment—not the humiliation he'd felt when she left, nor the anger or frustration he'd suffered when she chose to file for a divorce. What he was sure about more than anything was that he wanted her and if given the chance to repair the damage, he would handle things differently. What he was unsure about was whether or not she wanted another go with him. There was one way to find out.

It was time he was driven by a different motivation, not of revenge but of resolution. He moved toward the pool and dived in after her.

It was time to get his wife back.

Nine

Carmen surfaced when she heard a big splash behind her. Seeing Matthew in the water, she decided it was time to get out of the pool and began swimming toward the other side.

She eased herself out to sit on the edge and watch him, studying his strokes, meticulous and defined, and the way he was fluidly gliding through the water. He was an excellent swimmer, of course—after all, he had attended UCLA on a swimming scholarship.

He swam toward her until he was right there, treading water between her legs. And before she could catch her next breath, he reached up and pulled her into the water.

"Matthew!"

Carmen wrapped her arms around his neck so she wouldn't go under, but that ended up being the least of her worries as he tightened his hold on her and pressed his mouth to hers. She whimpered when his tongue grabbed hold of hers, stroking it hungrily. And when he deepened the kiss, she automatically wrapped her legs around his waist, feeling the strength of his thighs and his hard erection through his wet swim trunks.

She returned the kiss, realizing that she was powerless to resist this intense interaction, this outburst of sexual chemistry and reckless behavior. Heat and pressure were building up inside her. The feel of the water encompassing them captivated her, making her all too aware of the way he knew exactly what to do to her.

He began licking and nibbling around her lips, and she knew instinctively that this was a man with outright seduction on his mind. The only thing wrong was that she was supposed to be seducing him, not the other way around.

She couldn't resist the urge to clamp her mouth down on his, needing the feel of his tongue tangling with hers. She could truthfully say she'd never enjoyed kissing a man more—she had missed this intimate foreplay tremendously. Though she hated to admit it, being here with him was long overdue and she needed it like she needed to breathe.

When he began wading through the water toward the steps, she saw they'd somehow made it to the shallow end. Pulling his mouth from hers, he shifted her body in his arms as he walked up the steps from the pool. Cool air brushed across her wet skin and her entire body shuddered in his embrace.

She didn't ask where they were going. It didn't matter. She was overwhelmed by the way he was staring down at her with every step he took. And when he placed her on the lounger, she reached out, not ready for him to release her.

"I'm not going anyplace," he whispered in a deep husky

tone, running his hands along her wet thighs. "I'm just grabbing a couple towels to dry us off."

He only took a step or two away from her but Carmen instantly felt desperate for his touch. The loneliness of the past year loomed over her and she felt a stab of regret, wishing she had handled things between them differently.

She had known from the first that Matthew was a proud man, a man who'd had to work hard for anything he'd ever had in life. That was the reason he was so driven. When they'd married, he had vowed to take care of her and in his mind, working hard was the only way to do that. And although she'd told him over and over that all she wanted was him, he hadn't been able to hear her, mainly because he was who he was—a man determined to take care of his own.

At that moment, something in her shifted and she felt something she hadn't felt in a long time—peace and contentment. When he returned to her with the towels, she reached up and touched his face, tracing his lips with her fingertips before leaning in and kissing him softly on the mouth.

She felt his hold tighten and she detected the raw hunger within him, but he let her have her way. Knowing he was holding back caused a surge of desire to flood every part of her body.

She released his mouth and he wrapped her up in one of the towels, wiping her dry. She moaned in total enjoyment over the feel of the soft terry cloth against her flesh. He slid the towel all over her body to absorb the water from her skin, leaving no area untouched. She knew she was being lured into a temptation she could not resist.

He dried himself off, as well, and she watched, enjoying every movement of the towel on his body, looking at his chest and shoulders and legs. He was so well built—watching him had to be the most erotic thing she'd witnessed in a long time.

Tossing the towels aside, he leaned down and covered her mouth with his once more while stretching out to join her on the lounger, her body under his. He broke off the kiss and used his teeth to lift her bikini top. Before she could utter a sound, his mouth was at her breasts, sucking the hardened tips of her nipples between his lips.

Matthew had always enjoyed her breasts and that hadn't changed. Carmen could tell that he refused to be rushed while cupping the twin globes in his hands, using his mouth to tease them one minute and lavish them the next.

And then she felt him tugging at her wet bikini bottoms, removing them from her body and tossing them aside. He stepped back and began lowering his swim trunks down his legs.

She shifted on the lounger to watch him like she'd done so many other times. Her breath caught at what a fine specimen of a man he was in the raw—she had always enjoyed seeing him naked. And at that moment she was filled with a need to pay special tribute to his body the way she used to.

When he moved toward her, she sat up and her mouth made contact with his stomach as she twirled her tongue all around his abs. She felt the hard muscles tense beneath her mouth, and her hands automatically reached out to clutch his thighs as the tip of her tongue traced a trail from one side of his belly to the next, drawing circles around the indention of his belly button.

He moaned her name. Pressing her forehead against his stomach, she inhaled the scent of him. She then leaned back, her face level with his groin. She reached out and grabbed hold of his shaft, feeling the aroused member thicken even more in her hands.

The dark eyes staring down at her were penetrating, hypnotic and displayed a fierce hunger she felt all the way in the pit of her stomach. Although he wouldn't verbally express his desires, she knew them. She had been married to him for three years and she knew exactly how to pleasure him in a way that would give him the utmost gratification.

She opened her mouth and leaned forward, her lips and tongue making contact with his erection. She heard his tortured moan as she greedily licked him all over, focusing on her task as if it were of monumental importance—and to her, it was. He was the only man she'd ever performed this act on, and she derived just as much pleasure giving it as she knew he was getting from it.

"Carmen."

Her name was a guttural groan from his lips and when she felt his fingers plunge into her hair, she slid his erection inside her mouth and went to work, just the way he'd taught her, the way she knew that could push him over the edge. She so enjoyed watching him fall.

The thought that she was driving him crazy was a total turn-on for her. As her mouth continued its torment, she could feel his pleasure heightening. Soon, the same heat and passion consuming him began taking hold of her. He was the only man who could make her bold and daring enough to do something like this, the only man who made lust such a significant thing.

Was it wrong to desire her ex-husband so much? He was the very man who had broken his promise to make her the most important thing in his life, to cherish her forever....

She pushed those thoughts to the back of her mind, not wanting to dwell on all the things that had gone wrong.

Instead she wanted to dwell on him, on making love with the most irresistible man to walk the face of the earth.

"Carmen!"

The throaty sound of her name on his lips—the instinctive response of a man reaching extreme sexual pleasure—pulled her back to the here and now. When the explosion she'd been expecting happened, she was overwhelmed by her own passion and the depth of her love for him.

And then she felt herself being lifted into his arms. When he crushed his mouth to hers, she knew there was no stopping either of them now. Their wants and desires were taking over and they wouldn't deny themselves anything.

She wrapped her arms around his neck as she felt herself being carried up the winding stairs. She knew exactly where he was taking her—to the master suite, their bedroom, their bed.

She pulled in a deep breath when they reached their destination and he eased her out of his arms and onto the bed. Before she could draw in another breath, he was there with her, reaching out to her and pulling her back into his arms.

His hands touched her everywhere, and where his hands stroked, his mouth soon followed. He moved from her lips down past her neck to her chest where, after cupping her breasts in his hands and skimming his fingertips across them, he used the tip of his tongue to lavish the twin mounds and hardened tips.

Matthew then glided his hands down her hips and between her legs to cup the warmth of her womanhood. And then his mouth was there, pressing against her feminine folds, as if needing the taste of her on his tongue.

"Oh, Matthew."

She rocked her body against his mouth and he responded

by plunging his tongue deeper inside of her. The sensations he was evoking were so intense she could only cry out in a whimper once more before pleasure erupted within her, spiraling her into a shattering climax, the intensity of which brought tears to her eyes.

"You liked that?" he asked moments later when he slid back up her body and began licking her neck.

Unable to speak, she nodded her head. His mouth claimed hers again. Moments later he straddled her body with his arms, inching her legs apart with his knees. When he released her mouth, he peered down at her. "You sure about this, baby?" he whispered hoarsely before moving any farther.

She hadn't been more sure about anything in her life. "Yes, Matthew, I'm sure."

That was all he needed to hear. He continued to hold Carmen's gaze as his body lowered onto hers, his thick erection moving past her feminine folds and deep into the core of her. Her inner muscles clutched him and he groaned her name. He had missed this. He had missed *her*. He wanted to close his eyes and relish the feeling of being inside her this way, but he kept his eyes open. He held tight to her gaze as he continued moving deeper and deeper inside of her as she lifted her hips to receive all of him.

And when he'd buried himself in her to the hilt, he let out a rugged growl as pinnacles of pleasure began radiating through him starting at the soles of his feet and escalating upward. He felt every single sensation as he moved, his strokes insistent as he thrust deep, fully intent on driving her wild, over the edge and back again.

"Matthew, please..."

The longing in her voice revealed just what she was

asking for and his strokes increased to a feverish pitch, giving her just what she wanted. He understood her need, comprehended her desires since they were just as fierce as his own. He thrust deeper still as they moved in perfect rhythm.

She tightened her legs around his back when he groaned, triggering an explosion that ripped through their bodies. As he spilled into her, he lowered his mouth to hers and took her lips while an earth-shattering release tore through them.

He sank deeper and deeper into her as a pulsing ache took control of his entire body and he felt himself swelling all over again inside her. Moments later, another orgasm slashed through him, drowning him in waves after waves of intense pleasure.

The moment he released her mouth, she cried out for him. "Matthew!"

As she gazed up at him, he knew their lovemaking had proven what they'd refused to admit or acknowledge up until now, this very moment.

Divorce or no divorce, their life together was far from over.

Ten

Depleted of energy, Carmen lay still with her eyes closed, unable to move, her body still intimately connected with Matthew's. She could feel the wetness between her thighs where their bodies were still joined.

She slowly opened her eyes. Matthew's face was right there. He was asleep, but still holding her in his arms, his leg was thrown possessively over her, locking their entwined bodies together. It was as if he'd deliberately chosen that position so that he would know if she moved the slightest bit.

She glanced at the clock on the nightstand and saw that it was close to two in the afternoon, which meant they had spent the last five hours in bed. Closing her eyes again, she thought that she had never experienced anything quite like the lovemaking session they'd just shared, and she could still feel remnants of sexual bliss simmering through her.

Her body quivered at the memory of his mouth between

her legs, and of his tongue lapping her into sweet oblivion. She hadn't made love with another man since their divorce and now she knew why—her body didn't want anyone other than Matthew.

Suddenly, she felt him starting to swell inside her. She opened her eyes to stare right into the darkness of his. They lay there, gazing at each other while his shaft expanded into a huge, hard erection.

"Oh my goodness." The words slid from her lips as she felt him stretching her inside. Her inner muscles clamped tight and wouldn't let him go.

He leaned forward and kissed her, moving in and out at a slow pace. His unhurried strokes eased the tremendous ache between her legs and matched the rhythm of his tongue as it mingled with hers. She couldn't help moaning with each thrust into her body as she was overtaken with desire. He was so painstakingly thorough it nearly took her breath away.

Moments later she pulled her mouth from his when her body erupted into an orgasm so intense she screamed in ecstasy, totally taken aback at the magnitude of pleasure ripping through her. And then Matthew followed her into the thrill of rapture as his body exploded, as well. As he drove harder and deeper, she could actually feel his release shoot right to her womb.

"Matthew…"

She moaned his name from deep within her throat and when his mouth found hers again, she continued to shudder as her body refused to come down from such a rapturous high.

"I can't believe I feel so drained."

Matthew glanced over at Carmen and smiled. They had just arrived at Ray's Place, a popular hangout on the

Hamptons. She was leaning against his car and, dressed in a pair of jeans and a cute pink blouse, she was looking as breathless as she sounded. "I wonder why," he said.

She laughed and gave him a knowing look. "Oh, you know exactly why, Matthew Birmingham." She raked a hand through her hair and laughed again before saying in a somewhat serious tone, "You're pretty incredible."

His smile widened. "You're pretty incredible yourself. Come on, let's go grab something to eat to feed that depleted soul of yours." He took her hand in his and they headed toward the entrance of the establishment.

The one thing he'd always enjoyed about Ray's Place was that it was private and the paparazzi were not allowed on the grounds, which was probably why a number of people were there tonight, many of whom had ventured to the Hamptons for the polo matches.

Another thing he liked abut Ray's Place was the excellent service, and he appreciated that they were seated immediately. He glanced over at her and thought he didn't mind being guilty of making her tired. Making love to her most of that day had been the most erotic thing he'd done in a long time, and because it was her and no other woman, it had been special.

"Umm, so what do you think we should order?" she asked, looking at the menu.

He leaned back in his chair. "Whatever can fill me up. I'm starving."

She rolled her eyes. "You're famished and I'm exhausted. Go figure."

"My friend Matthew Birmingham and his lovely wife, Carmen. How are you?"

Matthew glanced up and smiled. "Sheikh Adham, I heard you were a guest this year at the Polo Club. How

are you?" he asked, standing and shaking the man's hand.
He had met the sheikh over ten years ago when, as a
college student, the sheikh had visited the United States
and participated in a swimming competition at UCLA.
They had become good friends then.

"I am fine, Matthew." And he leaned over and kissed
Carmen's cheek. "And you, Carmen, are as beautiful as
ever."

"Thanks, Sheikh Adham," Carmen said, smiling.

The man then gestured to the woman by his side. "And
let me introduce my wife, Sabrina. Sweetheart, Matthew
and Carmen are friends of mine."

The woman smiled as she greeted them. Matthew fought
not to show the surprise on his face. Adham married? The
woman was certainly a beauty. But he'd spent some time
with Adham just last year while working on a historical
piece in the Middle East when he'd claimed marriage was
the furthest thing from this mind. Matthew couldn't help
wondering what had happened to make him change his
mind.

"Would you and Sabrina like to join us?" Matthew heard
Carmen ask.

Adham shook his head. "We appreciate your kindness
but we've already eaten and were just leaving. Hopefully,
we can get together soon after one of the polo matches."

"Carmen and I would like that." They chatted for a few
more minutes before the couple left.

"Wow, I can't imagine Adham married," Carmen said,
speaking aloud what Matthew's thoughts had been earlier.
Matthew returned to his seat, remembering it was well-
known that Adham used to have a wild streak and be quite
a womanizer.

"They look happy," Carmen added.

Matthew wasn't so sure about that. For some reason he didn't quite feel that happiness that Adham and Sabrina were trying so hard to emit.

"I can't believe I ate so much," Carmen said when they returned from dinner.

She glanced over her shoulder and saw Matthew grinning as he tossed his car keys on the table. "And just what do you find so amusing?" She couldn't help but ask him.

He leaned back against the door. "I have to say I don't ever recall seeing you eat that much. You ate your dessert and mine."

Carmen chuckled as she dropped down on the sofa. "Only because you didn't seem as hungry as you claimed you were. I, on the other hand, was not only exhausted, I was hungry."

He nodded. "Are you full now?"

"Yes, pretty much so."

"And your energy level?"

She lifted a brow, wondering why he wanted to know. "Good. Why?"

"Keep watching, you'll figure it out."

And she did. First went his shirt, which he removed and tossed aside. His shoes and socks came next and Carmen watched fascinated. When his hand went to the zipper of his jeans she shivered in anticipation. The man had a body that could make her tremble while waiting for it to be bared.

Determined not to be undone, she eased off the sofa and began removing her own clothes. By the time she had tossed her last article of clothing aside, he was slowly moving toward her. "You're slow, Carmen."

She grinned. "And you look hard, Matthew."

"You're right," he said, pulling her into his arms.

She groaned out loud with the feel of his naked body against hers.

"Haven't you gotten enough yet?" she asked, smiling.

"No. Have you?"

She wrapped her arms around his neck. "No."

And then he pulled her back down on the couch with him.

Matthew gazed up at the ceiling. If anyone had told him that he would be spending a good part of his entire day making love to his wife—his ex-wife—he would not have believed it. Even now, while lying flat on his back, trying to regain his strength and listening to her moving around in the bathroom, he was still somewhat stunned.

Their lovemaking had been off the charts as always, but something had been different—he'd detected another element in the mix. An intense hunger had driven them to new heights, making them fully aware of what they'd gone without for twelve months and just how much they longed to have it back.

He had assumed leaving the house awhile would wean some of their sexual hunger, but it hadn't. No sooner had they returned, they were at it again. He could not get enough of her, and they had gotten it on every chance they got. Without any regrets. At least there certainly hadn't been any on his part and he hoped the same held true for her.

What if she was not feeling the same way that he was? What if it had been lust and not love that had driven her to sleep with him, and now that she had, nothing had changed for her?

Shifting positions, he lay on his side with his gaze fixed on the bathroom door. Carmen was an actress, and a damn good one, but when it came to certain emotions, he could read her like a book. At least he used to be able to.

But today she had made love with him as if they hadn't just spent an entire year not talking to each other. He wished he could let the matter go, but he couldn't. Their love had been too strong for him to just let things continue as they had before. He didn't want revenge anymore. What he wanted more than anything was an explanation as to why she had ended their marriage. As far as he was concerned, they could have worked it out if she'd just given him a chance, if she'd just communicated with him.

He drew in a deep breath as he waited for his ex to come out of the bathroom. It was time for all cards to be placed on the table. It was time for her to be honest with him and for him to be honest with her, as well. He wanted his wife back, and it was time he told her so.

Carmen stood at the vanity mirror after her shower, staring at her face, hoping that Matthew would still be asleep when she left the bathroom. She was not ready to see any sign of regret in his eyes. It had probably just been lust driving him to make love to her like that, and now that it was out of his system, it would be business as usual with them. He would remind her, in a nice way of course, that they were still divorced and nothing had changed.

Boy, was he wrong. Something had changed—at least it had for her. She could no longer deny that she still loved him. And she had to tell him about the baby—it wasn't fair to keep it a secret anymore.

At the time, she had been so hurt that all she'd wanted to do was wallow in the pain without him. She'd blamed him for not being there that night and had even gone so far as to tell herself that if he had been there, things might have been different. She hadn't wanted to believe what the doctor had said—that a large percentage of women miscarry a baby at some point during their reproductive years. According to the doctor there was no reason for her not to have a normal pregnancy when she was ready to try again. But at the time, she hadn't wanted to think about another pregnancy. She'd only wanted to mourn the one she'd lost.

She wished she'd handled things differently. She should have called Matthew and let him know what happened. She knew deep down that there was nothing, work or otherwise, that would have kept him from hopping on the next plane to Barcelona to be with her.

He would have held her while she cried, kissed her tears away and told her everything would be okay, that as soon as she was ready they would make another baby. He would have meant every word.

And when she'd been able to travel he would have taken her home and cared for her, pampered her and shown her that no matter how many hours he spent away from her, she was the most important thing in his life.

He had told her that many times but she hadn't wanted to hear it even though she, of all people, knew his family history and knew that taking care of her was important to him. But what she had done was turn her back on him and without telling him the full story, she had filed for a divorce. She hung her head, ashamed of her decision. He probably hated her for doing that, and their relationship could be beyond repair at this point.

She lifted her face to stare at her reflection again. Yesterday, she'd wanted to seduce her ex-husband in the name of revenge, but today she knew she needed him in her life. She loved him and wouldn't be happy until they were together again.

Somehow she needed to make him fall in love with her

all over again. But first she had to tell him the truth. She had to tell him about the baby.

Matthew held his breath when the bathroom door opened and the moment Carmen appeared in the doorway his heart began pounding deep in his chest. The sunlight pouring in through the windows seemed to make her skin glow.

Silently he lay there and studied the way her short silk bathrobe clung to her curves. He had every reason to believe she was naked underneath it. There was a damp sheen to her brown skin and her hair was tied back away from her face, emphasizing her eyes and mouth. As he continued to watch her, that mouth he enjoyed kissing so much slowly curved into a sexy smile.

There were no regretful vibes emitting from her and he let out a relieved breath as they stared at each other. They'd done that a lot lately, staring at each other without saying anything. But what he saw in her gaze now nearly melted his heart. She loved him. He was certain of that. He might not ever hear her say the words to him again but he could see it—it was there on her face, in her eyes and all around those delectable lips.

He intended to do whatever had to be done to remind her of what they'd once had. More than anything, he wanted her to accept that there was nothing the two of them couldn't work out together. That was the one thing he was certain about. Two people couldn't love each other as deeply as they did and still stay apart. In his book, things just didn't work out that way.

He watched as she slowly moved across the room toward him and he sat up to catch her when she all but dived into his arms. And then she was kissing him with a hunger and need that he quickly reciprocated. He fought for control, his body burning with a need that was driving him off the deep end. He wanted to do nothing more than bury himself inside her body.

Moments later, she ended the kiss and leaned back. Her robe had risen up her thighs and the belt around her waist was loose, giving him a glimpse of a tantalizing portion of her breasts and the dark shadow at the juncture of her legs. The scent of her was drawing him in, making him remember how he'd felt being inside of her.

Unable to resist, he reached out and slid his hands beneath the silk of her bathrobe and began stroking her breasts, letting his fingertips tease the hardened nipples. When he began moving lower, she whispered, "Matthew, let's talk."

He agreed with her. They should talk. He wanted to start off by telling her how he felt, but the moment he opened his mouth to do so, he realized he wasn't ready after all. He didn't want to revisit the past just yet. Instead, he wanted to stay right here, right now. "I'm not ready to hash out the bad times, Carmen. Right now I just want to forget about what drove us apart and only concentrate on this, what has brought us together."

He held her gaze, knowing as well as she did that there was no way they could totally forget. If this was about nothing but sex, then that was one thing, but deep down he knew it wasn't. The love between them was still there, which meant there were problems they needed to address. Had his long hours been the only thing that had driven her away from him? He was certain she knew he hadn't been unfaithful to her.

She nodded, and he drew in another deep breath. Eventually they would talk, and he meant really talk. Because now that he had his wife back in his arms, his heart and his bed, he intended to keep her there.

Eleven

Carmen had agreed to postpone their conversation at Matthew's request, and they had spent an amazing week together, enjoying each other. They were both fearful that an in-depth discussion of the state of their affairs would put them back at square one. And they weren't ready to go back there yet.

Instead they'd opted to spend time together, living in the present and not venturing to the past. At the polo matches, everyone was speculating as to what exactly was going on between them. And the *Wagging Tongue* wasn't helping matters. More than one snapshot of them together had appeared in the tabloid, and she and Matthew didn't have to work hard to figure out the identity of the person passing the photos to the paper. Ardella Rowe was the prime suspect. They had seen her at dinner the same night they'd run into Sheikh Adham, and she had tried pestering them with questions, which they'd refused to answer.

At one polo match, she and Matthew had stuck to "no comment" when a mic was shoved in their faces by a reporter wanting to know whether or not they'd gotten back together. The fact of the matter was, they couldn't exactly answer that question themselves.

One paper she had seen claimed they were having a summer fling with no chance of reconciliation while another had announced they'd remarried at a church on Martha's Vineyard. A third had even reported the real Carmen Akins was in Rome with Bruno and the woman Matthew was spending time with in the Hamptons was only a look-alike, a woman he'd taken up with who closely resembled his ex-wife. She could only shake her head at the absurdity of that.

Carmen stood at the huge window in the library, looking out upon the calm waters of the Atlantic.

This past week had been the best she'd known. And it hadn't bothered her in the least the few times Matthew had gone into Manhattan on business, even when one of those meetings had extended well into the late afternoon.

Now she could truly say that although she'd blamed him for the breakup of their marriage, a good portion of the blame could be placed at her feet. She of all people knew how demanding things could be for a director at times, dealing with temperamental actors, overanxious investors and too-cautious production companies. On top of that, there were a number of other issues that could crop up at a moment's notice. And because she'd known all of that, was aware of the stress, she could have been a lot more understanding and a lot less demanding of his time.

The sad thing about it was that she'd always been an independent person and had never yearned for attention from anyone, yet during that time she'd needed Matthew's. Or she'd thought she did. And when she'd lost the baby, she couldn't stand the thought of a future in which Matthew was never there for her, not even when she needed him most.

She selected a book of poetry and was sitting down in one of the recliners when she heard Matthew's footsteps on the hardwood floor. She glanced up the moment he walked into the room, surprised. He had taken a ferry to Manhattan that morning and she hadn't expected him back until much later.

The moment their eyes met, a sensation erupted in the pit of her stomach. And then the craving began.

She placed the book aside as he walked toward her with that slow, sexy saunter. She knew exactly what he had on his mind. Because it was on hers, too. But she also knew it was time for them to talk. They couldn't put it off any longer.

Carmen rose from her seat. "I think it's time for us to talk now, Matthew. There's something I need to tell you."

Matthew had a feeling he knew what Carmen wanted to talk about but he wasn't ready to hear it. The last thing he wanted to discuss was that she was beginning to feel as if there were nothing but sex between them. Given that they'd made love multiple times during the day for seven straight days, he could certainly see why she thought that.

But what she'd failed to take into consideration was that every time he was inside her body, his heart was almost ready to burst in his chest. And each and every morning he woke up with her in his arms made him realize just how much he loved her. What she didn't know was that making love to her was his way of showing her with his body what he hadn't yet been able to say out loud.

He knew things couldn't continue this way between

them. Time was running out and they would have to talk sometime, would have to rehash the past and decide what they would do about their future. But not now, not when he wanted her so much he could hardly breathe.

"Matthew, I—"

He reached out and pulled her into his arms, and within seconds surrender replaced her surprise. This is what he wanted. What he needed. He deepened their kiss, intending to overtake her with passion, to overwhelm her senses.

He closed his arms tightly around her and lifted her just enough to fit snug against his crotch, needing to feel her warmth pressed against him. The feel tormented him and he pulled his mouth away, turning her around so her back fit solidly against his chest.

"Hold on to the table, baby," he whispered.

Carmen felt the warmth of his breath on her ear and knew Matthew was trying to take her mind off her need to talk. And for now, she would let him. Her insides began to quiver and she pressed against him. Emotions she couldn't hold at bay consumed her entire being.

"I want you so much I ache," he added in a deep husky voice that had her body shivering. She loved him and wanted more between them than this. But she would settle for this for now. She didn't want to think about what would happen when she told him about losing their baby. Would he understand the reason she hadn't told him?

He slid his fingers into the elastic of her shorts and pulled them down her legs, leaving her bare. The cool air hit her backside and when he began using his hands to caress her, molding her flesh to his will, she couldn't help but moan even more.

She heard the sound of his zipper and then he tilted her hips up to him. She closed her eyes to the feel of the warm hardness of his erection touching her while his fingers massaged between her legs.

She tightened her grip on the table as he placed the head of his shaft at her womanly folds. The feel of him entering her from behind sent her mind spinning and when he pushed deep, she cried out as sensations tore through her. In this position she felt a part of him, enclosed in his embrace, in the comfort and protection of his body.

He began moving and her body vibrated with every stroke inside her. She closed her eyes, relishing the feel of something so intimate and right between them. He ground his hips against her, going deeper and deeper—she wondered if they would be able to separate their bodies when the time came to do so.

When he slid his hands underneath her top and began fondling her bare breasts, she threw her head back. She loved the feel of his hands on her breasts, the tips of his fingers tormenting her nipples.

The way he was mating with her, the hot warmth of his breath on her neck as he whispered all the things he planned to do to her before the night was over—all of that stirred heat and stroked her desire to a feverish pitch she could barely contain any longer.

She let go, sensations ripping through her. She began quivering in an orgasm from head to toe. Those same sensations overpowered him and he tilted her up toward him even more and drove deeper inside of her. He groaned her name as she felt his hot release. She felt it. She felt him. And before she could stop herself, she cried out, "I love you, Matthew."

She couldn't believe she'd said it, and part of her hoped that he hadn't heard it. Slowly, he turned her around and gave her the most tender, gentle kiss she'd ever had from him. But he didn't say anything. Not a word.

* * *

Matthew glanced around the bedroom as he leaned against the closed door. The last thing he had expected was for Carmen to admit to loving him, and as soon as he could escape her presence, he had. He should have told her that he loved her, too, but for some reason he hadn't been able to do so. Not that he didn't, but because he loved her so much. Had he confessed it at that moment he probably would have lost it—to know that she still loved him after all this time was more than he could handle. He needed to pull himself together before facing her. Before pouring his heart out to her and letting her know just how miserable his life had been without her in it.

He'd enjoyed being here with her for the past week and was looking forward to the rest of the summer. And he was doing a pretty good job balancing the work and spending time with her. They'd spent a lot of hours on the beach and had gone to several polo matches. And of course the media was in a frenzy trying to figure out what was going on between them.

Even with all the gossip floating around, things between them were almost like they'd been in the beginning. But not quite. He knew his time was running out. Given what she'd just said to him, they had to talk. And they had to talk today. He would take her for a walk on the beach, and they would finally hash it all out.

He opened a drawer and searched around for his sunglasses, smiling when he found the case buried at the bottom. He was about to close the drawer when he noticed a DVD case labeled, "For my Husband." And it was dated the day he was supposed to meet her in Spain.

Curious about the video, he took it out the drawer. After inserting the DVD into the player, he sat on the edge of the bed.

He smiled when Carmen appeared on the screen in what looked like a spoof of his very first job as a director, which was for a game show called *Guess My Secret*. She was talking to the camera, to him, daring him to discover her secret. The only clues she gave were a plate and a small clock. Soon she added a number of other clues into the mix—a pair of knitting needles and a jar of cocoa butter.

He was still scratching his head and laughing at her when she added more hints. Breath was sucked from his lungs when she placed two additional items on the table—a baby bottle and a bib. With a shaking hand, he reached over to turn up the volume while she smiled into the camera.

"Very good, Matthew. Since you're a smart man, I'm sure you now know my secret. We are having a baby! That's why I wanted to make our time here in Barcelona so special."

"Oh my God!" he groaned. Carmen had been pregnant? Then what happened?

"Hey, Matthew, I was beginning to think you got lost up here. What's going—"

Carmen entered the room and stopped talking in midsentence when she saw herself on the screen. Her gaze immediately sought out Matthew, and the pain she saw on his face tore at her heart.

"Is that true, Carmen? Had you planned to tell me that night in Barcelona that you were pregnant?"

She swallowed as she nodded. "Yes. I…I wanted to tell you in a fun way so…" Her words trailed off.

He nodded slowly and then asked the question she had been dreading. "What happened, Carmen?"

She lowered her head as she relived that night. The stomach pains that kept getting worse. Her not being able to reach him on his cell when she'd awakened that night, bleeding. Everything became a blur after that. Except the part about waking up and being told by a doctor that she'd lost the baby.

"Carmen?"

She lifted her head and met his gaze as her eyes filled with tears. And then she began speaking, recounting every single detail of that night. As she talked, she watched his expression. The shattered look on his face and the pain that clouded his eyes nearly broke her heart, and she felt his agony. A part of her was relieved to tell him the truth and no longer have the burden of keeping a secret on her shoulders.

"And you never told me," he said in a broken tone. "You never told me."

She pulled in a deep breath as tears threatened to spill down her face. "I couldn't. I wanted that baby so much. Losing it, and then not having you there with me to share my pain, made me bitter, unreasonable. I tried contacting you first and when I didn't get you, all I could think about was that I needed you and you were at work, away from me. In my emotional state, I blamed you."

He bent his head and when he raised his eyes to her again, the pain in them had deepened. "And I blame myself, as well," he said in a hoarse tone. "I blame myself because I should have been there with you. I don't know if I can ever forgive myself for not being there."

She saw the sheen of tears in his eyes and quickly crossed the room to him. As they clung to each other, tears she had held back since that night flowed down her face. She had cried then but it hadn't been like this. Her shoulders jerked with sobs she hadn't been able to let go of until now, until she was with him.

"I'm so sorry, Carmen. Now I understand. I had let you

down by letting you go through that alone. I know I won't ever be able to forgive myself for that."

She leaned away from him, wiping her eyes. "You can, Matthew, and you must. It took me a while to see it wasn't your fault, nor was it mine. The same thing would have happened if you'd been there. And being here with you this past week made me realize I can't be angry at you for something you didn't know about, something that was not in your control. I had tried telling you several times over the past week, but you kept wanting us to wait. I'm sorry you had to find out this way."

She wiped more tears from her eyes. "The woman who owned the villa called her doctor and made arrangements for him to take care of me there, figuring that I would want to keep it from the media. With her help, I was able to avoid the circus that could have taken place. The doctor said I can try again," she said, leaning up against him, holding tight. "But I so wanted that one," she whispered brokenly, burying her face in his chest.

Matthew swept her off her feet and carried her over to the settee. He sat down with her cradled in his lap. He bent his head, and felt his wet cheek against hers.

"It wasn't your fault, Matthew. It wasn't my fault. It was just something that happened. We have to believe that so we can move beyond it. There will be other babies."

He lifted his head to meet her gaze. "But will there be other babies…for us, Carmen? For you and me?"

Carmen knew what he was asking. He'd once told her that he didn't want any other woman to have his child but her. And from the look in his eyes he still wanted that. He wanted to know if their relationship would ever get back to the way it was, when he was her whole world and she was his.

She shifted slightly in his embrace to wrap her arms

around his neck. She wanted to make sure he heard what she was about to say. "I never stopped loving you, Matthew. The reason I wanted that baby so much was because it was a part of you, and a part of me. And the reason I hurt so much afterward was because I thought I had lost that connection. I thought the baby would bring us back together." She paused a second and then said, "But I've discovered that all it takes to bring us back together is us. Being with you here this past week has shown me there is still an us, and I want that back so badly. I was never involved with Bruno. It was all a publicity stunt. The only man I ever wanted to belong to was you. Can you forgive me for shutting you out of my life when I needed you most? Can you forgive me for running away? I will never leave you again."

"Oh, Carmen. I need you to forgive me, as well. I love you so much. I was so driven to give you the things you were used to having that I lost focus, I forgot about those things that truly mattered. You, and truly making you happy. I've been so lonely without you. And Candy, too, was just a publicity stunt. Hell, I was looking forward to spending time without her here. But when I arrived and discovered you, I wanted you to stay. At first I wanted revenge, to hurt you the way I was hurting, but I soon discovered it couldn't be that way with us."

She nodded. "I was going to make you want me and then leave again. Instead I ended up wanting you so badly I didn't know what to do."

"We're going to handle our business differently from here on out," he declared. "I've learned this week that I can balance my work and the rest of my life. Will you give me another chance to prove it?"

Carmen smiled up at him as he pushed back a strand of hair from her face. "I want that, too, Matthew."

"And will you marry me, Carmen?"

She felt more tears come to her eyes. "Yes, yes, I will marry you, and this time will be forever."

"Forever," he said, bending down to kiss her. And the kiss they shared was full of promise for a brighter and happier future. Together, knowing what they now knew about each other, they would be able to do anything.

Moments later he broke off the kiss and stood with her in his arms. She recognized the look he was giving her. "What about the polo match?" she asked.

He chuckled as he crossed the room to the bed. "There will be others."

Carmen knew he was right. Being in his arms and making love to him was what she needed. They were being given another chance at happiness and were taking it.

"It will be me and you together, Carmen, for the rest of our lives."

She reached up and caressed the side of his face. "Yes, Matthew, for the rest of our lives."

Epilogue

Ardella rushed over to them the moment Matthew and Carmen entered the tent, and from the anxious look on her face it was evident she was looking for a scoop. This time Matthew and Carmen didn't mind giving her one.

"So you two, what are you smiling about?"

Matthew pulled Carmen closer to his side. "It's a beautiful day and we believe it will be a good polo match."

The woman gave them a sly look. "I think there's something else."

Carmen decided to take Ardella out of her inquisitive misery. "There is something else and you can say you heard it right from us. Matthew and I have decided to remarry."

The smile on the woman's face appeared genuine. "I am truly happy for you two, but you know everyone will want details and facts."

Carmen threw her head back. "Sorry, but some things

we plan to keep secret and sacred." She refused to spill the beans about their plan to have a private ceremony on the beach here in the Hamptons this weekend. The first person she'd called was Rachel who had been supremely ecstatic.

"Matthew, will Carmen star in any future Birmingham movies?"

Matthew glanced down at Carmen and chuckled. "Ardella, Carmen can do anything Carmen wants."

Ardella beamed. "I will take that as a yes."

"You do that," Matthew said. And, knowing that Ardella probably had her secret camera ready, with the profound tenderness of a man who was in love, he pulled Carmen into his arms and kissed her.

No one would understand the emotions flowing through him at that that moment. They were the heartfelt emotions of a man meant to cherish the woman he loved. A man who'd recently realized that he really was husband material.

Carmen's heart was just as full and later, as she and Matthew sat beside each other watching the polo match, she couldn't help but wipe a tear from her eye. They had talked and together had promised not to let anything or anyone come between them again.

"You okay, sweetheart?"

Carmen glanced up at Matthew and nodded. "I couldn't be better." She paused and, still holding his gaze, whispered, "I love you."

A smile touched his lips. "And I love you."

She leaned closer to him when he tightened his arms around her shoulders. She was happy about the future that lay before them. He wanted to try again for a baby and so did she. But right now she looked forward to being Carmen Aiken Birmingham again.

She smiled, liking the sound of that and deciding to show him just how much when they returned home later. Life was good but being with the man you love, she decided, was even better.

* * * * *

THE SHEIKH'S
BARGAINED BRIDE

Olivia Gates

To the many fabulous ladies who made this novella
and this exciting collection come to life.
My senior editor, Krista Stroever, for the
wonderful premise and the unstinting guidance,
and authors Brenda Jackson, Yvonne Lindsay,
Catherine Mann, Katherine Garbera and Emily McKay
for all the fun and helpful collaboration.
It was a great experience working with you all.
I can't wait to do it again!

Olivia Gates has always pursued creative passions—painting, singing and many handicrafts. She still does, but only one of her passions grew gratifying enough, consuming enough, to become an ongoing career. Writing.

She is most fulfilled when she is creating worlds and conflicts for her characters, then exploring and untangling them bit by bit, sharing her protagonists' every heart-wrenching heartache and hope, their every heart-pounding doubt and trial, until she leads them to an indisputably earned and gloriously satisfying happy ending.

When she's not writing, she is a doctor, a wife to her own alpha male and a mother to one brilliant girl and one demanding angora cat. Visit Olivia at www.oliviagates.com.

One

Three weeks ago, Sabrina Grant married the man of her dreams.

Sheikh Adham ben Khaleel ben Haamed Aal Ferjani was a prince—literally—who'd charmed and captivated her from the moment she'd set eyes on him. He was everything a woman couldn't be creative enough to hope for. She loved him with every fiber of her being.

And she'd never thought she could be so miserable.

How had she ended up like this? Alone, discarded? This was the last thing she'd imagined when she'd said "I do."

But then, she couldn't have imagined anything that had happened in the six weeks since her father's heart attack.

It had been late May, less than a week after she'd finished her postgraduate courses, and she'd been about to go home with two master's degrees in hand, when she'd been hit with the terrible news. She'd hurtled to his bedside, struggling with her anxiety as well as his, while fielding those who'd come to pay tribute to her father, Thomas Grant, multimillionaire vineyard and winery owner. The stress had almost wrecked her…until his best friend had come to visit, accompanied by the most incredible man she'd ever seen. Adham.

She was bowled over. And to her stunned delight, he seemed as taken with her. The best part was that she was sure his interest had nothing to do with her father's fortune. Beyond being second in line to the throne of the staggeringly rich desert kingdom of Khumayrah, he was the owner of the largest horse farm in the States, with a fortune that made her father's look like change.

Adham started coming every day, enthralling her more each time. He kept her company in her vigil at her father's bedside, took her for meals and walks. His companionship bolstered her while each touch inflamed her. By the time she begged for him and he took her, it was only three weeks into their relationship, but she'd already stumbled head over heels in love with him.

Then the next day, her father told her that he was being discharged, and that Adham had asked for her hand in marriage. She was overwhelmed by relief and happiness. Her father was going to be okay, and Adham loved her as much as she loved him.

But she crashed down to earth when she talked to her father's doctors. They said they were releasing him only because he'd asked to die at home. There was no use performing open-heart surgery, or even a heart transplant, since his other systems had been severely damaged, and he had only a few days to live.

Both her father and Adham agreed on an immediate wedding so that her father could witness it. She wanted to give him whatever happiness she could in his last days, but it was heart wrenching to know he wouldn't live to see her building a family with the man of her dreams.

Hours after the wedding, her father slipped into a coma. He died twenty-four hours later.

After such a tragic start to their marriage, it was the last thing she expected to have Adham whisk her away from her family home in Long Island, to deposit her in a mansion of his in New England and return to his obligations and duties. He came home only fleetingly, but certainly not to her.

She at first thought he was giving her time and space to mourn, so she tried to show him that she wanted nothing but to lose herself in his arms, that his intimacy would be the best salve for her grief.

When that didn't work, she looked everywhere for a reason for his withdrawal. She got a possible explanation when Jameel, his right-hand man who also supervised her *hashyah*—her entourage as a princess—told her there was a forty-day mourning period in Khumayrah, where normal life was interrupted to observe bereavement.

Now it was three weeks later, and she could no longer buy this. It was understandable to cancel their honeymoon in their situation, but to not come near her at all? To treat her like a stranger and not the bride she'd thought he hadn't been able to wait to possess again? That, she couldn't understand.

Just this morning, she'd again tried to speak to him. And again, he hadn't given her a chance.

He whisked her to the Hamptons for the start of the polo season, informing her of his many interests there. He was a player on one of the teams, as well as a patron who provided their horses, and a friend and associate to many of the pivotal people in the Bridgehampton Polo Club.

And here she was, in another one of his mansions, this

one even more impressive than the last—a spectacular estate on a dozen acres in a prime Bridgehampton South location, with a stunning floor plan, top-of-the-line building materials and masterful finishes. Its three floors covered thirty-six thousand square feet, and the grounds included a unique recreation pavilion. He'd said he liked to have his own residence when he came every year for the tournaments, and he needed all that space to accommodate his entourage and security.

He'd installed her in the master suite that boasted Bordeaux walnut floors, exquisite decor and an expansive en suite bathroom with gold fixtures and onyx walls and floors. The only thing it didn't include was her groom.

"Sabrina."

She jerked out of her morbid musings. *Adham.*

His voice had come from the suite's sitting-room door. Fathomless, irresistible, the exotic inflections of his native Khumayran that mixed with his upper-crust British accent turning her name into an invocation.

In spite of the crushed expectations and confusion of the past weeks, hope surged, making her dizzy with it.

Maybe he would come to her at last. Maybe he *had* withdrawn to give her time to mourn her father, and had postponed their wedding night until he was sure she was up to withstanding his passion.

If that was it, she'd thank him for his consideration and adherence to his culture's mourning rituals, then scold him for not understanding the last thing she needed was to feel cut off with her grief. She didn't need space and time. She needed *him.*

Her breath caught in her lungs as she leaned back on the king-size, white-lace-covered bed. He'd walk in any second now.

Seconds stretched. Then she heard his receding footsteps.

She sat up, stunned. He'd called only so she'd come out, and walked away when she hadn't, rather than be in a bedroom with her? Why?

Then you call *him,* you moron. *Find out why. Once and for all.*

"Adham."

But she was too late. The door clicked closed behind him.

And she couldn't take it anymore. She exploded from the bed, running after him.

She called out again as she pursued him. But even though he must have heard her, he strode ahead undeterred.

This time, so would she. She had to get to the bottom of this or lose her mind.

She ran after him through the maze of a dazzling parterre, her heels grinding the gravel paths. She caught up with him before he lowered himself into the driver's seat of a gleaming black Jaguar that seemed like an extension of him, of his power and potency.

He turned to her, his eyes hidden behind mirrored sunglasses, his face blank. God. She missed his smile.

"Sabrina." That revving *R,* underlining his exotic origins, shuddered through her again. "I thought you were asleep."

"I'd be narcoleptic if I were asleep every time you think I am."

He didn't smile. Probably because of the bitterness that had stained her tone.

He looked down the eight inches between them—even with her three-inch heels—the wealth of his rain-straight hair gleaming like a raven's wing in the midday summer sun. She almost moaned as everything about him bombarded her. His scent, his size, his beauty. He'd changed out of the casual clothes he'd worn while piloting the helicopter out to the Hamptons into one of those designer suits that made him look almost intimidating. At thirty-four, he was the epitome of everything male, of what she'd never imagined could be gathered in one man. And he was her husband. Yet he wasn't really hers at all.

Suddenly, all thoughts, all existence disappeared.

Adham was taking off his sunglasses, his golden eyes flaring with their emerald highlights, reaching out a hand to cup her face in a possessive palm. His thumb stroked her cheek, skimmed over her trembling lips, dipping into their moistness, spreading it over them, setting everything he touched on fire.

"You look edible, *ya jameelati*."

Hearing him call her "my beauty," and the way he was gazing at her as if he did want to devour her, thundered through her.

Her response was so fierce, it sent indignation rippling through her. "I look exactly the same as I did this morning. I haven't even changed out of my traveling clothes."

"Then I beg your forgiveness for not noticing. I had too many urgencies on my mind. But that's no excuse. Nothing should have distracted me from *kanzi, aroosi*—my treasure, my bride."

Before she could process his words, or register the surge of joy they elicited, his hand slid to her nape, holding her head captive, the other gathering her around her waist and lifting her off the ground, plastering her against his steel-fleshed body.

"Adham…" was all she gasped before his lips took hers.

He drank her moans, thrusting his tongue inside her, occupying her, intoxicating her. "*Aih, gooly esmi haik*—say my name like that, like you can't draw breath with wanting me."

"I can't.…" She writhed in his arms, not caring that they were out in the open. She'd starved for him.

He turned, pressing her against the back passenger door, thrust against her, his daunting erection digging into her quivering stomach, his knee driving between her melting thighs.

One thing was left inside her mind, looping in a frenzied litany. *He wants me again.*

"I would say get a room, but we're standing in front of a mansion with sixteen suites. And by the look of it, you've probably made thorough use of each and every one of them."

The words, spoken by a deep, amused male voice, trickled through Sabrina's fevered awareness. She only understood that Adham was severing their meld and putting her back fully on her feet. She clung to him, panicked he'd drift away again.

But he brought her in front of him as he turned to the speaker, his arms gathering her tight, linking over her belly.

She blinked through the crimson haze of arousal at a tall, dark, handsome man standing a dozen feet away, his hands deep in the pockets of his ultra-chic pants. He looked highly entertained.

"And hello to you, too, Seb." Adham's voice above her ear had more moist heat surging between her thighs. She struggled not to rub them together, to ameliorate the pounding there. "It's great that you came, *ya sudeeki,* so I can have the pleasure—" his hands brushed her belly with insistent caresses, his hardness jerking against the small of her back "—of introducing to you the love of my life, my bride, Sabrina Aal Ferjani." Sabrina didn't know how she remained upright after such a declaration. "*Ameerati,* let me introduce Sebastian Hughes, my friend and associate. He runs the Bridgehampton Polo Club in his father's stead."

She extended a trembling hand to Sebastian, overwhelmed at Adham calling her "my princess" on top of everything else.

Sebastian placed a gallant kiss on her hand. "It's an honor and a pleasure to meet you, Sabrina." He raised green eyes full of mischief, before he straightened to a height a couple of inches shy of Adham's six foot five. "And a shock. I never thought the day would come when Adham entered matrimony's gilded cage willingly."

"I never thought it would, either." Adham looked down, his gaze singeing her. "Until I met Sabrina. And then nothing could have kept me out of it. Not that anywhere she is could be called a cage, gilded or otherwise, but a haven."

Sebastian barked a laugh. "Oh, man. You're spouting poetry! You must have potent magic, Sabrina. I can call you Sabrina, right?" Before she could blurt out an affirmation, Sebastian turned his teasing eyes to Adham. "You won't make me call her Princess Aal Ferjani, will you, Adham?"

Adham's smile flashed, riddling her vision in spots. "He's having a field day teasing me, since just before I met you, I told him that he'd never see me married. But then I can say the same about him. While we were falling in love, the world's foremost confirmed bachelor had a change of heart, too. It took his assistant almost leaving him to make him realize he can't live without her."

Sebastian nodded whimsically. "Yeah. One thing for sure, Sabrina, Adham and I are both lucky dogs. And you and Julia must be saints for not only putting up with us, but for forgiving our trespasses and loving us nevertheless."

"Why do you think Adham had any trespasses to forgive?" The question was out of her mouth before she could think.

Sebastian's lips twisted whimsically. "Because as an inveterate lone wolf, he must have committed some in his struggles not to succumb to his fate and his feelings for you. I know I did."

Suddenly it felt like floodlights went on inside her head.

Could that be what the past weeks were about? Adham trying to adjust to being married, after a lifetime of thinking he'd never tie his life to another?

"So what brings you here, Seb?" Adham asked, interrupting her musings. "I was just coming to the farm myself."

"I thought you wouldn't make it out on Sabrina's first day here, so I came to meet your bride and welcome her to our neck of the woods."

"And now you have." Adham turned his eyes to her. "And now that you're here, would you like to accompany me, *ya ameerati?* I'd love to give you a tour of the Seven Oaks Farm, where the polo club's tournaments take place."

She almost jumped in his arms. "Oh, yes, please."

Sebastian laughed. "And in case things get too hot for you during the tour, you can borrow my personal quarters at the farm to…cool off."

Adham shook his head. "Suffering in utmost discomfort doesn't matter, when one's waiting for the time to be finally right."

She twisted to gaze into his eyes, and saw it again. The pure, unadulterated passion of the life-changing night when he'd possessed her.

He meant those words. He had been waiting for her to heal, the incredible—if terribly misguided—man.

And she felt her life begin. Finally. For real.

TWO

The drive to the Seven Oaks Farm passed in a haze.

All Sabrina felt was Adham sitting beside her, his body radiating command and control, all she saw was his sculpted profile, all she could appreciate was his profound beauty. The man was gorgeous down to his last hair and pore.

And all she wanted was to carry on where they'd left off when Sebastian had interrupted them. She'd thought he'd intended to when he'd decided to have Jameel chauffeur them in a limo. But with the barrier between driver and passenger compartments down, and his bodyguards preceding and following them in other cars, she felt exposed. And then, even if she didn't, she wouldn't have acted on the desires churning in her mind, frying her body.

She wouldn't have run her hand up his inner thigh, wouldn't have leaned over him to rub his hardness with her leg and catch his maddening lower lip in her teeth. She had to face it. She was too inexperienced; she'd probably botch any seduction attempt. Worse, she was too shy to try, even if she was assured of the desired results. She still needed him to initiate their intimacies.

No such luck. He'd been inundated with one phone call after another since they'd entered the limo. She could only watch him, vibrating with his nearness, with ratcheting need.

"*Zain, kaffa*. That's enough," he growled under his breath as he ended the last call. "I'm turning the phone off. They'll have to live without me for a while." He turned to her. "*Aassef, ya habibati*. So sorry for all this. There will be no more interruptions. So tell me. What do you know about polo?"

Heat rushed to her face at hearing him calling her "my love." She'd memorized everything he'd said to her in his native tongue and investigated what it meant when he hadn't provided the translation. He'd called her that only once before—when he'd been deep in her, turning her inside out with pleasure.

She mumbled her answer. "Uh…not much."

"Let me guess. A group of men galloping on horses, hitting a tiny ball around a huge field with sticks to catapult it between goal posts." Her heat rose another notch in embarrassment. That was exactly how it seemed to her. The amused indulgence in his eyes poured fuel on her conflagration. "And you wouldn't be wrong. That's basically it. Want to know more about the sport and the events I'm going to be involved in for the next few weeks?"

"Please." Her heart kicked with eagerness to know more of what he enjoyed, what made up his passions and occupations. "Tell me everything."

Something she couldn't define came into in his eyes. He looked away for a moment, catching Jameel's eyes in the front mirror. Before she could wonder, his eyes were back, snaring hers, wiping her mind clean of anything but her yearning for him.

"I started playing polo when I was eight." Her heart melted inside her rib cage at imagining him at that age, the most beautiful boy, the strongest and smartest, already such an accomplished rider that he could excel in the fierce sport. "And I started breeding my own horses at sixteen. For the past ten years, I've played an integral role in every major polo tournament in the world, as sponsor, horse supplier and player. But I have a special interest in the one that takes place here every summer, especially since Sebastian took over after his father was diagnosed with cancer. For the past three weeks I've been commuting here for the preseason tournament, The Clearwater Media Cup, a run-up to the main season. Clearwater Media is the company Sebastian owns with Richard Wells, who's just become engaged to one of my best horse trainers, Catherine Lawson. Their engagement almost coincided with Sebastian's to his assistant, Julia."

She wanted to blurt out, "And with our marriage." But she hesitated, because it didn't feel real yet. She only said, "And the season hasn't even started yet."

"This summer's tournament *is* going to be memorable. It's always high stakes with the world's best athletes competing for one of the sport's most treasured prizes amid the splendor of the Hamptons summer scene." He suddenly cupped her face. "But this year it will be the best ever because you're here. With me."

She almost fainted with the surge of emotions as she gazed helplessly into the molten translucence of his eyes.

A scratchy noise came from what felt like a mile away. She didn't realize what it was until Adham withdrew his

hand and sat back. Jameel's discreet cough, alerting them
that they'd arrived.

She looked dazedly around. They'd stopped by a row
of stables. There were people outside. Some seemed to be
going about their business. Most seemed to be waiting for
them. With cameras.

She turned to Adham, apprehension shooting up her
spine. She didn't find him. Seconds later, he seemed to
materialize at her other side. He helped her out and she
stumbled up and into his containment as the glare and heat
of the summer day and the cacophony of the newspeople
bombarded her. He hugged her to his side as they walked
inside the stables, preceded by rabidly eager faces, snapping
photos and shouting questions.

Adham calmly confirmed the date of their marriage, and
that it had been a private ceremony because of her father's
condition. Then he nodded to Jameel, and bodyguards
appeared as if out of nowhere, clearing their path of
paparazzi.

There were still too many people inside the stables, too
many eyes, all on Adham and her. She felt more vulnerable
by the second under their scrutiny. She'd always hated
attention. She'd realized she'd get more than ever now
that she was Adham's wife, but realizing it was one thing.
Experiencing it was another.

A tremor shot through her. Adham's arm tightened,
making her feel he'd surrounded her with a protective force
field, as if she were the most treasured thing on earth.

"I want you to meet my most important colleagues."

Next second, all unease evaporated. It was replaced by
wonder.

His horses. Or as they were called in polo, his ponies.

The sight of the mind-boggling collection of magnificent

animals had delight bubbling inside her at being so close to such a manifestation of primal grandeur and beauty.

Adham introduced her to each pony, telling her its name, breed, measurements, character, quirks and strengths on the field. And throughout, people came to salute him, awe for him as clear as their curiosity about her, the woman this desert prince and celebrity entrepreneur had picked to be his bride.

He accepted their congratulations, deflected their adulation and introduced her with supreme pride, then made it clear that he expected privacy to show his bride around.

Once everyone had retreated to an acceptable distance, Adham resumed his explanations. "My ponies travel with me wherever my team goes. Each member must have six to eight horses per game. But to make allowances for injuries and other crises, I transport around sixty to seventy horses during each season."

Just when she thought she couldn't possibly see anything more perfect, he introduced her to his pride and joy, his prize ponies.

"Aswad and Layl, 'black' and 'night' in Arabic, are brothers. Their sire was Hallek, or 'deepest dark,' my very first horse."

She caressed one glossy velvet neck after another in wonder, flashing Adham a delighted smile. "Any relation, since your own name means 'deepest black'?"

He let out a peal of laughter that had every head in the stables turning, relinquishing any attempt to appear as if they weren't intently watching their every move.

"My family always wondered if I have horse genes in me, the way I'm as one with them. But it's true that I feel like they're my kin, my children even. I oversaw the breeding of each and every one of my ponies myself, followed their lives since before they were born."

"You do share all of their unrivaled magnificence."

At her fervent statement, his eyes flared. He plunged his fingers into the mass of curls at the back of her head, cupped her neck in his large palm as he crowded her against Aswad. "It's your magnificence that can't be rivaled, *ya jameelati*."

At the periphery of her fogging awareness, she heard a whirring sound. It was only when Adham removed his hand and shifted his eyes to the source of disturbance that she realized what it had been. One of the paparazzi had managed to slip by the bodyguards.

Adham glared at him. The guy only grinned, taking more photos. Adham advanced on him and the thin, seedy-looking guy clambered back out of the stables.

Sabrina put her hand on Adham's clenched forearm. "Aswad and Layl are Arabian?"

He looked back at her, the knowledge that she was trying to defuse the situation filling his eyes.

He let her have her wish, visibly relaxed, smiled. "All my ponies are purebred Arabian stallions and mares. You can tell by this." He ran his hand lovingly down Layl's head. The horse nuzzled him back in delight and affection. She knew exactly how he felt. "A refined, wedge-shaped head." He grabbed her closer, pressing his length to her back, running his hands down her arms until he entwined their fingers before he raised her hands so they could caress each feature of Layl he mentioned.

"They also have a broad forehead, large eyes and nostrils, small muzzles, an arched neck and a high tail carriage. Most have a slight forehead bulge, what we call *jibbah* in Khumayrah." He guided her fingertips in investigating the protrusion. "It's an enlargement of their sinuses that helps them weather our desert climate. And with compact bodies and short backs, even small Arabians can carry heavy riders with ease. They're known for stamina and courage. But I've never known a horse with half of Aswad's and Layl's endurance and fearlessness. I ride them in games at critical times. They play to win."

By now she was feeling he'd explored every inch of *her* body. Then he made it even worse, turned her to him. "The season's tournaments are played on six consecutive Saturdays and proceeds benefit charities. A match lasts about two hours, divided into six 'chukkers,' seven minutes each. During half time, spectators indulge in the social tradition of divot stomping, or evening out the ground for the players."

His informative discourse clashed with the hunger in his eyes, the coveting in his touch. Her state was only ameliorated when he gave her space to breathe, to play with the horses.

Then he hugged her off the ground, pressing his lips to her neck. "How about we meet my biped friends now?"

She twisted around and looked up at him. The solitary dimple in his cheek had her heart revving like a car with its accelerator pedal floored.

"Only if you promise I can see your ponies again." She sounded as if she'd been running a mile.

"I promise you anything you want, whenever you want it." She wanted to cry out that she wanted only one thing— him. "Everyone must be at the VIP tent, and I'm certain they can't wait to meet you. They're a great group of people. My friends are, anyway. These tournaments are celebrity populated, and they can be a magnet for all kinds."

She nodded. She knew only too well what kind of people were attracted to fame and fortune.

He hugged her to his side again, leading her out to the tent.

She searched for something to say. Preferably something intelligent this time. She'd been a swooning idiot in his arms so far, and a giddy child with his horses. "So, what makes a good polo player?"

His eyes crinkled with pleasure at her attempt to engage him. "The ability to ride like a desert raider, to hit the ball like a medieval knight and to work the game like a champion chess player all while someone is trying to beat your knees off."

"Yikes!" He threw his head back at her alarm, letting out a guffaw of sheer amusement. She leaned deeper into his body, delighting in having his large, solid form pressing against her again. "Have you ever been injured?"

"Injuries are part of such an intense contact sport where the competition has always been dubbed 'bruising.'"

Her heart pounded. "But that's it, right? The worst of it is bruises?"

His eyes stilled on hers. With doubt? Disbelief?

Next second she saw nothing in them but indulgence. She must have imagined what she'd thought she'd seen. "The more experienced a player is, the fewer injuries he'll have. Sometimes everyone gets away with nothing, sometimes with a few bruises, but there's always the possibility of a more lasting souvenir. Injuries throughout polo history ranged from lacerations to fractures to brain injury to death. The worst injuries happen if a saddle breaks, or ponies collide at top speed, or someone gets thrown off."

"Oh, God." Her stomach squeezed into her throat as she imagined him sustaining an injury—or worse.

Her heart contracted violently with the need to beg him to never play again. But she couldn't voice her plea. She didn't feel like his wife for real yet. Not that she believed spouses could interfere in each other's passions anyway. And then she was certain he was careful, in control of his game.

But what if…?

She couldn't bear it. She had to articulate her dread, to make sense of it all. "But if there are such risks, why play?"

He shrugged. "Life is filled with risks. People who are totally safe are already dead."

"But you're super careful, right? No saddles of yours can break, and you always watch out for rabid antagonists?"

Again his eyes took on that enigmatic cast. "If you're asking if I'm a risk taker, I'm anything but. I'm a planner. A strategist. I set a goal, put everything in motion and invariably see my plans through to fruition." Suddenly an edge of harshness flashed in his gaze as he added, "But then, so do you."

Three

Sabrina stared at Adham, a frisson of unease slithering in her gut. The way he'd said that…

She had a feeling he meant something beyond polo playing.

Which only figured. He was a businessman, who played the real estate and horse-breeding worlds like a virtuoso.

But what did he mean, so did she? Did he mean that she'd let nothing stop her from acquiring the degrees she needed to take her place beside her father in their family business? Yes, that must be it. And the hardness she'd imagined accompanied his words must have been a trick of her still-agitated mind. Now settled on this front, her mind swung back to her main concern. "So you've never been injured?"

"I didn't say that. You remember that scar on my thigh?"

She'd never forget. She'd been horrified to see it. She'd

touched it in trepidation, the pain he must have felt on
sustaining it echoing inside her.

"That was my most severe injury. My pony fell on top
of my leg. My femur fractured and ripped through my
thigh."

She felt darkness encroaching on her as she imagined
his flesh being torn, his blood pouring out. Her fingers dug
into his arm, as if she could pull him away from hurt and
injury, give him her own vitality to heal any pain he'd ever
suffered.

He pressed her tighter against him, accepting her
concern, paying her back in sheer mind-numbing sensuality.
"But you made me glad I have this scar."

She felt blood rushing to her head, pooling in her loins
as she remembered how she'd traced it. He'd sprawled back,
letting her explore it, stroking her in turn. She couldn't help
it, had opened her mouth over it, sucked at its ridges as if
she could smooth them out.

And she'd gotten her first look at what he was like
aroused. She'd been too shy so far to do more than open
herself to him, take him inside her body, not daring to look
at the huge hardness that had invaded her, had her sobbing
in an excruciating mixture of pain and pleasure. Her head
had spun at the sight of him. Then she'd been compelled
to explore his daunting beauty. She'd quaked with his feral
rumbles at her ministrations. Then he'd taken her over,
given her the hard ride she'd been disintegrating for.

She was suffering from the same need now. But first
she had to suffer more deprivation, be his bride to the polo
community, make him proud. They'd arrived at the VIP
tent.

At their entry there was an uproar of welcomes and
congratulations, with more camera flashes from sanctioned
celebrity reporters, and many of the guests.

She'd thought she was ready but she found herself wishing that floors really opened and swallowed people. And she'd thought she'd known social attention as Thomas Grant's daughter. She'd known nothing. Now she was Sheikh Adham Aal Ferjani's bride, she had a feeling this was just the tip of the iceberg.

The next thirty minutes was a maelstrom of introductions to hordes of beautiful and high profile people. She tried her best to be as gracious as Adham in accepting the tribute everyone was paying her as the bride of their most valued guest and invaluable sponsor. She had a feeling she was doing a miserable job.

Most of the women around gobbled him up with their eyes. Many ignored her, making blatant offers of availability. It was only because Adham looked at them as he would bales of hay that Sabrina's chagrin was held at bay. And then she realized she'd better get used to it. After all, what woman could be around Adham and not lose all control?

It was only when Adham took her to meet his core group of friends and associates that her mood improved.

There was Sebastian and his fiancée, Julia Fitzgerald, with Sebastian's partner, Richard Wells, and his fiancée Catherine Lawson, Adham's horse trainer. They were accompanied by Nicolas Valera, a renowned Argentinean polo player and model who played on Adham's team, the Black Wolves.

After a stretch of small talk, Julia said, "Tell us about your vineyards and winery, Sabrina. I'm ashamed to say I didn't even know that Long Island had vineyards."

"Many people don't know. My father was among the first to realize that the microclimate here was similar to that found in Bordeaux. He released his first wines in 1975. During the last three decades, the Long Island wine industry has expanded—today there are dozens of vineyards planted on thousands of acres. The vines yield high quality grapes similar to those used by the French and Californian winemakers. Grant Vineyards produces world-class merlot, cabernet franc, cabernet sauvignon and chardonnay."

"Wow!" Catherine exclaimed. "You sure know your business. Did you start working with your father when you were young?"

A vise clamped Sabrina's heart as she remembered her frustration at her father's misguided overprotection. "Actually, he didn't want me to, but I insisted on learning everything about the vineyards and winery. I have master's degrees in business and administration, *and* brewing and winemaking. I was determined to help him run the business, and take over for him when he decided to retire. But he didn't get the chance to...."

Her words faltered as her eyes filled with tears. Julia and Catherine reached out to her, empathy etching their faces. Sabrina felt solace pouring from them but it was Adham's tightening hold that eased the anguish.

Responding to Adham's subtle prompt, Nicolas changed the topic, engaging Adham in a verbal game as exhilarating and bruising as any of their polo matches, which had the ladies dissolving in laughter. Seeing the intention behind Adham's maneuver, Sabrina felt herself stumbling deeper in love with him.

But though she enjoyed his friends' company, after an hour, the need to get away rose. She needed to be with him, alone, to settle her mind about their situation.

She was trying to figure out how to let him know that without sounding like a clingy, demanding wife, when he again seemed to sense her need. He suavely thanked his friends on her behalf for their fabulous welcome, and slipped her away.

He took her to the far end of the tent, and she blurted out the first thing that came to her, unable to say what she truly wanted to say. "So, you told me what makes a good polo player. What makes a great one?"

He looked at her for a second, then said, "Apart from having thoroughly trained ponies, and an ability to read them, it's focus."

"If that's what it takes, I bet you're the greatest."

He smiled down at her, clearly amused by her adulation, and—pleased, too? Even touched? "I don't know about *the* greatest. But I am one of the few who've been ranked at a ten-goal handicap."

"What does that mean?"

"Polo players are rated yearly by their peers on a scale of two to ten goals. The term 'goal' doesn't refer to how many goals the player will score in a match, but indicates the player's value to the team. Player handicaps range from novice—or negative two—to ten, which is perfect. A rating of above two goals indicates a professional player."

"And you're, of course, perfect. But I already knew that."

He put a finger under her chin and tilted her head up. His gaze blazed down on her for a long moment as he seemed to vibrate with something vast and uncontainable, sweeping her in a swath of lust that singed her down to her bones. Then he kissed her. She pressed against him, her head falling back, sending her heavy curls cascading over his arm as it clutched her waist.

When he relinquished her lips in agonizing slowness, he left her panting for more. The ferocious appreciation in his eyes made her feel intoxicated, brazen.

"So that's your handicap," she whispered, her voice husky with arousal. "What's your preferred...position?"

At her barely veiled innuendo, his pupils engulfed the gold of his eyes like a black hole would the sun. "Any and every position. As long as it fulfills the purpose of the... game." She shuddered with the need eating through her, to have him pleasure her in all those positions. She'd been going crazy reliving the memories of the times they'd been together. "But my preferred position is number three."

For a moment she thought he meant the third time he'd taken her, that next morning, when he'd had her riding him as he'd suckled her nipples and fondled her triggers. He went on, a devilish smile on his masterpiece lips. "It's similar to a quarterback in football, usually reserved for the highest handicapped and most experienced player. It entails attacking the opposing offense and turning the ball up field, requiring long-distance hitting accuracy and superb mallet and ball control."

"And we all know what kind of control you have." She actually meant his ability to stay away from her, but he clearly thought she meant his control during lovemaking. His gaze smoldered until she felt he was burning her up from the inside out. Unable to deal with the unease and embarrassment of explaining her true meaning, she reverted to her earlier worry. "So, after your injury, didn't you hesitate before getting back on a horse, embroiled in another bruising polo match?"

"Not for a second. There's nothing more exhilarating than going at a speed of thirty-five miles an hour on a horse you feel as one with. It's such a pleasure and privilege to form a bond and share the synergy of the play with a horse. And then there is the breeze rushing against your face as time stands still while you swing the mallet knowing the exact second you'll hit the ball, feeling the satisfaction of catapulting it exactly where you want it, setting up the play that will end up in a score."

She sighed. "You make me wish I played polo."

"If you so wish it, then so shall it be."

She shook her head wistfully. "I can't even ride a horse. My father never let me. At first he said I was too young, too slight. Then after my mom died, he became even more overprotective. I had to fight for each inch of independence, and riding horses was one of the things I decided to forgo in order to have other things. He even made me swear I'd never ride while I was away at college. I always felt so... deprived. I contented myself with taking every opportunity to visit with our vineyards' horses."

"I can tell you love horses. Aswad and Layl took to you immediately. I'm sure they'd love to have your company whenever possible."

She sighed again. "But now that you've outlined the real dangers of riding, I can better understand my father's worry."

Something strange came into Adham's eyes again. What was this? Was he angry? At whom? Her father, for limiting her? Or at himself for planting in her mind worry over his beloved sport?

Next second, the ominous cloud disappeared and the world was bright and shining once more. He bent to press the warmth of his magical lips on her pulse. It went haywire. "Don't worry, *ya galbi*. Not about me."

"I couldn't bear it if anything happened to you. Please, be careful."

He pressed her closer. "I always am. But I now have more reason than ever to be so."

She felt her consciousness receding. She was *swooning*, like a heroine from a Victorian novel. Before she'd met Adham, she'd suspected she might be really frigid, as many men had accused her. If those small-minded, vicious men could see her now.

A discreet cough came from behind Adham. Jameel.

Adham half turned to him. Their exchange in Arabic was rapid. She didn't get one word. Then he turned to her, his lids still heavy with desire but with an apology on his lips. "I'm sorry, *ya ameerati*. Urgent business has come up. Please stay, mingle some more. Jameel will drive you home when you're ready."

Disappointment spread through her but she smiled at him. "Oh, no. You attend your business and I'll go home now. I'll...I'll wait for you."

"As you wish." He swept her around and walked her out of the tent, nodding to everyone who seemed more curious than before, if possible. She'd sure given them a spectacle worthy of curiosity. The blushing bride who now had plenty to blush about.

Thirty minutes later, she was back in the Hamptons residence. She had no idea how long his business would take, but she rushed to get ready for his return.

An hour later, she'd bathed and dressed in what she hoped was an irresistible creation.

Two hours later, she called him. His phone went straight to voice mail. She didn't leave a message.

What was going on? Where was he? What could possibly keep him away after the enchanted day they'd shared?

She tried to tell herself that she'd married a businessman and a man of state, and that his time wasn't his to control.

It didn't work. While all that was true, a simple call would have allowed her to go to sleep knowing that their marriage was not a mirage that could appear and disappear at his whim. His reverting to the man who didn't bother to tell her where he was or what he was doing tossed her back into her former state of turmoil.

The last thing she knew before she succumbed to exhaustion was that Adham hadn't come home.

Her nightmares throughout the night said he never would.

Four

She woke up alone. As she had all her life.

The first thing that came to her was a conviction: that she'd wake up alone for the rest of it, too.

She'd also gone to bed alone. As she had since she'd married Adham.

She'd thought after that first day in the Hamptons that the inexplicable hands-off phase had passed.

It hadn't. The past week had followed the same pattern. He'd be all over her during the day, then would disappear at night, every time with one excuse or another.

She dragged herself out of bed. She felt as if the silky sheets and downy covers were spread with thorns.

The room was swathed in cool, dark silence. She knew out there another day blazed with heat and light, bustling with the sounds of Adham's housekeepers tirelessly keeping this place immaculate. Blackout blinds and soundproof doors and windows shielded her from it all. The room echoed with isolation. Inertia.

She felt as if she'd been on a roller coaster without a harness, one that catapulted her up, made her feel she was soaring, only to crash her to the ground, leaving her stunned and crushed, only to start all over again.

If it weren't for that one night, when he'd proved he was as over-endowed sexually as he was in every other way, she'd have thought his lack of interest in intimacy stemmed from some deficiency. But since his potency was indisputable, she'd feared he'd somehow lost interest in *her.* Yet over the past week, he'd showed her proof, physical and verbal, of his need to possess her. But he'd left her alone again, every night, and now she feared he might be accepting those women's offers.

She couldn't really believe that, but she'd run out of excuses for his behavior. Not wanting to rush her after her bereavement no longer made sense. Preoccupation didn't hold water, either.

What kind of game was he playing?

Her cell phone rang. She stared at it numbly before she realized it was the special tone she'd assigned to Adham.

She pounced on it, sending it flying off her nightstand.

By the time she answered, she was panting. Air crammed in her lungs when his dark voice poured into her ear.

"Sabah'al khair, ya galbi."

Just hearing him say good morning in his mother tongue would have been enough. Hearing him say anything. But when he called her *his heart,* in that intimate, possessive way...

Before she could cry out her confusion, he went on, "I hope you've had some...rest."

The way he paused before he said *rest.* He thought she

was so distraught, she couldn't rest even when she managed to fall asleep?

No. There was satisfaction, not concern, in his voice. As if he liked the reason she needed rest. Anyone hearing him would assume he'd been that reason, after he'd tested her stamina in an exhausting session of passion and possession.

More confused than ever, she breathed, "I slept. Sort of. I—I missed you."

"And I more than missed you, *ya kanzi*. But I have to be here the whole day. I have back-to-back practice sessions. If you're up to it, Jameel will drive you over. You can watch me practice, or you can mingle with the ladies. You don't have to stay long."

"I want to watch you. I'll stay as long as you do, and go home with you."

"Then—come."

The way he said that—her nipples stung, her core clenched.

And suddenly, she was angry. Enraged.

She felt like a mouse after a capricious feline had taken turns licking and petting it, then knocking it around. She felt battered and desperate.

And she'd had enough.

"On second thought, I won't."

There was a prolonged silence on his end after her sudden change of tone. She could feel tension mushrooming through the ether, sending its electrifying tentacles into her body.

But when he spoke again, his voice betrayed no surprise or irritation. "I thought so, *ya ameerati*." His voice dipped into its darkest reaches, like it had only once before when he'd been driving inside her, scalding her with growls of praise and pleasure. "Do get all the rest you can. You'll need it."

Then he ended the call.

She felt she'd explode with frustration. She quaked with the force of it, with the urge to storm to the farm, grab and shake him, scream at him, demanding an explanation for his tormenting behavior.

Then the seizure passed. The calm of resolution slowly descended.

She'd take his advice. She'd get all the rest she could. She *was* going to need it. For the showdown she'd have with him.

She'd have this out with him, even if it was the last straw that would break their marriage. Their non-marriage.

Anything was better than this limbo.

She didn't rest.

Adham must have known she wouldn't. Couldn't.

Not that he cared. He'd come home very late and disappeared somewhere. As usual.

At eight in the morning, she'd been sitting in the grand foyer for two hours, waiting for him to make an appearance. She would intercept him before he pulled another disappearing act.

Then she heard his steps. Her heart clanged in her chest as he approached. Then its beats scattered as they receded. He'd made a detour, entered his study.

She rose on quivering legs. Her breath jammed in her chest as she approached it. She felt as if she was nearing a landmine.

She grilled herself over her stupidity and weakness.

Just get it over with. Once and for all.

She ground her teeth as she turned the handle. Then with one last bolstering gulp of oxygen, she walked in.

She knew he felt her come in, but he didn't raise his eyes from the dossier he had open before him on his hand-carved, polished mahogany desk.

Well, she was damned if she'd let him ignore her again and continue playing this sadistic game with her.

This ended now.

"Adham."

It took him several nerve-fraying seconds to raise his eyes at her curtness, his face a study in blankness.

There he was again. The remote stranger he reverted to when they were alone. She suddenly realized they had only been alone for minutes since their wedding. Someone else had almost always been around.

So what was it with the Jekyll-and-Hyde reaction to privacy? Had it been triggered by their wedding ceremony? He sure hadn't suffered from this affliction before it.

"I'm busy, Sabrina." His voice was as expressionless as his face. "This can wait."

Her outrage crested. "No, this can't wait. You're not putting me off again."

He put down his pen, adjusting his pose to that of someone bent on suffering a pest's interruption with utmost forbearance. "When have I put you off in the first place?"

"Oh, boy." She huffed a chuckle fueled by all her fury and frustration. "You are a piece of work."

"I fail to grasp your meaning. It must be a breakdown in communication, originating from our different grasps on the nuances of language."

"Don't play the 'cultural difference' card. You were educated in the West, and you've lived here for big chunks of time since childhood. The only one who has a problem understanding anything is me. But now you're going to explain. Start by enlightening me about your view of marriage, since it seems it doesn't coincide with mine."

The stillness in his body seemed to deepen. "And what is your view of marriage?"

"That of almost everyone on the planet, in any culture. A man and a woman who actually live together."

"I live with you."

"You mean you grace whichever residence you happen to install me in with your fleeting presence."

He gave a slight shrug of one formidable shoulder. "To the world, I do live with you. I come home to you every night."

"What does the world matter here? *I* know you don't. And I demand to know what you're playing at."

His body seemed to harden to rock, his face becoming almost inanimate. "I don't appreciate your tone."

A frisson of danger arced through her but she ignored it. He could think again if he thought she would be daunted by his dismissal or displeasure. "Well, tough. This is the only tone you're getting since you refuse to acknowledge my questions. I won't be brushed aside again until you suddenly remember I'm supposed to be your wife. Only in public, of course."

His gaze became arctic. Then his baritone drenched her with its pitiless coldness. "If you're worried this indicates I'm thinking of reneging on our deal, put your mind to rest."

She dazedly stared at him. "Our deal?"

"Is still in effect. You have no reason to fear I won't keep my end of the bargain. My father's edict remains unchanged, and I still need an heir. You know that I already settled your father's debts, securing the Grant name. And I will, in due course, secure your future." His gaze panned downward, obscuring his expression, before he looked back up, impaling her on icicles. "But I now realize the source of your anxiety. It seems your father, either due to his rapid deterioration, or because he thought that you knew enough, didn't inform you of the specifics of the deal he negotiated on your behalf."

His father's edict. An heir. Her father's debts. The Grant name. Her future. It all made no sense.

She heard her own hoarse rasp. "What specifics?"

He rose from his seat. The room felt as if it were shrinking, as if its walls were closing in on her. "As per the contracts I signed, I'll run the winery and vineyards until you conceive, then I'll give you back their rights. When you carry my child to term, I'll give you the capital and the experts you need to run them. I'll keep the two hundred acres your father never got around to planting. But since *my* father's terms specified that my wife must be pregnant a year after the wedding, and since I've already consummated our relationship, I can afford to wait to see if you are already pregnant. In a couple of weeks, if you aren't, I'll take you to bed again." He moved from behind his desk, seeming to vacuum the last wisps of air from her lungs. "Now, if that is all, I have important things to attend to."

She stood rooted inside the doorway as he advanced on her. She felt as if she was staring at an incoming train.

He brushed against her as he left, leaving her buried under the debris of every belief she'd held dear. About him and her father. About herself.

It had all been a *deal*.

"I want to know everything, Mr. Saunders."

"I thought you were aware of the basics, Ms. Gra..." Ethan Saunders, her father's attorney, halted on the other end of the line. "Excuse me. Princess Aal Ferjani."

Princess Aal Ferjani. She'd never felt this name applied to her. She'd thought it was because of the state of her marriage. Now she knew it was because it didn't apply. And it never would.

"*Sabrina* will do, Mr. Saunders," she said tightly. "And I want to know more than the basics. I want every detail. There are no legal provisos that stop you from filling me in, are there?"

"When you put it that way, no," the man said cautiously. "I just got the impression that your father didn't want to bother you with particulars. I assumed that was why you weren't present during negotiations or contract signing."

Wading deeper into the nightmare, needing to hit rock bottom and be done with it, she prodded, "I do need to be bothered with the particulars, Mr. Saunders. My future depends on it."

There was a protracted silence on the other end. Then he exhaled. "Very well, Sabrina. While you were involved in your graduate studies, your father's health deteriorated, plunging him into a deep depression. He made catastrophic financial decisions—against my advisement, I must add. They ruined him. It was then that Sheikh Adham moved in. He'd been circling your father's land, and had tried to purchase it more than once. He knew he could finally acquire the land he'd long coveted with your father no longer in a position to refuse the sale. He had clear plans to close down the winery and plant other crops, while using the rest of the unplanted land as a horse farm.

"But your father was not without his own strategy. He investigated Sheikh Adham in turn, learning of his need to produce an heir within a certain time frame."

Her heart detonated at the confirmation of her worst fears. "And he offered me to him."

"You did fulfill all of Sheikh Adham's requirements,

and your father was still an astute enough businessman to know that. You are of impeccable lineage, physical qualities and…reputation."

Sabrina felt another red-hot lance skewering through her.

So that was why Adham had pretended to want her. He'd been out to assure her purity when he'd taken her for a test drive before deciding to marry her. A test drive he'd hoped would bear his required fruit, that he'd been loath to perform, judging by his aversion to repeating it, except when necessity dictated.

He'd been another of her father's arranged grooms all along.

But he'd gone far beyond any of them ever had. He'd seduced her to make sure she'd consent to the marriage. The mutually beneficial deal. For her father and for him.

And instead of being an heiress, she was actually indebted to him and would regain her legacy only when she provided him with a child. A child he wanted in order to fulfill his father's demands.

He'd never wanted to marry her, and felt nothing sincere for her. She was nothing to him.

No. She was worse than nothing. She was an annoyance, a burden. One he probably would get rid of the moment he could.

Mr. Saunders was going on about fine print. She'd heard all she'd wanted to hear, all she couldn't bear hearing. She didn't notice when the call ended. She might have hung up on the man.

It was worse than she'd feared. She'd been the only one under the misconception that this was a real marriage. Everyone else knew what it was—another of Adham's breeding ventures.

She'd been offered and accepted as a desirable mare.

But worse, Adham had believed all along that she was in on the deal.

Rage rose inside her again. She wiped fiercely at the tears.

It didn't matter what he'd believed. Only one thing mattered. He had to know she wanted no part of his plan, had agreed to none of it. She'd take nothing from him. She'd do anything, give up everything, to prove it.

And if fate should have it that she gave him his coveted heir, it would be on her terms, not his. She'd make sure her child didn't grow up a pawn in a royal chess game like her—or a heartless, cold-blooded manipulator like him.

Five

Adham swung the mallet with such force he catapulted the ball off the field, sending mud and grass exploding in the air.

How dare she.

Acting the neglected wife. Taking him to task about not fulfilling his marital duties. As if she'd ever wanted more from him than his wealth and status.

But he knew otherwise.

It had all been a tightly woven plot between her and her father. It was why he couldn't bring himself to touch her again, even though the lust he'd felt from the moment he'd laid eyes on her was intensifying, was corroding his restraint. And damn her, every time he saw her, the wholesomeness of her beauty, which needed no enhancements, overrode his senses. He didn't even have to see her. He only had to close his eyes to see her stunning honey-tan skin, to feel it beneath his hands, his lips, to imagine the waterfall of glossy mahogany hair sifting between his itching fingers, to remember her mesmerizing chocolate eyes gleaming with passion and her flushed lips trembling with pleasure. He woke up in a cold sweat every night, aching, remembering how her voluptuous body had exuded sensuality out of every pore, a sensuality he'd once thought unconscious. How she had wrapped around him, writhed beneath him. It was almost impossible not to storm her bedroom every night and lose himself inside her again.

Just before he'd met her, he'd been about to tell his father that he'd never take a wife by command like that. Then she'd walked into her father's hospital room and into his life, and suddenly the idea of marriage was no longer abhorrent to him, becoming all he could think of. The more he'd seen of her, the more he'd become convinced the fates had conspired to bring him his bride, the one woman he could contemplate having children with.

Then he'd taken her. And if he'd had any uncertainties or hesitations about her, her honest and limitless passion, the unprecedented intimacy he'd experienced with her, the unimaginable pleasure, what she'd so explicitly shown and told him had been reciprocated in full, had solidified his resolve, sealed his fate.

The next day, while Sabrina slept in his bed, he'd gone to Thomas Grant, to ask him for her hand in marriage. But the man had spoken first. And Adham had realized.

Grant had targeted him as the best groom for his daughter and the surest way out of his debts. And he'd set Sabrina on him. All her artlessness, her eagerness for his company, her hunger for him had been an undetectable act. And it had worked. Spectacularly.

But Grant had grown desperate in his illness. He'd thought he could no longer afford to let things develop at their own pace, to maintain the illusion of spontaneity. So he'd exposed their plan, laying it out in distasteful terms of give and take.

The wretched man must have been in worse shape than anyone had realized, or else he'd seriously underestimated his daughter's seductive powers. He'd asked for far less than what Adham had been resolved to offer when he'd thought he was pursuing a marriage built on mutual desire.

Adham had been so enraged, his first reaction was to snatch everything from father and daughter, leaving them with neither land nor deal. But pity for Grant's desperation had won. Not to mention lust for Sabrina. Even though he'd hated himself for it, he could think of nothing but repeating that night of delirium—and that even more addicting morning after.

Then Grant had died, and Sabrina had been broken up over his death. And although he'd discovered her deception and manipulation, he had recognized her anguish as real. He couldn't have assuaged his lust for her, no matter how it had gnawed at him. Not even when she'd let him know he could. Especially when she had. He'd been disgusted—with her, with himself—and conflicted about her bereavement, enraged at his decisions, his desires. He'd thought it safest to stay away from her until he regained his sanity and decided how to deal with it all.

But the more he let time pass, the more he realized it had been a grave mistake to marry her. He desired her for real, while she desired him only as a sponsor to maintain her family name and boost her lifestyle. He'd never paid for his pleasures and he'd be damned if he'd start with her. Not even if she was the one woman he craved. Especially since she was.

But he couldn't even let her go, washing his hands of this sordid mess. He'd trapped himself forever.

Men in his family married for life, if at all possible.

Even if separation occurred, it remained private, with a solid family front presented, for the sake of all but the couple. Considerations far bigger ruled. The royal family's traditions, Khumayrah's veneration of marriage, the Aal Ferjanis' allies and rivals. A man who wasn't bound to the wife he'd chosen and the family he'd made with her couldn't be trusted.

Which brought him to that heir his father had revealed was necessary to help stabilize the currently volatile internal affairs in their kingdom.

For that alone, he couldn't let anyone suspect that his marriage was a mere business deal. It would be the perfect way for his enemies to slander him.

They had done it to his father, spreading rumors that Adham and his younger sister weren't his, that his bargained wife had cheated. The repercussions had been far-reaching, and it had taken half of Adham's life to disprove the lies and wipe clean their stain.

This alone should have stopped him from following in his father's footsteps. His parents' marriage had developed into a love match, but this wasn't his own situation, and he should have factored in that if the conditions of his marriage were exposed, it would affect the royal house and the kingdom's stability.

So here he was. Trapped into playing the doting, replete groom. And to his fury, his desire for her, having his eyes and hands all over her in public, hadn't been an act. The act had been the distance he'd forced on them in private, the disinterest and detachment he'd pretended when she'd confronted him.

B'Ellahi, that confrontation. He'd used up his last drop of will holding himself back from pouncing on her, dragging her to the ground and giving her what she'd been indignantly pretending to demand. His mind roiled still with conjectures over why she had.

He again slammed into the same conclusion. That she'd become worried. She hadn't seen the contracts, and had probably been trying to find out if their terms were worth the act she'd been putting on. After all, she'd made a tremendous effort so far, and hadn't missed a beat since they'd met.

But now that he'd assured her of the extent of her gains from their arrangement, she'd resume playing her part with even more commitment. This past week, her performance had surpassed his wildest expectations. He'd felt her dissolving in his arms, inundating him with hunger, with urgent need for everything he'd do to her....

How is she faking all this?

A thought struck him with the force of a mallet to the head.

What if she wasn't? What if, apart from her mercenary motives for their marriage, she lusted after him for real?

If this was true, it changed everything....

"Adham. Earth to Adham."

He raised burning eyes to the booming voice. He found he'd come to a full stop in the middle of the field with Nicolas staring at him in surprise and concern. He and the other players were wiping off the clumps of mud and grass they were covered in.

"The game is right here, buddy." Jacob Anders, who played his team's number one position, smirked. "But it's clear you're not."

"*Sí,*" Nicolas agreed. "Why don't we resume our practice when you don't feel the urge to take whatever's eating you on the lawn and pelt us with it?"

Adham grimaced at his teammates. He wasn't up to their teasing. He swung Layl away and galloped off the field.

They were right. He had to take this out on the cause of his turmoil. On Sabrina.

If she wanted him, she was going to get him.

If mind-blowing pleasure was all they could have out of this "deal," then they'd have it. They'd never stop having it.

He snapped his cell phone out, pressing her speed-dial number.

Her phone rang until the line disconnected. He dialed again immediately. Four more disconnections later, and he was ready to commit violence.

She answered the fifth time. Or rather, the line opened. She said nothing.

But he could feel her on the other end. He could swear he felt her breath flaying his face in its heat and sweetness.

He growled with a spike of anger and arousal, "Why didn't you answer right away?"

Silence on her end. Then her unsteady inhalation skewered his brain, forked more steel into his erection. How he remembered those fractured breaths that had driven him mad as he'd plunged inside her....

"I answered now." Her voice was clipped, distant, yet it was still the mellow caress he'd replayed in his memory nonstop, crooning her need for him, crying out as her urgency rose, sharpening with the pain of his first invasion, then losing all inhibition as he occupied her, as her pleasure peaked. "Anything you want?"

I want everything, he wanted to roar.

But he *was* going to get everything. Starting tonight. No more holding back. For any reason. For better and probably for worse than he could imagine, she was his wife. And he planned to gorge himself on all the advantages of that fact. He'd suffer the disadvantages gladly when he had her total abandon to negate it all.

Her father's bargain might have blinded him for a while, but he could see clearly now. There was no way she'd faked her responses. Her soul might be that of a mercenary, but her body was that of a hedonist. But what mattered was that he was convinced now that she suffered his same predicament. She craved the pleasure only he could bring her.

"Sebastian is holding a gala party tonight in the VIP tent," he said, his voice thick with pent-up hunger. "It's to celebrate our marriage. It's imperative we show our hosts that we appreciate their thoughtfulness and efforts."

After another protracted silence, she asked expressionlessly, "How do you suggest we do that?"

"Sebastian requested that we attend the party in full royal garb. Have Hasnaa advise you on how to dress. I'll send you outfits and sets of jewelry to choose from. I want you to be my princess tonight."

Another silence stretched in the wake of his directives. Then a tremulous inhalation spilled from lips he knew to be petal soft and cherry flushed and dewy. He hardened beyond agony. "Anything else?"

"Yes," he hissed with the abrasion of arousal, the knowledge that it would be unendurable hours before he could assuage it. "Don't straighten or restrain your hair. Leave its curls wild."

She muttered what he assumed was an agreement, then hung up.

He stared at the phone as if he expected her to call back, to say more. He knew she wouldn't.

The dynamics between them had changed. Just hours ago there'd been no acknowledgement of how it was between them. Now it was out in the open, and she'd dropped the adoring-bride act in private.

But her indignation this morning had been about

more than her worry for her future—it had contained true frustration. No matter why they'd ended up married, she'd expected him, *wanted* him, to wallow in the carnal connection they shared.

That must be the reason behind her standoffishness just now. She must think he still intended to deprive her of what she needed.

She'd be relieved that he'd decided to disregard how she and her father had set him up and would drag her into the tumults of passion. At every opportunity.

And if they'd attained that much pleasure when he'd been so careful with her, when she'd been so untried, now that he could unleash his passion...well, he couldn't even imagine how it would be between them. In fact, exacting retribution on her through sensual torment would only take it all to explosive levels.

Starting tonight.

"I think you've chosen the outfit that best showcases your beauty, *ya Ameerah* Sabrina."

Sabrina caught the genial Khumayran woman's eyes in the mirror. Hasnaa was truly a beauty, as her name proclaimed her to be. She was Jameel's wife and now her head lady-in-waiting.

She attempted a smile, to thank her for her reassurance. She could see for herself it came out a grimace.

Thankfully, Hasnaa didn't notice her forced attempt as she fussed around her, adjusting her outfit. It was the first time that Sabrina had availed herself of Hasnaa's services. And only because Adham had demanded it.

He wanted her to be his princess tonight. To look the part, that was. She felt obligated to meet his demand. To honor the pact that her father had made. She wouldn't give Adham a chance to say a Grant didn't uphold her end of a deal. Even if she herself felt there was nothing more to uphold, felt mired in a nightmare she'd never wake up from. A prison her father and Adham had conspired to throw her into.

She'd felt desperation before, with each loss in her life. But each time, she'd forged on, because there had always been something to strive for, someone else who mattered. Someone who'd been there for her, too.

When her mother died when she was twelve, she turned her grief into more love for her father, even though it wasn't easy being his daughter, especially after his bereavement made him even more ultra-protective of her. Then years passed and she realized the hardest part of being his daughter had nothing to do with his actions and everything to do with who he was.

She realized the magnitude of the problem when she entered college. She lost count of the men who pursued her for her father's assets. To make things worse, her father, in his attempts to protect her from opportunists, started supplying one suitable bachelor after another. She considered those men not much better than the vultures, since they also wanted to acquire her because of her father's assets, if in a merger rather than a takeover.

So she told him that she wasn't interested in marriage, but in graduate studies and a career.

After years of pursuing her with insistence that marriage didn't preclude a career, Thomas gave up, leaving her to her plans. She now realized he only did because he'd plunged into depression and debt. Then, just after she obtained her degrees, he had his heart attack.

But all through her dread and desperation, she'd been strong for him. Then he'd died. But Adham had been there, and she wasn't alone. She had him. Or so she'd thought.

She *was* alone. She had no one. Certainly not Adham.

She gazed at her reflection in the gold-framed, full-length mirror. It felt like she was looking at herself inside a gilded cage. Completing the picture of captive luxury was one of the outfits he'd sent her. They'd all been beyond breathtaking. Not that she'd appreciated their exquisiteness. She hadn't chosen the outfit she was wearing now, discerning that it would best suit her as Hasnaa had implied. She'd dragged it haphazardly off the rack.

She looked at it now, seeing it for the first time. A ravishing red outfit that blended all the ornate lushness of Adham's native Khumayran culture with stunning modern twists.

The sarilike, handmade, intricately worked and embroidered creation and its *dupatta*—what Hasnaa was now busily securing over her "wild curls"—were a masterpiece. A dream of silk, georgette and organza worked in fine gold threads, semiprecious stones, sequins, cutwork, mirror, pearl and crystal work.

To top it all off was one of the sets of jewelry he'd sent her. Hasnaa had chosen for her what she deemed went best with her outfit, a set consisting of two necklaces—a choker and a longer piece that framed her cleavage to maximum effect—earrings that reached to her shoulders, and bangles that covered half of her right forearm. Each piece had carefully cut and polished multicolored gemstones embedded into delicate twenty-four karat gold.

And to think she'd thought he was being indulgent when she'd found the enormous collection lining that extensive dressing room. She'd felt uncomfortable, accepting all that, even from the husband who could afford endless luxuries. She hadn't wanted the shadow of materialistic considerations between them. But she'd reluctantly conceded it was part of looking the part in appearances vital to his status.

But now she knew the truth. This wasn't an indulgence.

This was part of her price.

And she was to wear it, like a tag. Another check on his status report.

A bubble of nausea pushed against her diaphragm. She thanked and dismissed Hasnaa, and collapsed on the nearest chair the moment the door closed. She lowered her forehead to her knees.

She fought back a wave of sickness that seemed to rise from her soul. Suspicion struck her, deepening her distress.

This could be what Adham had hoped for.

She could be pregnant. It would be so easy to find out.

She couldn't find out. Not yet. She didn't want to know one way or another when she asked him to end their pact.

But first, she had to play the delirious bride again.

This time she would indeed have to act.

But it would be the last time she did.

Six

"Oh, my, Sabrina. You look a-*mazing!*" Julia exclaimed, her chocolate-brown eyes wide with admiration.

"You look like a princess right out of a fairy tale!" Catherine exclaimed, awe sparkling in her eyes.

"Okay, the verdict is in!" Vanessa Hughes, Sebastian's sister, said as she finished her inspection of Sabrina, looking every bit the fashionista with her killer body wrapped in a gold second-skin, plunging-neck, floor-length gown. "This is the most incredible outfit I've ever seen in my life!"

Sabrina flashed a smile at the women she'd come to like immensely, a smile as genuine as her condition allowed. "You are just too kind, ladies. I feel like a prize idiot here, coming all dressed up as if for a masquerade, while you're all floating around looking like supermodels fresh off the runway."

"Are you kidding?" Vanessa scoffed. "I'd give anything for an outfit like that. But I doubt I'd carry it off half as well as you do. You have that exotic tinge to your looks, that…heat to your coloring—you just set the whole thing on fire."

"See?" Sabrina smiled again. "Too kind, I tell you. But let me say something else. All the ego boosting is very much appreciated."

"As if you need our ego boosting," Julia said, winking, "with a man like Sheikh Adham, who has the female population drooling, literally composing odes in homage to your charms."

"*And* accompanying every word of his sonnets with a white-hot look," Vanessa added. "The guy showers you with more ego boosts than most women could handle."

"Ah, those hot-blooded desert princes." Julia sighed. "If only our men were that demonstrative and vocal."

"But Sheikh Adham is far from being either," Catherine, who knew Adham well, interjected. "He's certainly the best employer I could ask for, but in my opinion, reserved and uncommunicative are his middle and last names."

"Then this is an even greater testament to your charms, Sabrina." Vanessa held her hands together beneath her chin in a swooning gesture. "And their effect on him. I've never seen a man so overtly in love before!"

Each word hit Sabrina like a whip. She wanted to beg them to stop, to tell them that he'd only been putting on a show. That it had fooled them, these intelligent, discerning women. Just as it had fooled her. Until he'd slammed her with the truth about his emotions—or rather, his lack of them.

The memory of his passionless gaze as he'd decimated her world lanced through her once more. She felt her smile splintering, its cracked edges driving into her flesh.

She had to excuse herself before the heat pricking behind her eyes dissolved into an unstoppable flood.

Yeah, that would ruin her image as "his princess."

Perhaps she shouldn't fight the tears after all.

No. She wasn't only his so-called princess, she was a Grant. Foremost, she was herself. She didn't break down. Not in public. And she *would* stop doing it in private. She was done letting him control her emotions, her life. She was taking control, as of now.

"And I thought *you* looked right out of *Arabian Nights,* Adham."

Sabrina swung around at hearing Sebastian's amused comment. He faded from her awareness the moment she registered him.

Adham was beside him. Adham as she'd never seen him. In the garb that revealed what he was underneath the projection of modernity, the polish of advancement.

A raider of the desert who seized whatever he wanted, made willing slaves of his conquests, whose ruthlessness was only matched by the heartlessness of his seduction. A being from another world where everything was laced with mystery and magic, edged by danger, drenched in excess, in passion.

In a pitch-black *abaya* that spread over his endless shoulders and billowed around him like a shroud of mystery, a high-collared top embroidered with *zari* gold thread, and pants fitted into leather boots, he looked like a supernatural being who descended to earth to rule, to conquer, an avenging angel from the realm of oriental fables.

She swallowed. What felt like ground glass slid down her throat. His beauty, his majesty…hurt. Her stupidity, in believing he'd fallen for her as totally as she had for him, hurt more.

"I did tell you to wait until you saw Sabrina, Seb," Adham murmured as his arm snaked around her waist, his hand dipping beneath her top's edge to singe her flesh with the heat of his electricity-wielding fingers. "But even I couldn't have imagined how spellbinding the trappings of my culture could be until her beauty and grace adorned them."

Her instinctive reaction was to swoon at the extravagance of his praise, to melt into the possession of his touch. It took all of three heartbeats before reality sank its fangs into her and had her lurching away as if from burning tentacles.

Adham's eyes didn't betray any change of expression, apart from the fluctuation in his pupils' size. Without missing a beat, he pulled her to him again, as if he hadn't realized she'd pulled away. Or maybe he wouldn't let her in front of those whose opinion mattered to him. "I hope I didn't leave you waiting long, *ya jameelati*. I should have escorted you here or at least been here to receive you, to be the first to look on your enchantment tonight. But there was an emergency with one of the ponies."

"What?" Catherine eyes widened, her smile fractured, alarm catching her off guard. "What happened? Which pony?"

"Rahawan," Adham answered, sparing her a glance before returning his sizzling focus to Sabrina. "He had severe colic. I called Dr. Lima and stayed until Rahawan started recovering."

"Oh, I'll go."

This made Adham relinquish his hold over Sabrina's eyes, stretch an arm in Catherine's way, cutting her movement short. "Of course you won't, Catherine."

"But I am still working for you until the end of the season," Catherine protested. "Even if I weren't, your horses will always be mine, too, Sheikh Adham. I have to make sure he's all right."

"He is. But thanks for your continued caring and

commitment. Richard is a lucky man to have such a loyal, compassionate woman. Now put your mind at ease and enjoy the party. I intend to." He turned to Sabrina, hugging her closer. "Now that I'm with you, it's a certainty that I will." He looked to the women. "May I borrow my bride, ladies? It's been a long day without her."

The women giggled and fanned themselves, winking at her as he swept her away.

Once they were out of earshot, she tried to step back from his embrace, struggling to make it look like she wasn't pushing him away. He only tightened his hold, bearing down on her with his heat and voracity. His fake voracity.

He bent to take her lips. She turned her head at the last second. His lips latched on her cheek instead. He burned it with his kiss. "I thought I could wait for later, but I can't."

She pushed harder at him, managing to put him at arm's length. "Listen, nobody can hear you now, so you can quit it."

"Quit what?"

"The act. Go light on the theatrics. Less is more and all that. Look around and learn from your friends how a man in love is supposed to behave. Sebastian and Richard are not oozing all over their women."

"Oozing?" His frown was spectacular.

"Yes, oozing. You better watch it. You're crossing from convincing underacting to ridiculous overacting."

His glower deepened. Then something flared over his features, so sexual and savage she felt her core melt in ferocious response.

"*Suheeh?*" he drawled, slow and devastating, a predator certain his mate was in the bag, certain he could prolong her torment and his gratification to his heart's content.

"Really? The only under and over I'm interested in are when they involve you and me during lovemaking. So let's drop all acting and get down to the truth." He tugged her hand and brought her slamming against his steel length. One hand splayed across her back, searing the flesh exposed by the dipping back of her top through the sheer *dupatta* covering it, the other hand sinking into her left buttock, yanking her to him, grinding her against his thigh. A moan of unwilling stimulation bubbled from her depths. Her head fell back, her mouth opened, her lips stung and swelled as if he'd already ravished them. He documented her reaction, merciless satisfaction blazing in his eyes. "*This* is the only truth. That you want me. As much as I want you."

She tried to break free, feeling as if she were drowning. As she was—in sensation, in yearning. Every syllable he uttered, every press of his fingers, every abrasion of his clothes on her exposed skin, every gust of his breath brushing any oversensitive part of her, was an aphrodisiac overdose. She felt she was being submerged in him, in her need for him.

It made her angrier.

He was only manipulating her, feeling nothing himself. And she'd be damned if she'd let him pull her strings like that.

She wrenched free, any attempt to make this look like anything but an all-out fight dissipating.

For she was fighting. For her sanity, her sense of self. What he was taking over, with such ease, just because he could, not because he wanted her.

"Oh, no, you don't," she spat. "You told me how it is this morning. You don't get to change the rules as you please. I don't know why you're doing this and I don't care. Just let go of me."

He hauled her back, crashed her into him once again, his arms a vise. "I'm never letting go of you."

She stilled in his arms, chagrin and embarrassment drenching her. "For God's sake, stop. Everyone's watching us."

"Let them watch."

"But this isn't what you want them to watch. At least, if you don't let me go, it won't be."

"Is this how you want to play it now, Sabrina? You want me to make you succumb, take it out of your hands? You want me to arouse you out of your mind and take you so you can have what you want and not be responsible? I'd be happy to oblige. I made you beg for me once. This time, I won't have to take it easy or go slow, to make allowances for your inexperience and discomfort. This time I can show you just how much you inflame me and hold nothing back, exploiting every inch of your made-for-pleasure body, giving you so much satisfaction you'll faint with it."

She felt the world distorting, as if she'd pass out from testosterone overexposure. She struggled to focus, choking, "Stop it, Adham. If you don't, I *will* make a scene. And not the kind of scene you want your friends and the paparazzi to witness."

The sensuality on his face deepened as he leaned back, his hands shaping her, exploring her curves, cascading fire through every cell. He stopped at her breasts, kneaded and weighed them, rubbed circles of insanity around her nipples through the layered material of her top. "Show me, Sabrina. Do your worst."

A second before she felt she'd faint for real, she smacked his hands off her and spun around.

She didn't get far. He caught her at the tent's entrance, turned her and snatched her off her feet. His hands clamped her back, her buttocks, opening her thighs in her flaring *lehenga* over his hips. One hand held her in place as the other snatched her *dupatta* out of the way to sink into her curls, holding her face upturned to his, her neck arched back.

He swooped down to latch his lips on her pulse, growling against its frantic beating, his voice feral. "I shouldn't want you, I should keep this cold and all business. But you inflamed me, drove me mad, from that first moment I laid eyes on you. *W'hada gabl mat'sallemeeli nafssek*— And this was before you surrendered yourself to me. *Men hada'l yaum w'ana fen'nar*—I've been in hell since that day, craving you and knowing I shouldn't. But I don't care anymore why we married. You're caught in the same trap, you crave me just as much. And desire this fierce can't be denied."

Everything stilled inside her, desperation and anguish extinguished like a candle in a hurricane.

He wanted her, too? It hadn't been an act to make her succumb to his plans? He'd tried to keep it business, but his desire for her was overriding his intentions and his control?

If this was true, then his desire was fiercer than anything she'd wished for. This meant there was hope for their marriage. Far more hope than she'd dared imagine.

"Adham…I don't…"

He misinterpreted what she'd started saying and overrode her. "You do. I can feel your desire, can sense it. Your body is humming with need for me against your will—seeking, offering, begging for mine. I can feel your heart racing mine, your blood thundering below my fingertips."

She would have been mortified that he could read her reactions so explicitly if her reserves of mortification hadn't been depleted thinking of the scandal they were creating.

And if she didn't want him to know how he made her feel. But now she did.

Then everything ceased. Adham wrenched his lips from her neck, raising his head only to swoop down again to claim her mouth.

She cried out at the feel of his heat and moistness, of his tongue driving inside her, rubbing against hers. His growls poured into her, welling in surges of pleasure throughout her body.

He finished her, drained her, layering arousal in bolts to her breasts, her gut, her core. Heat built until she writhed with it, opening herself up, inviting his domination.

He raised her, brought his erection grinding into her long-molten core. Sensation sharpened, cleaving a cry from her depths.

And despite the pounding in her head, the shearing from her lungs and his, she felt it.

The commotion of curiosity and amusement and disbelief. The shuffling and whirs and flashes of people rushing to document their mindless disregard of everything but their conflagration.

He raised his head, his eyes almost black and unseeing as they panned the crowd surrounding them. Then, with a growl, he bent, hauling her high in his arms.

"I'm taking you home, Sabrina." His words held the conviction and power of a pledge. "And I'm making you mine, in every way. Tonight and forever."

Seven

Sabrina clung to Adham's neck as he strode out of the tent, the whole world receding from her awareness, shrinking to the confines of his body.

She registered nothing but its powerful perfection moving against hers with his every stride, his hands rhythmically squeezing her flesh. She saw his face clenched on such drive and felt weakness invading her every muscle, in preparation to have all this ferocity unleashed on her.

She didn't know how long he'd walked or what distance he'd covered. Time was suspended, space was compacted, until she found herself inside a limo with dark windows and a soundproof, mirrored partition. Adham laid her down and came to rest on top of her. Her legs opened in eagerness to accommodate his bulk. He lay over her, giving her what she needed of his weight, supporting enough of it so as not to oppress her. He devoured her lips, his hands everywhere, creating erogenous zones all over her, his hips driving between her splayed thighs in a simulation of the possession she was quaking for.

She heard her voice, thick and choppy, pleading for him. He rose off her, dragging her up. She swayed with the car's smooth movement as it shot across the streets, with the imbalance he'd struck inside her, feeling as if the burn in her blood would consume her if she didn't get under his skin.

"Sabrina, *galbi,* I need to feel your desire, taste your pleasure."

Before she could understand what he meant or tell him he could do whatever he liked with her, he hauled her on his lap, her back to his front, her thighs splitting wide over one of his. He stretched back so her upper body fell to the side and into the curve of his left arm. His hands came around her, undoing her front fastening.

She moaned his name as her breasts spilled out of the imprisonment of the corsetlike top and into his hands. He bent, leaning around her, engulfing one nipple and then the other in the moist heat of his mouth. Her cries rose, lengthened, her writhing getting more frantic. He didn't give her a chance to process the feelings as his right hand dragged her *lehenga* up, yanking her panties down. Then his palm was cupping her mound, squeezing it, condensing the throbbing there into a pinpoint of insanity.

He let go before it all spilled over. In her haze, she realized. He knew that she needed intimacy, not release. And he was giving it to her. The closeness of owning her flesh as intimately as she did.

Two strong, certain fingers parted her feminine lips, delving into the desire flowing there for him. He lifted his head from her breasts to swallow her sobs of overstimulation. He glided in her moistness, from her bud to her opening, until she bucked, begged. Only then he slid inside her, adding a third finger, replacing his fingers at her bud with his thumb. Her keen poured into his mouth. He withdrew his fingers, corkscrewing the tension inside her to a weeping pitch.

"Take your pleasure, *ya jameelati. Areeni jamalek wenti b'tjeeli*…show me your beauty as you come for me."

She'd been trying to hold back, needing to come with him deep inside her. But he was, if in another way. And he wanted her to give him this surrender. She'd give him anything he wanted.

He thrust his fingers back in, along with his tongue deep inside her mouth. And the tension snapped, over and over, uncoiling then folding back on itself, only to lash out again as her orgasm quaked through her like the ebb and flow of a stormy sea.

His gaze bathed her in his possessiveness, in his profoundly male satisfaction at the sight of her racked with pleasure, begging to be at his total mercy, to be taken, pleasured any way he could think of.

He held his fingers deep inside her, letting her quiver to the last tremor of satisfaction around them, before he slowly removed them, brought them up to his lips, licked them, growling his enjoyment at tasting her.

He gathered her, folded her, held her tight in his arms. His eyes were incandescent in the dimness, flaring gold with each passing streetlight filtering through the darkened windows.

"Do you know what it is, seeing and feeling you taking your fill of the pleasure I bring you, *ya hayati?* Tasting it? It's the most beautiful thing in my world."

Her heart swelled so hard, so fast, she whimpered with it. She couldn't utter a word. She'd been at her lowest point, and had given up on him. She'd been trying to contemplate a life of emotional exile, loving him and knowing he'd never love her back.

Now he'd given her this. And it wasn't only sex, or pleasure. He was opening himself up to her, letting her see inside him. This was for her, not for the eyes and ears of the world. And it was sincere. She just knew it was.

Tenderness swamped her, welled from her in feverish kisses and caresses all over his face. He rumbled a string of native praises to her as he kissed and caressed her in return.

The car stopped. In seconds he'd helped fasten her top and had her out and in his arms.

He took her where she'd thought she'd never be—the room he'd chosen as his in this sprawling house.

It was not as enormous or extravagantly decorated as the one he'd given her, but because it was permeated by his scent and presence, it was in a class of its own. Any place where he chose to live his most private moments was the best place she'd ever been.

He laid her down at the foot of his bed and proceeded to strip from her the outfit and jewelry in excruciating slowness, pausing at every inch of flesh he exposed to fondle and worship and praise. By the time he had her naked, her teeth were clattering, her heart in hyperdrive, desperate for an end to the sensual torment.

He then stood up to admire her sight, arranged among black silk pillows and sheets. Then, as if he hadn't tormented her enough, he started his own striptease.

He first shrugged off the silk *abaya*. It slid from his daunting shoulders and slithered to the floor with a resigned sigh. His gold-embroidered top, wrapped cummerbund and boots followed. He left the low-riding loose pants on.

Before she could cry out her indignation, he kneeled before her. His hands traveled up legs that went boneless at his first touch, his to do with as he chose. It pleased him to spread them, to drag her by them, to bring them over his shoulders.

"*Daheenah adoogek men jedd*—now I taste you for real. I've been addicted to your taste from that first time. I've been starving for more of you." He opened her lips, gave her core one long lick, groaning in response to her cry. "Say you'll always let me taste you, always want me to."

She wanted to tell him but her tongue twisted in her mouth, paralyzed with anticipation. She only keened, her hair falling all over her face with the vigorousness of her nod. Satisfied with her condition, with her response, he clamped her feminine lips in a devouring kiss. He licked and suckled at her swollen flesh, thrust inside her with his tongue, drank deep of her pleasure. He took her to the edge again and again, only to pull her back, set her to a simmer, then build her desperation once more until she felt the ache inside her reaching critical mass. She begged him with her hands in his hair, with her body writhing in mounting agony as she tried to pull him up, to have him penetrate her, ride her, put her out of her misery.

He resisted her, lashed her trigger and sent her convulsing and shrieking into another racking orgasm.

He drank her dry, kept licking her, soothing, defusing the surplus of sensations, until her oversensitized flesh subsided. And she wanted him more than ever.

She struggled to her elbows, looked down on the magnificent sight he made, kneeling between her legs, his lion's head rubbing her thighs, his lips worshipping them. Her heart spilled a fresh batch of palpitations.

"Adham, stop tormenting me. Don't make me wait anymore."

He raised eyes blazing with satisfaction at her renewed agitation, at his own pent-up arousal. He rose, pushing her back across the bed with his shoulders against her legs until he had her in the middle. Then he rose above her on all fours.

"Release me."

At his command, though her hands felt like they were no longer under her control, she fumbled with his pants. She somehow undid the zipper and pushed them halfway down his muscled thighs, exposing their bronzed splendor. He took pity on her, pushed them all the way down, kicked them off. He held her hands and guided them into removing his tight boxers. And she gasped.

His erection sprang hard and long and heavy, slamming against his belly. Just the sight exacerbated her swooning state.

He noted her reaction with those all-seeing eyes as he again had his hands and lips all over her triggers.

"I pleasured you in the car, and again now," he groaned against her nipples, her pulses, her lips, "not only because I crave your pleasure as much and more than I do mine, but because I need to know that your desire is all mine, all about needing *my* possession. Tell me."

"I want you," she moaned. "I've been going out of my mind with wanting you. I want you all the time, doing everything to me. Please, Adham, *habibi,* take me."

He rose to loom over her, a god of virility and beauty, almost menacing in the fierceness of his focus, the ferocity of his lust. He pushed her with gentle power until she lay flat beneath the cage of his muscle and maleness. He drove one knee between hers, winding the throbbing between her thighs to a tighter rhythm.

"How do you want me to take you? The first time?"

She didn't hesitate. She knew just how. "Fill my arms, let me wrap myself around you as you fill me."

"And the second?"

"Cover me, lie on top of me, over my back, let me feel all of you pressing me into the bed as you possess me."

He bent to pull hard on one nipple, grazing the other with his blunt fingernail. "And the third and fourth and fifth time?"

Her delirium intensified with each suckle and flick. "Anything—anything at all. Just do it all."

He rose over her again. "Then give it to me. Everything you have, everything you are. I will have it all."

"Yes. *Yes.*" She stabbed her fingers into the mane raining around his face, brought him down to her for a compulsive kiss. She tore her lips away, needing to know, panting. "And you'll give it all to me, too?"

"All that I have. All that I am. It's all yours, *ya malekati,* my owner. Take it. Take me. All of me." He reared back between her splayed thighs, his erection throbbing over her mound and reaching up to her belly button, heavy and engorged. He glided its underside between her lips, nudging her trigger over and over. She arched up, opening herself, hurrying him. He only rose on one knee, taking her one desire out of reach. "Show me what you want."

Unable to heed any inhibition, unable to wait to take advantage of the freedom he was offering her, she reached a trembling hand to his erection. She couldn't close around his girth. Intimidation shuddered through her even as another surge of readiness flooded her core. She stroked the velvet-over-steel shaft in wonder, rubbing the smooth head with the fluid silk seeping from its slit, her tongue tingling with the need to taste it. Promising herself she'd beg for the privilege later, she tugged at his shaft.

He growled, deep and dark, thrust his hips at her, watching her with an intensity she felt left its marks all over her skin. He let her drag him closer to her sex, still keeping his eyes on hers. But with the first touch of their intimate flesh, he threw his head back in an agonized growl, a duet with her keen. Then, as if they'd agreed, they both lowered their gazes to the sight of the intimacy she was performing.

She slid his head along her inner lips, bathing it in her moistness. Unbearably aroused, rumbles reverberated from deep within him on every glide, a sharper cry from her each time it nudged her slit. She kept going on and on, until he was shaking as hard as she was, his breathing as labored as hers. She knew she'd tumble into oblivion any second now, had to do it with him buried deep inside her.

She could no longer hold herself up, could no longer bring her hand to close around him. She slumped back to the bed, legs splaying. His erection was throbbing at her opening where she'd left it before she lost all coordination.

"Please," she sobbed.

"Please what?" It came out the growl of a great feline at the end of his tether. "Tell me. Let me hear you say the words."

"Fill me."

Rumbling something driven, he did, on one lunge.

She wailed as her flesh yielded to his invasion, as he stretched her beyond capacity. He forged on through her molten core until she felt him reach her womb.

The coil of sensations that had compacted inside her unraveled so violently, it lashed out through her system, shredding her with a release so profound, she convulsed as if with a seizure, as if with a chain reaction of explosions. Gusts of sharpness shrieked from her depths on each detonation.

"*Sabrina.*" She felt him expand to a size she couldn't accommodate as he drove deeper inside her body, lodged into her recesses. She jerked like a marionette with her strings being pulled haphazardly, her inner walls squeezing him until he hissed. "*Aih, ya habibati, eeji alai*…come all over me."

And all that was left inside her was one need. She sobbed it. "Come with me…come inside me…fill me.…"

As if he'd been waiting for her plea, her command, his seed splashed against her spasming walls. She shook and wept as another breaker of pleasure crashed down on her with each jet hitting her most intimate flesh, as his erection shuddered inside her, as his roars of release harmonized with her cries.

Time expanded. The perfection of it. The totality. The oneness.

Pleasure raged, each slam of his inside her unhinging the foundations of her very soul until she felt he'd uprooted it, until she felt it roamed free, releasing her body of its limitations.

Then she slammed back to the bed beneath him. Aftershocks surged in a current inside her. He'd drained her of every spark her nervous system was capable of. She felt irrevocably sated.

But she knew better. He'd whisper in her ear, touch her with his gaze, beckon with his fingers and she'd go up in flames again.

He came down on top of her, letting her feel his beloved weight for a minute, before he twisted to his back, taking her with him, draping her over him like a blanket.

He caressed her back and hair, still hard inside her. "It was merciful I lived these past weeks with only the memory of our first night together. If I'd known that our belated wedding night would be a thousand times better, I would have probably lost my mind."

She smiled into his chest, gratification sweeping through her that his feelings so exactly echoed hers. "Or you might not have tormented us so long. If I'd known, I might have provoked you into losing your control much sooner."

"So you're admitting you provoked me on purpose."

She giggled. "If only I could claim that I did."

His chuckles revved below her ears as his arms tightened around her. Feeling him stir inside her, feeling her own body blossom once more for him, she sighed in contentment, "You know, you're overwhelming anyway, but in passion, you're annihilating."

"Look who's talking." In one swift move, he rolled her over, bringing her facedown as he mounted her from behind.

She arched into him, ready again, impatient. "That's not a complaint. I can't wait to be devastated, over and over."

And throughout the night and early morning hours, she was.

Eight

Sabrina opened her eyes in her husband's bed.

Adham. Her husband. For real. At last.

For several golden moments, tranquil and content, she lay there, savoring the knowledge, the soreness of satiation.

But it had been so much more than sex they'd shared. Adham had deep feelings for her. They might not be as complete as hers were for him, but they were pure and powerful. And they were growing. She'd make sure they never stopped.

They might have started out the wrong way, for the wrong reasons, but it didn't matter. They were right for each other. Perfect. And her love for him had broken through his preconceptions, had made him release all the emotion he'd struggled to suppress, thinking he shouldn't feel anything for her, his convenient bride.

She now relived the moments when she'd opened her

eyes hours ago, arched into his embrace, offered herself to him. Even three-quarters asleep, she'd been disappointed to feel clothes instead of his nakedness pressing down on her. He'd said he needed to see Sebastian, telling her to sleep off the exhaustion he'd caused her. She *had* blinked out the moment he'd closed the door.

But her battery was charged now. Overcharged. And there was no way she could bear waiting for him to come home.

She'd go bring him back to bed herself.

Thirty minutes later, she parked her car in the driveway of the Tudor-style Hughes Mansion.

She was let into a cathedral-ceiling hallway, and the butler informed her that Adham and Sebastian were in the living room. She told him to point her their way—she'd announce herself. She wanted to see Adham's reaction to her presence—the first surge of pleasure that would light his eyes—firsthand.

She approached the door, debating whether to knock or just enter. The decision was made for her when she found the door ajar. She was about to make her presence known when something Sebastian was saying froze her in her tracks.

"I have to give it to you, Adham, that was one hell of a show you put on yesterday. I can't buy publicity like that. The Bridgehampton Polo Club will not only be associated with priceless horses and A-list celebrities but with the drama of the uncontrollable passions of desert princes and their gorgeous, rebellious American wives. I project attendance will triple next year."

"Not that I'm unhappy the club might benefit from my actions," Adham said, "but that wasn't among the things on my mind yesterday."

"*If* you had anything on it at all, that is," Sebastian

teased, "apart from chasing down and capturing your defiant bride. Defiant at first, anyway. Then you caught her, kissed her and...whoosh. She went up in flames in your arms. I bet all those enemies who're watching you for proof that your marriage isn't real no longer have a leg to stand on."

There was a long moment of silence.

"How do you know about that?" Adham asked slowly.

"A sleazebag posing as a reporter came a few days ago to interview me, but mainly asked about you and your recent marriage. He tried to get me to give him anything that would paint your marriage as a business deal. He went on to say it's a common belief in your land that a bargained wife is an unsatisfied one who cheats to get back at the man who acquired her."

"It's not a belief, just a rationalization to explain cheating wives and an effective weapon to smear men in high places, since the greatest dishonor in my culture is to have a cheating wife. It is a death sentence to a man's reputation if her infidelity results in children whom she passes off as his. This happened with my own parents. My father's political enemies used the marital difficulties my parents had after my older brother was born to cast doubt on my younger sister Layla's and my paternity."

Sebastian whistled. "Well, I investigated that jerk, and found that he was sent by one Nedal Aal Ajam, renowned political enemy of the Aal Ferjanis, denouncer of the King and number one beneficiary if ever the royal family of Khumayrah was overthrown."

"*Aih, hadda suheeh.* That's true. He would have latched onto any public discord between Sabrina and me to plant doubt about the authenticity of our marriage. Just like in my mother's case, who was herself only half Khumayran, they would have played on the fact that Sabrina is a foreigner.

In my mother's case, they said that she sought revenge as well as emotional and sexual freedom outside the restrictions of the loveless union. The lie that Layla and I were not the King's offspring chased us through half of our lives, until my father was forced to refute the allegations with medical evidence. Of course, his wrath was severe. Anyone who'd help spread the rumors paid dearly for their transgressions."

"I can imagine. To force a king, from a culture as big on macho pride as yours, to defend his wife's honor and his children's legitimacy—that's huge. But the example he'd made of those who'd defamed you hasn't deterred others from trying the same trick?"

"The potential gains are great enough to risk consequences. And they don't need to go as far as the others went. If they can prove any of the royal wives unsatisfied, they won't need to cast doubts over the legitimacy of the union's offspring. It's enough to start a campaign of ridicule that a man who can't govern and fulfill his own wife isn't fit to govern a nation or fulfill its needs. Our political situation is complex enough at the moment that a battle on this front might tip the balance in our enemies' favor."

"But you have nothing to worry about," Sebastian assured. "Whatever those backstabbers are trying to do, after last night, there's no way anyone could say that Sabrina is unsatisfied. The woman is clearly crazy in love with you. The whole world now has photographic evidence of that fact."

There was another moment of silence. Then Adham exhaled heavily. "I guess they do."

Sabrina turned around, stumbled away.

She somehow found herself back in her car, agony clamping each muscle, her heart flapping in her chest like a wounded bird. She dropped her head to the steering wheel.

It was far uglier than the worst thing she'd believed before.

She'd believed he'd seduced her for the land and a necessary heir. She'd thought he'd only put on a show in public, as Sebastian had so astutely realized, as a preventive measure against wagging tongues and social nuisance.

Then last night she'd come to believe he'd always been attracted to her but her father's deal had hardened his heart, making him treat their marriage as nothing but a business deal. She'd believed he'd lost control when she'd pulled away in public, acting spontaneously for the first time, baring his real desires, which he'd hidden from even himself.

She'd been a fool. He hadn't lost control. His actions had been *damage* control. Which he had to perform indefinitely. As long as his enemies watched him.

Her public rejection had been what he'd been guarding against all along, as it would have destroyed his projection of a blissful marriage that was vital to his image, to the stability of his ruling house.

So he'd seduced her again, to make her fall in with his plans. *Again.*

And if she hadn't been so desperate to be with him again, she would have remained in his bed, unaware of the truth. She would have continued putting on the show he needed, fooling his enemies with the sincerity of her ardor.

And being made a fool of for the rest of her life.

Adham had left Sebastian an hour ago.

He'd been driving aimlessly ever since. For the first time in his life, he felt at a loss.

He needed some time to come to terms with what had happened last night. It had been more than explosive sex. It had been nothing like the first time he'd taken her.

This time, when he'd made her his, she'd made him hers.

His father had said this would be his fate, just as it had been his own—to find one irreplaceable woman where he least expected, to want her with everything in him, to love her till the end of his days.

But did she love him?

He'd felt his heart clench as if on a burning coal when Sebastian announced that she did, as a forgone conclusion.

For he truly didn't know.

He had no doubt she wanted him with every fiber of her voluptuous body. But what about her heart?

There were too many considerations that made him fear her heart wasn't involved. Or worse, couldn't and wouldn't be.

She had been at her lowest moments when she'd fallen into his arms. She had needed his support, in more ways than one. Now, she might still be reeling from her father's loss, needing to cling to him to fill the void of security. What if her feelings for him were gratitude and need mixed with lust? The gratitude he could do without, the need he accepted as her right as his wife, the lust he craved. But none of this constituted love. And he couldn't live knowing she didn't love him as wholeheartedly as he loved her.

There was one way to discover the truth. A test.

He dreaded the result. He didn't know if he could live with it if he learned that she didn't and could never love him. But he had to do it.

He couldn't live not knowing for certain, either.

Hours later, he returned home, and felt it immediately.

A psychic vacuum. An absence.

He tore through the house looking for her. But even as he dashed from one place to another, calling out her name, he knew.

She was gone.

On his third time storming to his bedroom, which had been theirs for only one night, he saw something he hadn't noticed before on his bedside table.

A note.

He approached it as if it were a live grenade, unfolding it with the care of someone defusing a bomb.

But there was no defusing the destruction in the note.

Only four words. *I want a divorce.*

Nine

After the disbelief and devastation, Adham called Sabrina's cell phone for thirty minutes straight.

Each time the phone rang until it disconnected.

He careened through the house, raising hell, interrogating everyone within sight, not caring that he was revealing to his subordinates that he had no idea where his wife was.

He was at his wit's end when the bodyguards he'd asked to keep an eye on her, and whom he'd forgotten about in his madness, called. They'd said she'd gone back home. Her family home.

The two hours it took him to get to Grant Vineyards and Winery taught him the meaning of agony.

By the time he spotted her, a bright white figure in the distance among the verdant vines, he felt he'd aged two decades.

He strode after her receding figure through the uniform rows of vines that seemed to stretch into infinity, adding to his impression that he'd never reach her. So much crowded inside him—anger, dread, heartache—he felt he'd explode with it all.

It felt like the distance between them widened instead of narrowed with each step. It was too much.

He bellowed with it. *"Sabrina!"*

His shout seemed to freeze her and everything else, as if all existence had been paused. He felt as if his feet barely touched ground as he closed the distance separating them.

He came to an abrupt halt a foot away, vibrating with emotion. Her scent flayed him. He could discern every hair in the gleaming mahogany waves that cascaded down her back, feel each tremor her heart sent through her flesh. And he knew.

He was damned to love her, even without hope of reciprocation. What she evoked in him was the only thing he would ever want or need. And she didn't feel the same.

He could do nothing but accept it, and take whatever he could from her.

Feeling defeated for the first time in his life, he declared his surrender.

"So now you realize your power over me," he rasped. "You're raising the stakes. Go ahead, Sabrina. If you want to make a new deal with new terms, then make it."

She turned to him then, her face and voice inanimate. "I want one thing. To never see you again."

He advanced on her. She tried to retreat. He wouldn't let her, grabbing her arm, shoving the dossier he'd brought at her.

Her fingers closed around it instinctively, her eyes blank, making him feel as if she didn't even see him.

But he had to try to make her see, try to make her

respond to him. "I thought this would show me if you felt anything real for me, but it's no longer a test. I can no longer afford it. You can consider all of this an incentive. And you can ask for anything at all in addition. Just stay with me, give us a chance. I know we started badly, but we can make this work. I know we can."

She wrenched away as if his hand burned her. "This act will never work."

So she'd been acting all the time?

The thought swamped him with a despondence so profound, it made him realize one thing. The most important thing.

Even if he found the right price to make her stay, it would kill him knowing she felt nothing for him.

He had to let her go, no matter the damages to himself, his heart, or his kingdom. No matter if she were already pregnant with his child. He'd rather be exiled from his homeland than live knowing he had her in every way but was forever exiled from her heart.

Unable to face her or bear the agony, he turned away.

"What *is* this?"

Her exclamation hit him between the shoulder blades, making him turn against his will, against his better judgment.

He found her flipping through the dossier, her frown deepening. The shuffling sounds chafed his nerves, snapping them one by one. He waited with thorns in his heart for delight to invade her eyes, once she realized all she wanted was hers for the taking, with nothing required on her part.

But it wasn't delight that filled her eyes. It was rage.

His confusion turned to stupefaction as she threw the dossier to the ground and proceeded to shred the contracts and deeds for everything he'd promised her once she fulfilled her part of the deal.

"See this, Adham?" she shouted. "This is what I think of the deal you and my father made! You can take your land and assets and terms and shove them! You think I want to inherit my father's land and business? I want them *gone*. I want them to have never existed. They've been the cause of all the alienation I've felt my whole life. Everyone who's ever come within five feet of me had their eyes on them, including you. So if *you* no longer want the land, you can give it to charity or let the wild reclaim it for all I care.

"*I* never wanted any of this. The only thing I ever wanted from my father was love, the only thing I wanted to do was help him. I chose my fields of study so I'd be the right hand he'd always implied a *son* would have been. I'm good for more than being married off and making babies like he—and you—thought. I certainly don't need either of you to 'provide' for me. I am a professional any winemaking business in the world would hire in a flash at the salary I demand."

Adham could only gape at her as she continued her furious tirade.

"As for you, the only thing I ever wanted from you was caring and respect. But those are alien concepts to you and the only thing I now *need* from you is an uncontested divorce!"

With each word from her trembling lips, realization and heart-bursting delight dawned on Adham.

She'd never wanted the things he'd thought she'd married him for. She hadn't been in on her father's deal, and had always thought their marriage was real.

She'd *wanted* to marry him. Because she wanted him. Because she loved him!

So why did she want to leave him now?

"*Arjooki, ya habibati,* I don't understand. I love you—"

"Stop it!" she screamed. "Stop acting. I heard you, Adham. Today, with Sebastian. Your only concern is to allay doubts about our marriage so your enemies won't undermine your family's power. I understand it's a noble cause but count me out. Go acquire some other woman to do this job. I want—I *deserve* someone who doesn't have to pretend to want me."

And everything fell into place.

He surged toward her. "*Habibati,* I beg you, listen to me—"

She beat his hands away. "Oh, I did. I've done nothing but listen to you and your lies since the day I met you. But I've listened to the truth today, and nothing you say can change that."

He still vibrated with the elation of discovering her reciprocated emotions. But now, as her anguish flayed him, anxiety rose to supplant it as the extent of her misapprehension registered. He rushed to explain.

"But you misunderstood. I was discussing with Sebastian my predicament in retrospect, answering his questions about what my enemies had hoped to gain by approaching him."

"Oh, please. Last night was about bringing me back under your spell, to be your worshipping fool and provide your enemies with photographic evidence of my enslavement. You must have also deemed it necessary to sleep with me again, to get working on the heir you need."

His aching hands clenched on the need to drag her against him, make her listen to him, make her believe him. His heart stampeded with the rising dread that she might not, might close her heart to him, that he'd done it too much damage to fix. But he couldn't accept that, never would. He'd make her believe him.

"No, Sabrina, that isn't how—"

She cut him off. "That is exactly how it was. But don't worry. There won't be any repercussions from divorcing me. You were lucky—the two times you slept with me happened to be at the exact wrong time."

"I don't care if you never get pregnant," he protested.

"Save it, Adham. And look at it this way. Our divorce will bring in even more business for the club. More people will be rabidly curious to see you next season with a new acquisition."

He stared at her. Sabrina as he'd never seen her. A spirit that needed nothing and no one, that could not be tamed or bought, but would give her all willingly, endlessly only in the name of love. A tigress capable of slashing anyone who trespassed against her to shreds.

He knew he was fighting for his life here—for she was his life—but he couldn't control the thrill that took him over at discovering these new facets of her. The knowledge of the barbed steel beneath the silk and surrender would make him revel in them more. He couldn't wait to unearth more complexities, which he was now certain she possessed. But none of that would happen, his very life would be over, if he didn't convince her of his sincerity. As he must.

Ready now to take her bitterness, welcoming its pain in atonement for the pain he'd caused her, determined to wipe it away, he closed the distance she'd put between them.

"It was Sebastian who said what happened between us last night was good for business. But he was only right about one thing—I had nothing on my mind but you. I'd come to claim you, thinking that if desire was all you felt for me, that I was a fool not to let you have me. But you turned away and I lost all sense of place and purpose. All sense, period. I had to get you back, make you succumb to the hunger that was eating at both of us."

She shook her head, wrenched away. He caught her back, persisted. "But after last night, I was in agony. I didn't know if you were just taking whatever benefits you could from our situation while your heart remained untouched. I went back to our house to give you what I just gave you now, what you tore apart, what would have released you from any fear about your future. I thought if you chose to stay with me when you no longer had to, that it would mean you do want me beyond what I can provide.

"But you have given me more than I ever dreamed. As you have from day one. It was so good, so unbelievable between us from the start, that when your father approached me with his offer, I found it easier to believe that none of it had been true, that *you'd* been too good to be true. But you are my miracle. And the fact that you love me, after all your father and I did, is beyond a miracle."

Her tear-filled eyes hardened.

His heart sank. "You don't still love me?"

"You are still acting. You just need a baby to tick off some royal requirement and don't want to go through the trouble of acquiring another wife. It was a very time-consuming enterprise for you, acquiring me. All those times you pretended to be interested in me must have been torture for you. A word of advice. Next time, forgo the pretense and just lay your terms on the table. I'm sure hordes of suitable women will snap up you and your cold-blooded deal in a second."

"I only ever wanted you. The only pretense was when I pretended I didn't." He stopped as more tears escaped her eyes, groaned. "But I can't ask you to believe me. Words mean nothing. I have to prove the truth of my feelings with actions."

He got out his cell phone and dialed a number.

He spoke as soon as the line opened. "Angus Henderson? Sheikh Adham Aal Ferjani. I have a scoop for you. Record what I'm going to say so you have it in my own words. Are you ready?" He waited a second, gazing back at Sabrina's confused, apprehensive stare. Then he started. "This is Sheikh Adham Aal Ferjani of Khumayrah, and I'm here today to divulge the true circumstances of my marriage.…"

Sabrina gaped at Adham as he recounted everything from the start. He painted his actions in their worst light, closing by saying he was fighting to convince his wife, the love of his life, to give him a second chance to atone for his sins against her, so he could prove his love and dedicate his life to her.

Then he ended the call. "Do you understand now I care only that you believe me and remain my wife, lover and soul mate?"

Sabrina could only stare at him in shock. Angus Henderson was one of the country's most famous celebrity reporters, who produced and hosted the most notorious shows in the history of modern media. And Adham had just told him everything about their marriage. Everything.

That Adham would expose himself like that! That he would think nothing of offering himself to the media to eat him alive as long as it proved his sincerity to her.

Her paralysis suddenly snapped, and she snatched Adham's phone, redialed the reporter's number. Angus answered at once. No doubt the reporter was rabidly eager to answer in case Adham had forgotten more juicy details to add to the explosive scoop he'd just secured.

"Mr. Henderson? This is Sabrina Grant—Princess Aal Ferjani—Mrs. Adham Aal Ferjan…" She panted, her words and thoughts tangling. "Oh, you know who I am. Everything Adham told you was a joke. A dare. There is *no* truth in what he said, so please don't publish anything."

There was a moment's silence on the other end, before the man's signature raspy voice answered, "I'm sorry to hear that, since I just broadcast his recording live. In fact, you, too, are on the air with me right now."

"Oh, God, no...."

She felt she'd burn to ashes with mortification. Adham took the phone from her, assuring their live audience that he'd meant every word and wouldn't be issuing a retraction. Sabrina squirmed, protesting, but Adham only smiled down on her, hugging her to him as he terminated the call.

"Do you believe me now, *ya rohi?*"

She tore out of his arms and stumbled back. "Believe you? You painted yourself blacker than I ever had! What will that mean for you in your kingdom? I can only assume the worst. You big fool!" Then she threw her arms around him and smothered him in kisses. Tears flowed faster as his mingled with hers. He'd just proved he was as far gone in love with her as she was with him, and feared losing her as much. "Oh, *ya habibi,*" she sobbed, "I might have been reluctant to believe you right away, but I would have eventually. You didn't have to go to this extreme."

He shook his head. "I did. I couldn't let you doubt my love for you a moment longer. I couldn't risk that you'd always feel some distrust. I had to *agt'a ash'shak bel yaqeen*—cleave doubt with certainty, once and forever."

"You don't have to," she insisted. "I will never doubt you again. Please, tell that man to announce a retraction."

"I won't. It's my punishment for letting myself be blinded to the truth, your truth. It's my thanks to you for saving me from spending my life without you, and in misery."

"If you want to thank me, you won't punish yourself.

I can't bear seeing you suffer in any way. And what will your family, your father, think?"

"I couldn't care less. I'll take care of any fallout. The only thing that matters to me is what you think and feel, and that you give me the chance to prove my love to you."

A fresh stream of tears, of delight and gratitude, poured down her cheeks. "More than this?"

He pressed her against his body that trembled with emotion. "I haven't even started. I intend to do everything in my power, everything I can think of. And believe me, I can think of endless ways to prove my love."

"I promise you the same." She looked up at him, felt her heart quivering with adoration for this magnificent man, *her* man, for real, forever, even as a mischievous grin played on her lips. "Wanna bet I'll think of more things than you can?"

"Hmm, sounds like we've got a challenge on our hands. I like that. You know me and challenges—I never lose."

She melted back into his arms, sighing her bliss. "And I might just let you win...."

* * * * *

PREGNANT WITH
THE PLAYBOY'S BABY

Catherine Mann

To my incredible editor, Krista Stroever,
and her amazing assistant, Shana Smith.
Thank you both for making my job a joy!

USA TODAY bestselling author **Catherine Mann** resides on a
sunny Florida beach with her military flyboy husband and their
four children. Although, after nine moves in more than twenty
years, she hasn't given away her winter gear! With more than
thirty-five books in print, she has also celebrated wins for both a
RITA® Award and a Booksellers' Best Award. A former theatre-
school director and university teacher, she graduated with a
master's degree in theatre from UNC-Greensboro and a bachelor's
degree in fine arts from the College of Charleston. Catherine
enjoys hearing from readers and chatting on her message board—
thanks to the wonders of the wireless internet that allows her to
cyber-network with her laptop by the water! To learn more about
her work, visit her website, www.CatherineMann.com, or reach
her by snail mail at PO Box 6065, Navarre, FL 32566, USA.

Prologue

Two Months Ago
Seven Oaks Farm, Bridgehampton, NY

"I told you to stay the hell away from my sister!"

The growled threat from her brother rumbled over Vanessa Hughes's ears a second before her Argentinean lover blocked the fist coming toward his chin.

Damn. She'd landed in the middle of a mess. Again. No surprise, since she'd always been the official family screwup. And now, she'd dragged polo player Nicolas Valera into her chaos for the second time in a year.

"Stand down, Hughes," Nicolas warned, his accent thickening. Desire and sweat still slicked her skin from their steamy encounter. Thank goodness they'd picked up their hastily discarded clothes and dressed again rather than risk being seen together in towels or robes.

Nicolas tucked Vanessa firmly behind him and faced her

pissed-off brother, Sebastian, who'd somehow found out about their surprise encounter. A feat in and of itself, since neither she nor Nicolas had planned on bumping into each other in the sauna room at Seven Oaks Farm's lavish gym.

They certainly hadn't planned on stumbling back inside together for an impulsive hookup.

Thank goodness the place was all but deserted, with most everyone at the charity fundraiser Sebastian should have been attending, the one she'd blown off to come here, only to find Nicolas had ditched the gala as well.

Sebastian pushed forward. His gaze tracked along their hastily donned clothes, his jaw flexing. "I'm not backing off until you're no longer in Vanessa's life."

"Nicolas, look out!" she interjected, hoping to forestall another blow.

Nicolas raised his forearm to block the punch. Vanessa could hardly blame Sebastian. He was right, after all. They had been doing exactly what her brother suspected, even though she and Nicolas had broken up a year ago, bitterly and publicly.

Again, her fault. Her mess.

Pivoting, Nicolas flattened Sebastian against the wooden wall with the speed and agility expected given his world-class reputation on the polo fields. He had her brother pinned with an arm across the chest, but Nicolas wouldn't be able to use his athlete's edge indefinitely. Sebastian's forehead throbbed with an angry vein.

"Calm down, Hughes," Nicolas said quietly again. Of course, he never lost his control. Except during sex. "We do not want a scene here, especially with your sister involved. Vanessa, close the door, please."

She shut the door softly.

Given that the Hughes family's Bridgehampton Polo Club sponsored the polo season at the Seven Oaks Farm, it was considered bad form for her to date any of the players. She'd made plenty of mistakes in her life, but she'd made that particular error only once before, with Nicolas.

After their breakup last year, she'd sworn never again. Until she saw him. Tonight. On the worst day of her life, when she'd been at her weakest. Not that she was renowned for demure restraint even on her best day.

Her brother stared at Nicolas with steely determination. She and Sebastian were alike in that at least, even though they didn't resemble each other, with her being the only blue-eyed blonde in her family. And oh, God, how it hurt to think about that. How it hurt to know her parents had lied to her—

Sebastian pushed free abruptly, his tuxedo tie knocked askew. "Stay the hell away from my sister, Valera." The two men faced off. "Or I swear, I'll bury you."

Vanessa tamped down bitter tears and slid between the two battling bundles of testosterone. "Oh, cut the drama, Seb. There's no law that says I can't see him. Besides, I'm twenty-five years old. It's my business who I choose to spend my time with. I don't appreciate your following after me like I'm some underage kid."

She stomped her foot, tangling it in a discarded towel she and Nicolas had left behind.

Sebastian cursed softly and grasped her arm. "There are plenty of things that aren't against the law that you still shouldn't do. Nessa, if you won't look after yourself, you leave me no choice but to intervene for your own good. I'm taking you home—"

"Hughes," Nicolas growled, his chest expanded, his onyx eyes narrowing. "I cannot just turn away, not until I am certain Vanessa is safe. So listen to me carefully. Let. Her. Go."

She winced. Talk about fuel tossed on a fire in a room already heavy with heat. She wasn't sure she could deal with this, too, not while she was still so off balance from coming face-to-face with Nicolas again, with the scent of him still all around her, the feel of his touch still tingling along her skin.

Sebastian stared down his nose at Nicolas. "Don't you dare insinuate I would harm a hair on Nessa's head. You're the one who's hurting her, cruising back into her life when you know damn well you have no intention of staying."

Her brother was right, but it smarted all the same how he blithely assumed no man would want to stick around for the long haul with her. She shrugged off her wounded feelings and focused on the combustible situation in front of her. Nobody had come to investigate the ruckus thus far, but she couldn't count on that much longer. She needed to end this confrontation ASAP.

Her eyes trained on Nicolas, she saw him trample the urge to let the fight play through. Just a flash of emotion, and then his face was impassive again.

"Your sister and I still have some things to discuss. We're all adults here." He gestured to the door. "If you would step outside."

Sebastian stepped in front of Vanessa, tucking her behind him protectively. "My sister may be twenty-five, but she has never in any way acted remotely like an adult."

"Hello?" Angry, hurt and about to lose control, Vanessa waved her hand in front of her brother's face. "Your sister happens to be standing right here, in case you didn't notice."

"Believe me," Seb said, lasering her with a censoring stare, "I noticed."

"Then let's talk about this later," she said soothingly, desperate to pacify him long enough to buy them all time to cool down. "I need to say good-night to Nicolas first, without you glaring at us."

Sebastian's face lightened for the first time. He cupped her elbow. "After the scene you two caused last year, don't you think you've had enough playing with fire?"

She squeezed her brother's arm to soften her words. "That's not your call to make."

The polo world had been stunned by Nicolas's liaison with such a flamboyant woman. Her polo-champ lover had a reputation for complete, cool control, whether on the field or in front of camera shoots for sportswear endorsements. Vanessa was anything but cool and in control.

Her brother's face hardened again into that of a calculating businessman. "As long as what you do affects our father and the reputation of the Bridgehampton Polo Club, that makes it my call. I'm the one running the family's business interests in his place. And I'm the one who'll be picking up the pieces of your wreckage."

Vanessa gasped at her brother's low blow, her skin burning as the blood drained away. Their father had cancer and was very likely dying. She might be known as the drama queen in the Hughes clan, but today had doled out even more than she could take. She swayed, growing light-headed.

Nicolas touched her back, his hand calming and exciting all at once. "Nobody wants the fallout from a scene now or anytime. Your family's reputation will be safe. Your father can rest easy."

Glancing at Nicolas's stony features, she found no sign of emotion, not even a hint of the passionate lover of a half hour ago. That shouldn't sting, but God, it did.

She turned back to Sebastian. "Nicolas and I broke up a year ago and nothing that happened here changes that."

Her brother studied her intently—she had lied often enough in the past to sneak past the constraints of her family rules—then nodded curtly. "I've said what needed to be said, Valera." He straightened his tux tie. "And Nessa? We'll talk tomorrow when we're both calmer. You owe our father peace this summer."

She bristled at the arrogance of Sebastian advising her on how to please their dad, ready to tell him as much. But he left, taking the anger and outrage with him. Vanessa deflated enough to realize he was right. She couldn't afford to follow her impulses the way she normally would. She couldn't say to hell with the world and be her regular headline-making "celebutante" self—not now.

No matter what lies her father had told her, he'd still been her rock for twenty-five years. She owed him a headline-free season.

The sound of the door closing firmly echoed. Sebastian was gone. She was alone in the spa with Nicolas for a second time.

The bench beckoned. But the weight of what they'd done washed over her. She'd actually had sex with him again— steamy, impulsive sex that left her stunned and a little bit aghast. Not that she had a clue what he felt. Ever.

Where would they go from here?

Nicolas stuffed his hands in his pockets, his eyes as dark as the black clothes he always wore. "I am sorry about your father's illness."

Weighing her words, she allowed herself a moment just to look at her enigmatic lover. She hadn't spent much time looking earlier, simply touching, tasting, savoring. *Nicolas.*

At thirty-two, he was seven years older than her, and according to the tabloids, far more mature. Leanly fit with muscular shoulders and arms to die for, he filled the room with his magnetic good looks as much as his honed size. His deeply tanned complexion attested to the hours he spent outdoors riding and training. He wore his ebony hair wavy and not quite long enough for a ponytail, just enough to appear bedroom-mussed. Thicker in front, it tended to fall over one eye. With a toss of his head, he cleared it off his forehead and turned away.

That was it? He was leaving? He took reserved to a whole new level.

Nicolas clasped the doorknob. Stunned, she opened and closed her mouth twice before speaking.

"That's all?" Rage bubbled along with frustrated tears as she kicked a damp towel aside. "You're walking out after what just happened?"

Slowly, he turned, his black shirt showcasing his too-damn-perfect shoulders in a way she refused to let distract her.

He spread his hands, palms and fingers callused from handling horses and mallets. "What do you want, Vanessa? You made it clear to your brother we are through. This was a chance encounter, a fluke, a bit of unfinished business from last season perhaps. Because God knows, you made it clear we were through to the whole world then, on national television, no less. You even accused me of cheating on you, which we both know wasn't true."

She winced at the memory of the scene she'd caused on the polo field during the stomping of the divots. Blogs had been ablaze with photos and stories. They'd even been the opening segment of cable TV's *Celeb Tonight*. She'd been running scared then. The same fear squeezed her gut now, fear of how deeply he moved her, of how badly she could be hurt. She'd run then rather than take the risk. What would she do now? "I've never had any self-control when it comes to you. And after a day like this…"

His forehead furrowed, his first real show of emotion since he'd pressed his face into her neck after they'd climaxed together. "A day like what?"

A day like this. When she'd learned she was adopted.

She could barely wrap her brain around the fact that her parents had kept her adoption a secret for twenty-five years. Her family would have continued to hide the truth if she hadn't found out by accident during discussions about whether her brother could donate blood for their father in case of emergency surgery. At first she hadn't paid much attention, since the levels of her insulin injections made her ineligible. But as she listened to the discussion of different family blood types…something wasn't right. Once the issue was raised, she'd asked too many questions to avoid the truth. At least she was the only one who knew.

And she wanted to keep it that way until she figured out how to deal with the life-changing information. But she had to do it soon, because her father—the man who'd adopted her—might not have much longer left.

After a private detective verified the truth about her adoption, she'd come to the spa to ease the confusion, not to mention the sense of betrayal. Then she'd run into Nicolas, who'd just arrived for the preseason games, and they'd fallen into old habits as fast as they'd fallen onto the sauna bench.

She pushed back the urge to haul him down with her again and forget everything for another half hour. "Does it really matter what kind of day I've had?"

"What is wrong?" His accent thickened with his persistence. He was a determined man who never gave up on the field. Although he'd sure walked away from her fast enough last year, firmly ignoring her apology.

"Drop it, Nicolas. We don't do the whole serious routine, remember? We were all about keeping it light and uncomplicated. God knows neither of us needs another scene." She drew in a shaky breath. "I can't risk worrying my father, and I know you won't risk your career."

"Except I already did that here tonight with you. As you said, we never had self-control around each other." He slid his hand into her hair, slowly, almost as if against his will.

"Something that apparently has not changed during the past year."

She stared up into his face as he loomed over, a full twelve inches taller. His eyes glinted with every bit as much desire as she felt searing her insides. Then his mouth was on hers. Heat and strength and memories—lush and intense memories of all the ways they'd pleasured each other a year ago, and again tonight—rushed through her.

Vanessa plunged her fingers into Nicolas's hair and held tight. She moaned her need against his mouth. Now, just as then, he made her forget everything but the bold brush of his tongue exploring, the feel of his hands stroking up her back, drawing her closer. She let herself slide into the convenient amnesia he offered. So unwise, so undeniable.

He eased back. "Vanessa, we can't. Not here."

Even though she knew he was right, she shook inside at the prospect of letting him go. When would she ever be able to resist him? How would she watch the games this season, watch *him* and hold strong to her promise not to bring any stress to her father's doorstep?

Her father.

The anger rose again, the betrayal of the lies he'd told her every time she asked who she looked like, since she was so different from her brother, her father, her mother. She couldn't even turn to her mother now, since Lynette had died in a car accident several years ago.

It would be easy enough to say to hell with gossip and rules, but she couldn't. Not with her father dying. There had to be a way to balance it all without combusting.

"Vanessa? Do you hear me?" Nicolas's accent stroked her like a sensuous, private promise.

And then it came to her, the perfect plan for keeping the peace in public while finally, *finally* purging this seemingly unquenchable need for Nicolas Valera.

Vanessa leaned closer, her body molding to the hard, familiar heat of him. Desire pooled low and lush. "I do hear you, and you're right. We can't continue this. Not here, anyway. But what if we pick the time and place for you to…romance me? We keep what we're feeling totally secret." *Forbidden.* "No one knows but us. Nobody gets hurt."

As she urged his head down toward her again, she could almost believe her own words. No one would get hurt…

He stopped just shy of kissing her. "You propose we have discreet sex all summer long?"

His arousal throbbed harder against her stomach.

"Not exactly." She teased his bottom lip between her teeth, trailing her fingers down his chest. "I suggest that during this polo season, you convince me, in private, that I *should* have sex with you again. If you don't succeed, then we're through. No harm, no foul. We can rest assured knowing we've learned to resist each other. And if you do succeed—" she traced his mouth with her tongue, slowly, torturously "—we'll have one helluva night to finally burn this fire out once and for all."

One

Present Day
Seven Oaks Farm—Bridgehampton, NY

Vanessa Hughes had been burned. And it had nothing to do with the summer sun beating down overhead as she stood on the sidelines watching the polo match in action. The earth vibrated beneath her high heels from the thundering hooves passing by.

The calendar didn't lie. She was late. Scary late. Maybe pregnant late.

Her stomach bubbled with nausea. She'd forced herself to eat. She had to regulate her blood-sugar level for her diabetes, but fear had her ready to upchuck. Clamping her hand on top of her broad-brimmed hat, she peered through her overlarge sunglasses at one particular player in all black, riding his favorite chestnut sorrel.

Two months of being romanced by the intense and

passionate Nicolas Valera had been magical, soothing and stirring all at once. Although they hadn't slept together again since the sauna incident, he'd provided her much-needed distraction from confusion over learning of her adoption. Those moments of being secretly whisked away in a limo, finding anonymous flowers on her pillow, even stealing kisses in a kitchen pantry, had carried her through. She'd thought she'd found the perfect solution, and she had even considered giving in to temptation and indulging in uncomplicated sex.

That was impossible now. She was ninety-nine percent sure she was pregnant. Even thinking about the possibility made her sway in her high heels. She just had to get up the nerve to take the home pregnancy test stashed in the bottom of her voluminous purse. And she would. After the match.

Thank goodness sunglasses kept her eyes from betraying her fear to the crowd around her under the large white tent—the mainstay of old-money New Yorkers, Europeans, artsy and cultured Hampton royalty mixed with a couple of Hollywood celebrities. And right beside her stood Brittney Hannon, a high-profile senator's daughter.

Vanessa fanned her face with the program booklet. Her ever-present shades enabled her to watch Nicolas undetected as he rode across the field, mallet swinging.

Maximo's coat gleamed like a shiny penny. Nicolas loved that horse, a Crillo/Thoroughbred mix. Maximo wasn't the largest, but he was absolutely fearless.

Like Nicolas.

How would he react when she told him the news? It wasn't as if they had a real relationship beyond attraction. She wasn't sure how much more upheaval she could take.

Her heart nearly cracked in two to think of her father lying to her about being adopted. He'd always been there for her before. Her mom, however, had ignored Vanessa unless cameras were present. Not so nice to think ill of the dead, but then Vanessa didn't have much experience tempering her thoughts and emotions. This whole "good girl" gig was new to her.

She'd tried her best to clean up her act this summer, for her father's sake. No more wild-child acting out in public.

Private indulgences were another matter altogether. She just couldn't stay away from Nicolas, and that could cost her big-time. Their secret affair wouldn't be so secret once her pregnancy started showing. She glared at the ever-present cameras from behind the protective shield of her sunglasses.

"Damn paparazzi," she muttered, tapping her large black sunglasses in place.

Pulling a picture-perfect smile, Brittney Hannon linked arms with Vanessa. "As I've learned the hard way, press photos are an unavoidable part of the game. Don't let them ruin the match for you."

Vanessa turned to the senator's daughter, who'd weathered a bit of scandal herself at the start of the summer. Who'd have thought she would find a kindred spirit in the conservatively dressed Brittney, who had a reputation for being the antithesis of her showgirl mother?

"Don't you ever get tired of it?" Vanessa asked. The press had splashed racy photos of Brittney and a well-known playboy, only to learn later the two were engaged. "Don't you want some privacy? It's not as if we asked to be born into this."

Brittney blinked in surprise. And no wonder. Vanessa was known for welcoming the limelight. She'd never even considered that one day she might feel differently, and she sure hadn't realized how difficult it would be to step into the shadows.

The politician's daughter shrugged an elegant shoulder. "My father has the chance to make a real difference for our country. He takes a lot of heat as a natural byproduct of the job. The least I can do is keep my nose clean and smile for the paparazzi. Besides, none of this is real. It's all just for show." The outwardly reserved woman struck a subdued pose for the cameras, dimples showing in her cheeks. She spoke quietly out of the side of her mouth as she said, "But when I get away from all this, I'm finding it easier than I expected to simply indulge in being happy."

Vanessa wasn't even sure she knew the meaning of happy. The closest she'd come was the excitement of being with Nicolas, yet even that left her hollow inside afterward. Aching. Feeling she was missing something.

Brittney tapped Vanessa's arm with a French-manicured nail. "You have some dirt on the hem of your dress."

Gasping, Vanessa looked down at her simple, white Valentino Garavani original. "Really?" She twisted to look behind her. "Where?"

"Just teasing so you'll lighten up. You never have so much as a speck on you. Now smile."

Halfway through the round of clicking cameras, halftime started. Finally, she would be closer to Nicolas.

Vanessa slid her Jimmy Choo Saba bag from her shoulder, slipped off her heels and pulled on a pair of simple flats. Waving a quick goodbye to Brittney, Vanessa tucked her strappy heels into her oversize leather purse.

Time to divot-stomp. One of her earliest memories of coming to the matches was of holding her daddy's hand and stomping down the chunks of earth churned up from the polo ponies' hooves. She would jump up and down, smashing the ground until her Mary Janes were covered in mud.

Her mother had hated how she came home dirty, her huge hair bow lopsided. Vanessa stifled a wince. She'd despised those bows that weighed a ton and pulled her ponytail back so tightly from her face that she had a headache by the end of the day.

Smile nice for the camera, Nessa.

What a pretty baby.

The only way to get her mother's attention had been to go on shopping trips or sit still for a hair brushing. Her mother touched her only during those primping routines or when posing her for the camera.

Once she'd gotten out from under Lynette Hughes's fashionista thumb, Vanessa wore white. All the time, every day. She'd already spent two lifetimes in front of a three-way mirror as her mom put together perfectly color-coordinated outfits.

No more picking or choosing for Vanessa.

These days her hair stayed straight and free in the wind, or simply sleeked back in a low ponytail. Sunglasses covered her eyes so she never had to blink back dots from camera flashes.

People called her an eccentric drama queen. She was just tired of being a baby doll.

Baby?

Her brain snagged on the word. Her breath caught in her throat as she thought of having to tell Nicolas, of ending the fragile, tantalizing truce they'd forged. And her gaze zipped right back to the only man who could have fathered her baby, if she was indeed pregnant.

Nicolas would mingle with the divot-stomping crowd at halftime, even autograph some polo balls. He was a renowned six-handicap player after all, in the top five percent of players in the world. With fans—and with her—he would be coolly reserved, as always.

They wouldn't be able to talk, according to the rules of their summer-seduction game. Normally, she would have enjoyed playing out the moment. But today, she resisted the urge to check her watch. How long before she could slip away and use the pregnancy test tucked deep in the bottom of her purse? As much as she feared the answer, she couldn't afford to wait, not with her health concerns. Her diabetes could place both her and a baby at risk. She stomped a chunk of dirt back into the ground with extra oomph and wished her fears were as easily addressed.

Tingles prickled along her arms as Nicolas approached. She could feel him, could have even sworn she caught a whiff of his signature scent on the wind, a soap-and-cologne combo that smelled enticingly of bay leaves. He drew closer. If she hadn't known by his scent, she would have been able to guess by the reaction of those around her. People slowed, their eyes fixed on her as if waiting for her to react.

Nicolas stepped alongside her, nearly shoulder to shoulder. Her fears and wants tangled up inside her until she almost lost her balance. Nicolas pressed his booted foot ever so precisely in front of her, leveling the ground, then walking past with only the barest brush of his hand against hers. He never looked at her, didn't even miss a stride even though his simple touch had set her senses on fire.

Her fist closed around the scrap of paper he'd slid into her palm. She might not yet know the specifics of what he'd written, but she knew without question she would be seeing him alone soon.

Nicolas had arranged the location for their next tryst.

Six hours later, Nicolas added a twist of lime to his sparkling water. Nothing stronger for him at tonight's party. He never drank during the season.

Even if the timing had been different, he needed to keep his mind sharp. His instincts told him he was close to his goal of getting Vanessa back into his bed. Yes, he knew one misstep could cost him the whole game, but he had hope.

He glanced at his Rolex—thirty minutes to kill at this party before ducking out to meet her at the Seven Oaks boathouse.

Bridgehampton polo season parties were always top notch. The highest of high society pulled out all the stops entertaining their friends and celebrities in for the summer. The extravagance was so far beyond his spartan upbringing in Argentina. His village could have eaten for a month off the food spread out at multiple stations. Most gatherings were fundraisers, which took the edge off some of the decadence. Between his polo earnings and sportswear endorsements, his bank balance matched that of most of the partygoers. Still, he wouldn't forget where he came from. Nicolas emptied half his high-priced water.

Tonight's benefit was for the Humane Society. Hollywood star Bella Hudson had flown out with her hotel-magnate husband—and their dogs. Bella was talking with fellow actress Carmen Atkins. The two movie stars held the press's attention for now. Nicolas took the rare free moment to look at Vanessa.

Twenty-five years old—she was young, so young with her pampered life—yet she charmed the hell out of him. The tabloids painted a party-girl picture and he'd bought into that last year, never bothering to look deeper, only thinking about their next sexual encounter. But over the past couple of months, he'd come to realize Vanessa was also smart, witty and sensitive.

Their breakup had been tumultuous last year—and tough. He'd never known he could want someone that much. Now? He couldn't even look away, much less leave. Abundant energy crackled from her petite frame, no more than five foot two inches, *if that*. She always wore high heels and still barely reached his chin.

Tonight, in her white satin dress, she was very much the

"celebutante," perfectly groomed to catch the camera's eye. For some reason he'd never learned, she always wore white and managed to stay pristinely clean whether outdoors at polo matches or under a big tent at a Humane Society fundraiser with pets on leashes all around. Since the sun had gone down, he could see her unshielded eyes, a pale blue that turned almost silver when he made love to her.

His body jolted at the mere thought of being with Vanessa. Their secretive romancing had him on edge. He clamped down the urge to simply haul her off to the nearest room. Except he couldn't afford a repeat of the scene she'd thrown last year. He needed to project a professional image, important for his dream of launching his own training camp, even someday owning his own team.

Nicolas shifted his gaze from her to the linen-draped table of food beside her and walked closer. Swiping a tiny napkin, he trained his eyes forward and spoke to Vanessa behind the cover of his raised drink. "Did you help with the party plans?"

"Why would you say that?" She also kept her attention forward, her gaze not even straying his way as she cradled a glass of sparkling water with lime—like his own drink.

He nodded lightly toward the gauzy tent. "Everything is white."

Hydrangeas rested in clear crystal containers. Mammoth flower arrangements sat on top of pristine pillars. At least a tenth of the guests had brought their pets, yet there wasn't so much as a muddy paw print marring the décor.

Smiling, Vanessa inhaled deeply. "I adore lilies and stephanotis."

A tuxedoed waiter passed, carrying a silver tray of hors d'ouevres. Nicolas popped a smoked salmon canapé in his mouth, while Vanessa reached for a portabella mushroom and herb bruschetta. Her hand shook.

Odd.

He looked from her arm up to her pale face. "Are you all right?"

"You played well today." Ignoring his question, she dabbed at the corners of her mouth, her lipstick leaving traces on her napkin.

All summer she'd made a point of leaving hidden lip prints on his body for him to find when he showered later. Yet he still hadn't sealed the deal.

God, he couldn't wait to get her alone in the boathouse. He'd even set up a few surprises for her there. He glanced at his watch. Twenty-seven more endless minutes.

At least he could talk to her now. The *shoosh* of the champagne fountain on one side and the bubbling of the white chocolate fondue on the other added extra cover for their conversation.

She sipped her sparkling water, as the band took to the stage after their break. "I can't meet you tonight."

Surprise hit him, and disappointment, too. "You are free after this gathering, and I know it."

"Are you spying on me?"

"I just listen well enough to know you do not have plans."

"Then listen now." She placed her cup on the table. "I can't always be at your beck and call."

Surprise shifted to irritation. "You are the one who set the rules for this game."

"Sometimes rules have to change because—" Vanessa bit her lip as another waiter passed. They'd spent the whole summer brushing elbows at cocktail and garden parties, softball tournaments and music festivals, alternately ignoring each other and pretending they hated each other, while he found creative ways to pass messages for meetings. He started with simple whispered instructions of a place and time and moved on to a note scrawled on a napkin tucked into her bag.

And she'd built the anticipation well. His need for her... there were no words to express the exquisite pain. But for her to cut him off at the knees now? He wasn't sure what game she was playing. Of course while Vanessa may have been behaving in public for once in her life, in private she personified unpredictability.

Perhaps it was time for him to turn the tables. He eyed the other guests and found the partiers gathering around the stage to dance and sing along to a chorus of "Who Let the Dogs Out."

He clasped Vanessa's wrist and tugged her deftly behind a trailing gauze curtain. He pulled her into his arms and kissed her, hard and fast. She gasped, but didn't say no or push him away. She wrapped her arms around his neck. Growling deep in his throat, he delved into her mouth, sweeping, tasting sweet hints of the lime twist from her drink. He backed her deeper into the pear orchard beside the tent, an orchard that sprawled all the way to Seven Oaks. With no prior planning for this rendezvous, he followed his gut and what he remembered of the estate from last year's fundraiser for the troops.

She nipped his bottom lip, then traced the sting with the warm tip of her tongue. "We should stop. What if we get caught?"

"We won't. They're all busy dancing, and it's dark over here." He tucked her deeper into the shadowy orchard, branches rustling overhead. "You said you have to leave, so let's be together now." He'd had a lot more in mind than a few stolen kisses tonight, but if that's all they could have, he would remind her of just how good things could be between them.

Vanessa panted lightly against his neck, the sweet swell of

her breasts rising and falling faster against his chest. "We can't take this all the way, Nicolas, not here. It's too big a risk."

Desire pounded through his veins, throbbing fuller, harder, lower. "All the way?"

"I didn't mean that." She shook her head, the slide of her hair along her shoulders shimmering in the starlight. "Damn it, Nicolas, you jumble my head."

"Come closer," he pulled her hips to his, "and I'll take care of your tension."

"You're arrogant."

"But you haven't walked away." He dipped his head again, stopping just short of touching her, watching, waiting.

Shadows skittered through her eyes, illuminated by the moonbeams filtering through the trees. She blinked fast, swallowed hard, then arched up to meet his mouth full on.

Her frenzy intensified. Adrenaline still surged through him from the match, from the competition, the win. And most of all, from Vanessa. Kissing her equaled the rush of scoring three goals on a muddy course in the rain. The effort and exertion and almost painful tension was worth every bit of payoff. This woman seared his senses.

She was wrong for him on all levels with her overprivileged background and her high-strung ways. She was the one person who'd ever threatened his control. He would learn, though, how to have her while keeping himself in check. He was determined. He'd pulled himself up from a poor upbringing to become one of the wealthiest and most respected athletes in the polo world. His father had been a farmer on the outskirts of Buenos Aires, their horses certainly not of polo quality, but Nicolas had felt the calling, the affinity from an early age.

Luck had played a part in the right person seeing him in a race at eight years old. Even at that age, he was already too large to be a jockey...but polo? Argentina's famed sport was a perfect fit for him. He'd nabbed a sponsor. Now his family lived in a mansion he'd purchased for them.

Yet, no matter how hard he worked, he never forgot that a fluke of fate and the largesse of people like the Hughes family had lifted him out.

Vanessa didn't have a clue. Still, that didn't keep him away from her, even knowing her volatile nature could land him back in hot water again with his sponsors. His hands roved lower, cupping her bottom, bringing her closer.

"You're addictive," he whispered against her mouth.

She laughed shakily. "You make me sound like crack."

He swept a hand through her silky hair trailing over her shoulders. "Seeing you, feeling you move, takes me higher than any drug."

"Quit with the outrageous compliments." She scratched a nail along his bristly jaw line. "You haven't seen me all day."

"I watched you from the field." He pressed her closer until she couldn't possibly miss his arousal. So close, memories of being inside her surged through him, sending his pulse galloping against his ribs.

"You were focused on the game."

"I am a master at multitasking." He ran his hand up her back to cup her face.

She swayed toward him, then froze. She clasped his wrists. "Wait, we can't do this."

"What do you mean?"

"I can't stay. I, uh…" Shadows chased through her eyes again. "I have something to do tonight."

Jealousy nipped with the strength of a horse's bite. "Then why did you come to the party?"

"To tell you personally."

Reason edged through the suspicion. If she planned to move on to some other guy, she wouldn't be here. Vanessa might be impulsive, but she'd always been honest with him. He could count on that much. If she didn't intend to see some other man, he could think of only one other reason that would make Vanessa miss a good party.

"Are you ill?" He searched her face in the dim moonlight.

Her eyes widened. "Why would you ask that?"

"The season's in full swing and you always represent your father. You look pale. Are you having trouble with your diabetes?" Not many knew about her health concerns. She hadn't even told him last year. She'd only recently divulged it to him after he'd teased her relentlessly over her refusal to share a fudge-covered dessert with him when he'd chartered a jet to fly them to dinner in a remote Vermont town last month. The isolated locale and distance from the Bridgehampton frenzy provided the anonymity they needed to enjoy an evening together.

She shook her head. "I know how to monitor myself. I've been doing it since I was nine."

After she'd set aside that uneaten sundae, Vanessa had told him about learning to overcome her fear of needles to administer her own injections as a teen. She'd vowed it hurt less than watching her father wince when he gave her the shots. She cared for her dad, that was patently obvious. Christian Hughes's battle with cancer had to be hell for Vanessa. No wonder she was moody.

Nicolas rested his forehead against hers. "You have had a stressful summer. I only want to make sure you are all right. I…care for you."

And he did care. He'd always wanted her, but somewhere around the time she'd sipped her diet soda to hide the tears over how much her father worried about her health, Nicolas had felt something shift inside him. He felt that same unsettling change rumbling around in his chest again now.

Her fingers clutched the lapels of his suit, her forehead furrowing. Something obviously weighed heavily on her mind, something that had made her want to cancel their evening rendezvous.

"Nicolas, I should tell—"

A rustling sounded through the trees, fast, loud. Vanessa jolted, her mouth snapping closed. Nicolas pivoted fast to shield her from view, because the crunch of underbrush left him with no doubts.

Someone was coming toward them.

Two

Vanessa clutched Nicolas's arm, her heart hammering as hard as the bass throb of the distant band. Frantically she scanned the shadowy clearing, peering through the surrounding trees. The underbrush rustled louder. A scruffy dog lunged from behind a pear tree.

Straight toward Vanessa.

She stifled a scream and ducked behind Nicolas. Not that she was scared of dogs, but this little beast rocketed forward at lightning speed, pink leash flapping behind. Nicolas shielded her, his stance planted. Vanessa gasped in gulping breaths to steady her pulse, the clean night air fragrant with ripening pears. The wiry-haired mutt ran circles around them, yipping, but thank heavens not nipping

"Thank heaven, it's just a dog." She rested her cheek against Nicolas's back, the scent of his bay-rum soap stirring arousing memories of showering with him last summer. But the rowdy little pet had served up a hefty reminder of how easily they could be interrupted. Discussing her possible pregnancy would require total privacy. "We can talk later. I'll just walk the dog back to the party before someone comes looking—"

A whistle echoed in the distance. "Muffin?" a female voice shouted through the night. "Muffin, come here sweetie. Come to Mama."

Rhinestone collar refracting moonbeams, Muffin's ears perked up, twitching like satellite dishes working for a better connection. She was one ugly-cute scrap of fur, and small to have made so much noise.

"Muffin?" the female voice sounded louder, closer.

Nicolas knelt to grab for the leash. Muffin scampered deftly out of reach. A branch swayed.

"Damn," Nicolas muttered. "No more time."

He gathered Vanessa tightly against his chest and guided her behind a tree. Muffin trotted toward them, all but pointing a paw their way. Vanessa's stomach clenched. They'd eluded the press, her family and Nicolas's Black Wolves teammates all summer long. They couldn't possibly be discovered now because of one persistent pup.

"Shoo, shoo!" She waved the dog away with her hand.

"Shhh," Nicolas whispered before brushing a kiss across her cheek.

Just a simple skim of his lips had her relaxing deeper into his arms, her legs more than a little wobbly.

Staying still and quiet was tough enough with Nicolas clamping a possessive hand on her spine, his fingers straying to dip inside the swooped low cut back of her silk charmeuse evening gown. The air grew thick, her breathing so raspy she feared Muffin's owner would hear. Damn Nicolas and his tormenting caresses that turned her muscles to marshmallows right when they were seconds away from possible discovery.

Who was the impulsive one now?

"Muffin," the female voice demanded, branches parting a couple of trees away, "no more playing. Come. *Now!*"

Muffin sighed heavily and turned away, trotting toward her owner, leash tracing a serpentine trail in the dust back into the trees.

"There you are," the woman said—to her dog, thank goodness. "You're a naughty girl…" Her voice faded as she left with her pet.

Vanessa sagged back against the tree trunk, ragged bark biting into her back. Her heart drummed in her ears in the quiet aftermath. "That was close."

"Too close."

His fierce scowl reminded her well how dangerous a game they played. Her liaison with him now would cause a bigger scandal, given how she'd ended things before. Her brother had been angry enough last year when rumormongers had dared impugn the Hughes family's impartiality just because she happened to be sleeping with one of the players…. Okay, her brother wasn't at fault for her decisions. She had known going in that it would look bad.

Yet, here she was again, with Nicolas. How was she any better now than last summer? Just better at deception.

Nicolas looked from the clearing back to her. "They're gone. We're safe. Now what did you want to tell me?"

A secret that would pour fertilizer onto the rumormongers. She should wait until she was sure. Why upset him for no reason? She still hadn't taken the home pregnancy test. Better wait to confirm the pregnancy. She would decide what to do then.

Vanessa smoothed his tuxedo lapels. The heat of him warmed through the fabric and tempted her to explore further. Desire crackled through her until she could have sworn her hair sparked with static, but for once she would be strong around him. "We will have to talk later. I'm not thinking clearly tonight. It was a long day in the sun. I should have skipped the party."

She *should* have skipped a lot of things this summer. But looking up into Nicolas's dark eyes melting over her like the dangerous chocolate she shouldn't have, she couldn't delude herself into thinking she was any stronger at resisting him now than she had been before.

He nodded curtly. "Okay then. No boathouse for tonight. But rest up, Vanessa, because by tomorrow I will have an even more enticing plan in place, one you can't resist." His hands slid in a seductive path from her back to her hips then back up, stopping just below her breasts. "We're going to be together soon."

His confidence would have irritated her, except she knew full well her ability to resist him was in serious peril. She would not be impulsive this time the way she'd been in their last encounter, not to mention all their assignations last year. With the possibility of a surprise pregnancy looming over her, she needed to stay in control now more than ever.

Carefully, Vanessa closed the front door of her childhood home with the barest click echoing up into the vaulted foyer. She was good at sneaking in undetected after years of practice.

The Tudor-style mansion still radiated the same formality, with bulky antiques, thick curtains and the heavy scent of lemon furniture oil. The hallway sprawled upward into a cathedral ceiling, open to the living room. Her father hadn't changed anything since Lynette died.

Vanessa grasped the banister, the wooden rail cool and familiar under her hand. Even from the stairs she could see the carved fireplace mantel with a massive oil portrait of her and Sebastian as children above. The rest of the art on the walls was polo-centric—horses in action with bold players, women in long dresses and umbrellas watching from the sidelines. She'd taken a marker to one as a child, muddying up a dress with a Sharpie.

Wow, she'd been a brat. Yet she'd never doubted her dad's love.

Once her father had gotten out of the residential treatment facility last month, she'd closed up her sleek little condo in New York City and moved back to the fourteen-bedroom family hub without even asking. Sure her dad had plenty of nurses, but she wanted to spend as much time with him as possible. She liked to think her presence comforted him, even if he didn't say so. And she could still continue her new job for the season, her pet project—increasing entertainment activities for the children of spectators. She was trying to make amends, but it was hard knowing where to turn when her world was flipped upside down.

Italian heels dangling from her fingers, she tiptoed down the hall, not wanting to wake her father. He slept so fitfully these days. Of course, he'd always been a light sleeper with an ear perked to listen for her as a teen.

"How was the party?" her father's voice called through his partially opened bedroom door.

Caught again. Had she ever fooled him at all? Her heart squeezed with love for him.

She stepped inside, hinges creaking softly. "Hi, Daddy."

Christian Hughes lay propped up by a pile of pillows in his four-poster bed. His face was chalkier than the ivory satin sheets. The thick comforter enveloped him, his body emaciated from the treatments. He seemed frail, as if the heavy bedspread could crush him like poured concrete.

He'd completely shaved his head after the second round of chemo robbed him of his freshly grown hair. He looked just like his son, Sebastian. Of course, Seb was the biological child. She swallowed down welling tears her ailing father didn't need to see.

Her father had always been fit and tanned from days on his horses, full of energy whether he was cinching million-dollar deals or stomping divots with his daughter.

Now his breathing rattled.

And her heart broke.

She stepped deeper into the muggy room, temperature cranked up because he was frequently cold. Setting her shoes and purse on the floor, she sat on the antique beech-wood chair beside his bed and tucked her legs underneath her. "Sorry to wake you."

"You didn't. I was waiting up." He raised a bony hand and patted her arm, his fingers so thin the wedding band he still wore almost slid off. "I know you're an adult, but even when you're fifty and under my roof, I will worry until I hear your feet hit the stairs."

His hand slid from her, skipping lightly along a framed family photo on the bedside table before falling to rest on the bedspread. The picture had been taken when she was around five, her sky-blue bow perfect for the start of polo season. She wasn't looking at the photographer, but rather staring off into the distance. She still remembered the day and how she'd wanted to play in the barn instead of attend a match that seemed endlessly long.

That day, she would have taken a Sharpie to the polo players' stark-white pants if there'd been one handy. Those feelings had been the driving force behind her ideas for expanding the activities offered to entertain the children of families attending polo matches. "I'm sorry I've given you reason to doubt me."

"You're high-spirited, but in a good way, like Sassy." One of his prized fillies, gone now from old age. Sassy had been past her playing prime when Vanessa was a child, but the horse still had spirit.

"Remember how I begged to ride her?"

A reminiscent smile tugged at his parched, cracked lips. "Scared the hell out of me that day I relented."

"I got tossed on my butt." She'd stained and torn her best riding pants, which had made her mom mad. Her dad had usually been able to tease Lynette out of her tempers. That day he'd been silent, shaken.

She understood the feeling too well now as she faced the possibility of losing him. "Thanks for letting me ride her."

"I never could say no to you."

"I meant thanks for letting me land on my butt. I learned more that way."

He laughed weakly. "That's my girl."

Too bad she still had to learn the hard way.

She glanced at the family photo in the silver frame. Her father had placed it there after Lynette died to remind him of his perfect family. Perfect except for Lynette's tantrums and how they'd kept a huge secret from their children. What had made them decide to adopt her? What had made her biological parents give her up?

Her hand slipped to her stomach and she thought of her own increasing nerves as each day passed on the calendar. She wasn't mother material any more than Lynette Hughes had been. Panic pounded her chest for a brief moment until she quickly realized she would never put an emotional wall up between herself and a child, no matter how different her child was from her.

Still, Lynette had chosen to bring her into this house. Why? She wanted to ask Christian, needing answers, though she couldn't make herself add another line of worry to his weary face tonight. But his frail frame reminded her time could be running out. Her answers could die with her father…. The last thought choked her.

She would hold on to her questions for a while longer.

Vanessa patted his hand, bruised from multiple IVs. "I'm glad you waited up for me so we could talk."

"I always wait up for my girl."

How many hours of worry had she caused him? Had pushing the envelope become such a habit for her she'd subconsciously chosen Nicolas to create a stir? The possibility unsettled her more than a little. Maybe, just maybe, she'd done that last year, but this year? Her attraction to him was undeniable. There was definitely no secret wish to get caught, because that would end things for him. Nicolas had been her one bright spot in a summer filled with pain.

"Vanessa?"

Her father's voice sliced into her thoughts. "I was, uh, just thinking about the party. The Reagerts always throw a fabulous bash."

"That they do. I'm sorry to have missed it, but I'm glad you were there to represent the family along with your brother." He skimmed a hand over his shaved head absently. "You've been a real comfort to me this summer. I know you'll keep the traditions alive."

"Daddy, don't talk like that." She rested her hand on top of his over his bald head and squeezed gently. "You'll be out there divot-stomping with me next year."

"I hope so, Nessa, I hope so." His eyes drifted closed, his chest rising and falling evenly.

Vanessa sat beside his bed and watched him sleep for a few minutes. How sad that she was tucking him in now, this once big, strong father who'd long ago created bedtime stories with her favorite horse puppets. Once she was sure he was resting peacefully, she slipped out into the hall to her suite. She locked the door behind her and sagged back with a ten-ton sigh.

Finally, she was alone.

Pushing away from the door with purpose, she strode toward her bed and upended her purse onto the mattress. Her shoes and wallet mixed in with a thousand other items, but her eyes zeroed in on one thing.

The home pregnancy test. A thin box would spell out her future with a plus or minus sign. Her health dictated she learn the truth soon. While she might be reckless when it came to her own safety, she couldn't risk the well-being of a baby.

Scooping up the pregnancy test, she willed her shaky hand to steady. She would know in minutes whether she was free to meet Nicolas in the morning.

Or whether she would have to make a last-minute appointment to see her doctor.

Three

Where is Vanessa?

Nicolas brushed down Maximo, each stroke faster and faster as his irritation built. She'd been a no-show this morning for their brunch date at a tucked-away inn. While she'd let him know, her format—a text message—had left him frustrated. The fact that she was ignoring his calls shifted his frustration to anger.

Even his favorite ritual in a quiet corner of the stable couldn't calm him. The scent of polished leather, hay and nature usually soothed his soul. No matter where he traveled, in a stable, he felt at home. Since he was usually on the road for polo matches or traveling to photo shoots for his sportswear endorsements, there wasn't much in the way of routine in his life. He'd made a mistake in getting comfortable with his "routine" with Vanessa this summer.

Most of their evenings were orchestrated around the parties they had to attend. So he'd made a point of surprising her with late brunches after he'd finished his morning workout with the team's owner, Sheikh Adham.

Now that he looked back, he realized she'd been disappearing more and more. He didn't expect to know her every move or thought like some possessive jackass, but he could see how distracted she was lately. Which concerned him, as well as surprised him. Their time together this summer was supposed to be about attraction, passion. Certainly last summer had been about all that, yet these past two months— with no sex—had added a need he hadn't expected. A need to know her, to figure out if he could trust this new wiser, more mature Vanessa.

Footsteps shuffled along the dusty floor behind him. He looked back over his shoulder just as Vanessa rounded the corner.

"Sorry I'm late," she said softly, her large sunglasses silver today. Her white jeans and button-down shirt hugged her body, made him think of just how fun it was to peel away those layers. "I had an unexpected appointment."

"I got your text message." He forced his focus back on her words.

She would *not* unsettle him. He couldn't afford disruptions during polo season.

So what was he doing with Vanessa at all?

"It was rude of me not to call." She slid her sunglasses on top of her head, shifting from foot to foot nervously. "I was distracted. Not that you're easily forgettable, far from it."

He set the brush aside and looked into her troubled blue eyes. His instincts itched in the same way they did on the field, when he knew his horse was off even if he showed no perceptible signs. "Something is wrong."

Her hand shook as she fidgeted with her sunglasses again. "I had to check in with my doctor."

"Are you all right?"

"Healthy as a, uh, horse."

She slid her sunglasses back over her eyes in a gesture he'd come to recognize well. She'd closed herself off. Time to move on. He wouldn't get anything more from her on that subject today. Best to advance again later.

A whinny sounded a few stalls away.

Nicolas recognized the pony's call even though it wasn't one of his. They all had distinctive "voices." It paid to know everything about the polo ponies as well as their riders on the field. "Careful around Ambrosia or she'll nip you on the butt. She's high-spirited. It'll take a while before she's ready to be played."

"Sounds like one of my dad's favorite horses—Sassy. She might have been high-strung, but she was all heart."

Like Vanessa?

The sound of Ambrosia's groom echoed around the corner as the woman crooned to the pony with an unmistakable New Zealand accent. Catherine Lawson was the head groom for Sheikh Adham ben Khaleel ben Haamed Aal Ferjani, the owner of Nicolas's team. Sheikh Adham not only owned the team, but was also one helluva top-notch player for the Black Wolves.

Vanessa's brow furrowed. "Maybe we should speak somewhere else."

Nicolas cupped her elbow. "Lawson won't be coming this way. She still has to tend Sheikh Adham's signature ponies, Aswad and Layl."

Except for Nicolas, all the Black Wolves rode Sheikh Adham's horses. Aswad and Layl, Arabic for Black and Night, came from the same sire, the Sheikh's first horse. They were solid and glossy black, damn near perfect. He saved these prized ponies for the most crucial parts of a match.

Still, Nicolas would put his money on Maximo any day of the week. He patted the polo pony's smooth neck, the mane roached—shaved—so as not to get tangled during competition.

Maximo wasn't some elite Arabian, but he was a hearty Argentinean criollo mixed with a thoroughbred for endurance and speed. All five of Nicolas's personal ponies were of the same breed, but Maximo? He was special. At fifteen hands high, he wasn't the largest on the field. Yet even with mallets flying and the largest of the large bumping him, Maximo never flinched.

Vanessa stroked the sorrel's nose with obvious affection. "Funny how we can trace their lineage further than our own."

Nicolas cocked a brow. "There are books written about the Hughes family tree."

She rubbed her cheek against Maximo without hesitation or fear. "I'm not a Hughes. I'm adopted."

Shock snapped through him harder than any nip from a horse, but he fought to shake it off fast for her sake. From the pained expression on her face, it seemed she hadn't quite made peace with the information. He searched for the right words.

He hated platitudes, so he settled for the truth. "You may not be biologically related to Christian and Sebastian, but you believe me, you are every bit a Hughes."

A smile flickered along one corner of her mouth. "I don't think you mean that as a compliment."

Damn, apparently he hadn't struck the right chord. He spoke English fluently but still missed nuances on occasion. "Sorry, I did not mean to make light of something that's obviously painful for you. How long have you known?"

"I only found out at the beginning of the summer."

Could that be the reason for her distraction lately? He wanted to haul her into his arms, but she was emitting hands-off vibes. "That must have been a shock, learning as an adult."

"That's an understatement."

"How did you find out?"

"Through Dad's treatments." She gripped the wooden stall plank until her fingers went bloodlessly white. "There was some discussion about donating blood to be stored if Christian needed transfusions. I couldn't give because of my insulin injections, but in listening to the discussions about family blood types, I started wondering. It's a lot of techno medical garble, but basically, I realized I couldn't be Christian and Lynette's biological child. I had a private detective look into it. He discovered I was adopted as an infant."

He wasn't sure why she was telling him this here, now, but she needed to talk and he couldn't deny the need to learn more about her. "What about your birth parents?"

"The detective hasn't learned that part yet, and I told him not to dig any further. What if my biological parents don't want to be found? I decided to ask my father—Christian—for any other information."

"What did he have to say?" The Christian Hughes he'd come to know over the years adored his only daughter to the point of indulgence. Surely he would have reassured her with his explanation.

She scrunched her nose. "I chickened out and never asked him. He doesn't even realize I know."

He could see the concern in her eyes for her father. She'd made a mature and thoughtful decision not to worry him. Nicolas squeezed her shoulders in quiet comfort. It wasn't just wishful thinking on his part that he was seeing a new side to this woman. She had a tender heart beneath the more impulsive instincts.

Nicolas stroked her neck with his thumbs. "You don't want to worry him while he's ill."

Last year, she hadn't given a thought to worrying her father, even when he'd been in the early stages of his battle with cancer.

"Actually, until now, I haven't even been able to discuss it with anyone." She squeezed her eyes shut for an instant, her shoulders tensing under his hands. "I was so upset when I found out, I ran out of the detective's office and came straight here to ride out my feelings. It didn't help. I was an even bigger mess. I didn't dare show my face in public, so I skipped the start-of-the-season party and went to the…" Her eyes shifted nervously.

Realization booted him as solidly as a horse's hoof to the chest. "You went to the sauna to steam away the pain and you found me."

And they'd made love in the heated enclosure, the sprawling gym all but abandoned while everyone else attended the party. Seeing her then had been a bigger shock than he'd expected. He'd prepared himself to see her on the field and had been determined to keep his distance. However, running into her when she wore only a towel, perspiration and vulnerable eyes had leveled all his best intentions.

He leaned back against the stall wall, crossing one booted foot over the other. "I wondered what made you cave in so easily after announcing to the entire world, on national television, that you wouldn't sleep with me again even if—" He held up a finger. "Now let's make sure I get this right…. Even if I was hung like the best stallion in the stable."

Unmistakable remorse flitted through her eyes. "Did I actually say that?"

"There are plenty of YouTube videos out there to document it." Damn, he'd been angry—and disappointed. He'd deluded himself into thinking the media frenzy surrounding her had been hype. Just like he was doing this year.

She rested a hand lightly on his arm, her eyes glinting with more of that contrition he wanted to believe was real. "I really am sorry for causing you embarrassment. You didn't deserve that kind of treatment."

While he wasn't sure he completely trusted her yet, he did appreciate the effort she was making now. "Thank you for the apology."

"I apologized last year, too."

"But I believe you mean it now."

Her hand rubbed lightly up and down his arm, just under the rim of his fitted black T-shirt. "You didn't say if you've forgiven me."

"I forgive you," he conceded. It was the truth, after all. Yet if he was telling the truth, more needed to be said. "I'm just not sure yet if I trust your change of attitude to last."

Vanessa's face froze into an expressionless mask—a beautiful, pale mask—until she finally nodded tightly. "Fair enough. Trust takes time. I'm not sure I trust myself to be quite honest about everything I'm thinking either."

He wanted to press her on what those other things might be, but they'd already made progress here. They weren't in bed, but they'd grown closer. She'd talked to him, shared a secret with him she hadn't told anyone else. That touched him as surely as her hand on his flesh.

Dipping his head, he brushed his mouth over hers, nothing deep or passionate. Hell, their mouths were even closed. But the feel of her lips under his, not pulling away, had a special intimacy all its own.

Easing back slowly, she squeezed his arm. "Be patient with me, okay?"

"I can do that."

Vanessa sketched her fingers over his eyebrows. "Would it help soothe the sting if I told you you're hung like the second-largest horse in the stable?"

His laughter burst free. God, he enjoyed the audacious way

she surprised him. "Tomorrow, spend the afternoon with me and we'll see."

Lucky for him, for the past few weeks he'd been working on the perfect plan to have Vanessa all to himself, no concerns about interruptions. He wanted Vanessa Hughes in his bed, even though he was quickly realizing one more time wouldn't be nearly enough.

Hooves thundered with the passing ponies. Vanessa planted her palm on her floppy hat as Nicolas's team approached the end of a short practice match. She'd considered keeping her distance but hiding seemed more conspicuous. Instead, she lounged in an Adirondack chair a few feet away from the small clusters of other observers.

The crack of a mallet connecting, the scent of earth churned under the ponies' hooves all wrapped around her with familiarity. She needed that comfort right now more than ever.

Her pregnancy test had been positive, a diagnosis the doctor confirmed. The physician had immediately recommended a high-risk OB but had assured her that while there were health concerns, she had every reason to believe she would deliver safely.

Provided she adhered to the doctor's monitoring and orders.

Equipped with prenatal vitamins, a rigid meal plan and stacks of reading material, she'd left the office—and run straight into Nicolas at the stables. Okay, so maybe she'd been hoping to run into him by showing up at the most likely place to find him. She'd needed to see him. She just wasn't ready to tell him yet. The news still hadn't settled in her mind. Polo season was almost over. Perhaps it would be best for all if she waited until then to share the news.

So here she was, seeking Nicolas out again. Dreaming of

what could have been if she hadn't screwed up so badly last summer.

Her eyes were drawn to the sleek lines of his body in motion as he swung the mallet, the way he moved as one with his horse. And most of all, she couldn't look away from his intensity. The way he poured himself into the game was mesmerizing. Much like the mesmerizing intensity he poured all over her while making love.

Would she ever feel that beauty again? He'd said he forgave her, but he still didn't trust her. How could she risk being with him when they were still missing such a fundamental element need to make a relationship work?

The sound of footsteps pulled her out of her reverie. She glanced over just as her brother drew up alongside her.

Sebastian dropped into a chair next to her, looking anything but relaxed in his business suit. "How's the practice match going?"

"They're almost through," she answered tightly. She and her brother hadn't spoken in private since the explosion at the sauna. "What brings you out here?"

"Saw you from my office window. Thought I'd stop by."

More like he was checking up on her to make sure his little sister was behaving. "I'm not stalking Nicolas, in case you were wondering. I'm simply showing my support the way Dad would want us to."

"Good, I'm glad to hear you're done with Valera."

"I'm glad you've quit punching out polo players." Well, technically he'd only punched out one. How much angrier would her brother be when he learned about the baby? Apprehension tightened her chest.

Sebastian laced his hands over his stomach. "Still mad at me, are you?"

"You behaved like a beast and you know it, not that you've

apologized. I was embarrassed and hurt by the way you acted in the sauna."

"But you obviously listened." He reached across to squeeze her shoulder. "You've really gotten your act together this summer, Nessa, and you have to know that's been a comfort to our father."

She noticed he still hadn't apologized for overreacting. She had such a short time to come to some kind of resolution with Nicolas before everything hit the fan with her family. The fear constricting her chest shifted to panic.

Vanessa pulled a tight smile. "Don't you have more important things to do than worry about my love life? Go back to work, or take your fiancée out to lunch. Scram."

Sebastian studied her through narrowed eyes before nodding curtly and standing. He started to speak again, then shook his head and walked away. Vanessa blinked back tears, wishing life wasn't so complicated. She looked back at Nicolas just as the practice match ended.

Morning sun beating down on him, Nicolas tugged his helmet off and sweat slicked his dark hair to his head. Her body ached to be near him again, but there was still so much unresolved.

Nicolas had asked her to spend the afternoon with him. Was it wise to spend time alone with him right now, while her feelings were still so raw over finding out about the pregnancy?

With time ticking away, she didn't have a choice. She had to resolve things with Nicolas one way or another before the rest of the world—and her volatile brother—found out about the baby.

Vanessa swung her feet up onto the sofa in the private railway car. Propping her chin on her hand, she stared out the tinted window as the Long Island shore whipped past. She was thrilled and entranced by Nicolas's idea to spend the afternoon together. Apparently he'd gone to a lot of trouble to arrange this in advance. That he would go to so much trouble, think so far ahead about them together, touched her heart. "How did you come up with this idea?"

Nicolas lifted her legs and sat beside her, resting her feet in his lap. "Train travel is more prevalent where I come from."

"Well, I'm totally a fan."

The sheen of polished mahogany wainscoting with a brass chandelier anchored overhead created an old-fashioned, time-away-from-the-world feel she desperately needed right now. The air was thick with the scent of orchids filling a crystal vase. White flowers. A small nod to her color preference that she couldn't help but enjoy. Antique linens covered a small table with a silver tea service at the ready.

And yet she was too nervous to enjoy it all to the full extent.

She looked away from the window, needing to focus on what was right in front of her, leaving everything else behind. The gilded mirror reflected her pale face, although she felt fine, wide awake, in fact, and all too aware of the double just beyond the archway.

Maybe she should focus on the table for two instead, where they'd shared almond chicken salad, cheese and fruit—all perfect treats to tempt her palate without risking sugar overload.

At least she could indulge her ravenous appetite. This probably wasn't the best time to indulge in sex, when her emotions were in such turmoil over the pregnancy. So far he wasn't pushing, simply rubbing her feet and talking.

The railcar rocked ever so slightly, just enough to sooth without overpowering. Exactly what she needed. And wow, he could continue that foot rub forever. "What an amazing idea."

"You inspire me." The words rolled off his tongue with a thicker accent than normal, one of the few indications of emotion from her stark lover.

"What a beautiful thing to say."

He paused his massage, his hands simply holding her feet. "Beautiful?"

"Don't get your testosterone in a twist. You're totally masculine, almost too much so sometimes. Be thankful you have that sexy accent to add a romantic edge to the 'oozing machismo.' I do believe that's the phrase I saw in a recent tabloid piece on you."

"You've been reading up on me, 'Fearless Vanessa'?"

She clamped her hands over her ears. "I hate that headline."

He rested his hands over hers and linked their fingers until she slid into his arms. "Vanessa," he said, his voice caressing her ears as surely as his thumbs stroking her wrists, "it's true. You have an unconquerable spirit."

"Spoiled, you mean," she said with a wince, remembering an old accusation.

He held her eyes with his, so dark, mocha-rich and mysterious. "I'm sorry for not taking the time to get to know you better last year."

"We were kinda busy with other pastimes."

Memories swirled between them—sex in the shower, in the stable, in her car, anytime the mood stirred…and it had stirred so very often. How strange this celibate summer was in contrast.

Slipping her hands from his, she crossed her arms over her stomach as if she could somehow hold on to her secret, on to this understanding between them, longer. "I'm a master at dodging the press when I wish, but even I never knew there were this many places to hide. You've outdone yourself these past couple of months."

"I see your world differently than you do."

"What do you mean?"

His thumb worked along the tender arch of her foot. "You've walked the path so often you see what you expect."

A shiver of awareness sparked from her foot upward. "You know all about my life here, but you never talk about growing up."

"As you said, we were too busy to talk much last summer." His thumbs worked with such seductive precision she began to wonder if the sensual massage was part of some grander plan.

"The way we handled things was a mistake."

"Perhaps." He worked along one toe at a time.

She swallowed hard, her body languid. How could she be so relaxed and turned on all at once? "Talk to me now, about your childhood."

"Pfft," he dismissed her question. "You can read my bio on Wikipedia the same as anyone else can."

"And of course I already have." She refused to be distracted that easily. This was her chance to ask more, to be more. "Wiki doesn't tell me about your paths."

"I'm a fairly uncomplicated man. My family wasn't wealthy, but we weren't hungry. My sisters and I had what we needed. I lucked into a chance to increase the family coffers, and I took it."

He said it all so simply, sparse with his words and emotions. She knew there was more to him, even if he offered few glimpses behind his impassive mask.

Regardless, she refused to let him dismiss his impressive accomplishments. "My father says the harder he works, the luckier he gets."

A rare smile twitched his seductive mouth. "I like the way your father thinks."

"I believe you look at paths and see opportunities."

"If it makes you happy to analyze me, feel free." His hands slid up to her ankles, clearly intent on distracting her.

"Am I an opportunity?"

"Woman, you are a walking, talking, mesmerizing liability, and you damn well know it." His fingers worked along muscles up to her knees, his hands hot and strong and tempting even through her jeans.

She clamped his wrists and stopped his path. "I think I'm insulted."

He held her hands and met her eyes again with intensity and even a hint of anger. "You slapped me in front of a dozen reporters—and your family. Such a huge crowd gathered to gawk, the other game had to be stopped. A senator and a visiting ambassador left—conspicuously, I might add. I don't know about you, but that is most certainly not the professional face I wish to display."

The power of his emotions stirred her own. He might be mad, but she knew he would never hurt her. In fact, he was so gentle with her sometimes she wanted to rattle him and shake free the powerful passion she knew they shared. "You shouldn't have called me a spoiled and immature princess."

"You shouldn't have acted like one."

The immature part had stung most, and still did. But she had to accept that she'd earned that reputation. Repairing the damage and regaining trust was her responsibility.

She was trying to make amends, but time was ticking away so fast for her this summer. She didn't know how much longer she would have with Nicolas. Who knew how he would react when he learned about the baby? Would he consider this yet another reason he couldn't trust her? But could she help it if she wanted to get closer to him, to earn back his trust before news of the baby weighed into his thinking? Either way, she could lose him altogether, and it hurt to think about a lifetime of wanting him.

Right now could be all she—they—had.

Decision made, Vanessa knelt beside him on the sofa, linking her arms around his neck. Before she could lean in to kiss him, Nicolas swept her up with the predatory growl she remembered well.

Months of waiting was about to end.

Four

His waiting had come to an end. Finally, he had Vanessa back in his bed. Or in this case, in the bed in his railcar, once he carried her from the parlor compartment through the archway to the bedroom.

He sensed the difference in her kiss, the subtle suggestive pressure of her mouth. Testing his perception, Nicolas traced her pouty bottom lip with his tongue, and she opened immediately. The taste of melon and cheese, Vanessa and him, mingled in a foreshadowing of the deeper connection they would share soon. But not too soon. He wanted to draw this out for her, ensuring an encore.

Nicolas settled her on the plaid spread piled high with decorative pillows and shams. The mattress dipped with the weight of his knee on the edge as he shifted over her. She must have come to some kind of peace about her adoption because there was no mistaking her intent focus on the moment. On him.

And he intended to work like hell to ensure she wouldn't be so quick to leave.

One button at a time he flicked open her blouse, exposing inch by tempting inch of creamy skin, see-through lace, more skin. After so long without her, he soaked up the sight of her, the curves of her breasts, the dip of her waist. In a double-edged torment he ruthlessly controlled the moment, drawing out her pleasure while sharpening his own to a painful edge.

He'd planned this afternoon on the private railcar to have her totally and completely to himself. No concerns about interruptions. Just Vanessa, with him, for hours on end. For once they didn't have an evening party to attend, so he'd arranged to have a limo pick them up at the train's after-dinner stop.

Meanwhile, he needed to use this time wisely, seductively. He thumbed along her rib cage, the fragile bones and translucent skin familiar under his fingers. Still he couldn't stop staring with appreciation, anticipation.

Her fingers worked down the fastenings on his shirt, mirroring his actions button for button until the cool conditioned air swept over his chest. She flattened her palms inside, branding him with her warm touch as she swept the crisp cotton away.

She raked her nails along his chest, lightly scoring. "This has been the longest two months of my life."

"I would have been happy to accommodate you at any time." He popped open her jeans and slid the zipper down, the rasp echoing the need grinding inside him. A low band of white lace peeked free, and he tucked his head to snap the elastic lightly with his teeth. "Thoughts of you, of this, have been killing me every second."

Nicolas inhaled, the erotic scent of her filling him. Throbbing, he nipped his way up her pale flat stomach, up to her breasts, her dusky nipples visible and taut and pushing against the peek-a-boo swirls of her lace bra. Her underwear was always white in her signature style, but in different patterns and cuts. Last summer he'd almost driven himself crazy watching her throughout the day, wondering what he would find once he undressed her.

Today, he knew. Lacey demi-bra and a thong. He took one hardened peak in his mouth, rolling it gently against his teeth, the dampened fabric a sweet abrasion against his tongue. She tasted like perfection.

Vanessa gasped, her blond hair tousled from his touch, one long strand pooling in the hollow of her throat. "How long does the train ride last? How far will we go?"

"As long—" he shifted his attention to her other breast "—and as far—" he tunneled his hand into the open vee of her jeans "—as you want."

"Don't make promises like that." She cupped his cheek and brought him up to her, face-to-face, her azure eyes stormy, intense. "We both know this ride has to end."

He couldn't miss her implied meaning about their future beyond this simple afternoon on the train. Of course nothing was ever simple with Vanessa, and he was quickly finding that intrigued him. If she wanted more, he would damn well provide.

Nuzzling into her silky hair, he peeled down her jeans while whispering in her ear, "Then we'll return again…and again…and again."

"I'm going to hold you to that promise."

His heartbeat pounded an extra thump in response.

She kicked her jeans off, her legs tangling with his, urging him to his side. She stayed with him until he rested on his back. He cupped her head, taking the kiss deeper, fuller. Her busy fingers roved, explored, disposed of his pants. And then he was in her hand.

His head pushed back into the pillows, his eyes closing as she stroked slowly, deliberately. A hitch in the train's motion provided tantalizing pleasure as they moved subtly against each other. He had to regain control fast or this would be over before they really got started.

Bracketing her waist with his hands, he lifted her as he sat up straighter on the bed. With a deft sweep of his hand, her bra came free, airborne as he tossed it away to land on the floor. She filled his hands, her breasts swelling into his palms with a sweet abundance his memory hadn't done justice. Her head lolled, her lashes sweeping closed.

Yes, he'd been right to find this time away, to dispense with their reservations as surely as their clothes. A quick twist and snap and he'd done away with her lacey thong, the final barrier between them. She straddled him as they sat face-to-face.

He looked his fill. Their time in the sauna had been fast and frenzied. This would be different.

Her silvery blond hair slithered over one shoulder, ends teasing along the tip of her breast. For a moment he noticed that she had the barest of tan lines—and then he could think of nothing but the slick press of her core against the throbbing length of him.

The chandelier swayed overhead with the gentle rocking of the railcar, shifting light and shadows over her skin like phantom fingers stroking her in all the places he ached to explore.

Fingertips to his cheek, she scratched lightly along the stubble he never seemed able to completely shave away. "I'm all for savoring the moment, Nicolas, but if you don't take me soon, the motion of this train is going to finish me."

She rolled her hips against him until the head of his arousal pressed closer. All he had to do was thrust and he would be inside her again. He clamped his jaw hard against the temptation to throw away caution again, and palmed the protection he'd tucked just under the rim of the tea set. Vanessa looked at the condom in his hand and frowned. Yeah, he understood her frustration—they'd come so close to forgetting about birth control altogether.

Frenetic need filled him now as it had that night in the sauna. He'd almost forgotten then, withdrawing just in time. He would do better by her this time. Vanessa stayed silent, chewing on her bottom lip while he sheathed himself.

Her hands on his shoulders, she lowered herself onto him and he clutched her hips as he wrestled with restraint—tough to do, given the soft feel of her flesh around him. Nicolas leaned back against the headboard as she hooked her legs around his waist, her arms around his neck.

Sighing, she teased his chest with her breasts, skimming kisses over his mouth. His tongue stroked in sync with his thrusts until he stopped thinking and just felt her around him. In his senses. It seemed right, given that he couldn't get her out of his thoughts even when they weren't together.

The humming vibration and swaying of the car intensified every movement she made, her sighs and moans of pleasure echoing in the dimly lit cabin. He rolled her onto her back, still intimately connected.

Vanessa's arms clutched him closer, her legs wrapping tighter until her heels dug into him. With each urgent rocking of her hips, she whispered her wants, and damn how he enjoyed the way she made it crystal clear what she needed and how he made her feel. Every sexy word and hitch in her breathing stoked him higher, harder, closer to the edge, but he wasn't going there alone. He thrust and waited, watching for the telltale flush spreading over Vanessa's creamy flesh. She arched and moaned, her fingernails biting into his back.

Finally, finally he could let go. Release jetted through him, intensified by her body gripping him in pulsing waves, drawing out the sensations until— He slumped to rest on his elbows before rolling beside her and gathering her perspiration-slicked body to his.

They must have drifted off because the next thing he knew, the sun was setting outside the window. He dragged the comforter from around their feet and draped it over them.

Stirring, Vanessa snuggled closer with a sigh and mumbled, "How late is it?"

"Almost supper time. The refrigerator is well-stocked. Would you like to take a look and decide what calls to your appetite?"

A sleepy smile dug dimples in her cheeks, still pink from stubble burn. "Surprise me. You've done well with that today."

He skimmed her shoulder with the back of his knuckles. "Spend the night with me. We can stay on the train. I can have the limo pick us up farther down the line."

Her smile faded and she fidgeted with the covers. "My father waits up. I know I'm an adult, but it seems cruel to worry him."

"What about telling him the truth?" The words were out before he thought about them, but once said... The secret meetings had been stimulating, and his conscience hadn't bothered him since they weren't sleeping together. But now? His principles demanded honesty. He would treat her and their relationship with respect. "A simple phone call, and your father will know we are a couple again."

She bolted upright, the comforter clasped to her chest, her hair tousled around her face in sexy disarray. "You're willing to take the scrutiny of dating me, of being connected to the Hughes family and the Bridgehampton Polo Club?"

Nicolas pushed to his feet to give himself distance from the distracting scent of their lovemaking, not because he was uncomfortable with her question, damn it. "People will gossip, but that should be of no concern to us."

He'd hesitated a second too long before answering her. He knew from the retreat in her eyes that she'd sensed his concern about possible bad PR and was upset by his gut reaction. Honor dictated he be upfront about their growing relationship, but that didn't mean he was comfortable with the decision. He had a professional reputation to maintain, something he thought Vanessa would understand better now than she had last year.

And what did she want? The flash of uncertainty in her eyes made him wonder if she wanted more than a last fling to get over each other.

Then she blinked, a smile curving her kissed-full lips. She wriggled to lean against the headboard, the rustle of sheets serenading him with promises.

To hell with food or phone calls. They still had hours left before they returned home.

The mattress gave beneath his knee as he returned to the bed. She opened her mouth and he kissed her before she could speak. Every word they'd spoken seemed to slide between them like layers of clothes, keeping them from the one way they communicated without confusion. Her fingers crawled up his chest and into his hair, urging him to stretch out beside her.

He understood her need to keep the affair private. Hell, he agreed. But he also knew he'd somehow fallen short in assuaging the concern that was evident in her eyes.

The next morning, Vanessa zipped up the side of her tennis skirt and stifled a yawn. She and Nicolas had made love until minutes before the train stopped. They'd tossed on their clothes and rushed to the waiting limo that had driven them home by midnight. She'd actually managed to tiptoe past her father's room with only a groggy "Night, Nessa" drifting out into the hall.

Still, the truth couldn't be avoided any longer. She would have to tell Nicolas about the baby, and soon. Her plan to wait until the end of the season was fatally flawed. She simply couldn't look into Nicolas's eyes while making love and keep such an important secret from him. How could she condemn her parents for concealing the truth, then turn around and do nearly the same thing to Nicolas? She refused to behave like a self-indulgent brat any longer.

Before she told him, she would need to prepare her father for the fallout. She had promised to meet Nicolas for lunch after a tennis game with her brother. She'd been surprised when her brother called to schedule the match. He was usually a workaholic, but he vowed he could step outside the polo club office for a quick game at the Seven Oaks courts.

After their tense summer, she was grateful he'd offered the olive branch. His surprise relationship with his assistant, Julia, seemed to be softening the harsher edge of her intensely ambitious brother.

That was how a relationship should be—two people bringing out the best in each other. While Nicolas challenged her and excited her, did she make him as happy? She tried to shrug aside the memory of the withdrawal in Nicolas's eyes when they'd discussed the possibility of going public. He might not want this kind of scrutiny, but she was certain he would stand by her during the pregnancy. Beyond that, she didn't know.

And her father?

As she slid on her tennis shoes, memories from her childhood streamed through her mind of her dignified mogul daddy waving two horse puppets around and putting on different voices. Her mother may not have been ideal, but her father had showered her with attention and affection. She had a fine parenting role model in him.

Shoelaces tied, she grabbed her racket and headed for the

hall. Her father's door was open wide and she could see he was awake in his sitting room with a breakfast tray. Wearing a paisley robe and matching pajamas, he sat in a wingback chair by the bay window, a cane propped against his knee.

A thousand words and explanations churned through her mind and she struggled for the right way to start the conversation.

She gripped the door frame to steady herself and blurted, "Why didn't you tell me I'm adopted?"

Hell.

That wasn't what she'd meant to say at all.

Except now that it was out there, she couldn't call the words back. She waited with nerves prancing in her stomach.

Christian stilled for just a moment, then placed his fork full of eggs back on the tray by the single rose. He carefully folded his hands under his chin, every movement slow and precise as if buying time to gather his thoughts. "How did you find out?"

Exhaling hard, she strode into the room and sat on the ottoman in front of him as she'd done a thousand times as a child, waiting for him to tell the next story. After a while, she'd started creating puppets for him, stretching her imagination to the limits to come up with whacky characters, delighted to find out how he would incorporate them.

Today, she needed something more than stories. She needed the truth. "Does it really matter how I know?"

"We'd always planned to tell you, but you had such a rough time of it during your teenage years." His eyes broadcast his apology and regret. "I was afraid of losing you altogether. Then your mother died…"

He cleared his throat, twisting his wedding band around his finger.

Understanding crept in even as she wished he'd made a

different choice. She rested her fingers over his bruised hand. "You've had a lot on your plate lately."

"I like to think I would have told you eventually, but I can't lie." He squeezed her fingers. "I honestly don't know."

It was not the answer she'd been hoping for, but at least they were talking openly. "Thank you for being honest about that."

He scrubbed a hand over his mouth. "I'm not a man who easily owns up to being wrong…"

His voice trailed off and he simply stared at her. She realized this was as close as her proud father could come to admitting he and her mother had screwed up. But she deserved to know more. She was no longer a child. And he could have died without ever revealing the truth.

What kind of hell would that have been for her if she'd found out afterward, never able to ask him about it face-to-face? Never been able to see the regret in his eyes that at least gave her some peace?

"Why did you adopt me? I would think after Sebastian, Mom would have realized motherhood wasn't her gig."

"Are you sure you're ready to hear everything?"

Her throat closed with nerves, but she wouldn't shy away— not when it counted. "I have to know."

"All right then," he said with a shaky breath. "One of my employees, a married man, had an affair with his secretary."

"She got pregnant?" She struggled not to press her hand to her stomach. While she couldn't imagine having an affair with a married man, she understood well the weight of secrets and fears for an unborn child. Vanessa pulled her concentration back to her father's words.

"They approached the company lawyer for help in arranging a private adoption for their baby. When your mother heard tests indicated the baby was a girl, she was insistent. We wanted to adopt the child, to adopt you."

"Because I was a girl?" Lynette had wanted a daughter? A bookend set of a son and daughter to round out the perfect family. Bitterness burned her mouth more fiercely than bile.

"She may not have been a warm, cookie-baking sort of mother, but she thought she was giving you everything by giving you what she wanted but never had growing up. I'm sorry she couldn't find it in herself to be a better mother to you and Sebastian."

She wanted to know more, to pry every bit of information out of him to better understand how her mother could have turned out so lacking in warmth or empathy. But the lines of exhaustion around her father's eyes stopped her.

Judging her mother wouldn't accomplish anything, wouldn't change the past. And wasn't she just as guilty in her own way of wounding other people because she hurt inside? She was trying to take steps toward being a better person, but she wasn't in any position to be sanctimonious.

Time to dig in and work if she wanted to be a better person.

A better mother.

She squeezed her father's hand again and started to stand. "Thank you for telling me."

"That's not everything."

Steeling herself for whatever he had to say, she sat again, determined to see this through even if it hurt.

"I went along with the adoption for your mother, but I hadn't counted on the way I would feel the first time I held my daughter." He leaned closer and cradled her face in his shaky hands. "You are my child, and my love for you isn't dependent on sharing the same DNA."

"I know," she said and realized she believed it without question. "Thank you for reminding me, though."

"We have to get everything right, Nessa, in case—"

"Stop." She clasped his wrists as if she could somehow root him in this life. "Please don't say it."

He reclined back in his chair, shaking his head sagely. "Not saying it doesn't make it any less real. Don't get me wrong, I'm thinking optimistically. I'm going to do whatever it takes to hang on. I've always wanted to bounce grandchildren on my knee."

Her breath caught in her throat.

Should she tell him about the baby? Would it be a comfort or a worry? She weighed the options. If he was nearing the end of his life… Vanessa swallowed hard.

She could tell him later, after she told Nicolas. Better to know where he stood before talking to her father. In an ideal world, she and Nicolas would tell him together.

"Daddy, I hope and pray you'll be around to applaud your grandchildren at their graduations, but if—" she gulped back tears that threatened to choke off words "—if that can't be, I promise I'll tell my children all the puppet stories you shared with me. And I'll teach them to stomp the hell out of those divots."

He smiled, big and broad, just the way she remembered from her childhood and in a way she hadn't seen the past year. Laughing, he held out his arms and she slid right into the familiar hug. His frame was surely slighter, but the hold was firm, steady. One she would feel lifting her up for the rest of her life.

She would need all that strength and more to put her heart on the line with Nicolas.

Five

"It was on the line!"

Standing beneath a striped awning outside the Seven Oaks gym, Nicolas heard Vanessa shout good-naturedly at her brother on the lush, green tennis court. The sound of her voice stirred memories of passionate hours spent on the train car together, stirring a need for more.

Sun already baking overhead even though the clock tower only said eleven, he slicked a hand over his hair, still wet from the shower he'd taken after his morning regimen with the team. The Seven Oaks Farm had top-of-the-line workout facilities as well as tennis courts…and, of course, a sauna.

Any more time spent thinking about the sauna and he would have to head to the gym shower again.

Stepping aside and nodding politely as Sheikh Adham left the building, Nicolas kept his eyes firmly locked on Vanessa arching back, tossing the ball in the air and swatting a clean serve. She swiped an arm over her forehead, shifting from foot to foot as she watched for her brother's return hit.

Yes, he could most definitely stand here and take in the view of Vanessa in her short white tennis skirt. All the other people by the pool might as well have faded away.

Vanessa and her brother lobbed and volleyed teasing comments back and forth with each sweep of the yellow ball over the net. There was no mistaking the bond of affection between them. Hughes would be pissed to find out about the secret affair—not that his sister's love life should be any of his business. But Nicolas didn't like the notion that he would cause trouble between the siblings.

In fact, he didn't much like the notion of sneaking around, either. He couldn't deny the growing realization that he wanted more with Vanessa, beyond the polo season, and that meant coming out with their relationship.

Once he had Vanessa alone—he'd arranged a private dinner at a local French restaurant—he would discuss the proper time and manner to reveal their relationship to her family. And to the press. Decision made, he started to leave. Better to let her enjoy her game with her brother. If Hughes caught him watching Vanessa, Nicolas wasn't so sure he could keep his face impassive.

Vanessa stumbled, missing the ball. Nicolas hesitated. She regained her footing and he exhaled. Hard. Damn, he never would have thought a time would come when he would wear his heart on his sleeve. He definitely needed to regain his own footing before he had the discussion with Vanessa.

Pivoting, he started back into the gym.

"Vanessa!"

Hughes's shouted call carried an urgency that made Nicolas freeze in his tracks. He turned, just in time to see Vanessa crumple to the ground unconscious.

Nicolas had considered himself fearless. Until now.

Seeing Vanessa sprawled on the ground, passed out on the court, dumped fear into his gut. To hell with waiting for the right time to reveal his feelings for Vanessa. He didn't care who saw how he felt about her.

Nicolas tossed aside his gym bag and sprinted toward Vanessa.

Vanessa pushed through the foggy layers of unconsciousness.

Had she overslept? Disorientation muddled her mind. She sank deeper into the cushiony surface beneath her. Voices swirled—in her dreams?

"What the hell are you doing here?" her brother demanded.

"Hughes, this is not the time or place," Nicolas answered, his voice worried.

The baby. Their baby. Oh, God.

Vanessa clamped a hand to her stomach and pried her eyes open. She felt fine, other than dizzy, but still, fear swept over her.

She blinked fast and saw Nicolas and Sebastian standing nose to nose a few feet away. A quick look around told her they were in Sebastian's office at the polo club's headquarters—her father's old office. Someone must have carried her to the large leather sofa. How long had she been out?

A cool hand touched her brow, and she found Sebastian's fiancée, Julia, kneeling beside her. Brass sconces illuminated the concern on her future sister-in-law's face.

"Julia?"

"You fainted. Have you checked your levels recently? Where's your meter so we can check now?"

"Fainted?" Because of the baby or low blood sugar? "My meter is in my purse back in the locker room."

Nicolas and Sebastian went silent, then bolted across the room toward her. Nicolas beat him by a step.

"Vanessa?" He stroked back her hair as she struggled to sit up. "Are you all right?"

His own damp hair was slicked back. Wearing black slacks and a gray polo, he must have just completed his morning workout. She should have considered that when agreeing to meet her brother here, but who could have foreseen this?

She touched Nicolas's chest lightly. "I'm fine. Just a little woozy. A quick check of my blood sugar levels and there will be nothing to worry about."

He clasped her hand in his.

Sebastian growled protectively.

Nicolas scowled, his dark Latin eyes turning even darker.

"Gentlemen," Julia said with calm command as she stepped in front of Nicolas, tucking a tapestry pillow behind Vanessa, "why don't you both help by stepping outside. One of you can go look for her purse. The other can see if the paramedics have arrived. Make sure they know about Vanessa's diabetes."

Both men eyed each other warily, then made tracks toward the door.

"Thank you." Vanessa reclined back on the pillow, her head still woozy. "I don't think I could have handled them arguing right now."

"Just lie still. The paramedics are on their way." Julia tucked another pillow under Vanessa's feet. "I can't believe we don't have a doctor playing tennis here this morning."

Vanessa tried to laugh at the joke, but fears for her baby overwhelmed her. "Julia? I need to talk to you. If I pass out again, be sure the paramedics know—"

"About your diabetes. Of course, I will," Julia reassured her.

"Not just that," Vanessa rushed to explain. This wasn't the

way she'd wanted the news to come out, but she didn't have the luxury of waiting. "Don't let them give me any drugs. Nobody knows yet, but, um, I'm pregnant—"

The echo of heavy footsteps stopped her short. Had the paramedics arrived already? She wasn't sure how long she'd been out.

Framed in the doorway stood her brother and Nicolas. The room swirled again, and this time it had nothing to do with blood-sugar levels or pregnancy. The stunned—then thunderous—looks on both men's faces left her with no doubts. They'd heard her revelation. Her secrets were out. Sebastian knew about her relationship with Nicolas.

And Nicolas knew about their baby.

Waiting outside the E.R. exam room, Nicolas struggled to keep his emotions in check.

He was known for his calm under any circumstances. But today had blown that out of the water. He was furious, wrecked, leveled by Vanessa's revelation at the polo club. She was pregnant with his child. And yes, he knew it was his. He could read that in her expression clearly enough when her eyes had met his.

Thank God he'd kept his mouth shut then, because he wasn't sure what would have come out once he learned she'd been lying to him for weeks. Nothing had changed. She was still keeping secrets—and may have endangered his child.

She was still the same immature woman. He'd been a wishful fool to think otherwise, simply because he'd needed to justify climbing back into bed with her.

Nicolas paced, shoes squeaking on industrial tile. He wanted to punch something.

At least Hughes and his fiancée were staying quiet. He and Vanessa's brother seemed to have reached an unspoken understanding that there would be no confrontation right now. Not that Hughes's fiancée would have let them exchange words. The woman was a velvet-gloved, stern taskmaster.

She was right. Vanessa's health was paramount. He was angry, without question, but he would hold himself in check.

And he wasn't leaving Vanessa's side.

At least her baby was okay—even if her relationship with Nicolas appeared uncertain.

Unable to get Nicolas's thunderous expression out of her mind, Vanessa finished dressing in the E.R. exam room. The paramedics had transported her to the hospital, a frightening five-minute ride. Her physician had met her at the hospital and checked her over. The doctor had reassured her that the fainting spell was not related to her diabetes and that everything appeared fine with the baby. Passing out had simply been a byproduct of pregnancy. He'd prescribed a lazy afternoon in bed and given her his pager number if she had any concerns.

She still had plenty of concerns. First of all, she needed to read a whole lot more about becoming a mother, because she did not want to screw this up. And if she was overdoing it, by God, she would make an art form of settling down.

Then there were other concerns, the ones centered on the baby's father. The sterile air stung her nose as she sniffed back tears. Nicolas had come to mean so much to her this summer, even more than she'd expected after a year of thinking about him, of missing him. Seeing that look of betrayal on his face had hurt so much—she wasn't sure how to begin making it right.

Vanessa stepped out of the exam room and found Nicolas right outside the door, leaning against the wall, waiting. Alone.

"Where's Sebastian?" she asked nervously.

"Julia persuaded him to leave once the doctor assured us all was well with you. Your brother put up a fight, but she convinced him that was the very reason he should leave. You need peace, not controversy." He touched her back. "I have arranged for a car to drive us."

She tried to get a read off his face, but her intense lover, the charmer of the past two months, had disappeared. The old Nicolas was back, the man in complete control of his emotions. She sure could use some tenderness. Maybe he was just waiting until they were alone. After all, they still hadn't officially come out about their relationship.

The sun blinded her momentarily, her eyes adjusting as a limo pulled up alongside her.

Nicolas slid his arm around her waist, steadying her, not letting go until she was safely inside. His care touched her ragged nerves as firmly as his hand held her body. He settled her into the backseat then sat across from her.

Across?

So much for warm fuzzies. She wished she could sink into his arms and rest her head on his broad chest while he reassured her he was excited about the baby.

After giving the driver her father's address, Nicolas folded his arms over his chest and watched her with the detached air of a physician observing his patient.

The limo glided out of the parking lot and onto the main road. The drive would be short back to her father's house. Even though every instinct inside her shouted to wait, to talk to him later when they were both calmer, she couldn't stop the words from tumbling out of her mouth.

She resisted the urge to grab him by his collar and shake him. Instead, she folded her hands carefully in her lap and wished she had on something a little more substantial than a tennis skirt. "Aren't you going to ask about the pregnancy? I know you overheard me tell Julia."

His jaw flexed, all his muscles visibly tensed even though he sat stone still. "All the more reason not to discuss this now. You need to rest and take care of yourself."

"Don't you think I understand that?" She pulled in the rising hysteria that grew with every second he stayed in that seat across from her. She needed to hear how he felt, damn it. "I went to my doctor right after I took a home pregnancy test. He's already referred me to a high-risk OB because of my diabetes. I understand the risks and I know how to be careful."

"You're keeping the baby then."

"Yes, I am." Certainty settled within her for the first time. She was her own person, in her own situation. "I want our child regardless of whether or not you're in my life."

"Our child," he said slowly.

She realized that until that moment, she hadn't officially confirmed that the baby was his.

No wonder he'd been distant. She leaned forward and rested a tentative hand on his knee. "Nicolas, this is your baby. I got pregnant that evening when we made love in the sauna."

"But you weren't going to tell me." A tic twitched in the corner of his eye.

Of course he was angry over being kept in the dark—but not necessarily because of the baby. Relief swamped her. "I was waiting until after the season."

"Why would that make any difference?"

His cold voice iced her relief. She pulled her hand back. "I didn't want to upset my father."

"What does that have to do with telling me? I can see waiting until after the season before telling him, but I have a right to know."

She couldn't argue with his logic, since she'd come to the same conclusion herself. "I had changed my mind about waiting and was going to tell you tonight."

"So you say."

Shock and anger rooted her to the seat. "You think I'm lying?"

He shook his head, going silent again.

She smacked the leather seat with her hands. "Talk to me, damn it. You're upsetting me far more by keeping your thoughts to yourself."

"I just think it all sounds convenient. Nothing's changed from last year."

The reminder of his recurring accusations about her immaturity drained the blood from her face. "That's not fair."

He looked out the window.

"Don't you dare clam up on me now!"

"You're being too emotional," he answered in the same low voice he used to calm his horses. "It's not good for you or the baby."

She was not an overworked pony! She was a woman with her heart on the line. "Of course I'm emotional. You're dumping me again."

"Now is not the time," he said, still using that cool voice as the limo pulled up outside her family home. "Perhaps you are right. We should wait to discuss this at the end of the season."

"You don't want your baby?"

His eyes went darker with emotion. "Make no mistake, I will be a part of our child's life."

But he said nothing about her, and she couldn't overlook that omission.

She bolted from the car and sprinted up the steps toward the double doors, brass knobs gleaming, welcoming her into the haven of home.

She'd been a fool all summer long, a fool to think she could make a game of her relationship with Nicolas, that somehow she could minimize the power of her feelings. Throwing him out of her life last year had been painful, but it was nothing compared with the ache twisting her heart now. She loved Nicolas Valera, a man who didn't trust or respect her.

A man who didn't love her back.

Six

He'd screwed up, big-time.

Nicolas shouldered through the scores of spectators gathered for the afternoon game. His team wasn't playing, but he needed to analyze the other ponies in action for future matchups.

Instead, he could only think of finding Vanessa.

She'd ignored his calls the night before and this morning. He wanted to apologize for not supporting her at a time when they should be banding together. God, how he regretted hurting her feelings with his insensitive behavior.

And if she wouldn't accept his apology? Then they at least needed to get on a more civil footing and make plans before the pregnancy became public knowledge. So far not even a whisper had leaked, but they couldn't count on that lasting much longer.

Sweat beaded along his back, the full force of the afternoon sun intact for at least another hour until it dipped below the tree line at the western edge of the field. Weaving around three men setting up a tailgate party on the lush green lawn, he searched—and still no Vanessa.

He wasn't accustomed to losing control. His sisters had a more stereotypical Latin temper, but Nicolas had always prided himself on his cool calm. Until he'd met Vanessa.

The woman tapped into emotions he'd never felt, good and bad. While wrestling with his anger, determined to keep things low-key for both her well-being and their baby's, he'd lost sight of how much she would need his reassurance.

She was carrying his child, a fact that still shook the ground beneath his feet. His brain filled with images of a little girl with Vanessa's face and his hair, tiny feet stamping divots and taking the world by storm.

He felt eyes on him and pivoted…only to find a pair of women in nearly identical sundresses and sandals staring, then waving and giggling. Groupies. He wasn't interested.

Finally, he spotted a familiar face. Down the sidelines, he saw Vanessa's father, Christian Hughes, in a wheelchair. The ailing man had lost at least twenty or thirty pounds since last season, but he still had a commanding gestalt that couldn't be missed. He may have made a concession to his illness with the wheelchair, but there was no sickroom blanket resting over his knees. The older man wore neatly pressed tan slacks with a polo shirt under a linen sports coat and a perfectly folded kerchief peeking out of the pocket.

A plaid driving hat protected his shaved head from the sun. And behind the chair, no nurse. Nicolas slowed his step. Sebastian Hughes stood watch behind his father.

How much had he told his dad about Vanessa and the baby? Time to find out.

Nicolas charged forward. Christian Hughes eyed him impassively, giving nothing away.

"Good afternoon, sir," Nicolas said carefully.

"Valera," Christian nodded, "always nice to see the players out mingling with the crowd. Good for the draw."

Sebastian silently assessed him with cool eyes.

"Actually, Mr. Hughes, I'm looking for Vanessa."

A spark of surprise glinted in the older man's eyes for an instant. Nicolas glanced up at Sebastian, who shook his head. Vanessa's father didn't know. Interesting.

He held on to his hope that he could stand by Vanessa's side when she told Christian Hughes. He wanted to be there for support, and to reassure her father he cared for Vanessa and the baby. He would be there for both of them.

Christian raised a frail but steady hand and gestured left. "She's about five tents down, away from the field. Look for the red-and-white-striped tent with all the children."

He couldn't have heard right. "Pardon me? Where did you say?"

"The red-and-white tent, the child care area. She's arranged activities for children during matches." He smiled proudly. "I believe it's story hour right now. She makes a point of dropping in then."

His perception of her shifted and settled as he heard of the considerate way she'd seen to the needs of others, from the spectators to their restless children. How could he have not known that about her? Now that he thought about it, this certainly fit with the impressions he'd gleaned this summer of added maturity, of a deeper sensitivity for the needs of those around her. She'd certainly been there for her father.

He could picture her with kids. He'd bet anything her impulsiveness and quick laugh—and the mischievous gleam in her blue eyes—would attract children by the dozen.

"Thank you, Mr. Hughes." *For the directions and the additional insight.*

He sidestepped the chair. A lowly spoken "good luck" drifted on the wind from her brother as Nicolas covered grassy ground quickly on his way toward the red-and-white-striped tent. Had he heard that right? Then again, maybe Sebastian wasn't rooting for him as much warning him. No doubt Vanessa was not pleased with him.

Shouldering past a pair of Shetland ponies set up for children to ride, he heard Vanessa's voice above the hubbub of activity. Her warm, inviting tone drew his feet forward even faster.

Then her voice changed. She lowered it as if imitating another person. Stopping at a large metal pole at the back of the tent, Nicolas peered into the shaded depths.

Vanessa came into focus.

Her sunglasses were off, her eyes bright and completely unguarded. A half dozen kids sat cross-legged around her while adults wearing Bridgehampton Polo Club uniforms stood along the periphery. He looked closer, frowning. Yes, Vanessa wore finger puppets.

A smile tugging his mouth, he leaned against the metal pole and listened. She gestured with a fairy princess on her pinky and then introduced the horse on her thumb with a mane made of fuzzy black yarn. She wove tales of a magical polo-pony adventure, featuring "Nessa" and "Nicky." Vanessa was so absorbed in her storytelling, she didn't even notice his arrival. At different points in the tale, she swapped out tiny puppets for other supporting characters hidden away in her huge purse, yet Nessa and Nicky stayed in place throughout. He wasn't so sure he liked being referred to as Nicky, but he appreciated being in her imagination because, God knows, she was featured in his every thought.

But it was more than the puppet tale that tugged him as he stood there. It was the space she'd converted into a child's haven that drove home that a sweet, dedicated and caring woman lived beneath her beautiful exterior.

She'd done more than blow up a few balloons and hire a

clown. The play area had backdrops that had been painted in rainbow colors with the carefree enthusiasm a child might use on an easel drawing. Various stations were set up in the corners—arts and crafts, snacks, even a few cots for tired tots. An inflatable slide hummed with air off to the side. A miniature basketball court awaited a game.

And at the center of it all was a woman he'd misjudged. A woman who guarded herself so carefully he hadn't seen the transformation she'd undergone, which was as vast as the changes she'd made to the red-and-white-striped tent.

His eyes and ears told him what he should have realized long ago. The Vanessa he'd gotten to know this summer was the real woman, a woman he would have understood better last year had he focused on more than getting her naked at every opportunity. He'd almost missed the boat again by failing to come through for her yesterday the way he should have. The truth stared him in the face as clearly as those finger puppets waving through the air.

And today, he intended to make sure Vanessa and the entire Bridgehampton community knew just how much he loved her.

Her heart still aching, Vanessa stood on the sidelines of the polo match, grateful for the sunglasses shading her tear-stained eyes. She forced herself to sample the luncheon buffet set up beside her under a tent, but the catered fare tasted like dust.

After story time with the children, she hadn't been able to hold back her sobs any longer. She'd cried her heart out in a bathroom stall—hurt, mad and downright lost. How could she make her world right again?

Watching the match now was pure torture, and Nicolas wasn't even playing today. How much worse would it be when she had to see him and know she couldn't have him?

Everyone else around her was abuzz with excitement over being at the epicenter of the Hamptons' social scene. The Bridgehampton Polo Club events had become Long Island's playground. The outrageously good-looking players were the main attraction, of course. As a teenager, she'd fantasized about scores of them. Now, her thoughts centered on only one.

The one she couldn't have.

She wanted to find her old spunk and fight for him, but she wasn't even sure where to begin. She couldn't afford to risk upheaval and discord when they needed to communicate peacefully for their baby's sake.

The halftime horn blew, jolting her from her thoughts.

Out of habit, she slid her purse from her shoulder and dug for her shoes. As she swapped out her heels, she found she simply didn't have the urge to stomp anything. She wanted to go back to that stall and cry some more.

This was so unlike her, and yet she couldn't bring herself to blame it on pregnancy hormones. For the first time in her life, she had no idea what to do. She'd always fought for what she wanted, but Nicolas had made it clear he didn't want scenes.

He didn't want *her.*

A hum started in the crowd. Vanessa looked over her shoulder to see what had caused the ruckus. She saw nothing, except a bunch of faces looking past her.

She followed the direction of their gazes. A horse galloped along the sidelines, a sorrel pony with a coat as shiny as a new penny. She knew the horse well, and the man astride Maximo. Confusion knitted her brows together. Nicolas wasn't playing today—it wasn't his match, after all—so why was he here? And why was he riding directly toward her?

Her heart flip-flopped in her chest. He pulled up on the reins, the horse stopping just an arm's reach away from her. An expectant hush settled over the throng gathering tighter and tighter around them. Maximo, unflappable as always, stayed still as stone. Nicolas's face, however, was full of emotion, his impassive look long gone. Heart in her throat, hopefulness fluttered to life inside her.

His shoulders back, head regally high, he winked at her before shifting his attention to the crowd. "Is there a reporter out there anywhere?"

Bodies jostled before no fewer than seven microphones poked through the crowd toward Nicolas.

What was he doing? Nicolas had never courted the media outside his carefully chosen endorsement spots. And heaven knew, he'd never wanted to share the spotlight with her. Hope fluttered faster.

"I have an announcement," Nicolas broadcast, his sexy accent rippling along the light summer breeze. "Last year I made a terrible mistake in letting a special lady slip away, a mistake I do not intend to repeat. I want to make sure the world knows I am in love with Vanessa Hughes. And whether or not she will have me, I want everyone to realize how much I admire this amazing woman."

Her knees turned as soft as the rice pudding she'd served the kids after lunch.

Dreamy sighs echoed through the crowd, but nothing was louder than the pounding of her heart, the gasp in her throat. Because Nicolas was here, in front of all of Bridgehampton, making a wonderfully uncharacteristic scene on her behalf, laying his heart on the line for her.

Flashes went off. Shutters clicked. Whistles and applause stirred the crowd. Happy tears fell unchecked down her cheeks.

He raised his hand for silence before continuing, "I have plenty more I could say about Vanessa, but it is best I save it for her ears only, you understand." He dismounted, his eyes meeting and holding hers for the first time. He extended his hand. "Would you please do me the honor of joining me for a ride?"

If she went with him on the horse, she would be deciding her whole future right now, embracing a lifetime with this passionate man who could hide his true feelings so well. Or… she could simply walk away.

The decision was easy. Hadn't she just experienced a small taste of how much it hurt to be without him? She trusted him. She loved him. They would figure out the rest together.

With a chorus of songbirds singing in crescendo, Vanessa placed her hand in his, happily sealing her fate.

The crowd roared their approval. With a strong but gentle touch, Nicolas lifted her onto Maximo before settling behind her. His arms bracketed her as he held the reins. A light click and Maximo trotted forward. Nicolas's chest offered an amazing place to rest her head, his signature scent swirling around her along with cheers and applause from the throng.

Vanessa caught a quick glimpse of her father and brother. Her dad lifted his hands, clapping. Even Sebastian shot them a thumbs-up. Peace settled inside her as she soaked in the support from her family. Any concerns or aches over the adoption scattered faster than chunks of turfs from under Maximo's hooves.

She tipped her face up to Nicolas, nuzzling his neck as he navigated his way out of the crowd. "I don't know what made you change your mind about us, but you'd better find a place for us to be alone, or I'm going to cause another scandal."

"As long as you're creating that scandal with me, count me in." His brown eyes glinted with amusement, arousal, love.

He swept her sunglasses up onto her head, the bright sun glinting off of the barn roof in the distance. Then she couldn't see at all as her eyes closed for his kiss. Her world narrowed to just the two of them, the taste of him on her lips, the bristle of his cheek against her skin, the sensuous way he dipped his nose toward her hair and inhaled.

Nicolas secured her against his chest with an arm and urged Maximo into a canter toward the pear orchard near the fields. Her heart pounded in time with horse's hooves. They slowed to a stop in the same clearing where they'd tucked away for a clandestine moment during a party. Now, glossy white ribbons and bows were draped from the branches.

"Oh, Nicolas," she gasped. "How did you manage all of this?"

"Bridgehampton Polo Club hires only the best staff."

Her laughter bubbled up and over like champagne freed from the bottle. "Of course. I should have known."

He slid from the horse and raised his hands to help her dismount with reverent tenderness. Then he knelt in front of her. She tugged his arm.

"Really, you don't have to do this. No one is looking now," she grinned.

His face went as solemn as she'd ever seen it.

"You're looking, and that is what matters most to me." He clasped her fingers. "Vanessa, will you do me the honor of becoming my wife?"

In spite of the sincerity and emotion she saw in his eyes, a final doubt lingered. "If you're saying this because of the baby—"

He squeezed her hand lightly to silence her. "I am asking because I love you. You already know how much I want you. But I also love you—the way you stand up for yourself, the way you care for your father, the way your eyes dance as you share finger puppet stories."

"How did you find out about the puppet play?" she asked, incredulous.

He traced her lips, caressing. "Does that matter? All that

matters to me right now is that you give me a lifetime to prove how happy we can be together."

Then her mind zeroed in on the most important part of his declaration. "You love me?"

"Completely. And I intend to make sure you never have to phrase that as a question again." His bold face furrowed with regret over the hurt he'd caused.

How easy it was to forgive him when he'd found such a dramatic way of making amends.

He continued. "I think we bring balance to each other, in addition to the love and passion. Together, we have everything."

The peace in his eyes matched the quiet joy in her heart. Her last reservation was put to rest.

"Yes." She knelt into his arms. "Yes, yes and again yes, I love you and want to be your wife."

Pulling her close, he kissed her firmly, shuddering with unmistakable relief. This unshakable man, her cool, collected lover, had been afraid she would say no? Tears of happiness stung her eyes. She pressed her face to the warmth of his neck, savoring the fact that she would have years to enjoy his embrace endlessly.

He nuzzled her hair. "So how does the story of Nessa and Nicky end? I had to leave before you finished."

Smiling, she looked up at him. "They worked together and won the match, of course."

"Hmmm…" He rested his forehead against hers. "I am sorry I didn't come through for you right away."

"We're here now."

She stayed in his arms and the moment until Maximo pawed the ground impatiently.

Nicolas glanced at his horse. "Thank you for reminding me, my friend." He looked back at Vanessa, a heated gleam in his eyes as he stood. "I have more planned for you today."

"More? But I already have everything I want right in front of me.

"I can think of one more thing that I want."

"What would that be?" She would do her best to deliver.

"I want to see an engagement ring on your finger by sunset. What do you say to a shopping expedition before dinner?"

Certainly filled her heart as surely happy tears filled her eyes. "I say absolutely yes."

He reached for her, his hand steady and sure, his thoughtfully romantic ribbons and bows rustling overhead like a sentimental bridal bower. Anticipation tingling through her, she clasped his hand and settled atop Maximo with him.

Nicolas brushed her ear with a kiss. "Don't you want to know where we're going after we pick out the ring?"

"Surprise me."

And she knew without a doubt this intensely driven, sexy man would always deliver a winner.

* * * * *

HIS ACCIDENTAL
FIANCÉE

Emily McKay

To the fabulous women (and men) of ARWA,
the best RWA chapter in the world.
Y'all are wonderful, supportive and just dang fun.

Emily McKay has been reading romance novels since she was
eleven years old. Her first romance novel came free in a box of
rubbish bags. She has been reading and loving romance novels
ever since. She lives in Texas with her husband, her two kids,
too many pets and a keeper shelf that has taken over most of
her upstairs. Her books have been finalists for RWA's Golden
Heart Award, the Write Touch Readers' Award, the Gayle
Wilson Award of Excellence and RWA's RITA® Awards. She
is an *RT Book Reviews* Career Achievement nominee. To learn
more visit her at www.JauntyQuills. com or at her website, www.
EmilyMcKay.com.

One

Connor Stone looked up from his drink and saw the next woman he was going to take to bed.

He knew it the instant he saw her standing by the bar in Riffs, the jazz bar where he was sipping away his Thursday night. The fact that she was there with a date didn't particularly worry him.

He had met his buddy Tim for drinks. Connor had been watching the gorgeous blonde since she'd arrived ten minutes earlier. Based on the way the guy was acting, they were probably on a bad blind date. He kept glancing at his watch and tugging at his tie.

Though why a guy would try to ditch a woman like her, Connor couldn't guess. Her face had an extravagant beauty that made her impossible to ignore. Her movements had a grace and sensuality to them, as if she moved in rhythm to the quartet playing standards in the corner. Through the constantly moving crowd, he could see her well enough to tell her body was made for sin. Unfortunately, all those lush curves were encased in a demure navy dress. Why would a woman with a body like that shield herself in a layer of protective armor meant to hide her most appealing attributes?

Connor was debating whether to wait for her date to leave before approaching her when Tim nudged him. "If you're thinking about hitting on her, I should warn you, you're going to strike out."

Something about Tim's tone irritated him. Tim was a work friend, and frankly, Connor had always thought Tim got by on family connections rather than hard work.

"Don't tell me you know her."

Tim smiled smugly, then leaned closer to be heard over the music. "Brittney Hannon. Daughter of Senator Jonathon P. Hannon. Just last week, *New York Personality* magazine did a big interview with her. Called her 'The Last Good Girl in America'."

Connor eyed his target. She did have a certain puritanical quality to her. She wore her blond hair long and straight. If Marcia Brady had come to the bar directly from Sunday school, this is what she'd look like.

He'd always had a thing for Marcia Brady.

"You think good girls can't be tempted?"

As he asked the question, Brittney looked up from her nervous date and met Connor's gaze. The awareness between them arced across the room. He felt it like a strong kick to the gut.

"I'll bet you a thousand dollars you can't get her into bed by the end of the summer," Tim said.

Brittney looked down at her drink, clearly disconcerted. Connor smiled. "I'll have her in my bed by the end of the week."

Tim just laughed. "You're going to have to work fast then. From what I've heard, she's a polo fan."

"So?"

"Boy, you really don't follow society news, do you?" Tim looked at him like he was a moron.

"I follow the financial news."

"Well, she'll be in Bridgehampton all summer for the polo season. While you're in town, working." Tim gave him a punch in the arm. "You should get your head out from under that rock and play a little."

Easy for Tim to say. His family was old money. All Tim had to do was sit back and make sure he didn't screw up too badly.

Connor, on the other hand, came from a blue-collar family in Pennsylvania. If he didn't work his ass off, his clients lost millions. And if that happened, his career as a hedge-fund manager would be over. "I gotta work hard so I can play hard," he explained.

But the truth was, he *had* been working too hard lately. It was time to cut loose. And Brittney Hannon was just the woman to do it with. As if on cue, her nervous date tossed down a few bills, gestured toward the door and made a run for it.

The guy was clearly an idiot, but at least he hadn't stiffed Brittney with the bill. But his loss was Connor's gain.

This is going to be too easy.

Being dubbed "The Last Good Girl in America" was killing Brittney Hannon's love life.

She sighed as her date abandoned her at Riffs. If her drink hadn't *just* arrived, she'd leave too. But she figured she'd earned the appletini.

In the two weeks since the profile had run in *New York Personality*, she'd had no fewer than three disastrous dates.

She blamed the article. She'd agreed to the interview as a favor to her college sorority sister, Margot. It was supposed to be an in-depth look at how Brittney was using her Web design background to manage her father's "cyber campaign." Instead, Margot had taken a few quotes from the actual interview and cobbled them together with bits and pieces of private conversations from over the past decade. The resulting "profile" made Brittney out to be a sanctimonious prude who was on the hunt for a husband and who encouraged women to withhold sex in exchange for an engagement ring. There was nothing overtly libelous about the article, but the title had not been meant as a compliment.

And this was exactly why she didn't talk to the press very often. She was too blunt. Too outspoken. Too honest. And it always got her in trouble. Which was why she hadn't confronted Margot after reading the profile. Why risk giving the woman more fuel? She had decided long ago she was better off giving reporters nothing interesting to say about her.

For now, her love life was taking a hit. The best she could figure, most men simply weren't interested in working any harder than they had to. They saw her as a pain, rather than interesting challenge. She was trying to view this as simply a way to weed out the men who scared easily. But it wasn't much consolation. She'd just have to suffer through it. It wouldn't kill her.

The truth was, she was more concerned about how the profile would affect her father's campaign. Zoe, her father's senior aide, had assured her the profile wasn't as bad as she thought. And then politely reminded her to schedule any dealings with the press through the senator's office. Most of the time, Brittney's own views came off as too socially conservative for her father's urban constituents, and she had no talent for tempering her opinions to make them more palatable. In short, she was a total failure as a politician's daughter. As if it wasn't bad enough that the circumstances of her birth had cast suspicions on her father's morals.

She'd grown up knowing that marriage to her showgirl mother had nearly destroyed her father's budding career. That, combined with the fact that she was the very image of her mother, motivated her to stay out of trouble. She certainly didn't want to do any more damage to her father's career. Her mother might not be around anymore to create scandalous headlines, but Brittney certainly didn't want to remind anyone of her. She'd learned long ago, her safest course of action was to smile serenely, pose for the photos and keep her mouth shut.

And then Margot had come along asking for an interview. Brittney hadn't imagined that an innocent profile of her work on her father's campaign could cause any problems. But once again, her honesty had come back to bite her on the ass.

Thank goodness the polo season was just around the corner. The rich, famous and dissolute would descend on the Hamptons. They'd stir up enough gossip to satisfy even the most inquiring of minds. Within a week or two, everyone would forget about the silly profile. Then Brittney could enjoy the rest of the summer at her father's place on Long Pond. The house was secluded enough that she could get plenty of work done during the week, but close enough to Bridgehampton she could enjoy the social scene on the weekends.

In a discreet, quiet fashion.

No more interviews for her. For the rest of the summer, she was going to focus on keeping her nose clean and her mouth shut. Maybe by fall she would find a man brave enough to date her.

Normally, she wasn't much of a drinker, but since her date had abandoned her, she raised her martini, gave a silent toast to the door through which he'd left, and then downed the rest of it.

When she lowered the glass, her gaze met a pair of piercing blue eyes from across the room. The same man she'd seen earlier was still watching her. She tore her gaze away, but then a second later, looked back. Still there.

That piercing gaze of his was just the tip of the iceberg. He had jet-black hair, disheveled in a way that could be bought only from a very expensive hairdresser. His shoulders were broad and encased in Armani. The intensity of his eyes was balanced out by a rakish smile, full of charm and humor. Dimples slashed his cheeks, making it almost impossible to resist returning his smile. The overall combination resulted in a 'berg big enough to sink the most titanic of female hearts.

Everything about the man exuded sensual promise. The scary thing was, just once she wished she were the kind of woman who would take him up on it.

But no, she was Brittney Hannon, daughter of a prominent senator. Stalwart defender and representative of middle America's values. She truly was the last good girl in America. Unfortunately.

She set down her empty glass and picked up her clutch, ready to leave. When she looked up, he was there, standing beside the chair across from her.

"Mind if I join you?"

She should tell him that she did mind. Or better yet, that she was just leaving. She *knew* that. Instead, she nodded, allowing her purse to slip through her fingers and land back in her lap.

He gestured to a passing waitress to bring her another drink. "A woman as beautiful as you shouldn't be sitting in a bar alone."

Somehow, she'd expected better from him. "Do pickup lines that cheesy ever work for you?"

He smiled ruefully. "Only when I really mean them."

She wanted to resist but couldn't help smiling back. "Nice save."

The waitress brought her drink over. Brittney blinked in surprise at the bright green concoction. "I had to wait twenty minutes for my first drink to get here." She took a sip. "Do you have a name?"

She looked up at him. The heat from the intensity of his blue gaze burned through her, hotter than the warmth from the vodka in her drink.

The connection she felt almost made her sorry she'd looked into his eyes. It wasn't just that he was handsome and charming—she encountered handsome, charming men every day. No, there was something else about him. When he looked at her, she felt enticing. As if she were the only woman in the room. As if she were a sex goddess. And for a second there, she'd wanted to be that person for him. She wanted to be sexy and alluring.

"Connor Stone," he said.

She blinked. She'd nearly forgotten the question she'd asked. He was watching her, waiting for her to tell him her name. For a second she hesitated. Normally, she was proud of who she was, proud of being good. So what was it about this man that made her want to forget all of that, just for one night?

She took another generous sip of her drink. "I'm Brittney."

He raised his eyebrows. "Just Brittney?"

"Just Brittney."

He leveled that shrewd, assessing gaze at her, and she could have sworn he saw right through her. To the lies she was telling herself even now.

"Like Britney Spears," he supplied.

And just like that, who she really was came crashing back.

"No," she shook her head. "Not like Spears. More like the spaniel."

He chuckled at her self-deprecating analogy. The sound was low and sexy. It made her want to keep saying funny things so she could hear it again, but she was all out of witty repartee.

Her sorority sisters—Margot included—had come up with that assessment of her personality. Brittney…not like Spears, like the spaniel. Steadfast. Loyal. Dependable. And even if she wanted to be more like Spears for one night—reckless, careless and fun—she wasn't that person.

She set down the appletini and leaned forward. "I have to be honest. I'm not really this kind of woman."

"What kind of woman?"

"The kind who lets a stranger pick her up in a bar for a one-night stand."

He smiled a knowing smile. "I didn't really think you were."

"So I should go. Give you a chance to try with someone else." She nodded toward the room in general, where there were countless other women who'd cheerfully fill her empty chair.

Now he leaned forward. His gaze shifted from amused to something more intense. "Then I should be honest, too. That guy that you think I am—the one who'll hit on one woman, strike out and then mindlessly move on to the next—I'm not that kind of guy."

Surprised, she asked, "Then what kind of guy are you?"

"I'm the kind of guy who gets what I want."

Her throat tightened even as warmth spread through her limbs. It was an odd combination of dread and excitement. To cover her discomfort, she stood up. "Well, then, Connor Stone, you should prepare yourself to be disappointed."

He stood as well, extending his hand. "And you should

prepare yourself to be surprised, Ms. Brittney. Like the spaniel."

His tone conveyed gentle teasing as well as a subtle warning. The part of her that clung desperately to her good-girl core screamed out a warning to flee through the nightclub door. But the tiny sliver of her that yearned to be less like the spaniel urged her to shake his hand.

The tiny sliver won out. After all, it had good manners on its side.

She slid her hand into his, ready to give it a brief shake. But his palm was warm, his touch strong yet gentle. Once again she met his gaze and had the curious sensation of pitching forward. As if she were falling into the vast rift between the two parts of her personality.

In that instant, she knew that Connor Stone, despite his charming veneer, was a very dangerous man.

She should have run when she still had the chance.

Holding Brittney's hand, Connor felt the full force of her allure like a punch to the solar plexus. Damn. She was not just beautiful. She was knock-him-over, sexy-as-hell beautiful.

And for an instant, he wondered if she even knew it.

That look of hers was half come-hither, half pure innocence. It stirred images of tousled sheets and lazy afternoons in bed. He knew in that instant that he didn't just want to sleep with her, he wanted to pursue her. To lavish her body with sensual pleasure. To seduce her very spirit. There was something magical about her. She was the kind of woman men went to war for and wrote sonnets about.

Then he blinked and forced the moment to pass. She was just a woman. More beautiful than most, even in a city like New York, which had more than its fair share of beautiful women. But there was nothing magical, nothing sonnet-worthy. Where had *that* come from?

Feeling slightly off-kilter, he released her hand. He glanced at the dance floor, wanting to ask her to dance, but when he looked back, she was gone, retreating through the door. She'd ditched him. She'd warned him, of course, but still, it was something that rarely happened to him.

This was not how he'd imagine tonight's seduction going.

He wasn't a long-term relationship kind of guy. He drifted in and out of affairs, all with women whose expectations were as low as his. He liked an eager bedmate as much as the next guy, but work was what was important to him. Which meant he should probably be glad that Brittney Hannon had disappeared from his life as quickly as she'd appeared in it. He had neither the time nor energy for sex with a complicated woman.

Walking away now without giving her a second thought was definitely the smart move.

"Told you she'd shoot you down."

"Don't worry," he surprised himself by saying. "I'll find her again."

"Boy, you're not giving up, are you?"

"She's the daughter of a senator," Connor mused aloud. "And you said something about her going to the Hamptons for polo. How hard can she be to track down?"

"Dude, this isn't going to end with a restraining order and me being interviewed by Nancy Grace, is it?" Tim raised his hands in a gesture of innocence as Connor glared at him. "Just checking. If you're going to stalk her, I want to know in advance."

"I've never had to stalk a woman in my life." He'd meant it as a joke, but the determination in his voice surprised him.

Tim gave him an odd look. "I've never seen you like this before."

And that was precisely the problem. If he never slept with

her, Brittney would slowly become more than just a woman he'd met in a bar one night. She'd attain mythical status in his life. The woman who got away. The woman he might have written sonnets for, if he'd had the chance.

And damn it, he was not a sonnet-writing kind of guy.

No, the only solution was to find her, arrange to run into her and seduce her. Once he slept with her, he'd lose interest.

The last good girl in America was going down.

Two

What is he doing here?

Brittney could only see his profile, but she recognized Connor instantly. The VIP tent at the Clearwater Media Cup tournament was absolutely the last place she'd expected to see him. Not that she'd actually expected to see him again. Yes, two nights ago, he'd tried to pick her up in a bar. He'd even hinted that he'd surprise her with his tenacity. But surely this was just some weird fluke.

Still, it was him. That slash of ragged bangs hanging almost in his eyes was unmistakable, as were his height and commanding presence. And if he turned just ninety degrees, they'd be staring right at each other.

Coming face-to-face with Connor Stone was the last thing she wanted right now, when she was struggling to make small talk with Cynthia Rotham, one of her father's most severe critics. Pretending to fuss with her hair, Brittney shifted so her back was to him.

"Who is it?" Cynthia asked bluntly.

"What?" Brittney asked stupidly. When all else failed, feign ignorance. Not that she really believed the tactic would work. Congresswoman Rotham had made a career of feeding off of others' mistakes. The woman's vulture-like skills of observation made Brittney nervous. Brittney just knew the older woman was waiting for her to inadvertently say something stupid or offensive. Of course, the only thing worse than putting her foot in her mouth would be to say something personal that Rotham could one day use against her.

Cynthia leveled a steely gaze at her. "You spotted someone from across the tent and went white as a ghost. And now you're trying to avoid looking at him." Cynthia peered beyond Brittney's shoulder as if trying to get Connor in her sights.

"It's no one. Just someone I ran into the other night."

"Point him out. Maybe I know him."

Ha! Like she'd point Connor out to Cynthia, world-class gossip and judgmental old biddy. "I doubt that."

Brittney didn't mean to look. Really, she didn't. But just then, he laughed that throaty laugh of his. The sound of it drifted over the chatter of the crowd as if meant just for her ears. Her gaze sought him just as he raised his hand to rake his bangs off his forehead.

Beside her, Cynthia gave a sound of barely repressed glee. "Oh, my."

Brittney feigned nonchalance. "What?"

"The man who has you so disconcerted is Connor Stone. He's a hedge-fund manager." She paused, then added, grudgingly, "One of the good ones. Very reputable. Very wealthy. But I'm afraid, my dear—" Cynthia put a hand on Brittney's arm "—that he has a terrible reputation as a ladies' man."

Brittney found herself gritting her teeth so firmly she had to pry her jaws apart to speak. Returning Cynthia's false smile, she said, "You don't need to worry about me. I barely know him."

Cynthia arched a disdainful brow. "Is that so? Because I've never seen him here before. You don't suppose you made enough of an impression that he followed you here, do you?"

Yes, she wanted to say, *the other night he flirted with me so outrageously, I wanted to rip my clothes off right there in the bar.*

That would shut Rotham up. For a full ten seconds, maybe.

"Absolutely not," Brittney assured Cynthia.

"Good. Because he has a reputation for not giving up until he gets what he wants. You better hope he doesn't want you."

Cynthia looked ready to salivate at the prospect. Vulture that she was, she'd no doubt love to see Brittney's heart devoured by a world-class playboy.

Brittney wanted to tell Rotham to mind her own damn business, but that was not the way for Brittney to keep her nose clean this summer.

So instead, Brittney pretended to be thankful for the advice. "I'm sure he hasn't given me a second thought," she said with what she hoped sounded like blithe confidence.

"You'd better hope so, because he's a bit out of your league."

Brittney ignored the insult. "Now if you'll excuse me, I'm going to find a seat and watch the match. After all, though most people come here to socialize, I actually enjoy the sport."

Cynthia eyed her with anticipation. "Just be sure that's all you're enjoying."

Connor spotted Brittney just as she was leaving the VIP tent for the bleachers. The sight of her straight blond hair sent a shot of adrenaline directly to his blood. Only a few days had passed since they'd met, but he'd already spent a significant amount of time and energy researching her.

Logically he couldn't possibly expect to get as much out of the relationship as he was putting into it. In simple terms, there would not be a solid return on his investment. But it wasn't about that.

It wasn't even about the stupid bet. Though he'd used that excuse with Tim, who'd gotten him the exclusive invitation to the VIP tent. Tim was so damn convinced Connor was going to strike out that he'd actually offered to help Connor run into her again. Thanks to Tim's persistence, Connor couldn't back off even if he wanted to.

Sometimes it wasn't about the catch, it was about the chase, as his grandfather used say that. His grandfather had been a recreational fisherman—up at dawn, he'd spend hours at the lake. It was a sport Connor had never understood. All that time and energy wasted on a fish you didn't even eat. But then Connor realized his grandfather never talked about the fish he caught. But he told countless stories about the ones that got away.

If Connor let Brittney go now, he'd be admitting failure to Tim. But he'd also always wonder if he'd backed off because he thought she wasn't worth the effort—or because he was afraid she was.

He excused himself from a conversation he was having with a client. The man, the heir to a chain of drugstores, looked surprised.

"Where are you going?"

"Isn't the match about to start?" Connor asked evasively.

The client chuckled as he jostled the ice in his bourbon. "Don't tell me you actually came here to watch the matches."

Connor just smiled. "Actually, I came here to do a little fishing."

He didn't stay to see it, but he could picture the man's expression. He left the bustle of the tent and searched the crowd outside for the sight of her already-familiar blond hair. He found her immediately, even though she'd donned a wide-brimmed straw hat draped with a pale green scarf. Amid the bright and often gaudy fashion of the flashier dressers, Brittney looked elegant and delicate.

She'd jockeyed for a seat high in the bleachers and had her binoculars already out even though the ponies hadn't yet taken the field. There were several seats open around her, since most people were still in the tents.

"Mind if I sit here?" He didn't wait for a reply before taking the seat.

Her gaze jerked away from the field, her expression registering surprise as she whipped off her sunglasses to stare up at him. She opened her mouth to speak, but then snapped it shut and shoved her glasses back on.

"Not at all." She returned her attention to the field, even though the match hadn't started yet. "It's open seating. You can sit where you want."

Her tone was as cool as if she were talking to a total stranger. Which, of course, she was. The sexual tension between them was off the charts, but they still didn't know each other.

He shifted on the hard bench. Despite the fact that some of the wealthiest people in the country attended these events, the facilities were an odd mix of extravagant elegance and rugged utilitarianism. A reminder that the season was supposed to be about the sport, not just the drinks and the fashion.

"You dashed out of the tent before I had a chance to say hello."

"I like to get a good seat," she said without turning her

attention from the field where the grooms were warming up the ponies for the first chukker.

"You left quickly the other night, too. You're good at making quick exits."

Finally she looked at him. "If you're implying I'm afraid of you, you'd be wrong."

"That's good. I certainly don't want to engender fear. If you were afraid of me, I'd feel obliged to leave you alone."

She pressed her lips together in a frown, as if wishing she could back out of the conversation. He wondered if she would fake nonchalance. Finally, she seemed to decide honesty was the best policy. "I have been warned about you, you know."

"So, you were curious enough to find out who I was."

For a long moment she sat there saying nothing, the pink creeping into her cheeks the only indication she'd even heard him. "Not at all. An acquaintance pointed you out just a few minutes ago. She said you were a notorious playboy. It's not like I was asking about you."

"You're lying."

She looked at him now. Through the darkened lenses of her sunglasses, he could almost see her eyes. But not well enough to judge if she were telling the truth—or merely wished she were. "Her opinions of you were unsolicited."

He smiled. "There's no shame in doing your research. I looked you up."

"How did you know—"

"Who you were? Turns out you're fairly recognizable. Brittney Hannon, Last Good Girl in America."

Her mouth snapped shut. He could nearly hear her teeth grinding down.

"I take it you didn't like that profile."

"If we had a week, I couldn't tell you all the things wrong with that glib assessment of my personality. How would you like to be summed up in a single catchy phrase for all of America?"

"A single phrase like 'notorious playboy'? At least they gave you six words. You only gave me two."

"Those were her words, not mine," she protested.

Still, he got the reaction he was hoping for: a wry smile and a voice filled with chagrin. "I'm sure you're more than just a workaholic playboy."

"I got workaholic, too?"

"It doesn't change anything." There was a glimmer of what might have been regret in her gaze. "You and I, we don't match."

He nearly chuckled at her straightforward honesty. It was hard not to admire that. "I think we'd match quite nicely."

He drew out the words, giving her imagination time to kick in—just as his had. She'd crossed her legs away from him when he'd first sat down, which had made her dress inch up, revealing a tempting stretch of thigh. Now, she shifted in her seat, obviously aware he was looking at her. The lovely pink of her cheeks deepened. "That's not what I meant."

"Of course."

"But it proves my point perfectly. You're all sexual innuendo and I'm…not. With me, what you see is what you get."

"That doesn't mean we can't be together."

"You're right. That doesn't. But there are plenty of other things that do. If you'd really done your research, you'd know that."

"Oh, I did my research."

"Did you actually read the profile?"

"That's where I started."

She uncrossed her legs, shifting toward him in her seat. "Then you know—"

"No one's that good. Besides, I was there the other night." That tempting stretch of thigh was even closer. He leaned forward, bracing his forearms on his knees, bringing his hands mere inches from her skin. No one observing them would notice—they'd just look like two people having an intense conversation. "You can't deny you're attracted to me."

"I'm not trying to," she said.

Her gaze was as direct as her words. With her, there were no attempts at deception.

He brushed his knuckle across the skin of her outer leg, just above her knee. A tiny, subtle gesture. He expected her to move away from his touch. When she didn't, a jolt of pleasure coursed through him. She hadn't taken the bait, but she wasn't swimming in the other direction either.

"I tempt you." He let his knuckle circle over her skin in a slow, lazy motion. "For all your talk about abstinence, you nearly let a stranger pick you up in a bar the other night."

He was surprised that she met his gaze head on. Her eyes were wide, her pupils dilated. Her breath was coming in slow draws that were too even to be anything other than forced. He was getting to her. But she wasn't letting herself be intimidated by his overt pursuit. Damn, but he liked her.

After a moment, her gaze hardened. "You really want to debate abstinence with the last good girl in America?"

He nearly chuckled. "I can think of things I'd rather do with you. But I'll settle for talking."

"Talking is all you're going to get."

"I'll take my chances, because whatever you claim to believe about chastity, you wish you could give in."

"But I won't. That's the point." She jolted to her feet, shoving her binoculars into her oversized bag. "Come on, then."

He stood. "Where are we going?"

"Away from here." She scanned their surroundings. "This is the opening match of the Clearwater Tournament. There are more celebrities here than on Broadway, which means it's the most photographed, talked about, gossiped about event of the season. I'm not going to sit here in plain sight of five hundred cameras and microphones and debate my morals with you."

"So we're going somewhere more private? You have a hell of a way of turning a man down."

Brittney led Connor down the bleacher steps, through the throng of people to the very edge of the field, where the crowd tapered off to a mere trickle. Gradually, the rows and rows of horse trailers gave way to open pasture divided by split-rail fences. Nestled against the tree line sat the massive barn dating back to Seven Oaks's midcentury days as a dairy farm. The odd groom wandered past, but they were far enough from the crowds that they were essentially alone.

They walked toward the old dairy barn, with its gambrel roof and icon silo towering behind it. Whenever they were within earshot of others, she narrated their progress with the history of Seven Oaks Farms and of the Clearwater Media Tournament. On the few occasions when someone stopped to greet her, she made a point of introducing Connor and explaining his recent interest in the sport. Anyone who overheard their conversation would probably pity Connor. But he showed no signs of boredom.

Her heart pounded in her chest, issuing a frantic warning: *Turn back now! This is a mistake!*

Nevertheless, she kept her hands firmly clasped in front of her, speaking partly to calm her fears and partly to dissuade him. "The thing about you, Connor, is you think you're going to get my attention by being shocking, but the truth is I've met men like you before."

"I doubt that."

"I know your type," she told him as they walked. "You've decided I'm a challenge. A prize to be won. You probably have some fishing or hunting metaphor you're using." She slanted a look at him from under her lashes, trying to gauge how close she was to hitting the mark, but he kept his expression carefully blank. A sure sign she was right. Dang it.

She didn't *want* to be right about this. Some tiny—stupid—part of her wanted him to deny it. When he didn't, she continued. "But I'm not worried. You'll lose interest as soon as you realize I'm not going to be easy to bag. Or whatever metaphor is suitable."

He stopped walking, forcing her to stop as well. She turned back to face him, only to find him studying her with that disconcerting intensity. His gaze felt heavy with appreciation. But unlike most men who gave her body heated glances, he was looking into her eyes. As if it were her thoughts that interested him, not her curves.

"I think," he stated baldly, "that you underestimate my endurance and my creativity."

And there it was again. That innuendo that sent tendrils of heat pulsing through her body. The man was too tempting by a mile. She could only pray that she *wasn't* underestimating him. If he was half as creative as he claimed, she was in serious trouble. Who was she kidding? She'd *been* in serious trouble from the moment they'd met.

Which was why she had to nip this in the bud. He made her want to give in to temptation. And that simply wasn't something she could afford to do. If her assessment of his motives was dead on—and she'd bet it was—then she was nothing more than a challenge to him. Something to accomplish. She wasn't willing to bargain away her morals for that, no matter how pleasurable the experience might be.

Intellectually, she knew that. It was her body she was having trouble convincing.

Which was why she couldn't risk having him pursue her for very long. What if her hormones overran her otherwise very logical mind? This had to stop. Unfortunately, the only way she could think of to deter him was with brutal honesty.

"Maybe I have underestimated you," she began, "but you have definitely underestimated me. My ideas about abstinence aren't something I came up with on a whim. I'm not a virginal teenage girl who's made a well-meaning but misguided pledge. I'm an adult woman. I know what I'm talking about."

His hands were tucked in his pockets. The heated look he gave her seemed to see into her very soul. In that instant, she could have sworn he could read her mind.

"And what exactly are your views about sex?"

She narrowed her gaze at him. "You said you read the article."

"Maybe I want to hear them straight from you."

"Or maybe you just want to hear me talk about sex."

His lips twitched. "Can you blame me?"

She sighed, trying not to let her exasperation get the better of her. Unless she got this out on the table, he'd never believe she really meant it. Maybe she'd even forget that she really meant it.

They'd wandered far enough from the field that they were truly alone. She had orchestrated this very situation, getting him alone so that she could be blunt without being overheard.

Plus, she figured there was a good chance her honesty would be a turnoff for him. That was certainly the case with the last man she'd dated seriously. Phillip Gould, a young congressman from Virginia—who'd been her father's protégé, in addition to being her boyfriend. Their relationship had ended badly. She wouldn't tolerate his cheating and—it turned out—he couldn't tolerate hardly anything about her. It seemed their mutual desire to impress her father had been all that they had in common.

During their last big fight, Philip had called her tedious

and a bore. Dull. Of course those men she'd dated since that blasted profile had found her opinions equally tedious. Maybe Connor would agree. Which would be a good thing. Right?

Yet now that it came down to it, she found herself reluctant to speak her views aloud. Which was odd because she'd never felt that way in the past. Or maybe she'd simply never before been in the position of talking about sex with someone to whom she was attracted.

"It's simple." Her words came in fits and starts. "I think women today sell themselves short. Real relationships take work, and a commitment from both the man and the woman. One-night stands are easy. But they're less enjoyable."

"I think that depends on who you have the one-night stand with."

"Well, sure, if you're a man," she countered. "A man can enjoy sex with anyone. It's more complicated for a woman."

"That's an oversimplification."

She shook her head. "I don't think so." Her words came more quickly as she warmed to her subject. "For a man, pleasure is straightforward. Orgasms are easy. It's not like that for a woman. Unless you're both emotionally involved, it's too easy for a man to take his pleasure and ignore a woman's needs. One-night stands aren't fulfilling, emotionally or physically."

"And you're speaking from experience?"

"I'm right," she said finally. "I know I'm right."

"How could you possibly know you're right when your theories have never been tested?"

"I'm not a complete innocent. I do have experience with men."

"So I suppose there are legions of men who weren't able to satisfy you."

She tried to glare at him despite her amusement. "You make me sound like a tramp on a warpath to punish men because they couldn't make me climax. Sex is more complicated than that."

"Was it legions or wasn't it?" he prodded, his tone gently teasing. "You can't be experienced and innocent. You can't have it both ways."

In that moment, under the heat of his steady gaze, she remembered a crucial detail. This wasn't a philosophical discussion. It wasn't a discussion at all. It was a seduction. And she was no longer holding her own against him.

"I have experience," she insisted. "Enough to know that I'm right."

"Okay, then," he agreed way too easily. "I'm sure you're right." Connor paused strategically, slanting her a look. "Just out of curiosity, who were these men?"

She scoffed, but trepidation was creeping behind her bravado. "You know I'm not going to answer that."

"Why not? It's only fair. You're shooting me down without giving me a chance because of some mysterious men in your past whom you found disappointing. If I'm going to be judged based on their bad performances, I should at least know who they are."

"Don't be ridiculous." She had such trouble reading him: was he just an arrogant jerk trying to get into her pants or was he just teasing her? She couldn't tell.

They'd reached the line of trees that ran along the edge of the property from the dairy barn to the main house. The soft whispering of the breeze through the willows and oaks almost drowned out the faint murmur of the crowd in the distance. A few more steps and the barn would block their view of the polo field.

Her heart rate picked up, and she wasn't sure if it was from the urge to run or the desire twirling through her belly.

She was about to flee toward the field when he snagged her hand and pulled her to a stop.

"Come on, I should know their names, these guys who are so bad in bed they've ruined you for other men."

"I never said—"

"What if one of them is dating my sister?"

She gave her hand a light tug, but he didn't release it. His palm felt warm against hers, and she didn't have the heart to wrest it from his. She smiled, bemused by her own reaction and by him. "Do you even have a sister?"

"Not the point." As he spoke, he started walking toward the barn, her hand neatly tucked in his. "It could be someone I know. Unless you give me some names, I won't know whom to trust. What if it's my best friend?"

This time she laughed out loud. "I seriously doubt that you're best friends with my prom date."

He stopped in his tracks. "Your prom date?" His face registered exaggerated surprise. "We're talking about your prom date here? We've gone from legions of men who've disappointed you in bed to a single, overeager teenage boy?"

From another man, the teasing might have offended her, but he did it in such a gentle way, she found herself laughing at her own foibles. "I never said legions. That was your word."

"But he was a teenager. You're assuming you know how I'm going to be in bed based on the experience of one boy?"

"It wasn't just *one* boy."

"I can't help but notice you emphasized 'one' in that sentence, not 'boy.' Which means we're still talking about boys here."

She felt the trap he'd been setting begin to close around her, finally giving her the strength to tug her hand free and walk away from him. "So?" she asked.

"Back when you were a kid, you had a couple of tumbles with teenagers and they couldn't satisfy you. So you developed this harebrained theory of yours."

"It's not a harebrained theory." *Is it?*

"It's not a statistically valid one."

She turned to face him. She didn't want to mention Phillip, who had not been a teenage boy at all but a full-grown man. In that case, she hadn't been the only one dissatisfied, so it hardly seemed part of the argument.

"What's your point?"

"My point is, you're not being fair." Before she could protest, he continued. "You're not being logical either. You've based all your assumptions about one-night stands on your experience with teenage boys."

"So?" she prodded again.

He chuckled gently. With two quick steps he had her backed up against the wall of the barn. He braced a hand by her shoulder and leaned toward her. In the dappled light streaming down through the trees, his expression was hungry. Predatory, but not cruel.

"Teenage boys," he said, "have no self-control and very little experience. Which means they don't know what they're doing."

His words left no doubt. He would know what he was doing. With Connor, there would be no awkward fumbling. No mumbled apologies. There would be only pleasure. Her whole body shuddered, and she had to bite down on her lip to hide it.

"If you really want to be fair, you have to test your theories. Not with a boy. With a man."

Her gaze met his. She knew what was going through his mind as clearly as if his imagination was projecting onto a movie screen behind him. He was picturing them in bed together. His body moving over hers. Into hers.

She sucked in a deep breath. "So what do you suggest? That I sleep with you, just so you can prove your point?" She tried to scoff, but her words came out too high-pitched.

He studied her face carefully. She had the impression he was trying to decide if she was the kind of woman who would back down from a challenge. "You can walk away from me right now. Maybe I'll even just let you go. Or maybe you're right and I'll get bored and stop pursuing you eventually. But the truth is, if that does happen, then all you'll have gained is the knowledge that you were more stubborn. Not that you were right."

"You're still suggesting I sleep with you just so you can prove your point."

He ran his hand up her arm. "No, I'm suggesting you just give me a chance. A single kiss. That's all I'm asking." He moved his thumb from the top of her arm to the underside, tracing a circle along the tender skin there. "You stop me whenever you want. If I'm wrong, you'll be completely unaffected by our kiss."

Her gaze skittered back to his. Her chest was rising and falling in short staccato bursts. Had he noticed? Did he know how aroused she was when he'd barely even touched her? "And if you're right?"

"All I'm asking is that you give me a try. One kiss. What harm can I do with just one kiss?"

She tilted her head to the side, considering her options. "Why is one kiss so important to you?"

"Why are you working so hard to avoid giving me one? What are you afraid will happen if you give in?"

She couldn't afford to be honest with him. *I'm afraid I'll lose control completely. I'm afraid I'll have no restraint.*

"Just one kiss?" she asked.

"I'll stop the moment you ask me to," he said evasively.

"Do you promise?"

"Absolutely."

Three

Connor knew he could afford to promise, because he knew she wouldn't ask him to stop.

He considered her for a moment. Between her wide-brimmed hat and oversized sunglasses, she had more body armor than a warrior about to go into battle. Without even touching her skin, he gave the end of her scarf a long, slow tug. When the knot released, he gently removed her hat. Of course, then he was stuck holding the ridiculous thing. Luckily, a tree branch hung nearby and he dangled it from the end. As for her glasses, he raised them to the top of her head.

When he looked at her again, he smiled. Her cheeks were flushed, her chest rising and failing rapidly. She was in expert hands now and she knew it.

He stood perfectly still, one hand on her arm, the other on the wall beside her, waiting for her to give the go-ahead before pulling her into his arms. She moved before he had a chance to, rising on her toes and pressing her chest against his. He barely noticed her bag dropping to the ground. Her hands burrowed into his hair, angling his head to meet her lips.

Everything about the kiss surprised him, from the way she took full command to the scorching heat of her mouth.

After all her talk of propriety and abstinence, he expected timidity. He thought that he'd have to be the aggressor, that he'd have to gently tease a response out of her. Instead, it was the opposite. Her kiss was bold, if a bit clumsy. Completely enchanting.

Her hands clung to him as her tongue traced the crease of his lips. She didn't have to ask twice. He opened his mouth to her, nearly shuddering with desire when her tongue darted into his mouth, eager and fast, like a ravenous hummingbird. He realized then how quickly this could get out of hand. She had it in her to dominate her lover completely. An inexperienced man might mistake her natural enthusiasm for arousal. Or worse, be so turned on that he couldn't wait for her. If she'd been like this at eighteen, no wonder the poor guys hadn't lasted.

He moved his own hands to the sides of her face and pulled his mouth from hers. She tried to follow him, rising higher onto her to toes. He nudged her down with his hands on her shoulders, pressing his forehead to hers.

"Slow down. It's not a race."

She pulled back, blinking as if dazed. He knew how she felt.

"Give me a second and then let's try this again." He sucked in a deep breath. The smell of her flooded his senses, sweet and somehow homey, with just a hint of citrus. Like lemon cookies. His favorite.

When he heard her breath slow down, he lowered his mouth back to hers, taking control, coaxing her mouth open, moving his tongue against hers in slow, sensuous strokes. Her body relaxed against his and he set about seducing her with his kiss. He'd promised her he'd stop the minute she asked, and he would. He just had to make sure she didn't ask. He wouldn't push her for more than she was willing to give. No, if there was going beyond a single kiss, she'd have to take it there.

And she did. Sooner than he thought, her hands were moving down his chest, tugging the hem of his shirt free from his pants. He sucked in a breath as her palm reached the bare skin of his abdomen. Her fingers were cool, her touch light and fluttering.

He might not have intended to push her, but turnabout was fair play. She was dressed in a simple wraparound dress, which made it all too easy to slip his hand into her bodice. All he wanted was to touch her bare skin, but she misinterpreted his actions and moved his hand to the tie at her waist. With a single tug of her fingers, her dress fell open. His surprise nearly knocked him off his feet. They were alone, but they were still outside.

He glanced down. The sight of her sent desire rocketing through him. The way the fabric of her dress fell across the sides of her body, the way her hot-pink bra encased the pale, creamy skin of her breasts. And, my God, that bra.

Because she dressed so conservatively, he'd thought he might have to brave a fortress of starchy white nylon to reach her skin. Instead, she'd shocked him with scanty silk and lace. It was a fantasy come to life. A miracle of engineering in fuchsia. He really could write a sonnet about the things that bra did.

What the hell was the Last Good Girl in America doing wearing a bra and panties like that?

Somehow the combination of hot-pink silk and her naked flesh in the dappled light was almost too much. She was too perfect, with the bright afternoon sun filtering down through the leaves of the tree, making her bare skin glimmer. He wanted to drop to his knees and worship her.

This was not how it was supposed to happen. He'd planned on seducing her. Pushing her to her limits. Not the other way around. That's when it hit him. He was in serious trouble. And he didn't even give a damn.

Watching the desire flicker across Connor's face, a surge of pure feminine power shot through Brittney.

She'd always known men found her attractive. A body like hers was designed to bring men to their knees. She knew that in the same way she understood foreign trade agreements—dispassionately. As if it were unrelated to her personally. It was like owning a chain saw but never choosing to use it. Why would she? She didn't need to chop down any trees.

But watching Connor's reaction to her body, for the first time, she felt the power of it. This man, this notorious playboy, whose affairs were so legendary people had warned her about him…he wanted her.

She saw it in his face more clearly than he could have told her with a thousand seductive murmurings. His reaction to her filled her with power. And his desire surprised him, too. She also read that in his expression. He was shaken by how much he wanted her. And she'd never seen anything more erotic in her life than that mixture of shock and raw lust.

Need shot through her, zinging every nerve in her body with energy. Her fingers trembled with eagerness as she shimmied out of her dress. A breeze drifted from under the tree, tantalizing her skin as her dress fluttered to the ground, leaving her clad only in her bra and panties.

For a moment, Connor merely stood there, his gaze raking over her exposed body. Then he smiled, looking like a kid on Christmas morning, set loose in FAO Schwartz. Brittney was damn glad that the lingerie she'd always considered her private indulgence was not so private now.

He closed the distance between them, pressing his body to hers, and thoughts of everyone and everything else vanished. Her skin felt overly sensitized, every nerve ending aware of the brush of his hands and the grazing of his clothes. He was still fully dressed and her hands tugged at buttons and fabric, desperate to level the playing field, to expose the smooth expanse of his skin to her touch.

His hands were hot and needy, one cupping her breast, the other her backside. He hitched her up, wedging a leg between hers. The pressure at the juncture of her thighs was an exquisite torture. She rocked her hips forward and back, shuddering with pleasure. His mouth nipped at her neck while he thumbed her nipple through her bra, matching the rhythm of her movements.

She felt her nerves tightening, an orgasm just out of her reach. Sucking in deep breaths, she tried to stay in front of it. "Please, Connor," she gasped, "tell me you have a condom."

"I do."

She was only vaguely aware of him fumbling for it. A moment later, he was thumbing aside the fabric of her thong and thrusting into her. He kept his fingers right at her juncture, rubbing the apex of her desire, pushing her over the edge as he reached his own climax, buried deep inside of her.

It wasn't supposed to be like this.

Connor'd had it all planned out. He'd sleep with her. Get her out of his system. Move on.

He wasn't supposed to lose control. *She* was.

Knowing that they'd both lost control was little consolation.

Her body was still trembling as he pulled away from her. Heart pounding, he straightened his clothes. And then picked up her dress. He scrubbed a hand through his hair and down his face. Picking her dress up off the ground was almost as disconcerting as taking it off had been. Nothing about Brittney was what he expected.

She blinked lazily, her expression dazed, her cheeks flushed, her lips swollen and red. Anyone who so much as glanced at her would know she'd just been taken up against a wall. Everything about her was erotic and tempting.

So much so that the sight of her might have turned him on all over again. If he hadn't just had the most fantastic orgasm of his life. And if he weren't fighting back panic. He got her back into her dress as quickly as he could.

She smiled up at him with dazzling trust. "That was amazing." Her hands fluttered to her hair and then to her chest, like she was trying to keep her heart from pounding out of it. "Is it always like that?" Then she laughed as she knotted the ties on her dress. "I mean, I know it's supposed to be good. But I had no idea…"

The tie of her dress was still askance. He reached to straighten it, but the small effort did little to help. "We've got to get you out of here. What's the fastest way back to the parking lot, where we won't see anyone?"

"Back behind the barn, I think." She looked confused. "Should we leave?"

"Definitely." He gripped her elbow and steered her in the opposite direction of the field.

"Can we do it again?" Her breath seemed to catch with excitement. She laughed again, that low, sexy rumble that stirred parts of him that had no business stirring. "Gosh, I sound so naive, don't I? I just—"

He cut her off, muttering a curse under his breath. "Let's just get out of here."

For several steps, she walked along beside him. Then she stumbled, and he could almost feel her tension building.

Suddenly she dug in her heels and stopped. "You're ditching me already, aren't you."

"I'm not ditching you," he countered quickly. Never mind that logic dictated honesty would be the best approach here. She looked too hurt for him to go with honesty. So he hedged. "I'm going to take you home. You said yourself you didn't want any gossip. If anyone saw you looking like this, there'd be talk."

She held up her palms as if warding off an attack. "Hey, it's okay. I get it." Her gaze traveled the length of his body, and he had the uneasy sensation she'd summed up the breadth of his soul, as well. "This is the kind of guy you are." Her lips curved in a wry, self-deprecating smile. "I knew it going in. I was warned. I saw it coming from a mile away. And I still fell for it. My mistake."

Her arms wrapped around her waist and she brushed past, heading for her car without looking back.

Let her go, his logical mind demanded. *Just let her walk away. That'll be easiest on everyone.*

And, damn it, that's what he would have done. If she hadn't paused and turned back to deliver one last barb.

"And for those in the audience keeping score, I won this point. Even when the sex is good, it's still not worth it."

With that she turned and walked away.

He wanted to let her go, wanted to pretend that he hadn't hurt her, that he wasn't acting like a complete ass.

But he knew he was.

"Wait a second," he called out, speeding up to catch her. "You're not even giving me a chance."

She eyed him shrewdly. "A chance to what? Dump me in a more humiliating manner?"

There was such vulnerability in her gaze, along with a liberal dash of sass. Before logic had a chance to beat him over the head again, he turned her to face him and cupped her

face in his hand. "Look, I have a client I have to see tonight."
The lie slipped out cleanly. "But I'll see you tomorrow."

Her gaze was suspicious. "You don't really want to see me.
You're just feeling guilty."

"I do," he argued. "Promise me you'll meet me somewhere."

Now he was begging her to meet him? How the hell had
that happened?

She bit down on her lower lip as she considered her
options.

"Let me take you to dinner," he offered.

Finally she shook her head, pulling away from him. "No.
Tomorrow night is the Harbor Lights Gala for the local
schools. I was on the planning committee for years. If I miss
the event, people will notice."

"I'll meet you there."

Her expression was blank, but he could tell she was
struggling to keep it that way. He walked her the rest of the
way to her car, wishing he had a better handle on her emotions.
Or, for that matter, on his own.

She swung the door open but paused before climbing in.
When she spoke, her tone was even, all traces of suspicion
gone. "Look, it's fine. I knew exactly what I was getting into.
You didn't mislead me."

There it was again. That blunt honesty. Her gaze met his,
her blue eyes almost painfully clear of accusation.

"Brit…" he began, but he didn't know how to finish the
sentence. She so clearly saw through all his crap. And she was
giving him a chance to walk away. Guilt-free.

Before he had a chance to stop himself, he brushed a hand
up her arm to her shoulder. He pulled her to him, intending
to simply hug her. But at the last second, her face turned up
to his and he found himself unable to resist the lure of that

tempting mouth. His lips found hers, coaxing them open with the gentlest of touches.

All those things he couldn't say, all those emotions he couldn't even name, he poured them into the kiss. The regret, the apology, even the fear. The sheer awe he felt at her stunning mix of innocence, honesty and sensuality.

She leaned into him and kissed him with knee-weakening passion. He felt the tendrils of her desire taking root deep within him as she arched her body against his, sliding a leg up along the outside of his thigh. It took every ounce of his self-control to break the kiss.

By the time he lifted his mouth, he could see he'd kissed away the last of her suspicion. As she climbed into her car and drove away, Connor was mentally kicking himself. He'd made things worse, not better.

Brittney should send him running for the hills. Yet he'd just promised to see her again. Begged for it, actually. What was it about this woman that turned him into a total idiot?

Four

Once, as a teenager, in a brief burst of curiosity about the mother who had left her, Brittney had spent hours at the local library reading interviews with Kandy Hannon. Most were from the time immediately after her scandalous affair and marriage to Brittney's father, the then-freshman senator. In those articles, her words were carefully guarded and most likely well rehearsed. But in the few interviews she'd done after leaving her husband and abandoning her three-year-old daughter, Kandy Hannon spoke freely.

To the teenage Brittney, the most memorable quote was, "Why on earth would I be ashamed of having sex? It's great exercise and makes my skin glow. Why not enjoy it as often as I can?"

For a brief time, Brittney flirted with adopting that philosophy for herself. She hadn't enjoyed it. At all. Since then, she'd eschewed her mother's ideas about sex in favor of her own, very conservative views.

One afternoon with Connor had changed all that. Despite her doubts about his intentions, she woke up the next morning with a feeling of smug contentment. She felt more in control of her sexuality than ever before. It almost didn't matter if he showed up at the gala. Her body hummed, her mind buzzed and her skin glowed. For the first time in her life, she felt like she really was the daughter of Kandy Hannon.

And it was all thanks to Connor and the miraculous things he'd done to her body.

He might not show up to the gala this evening, and if he didn't, she'd survive. One more life lesson learned.

But if he did show up, what then? Yesterday, she'd been unable to tell if he was motivated by guilt or if he genuinely wanted to see her again. She'd have to play it by ear.

That should be no problem. After all, she'd lived her entire life in the limelight of her father's political career, playing things by ear. If she could figure out how to get through dinner with the president and first lady at age twelve, she could darn well run into Connor at a gala. She'd made it through that crucial dinner, despite the nausea clutching her stomach, by taking tiny bites and smiling a lot. She'd do the same tonight.

Funny how much of her life she spent thinking about a woman she hadn't even seen since she was three. After abandoning her husband and daughter, Kandy had spent a few years stirring up trouble and living recklessly. She'd died in a skiing accident when Brittney was ten.

Though Brittney barely remembered her, Kandy had left an indelible mark on her life. They looked so much alike, Brittney felt as though everything her mother had done was a reflection on her. Between dodging her mother's past and trying not to impinge on her father's future, sometimes Brittney felt as though she barely had a life of her own. Until yesterday, in Connor's presence, when she'd forgotten both.

She spent an unproductive day trying not to think about Connor. By late afternoon, when it was time for her to dress for the gala, she was tired of contemplating her future. She was ready to simply be done with the evening.

She was prepared to face whatever met her. Except for what was actually there.

Connor stayed in his room at the B&B where he was staying for most of the day, catching up on world news and his backlog of e-mail on his laptop. He'd even downloaded an action flick and watched that. Anything to keep his mind off Brittney. He also did the unthinkable and kept his phone off. When he finally turned it on, he saw he'd received no fewer than seven phone calls from Tim.

As much as he wanted to avoid talking to anyone, he figured he had no choice but to return the call.

"Connor," Tim said as soon as he picked up, "did I underestimate you."

"What are you talking about?"

"When you said you'd get her into bed within the week, I thought you were full of it. Man, was I wrong. What can I say, other than I owe you a thousand bucks?"

Anxiety clutched at Connor's chest. He repeated his question slowly. "What. Are. You. Talking. About?"

"Brittney Hannon. You and her hooking up. That picture of you two on Headin-for-the-Hamptons.com was smoking hot."

Great.

Connor hung up on Tim. By the time he'd set down his iPhone, he was already loading the Web site. And there it was on the front page of the site's coverage of the polo tournament.

There were actually two pictures. The first was a grainy black-and-white photo that had to be at least thirty years old. A young Senator Hannon, dressed in a suit and looking clean-cut, with a blonde bombshell pressed against him in the risqué costume of an Atlantic City showgirl, her naked limbs entwined with his. The photo's combination of disheveled business suit and bare skin suggested an illicit embrace.

Connor had seen it before, when he'd searched Google for Brittney after meeting her. It was the photo that had nearly ruined the senator's career.

But it wasn't nearly as shocking as the photo beside it.

The second photo also portrayed a well-dressed man and a scantily clad blonde bombshell. But unlike the first photo, this one was in garish bright color. And it wasn't nearly thirty years old. It was less than twenty-four hours old.

It was a photo of Connor and Brittney, kissing outside her car in the parking lot at the match, her hair mussed, her clothing disheveled.

How the hell had they gotten that shot?

His breath came in short, ragged gusts as he fought to control his anger. His mind raced. He'd find out whoever was responsible. He'd have him fired. He'd sue him. Crush him financially. Hell, he'd kill him.

The prospect of some nameless member of the paparazzi lying trampled under the hooves of polo horses made Connor feel only marginally better. Only once his vision began to clear did he read the headline spanning the width of the two pictures.

Looks Like The Apple Doesn't Fall Far From The Tree!

He quickly scanned the article. Straight gossip would have been bad enough, but the site aimed well below the belt. It liberally referenced the interview that had run in *New York Personality*. Worse still, it implied Brittney only pretended to practice abstinence to pacify her father's constituents while actually sleeping around.

He cursed as he dug through his pocket for his car keys. It wasn't the papparazzi who deserved to die painfully. It was him.

The whispers of gossip were especially fierce when Brittney arrived at the Harbor Lights Gala on Sunday evening. She didn't pay any mind to the murmurs. Until she noticed that stares of barely veiled curiosity were pointed at her.

First it was just a glance here and there. The glare of a matronly older woman. The nervous snicker of a teenage boy who held her gaze too long. The knowing smile and faint nod of a woman who was known for her sexual escapades. But it was the lewd "Hey, baby" grin of a guy in his twenties that made the hair on the back of her neck prickle.

Suddenly nervous, she scanned the crowd, looking for a friendly face. She'd been socializing with some of these people for most of her life. But the only person who looked approachable at the moment was Vanessa Hughes. Though she and Vanessa had never been close, they'd been acquaintances for years. Vanessa shot her a look full of sympathy that made the bottom drop out of Brittney's stomach. Whatever was going on, Vanessa knew about it.

Brittney quickly crossed the lawn to Vanessa. As always, the beautiful blonde was dressed impeccably in a white sundress, her oversized sunglasses propped on her head. As if they were far closer than they actually were, Brittney gave Vanessa a quick buss on the cheek and then linked arms with her.

"Protect me from the circling vultures?" she asked under her breath.

Vanessa picked up Brittney's cue and smiled cheerfully. "Absolutely." Softly she added, "Am I wrong in thinking you don't yet know why the vultures are circling?"

Brittney's smile felt tight as she shook her head.

In a voice loud enough for passersby to hear, Vanessa said, "You've got to try these canapés." She guided Brittney to the edge of the lawn where the catering tents were set up. As they walked, Vanessa pulled her iPhone out of her enormous Jimmy Choo bag and surreptitiously pulled up a Web page. She slipped the phone into Brittney's hand as she loaded up a plate with appetizers.

Brittney recognized the Headin' for the Hamptons site. Then the world fell away as she saw the pictures. Her blood pounded through her head—all she heard was a distant roaring. She had to concentrate to read the headline. As bad as the photos were, the accompanying article was even worse.

One bad choice, one little mistake, and everything she'd ever stood for was in question. A single scandalous photo wouldn't be so bad for the average politician's daughter. But she'd always been so vocal about abstinence. Her entire adult life, she'd advocated women respecting themselves enough to eschew promiscuity and find committed, long-term relationships.

The Web site made sure to point that out. It made it sound as though she'd said those things merely to pander to her father's more conservative voters, while she was partying and sleeping around with men she barely knew.

And the horrible truth was, it was right. She had betrayed everything she believed in for a few minutes of mindless pleasure in the arms of a man she barely knew.

"I can't..." she muttered under her breath, but the sentence died in her mouth before she could finish it. Panic tightened around her throat, making speech impossible.

Beside her, Vanessa threw back her head and laughed, like she'd said something outrageously funny.

Stung, Brittney just gaped at her.

Vanessa gave Brittney's arm a gentle squeeze. "If they know it hurts you, it makes the feeding frenzy worse."

Brittney nodded in understanding. Vanessa had always had a reputation as a wild child. Just last summer, Vanessa had had a tumultuous fling with polo player Nicolas Valera. There'd been gossip aplenty about that.

Taking advice from someone who'd weathered her share of storms, Brittney gave a trembling smile. "Right. Thank you. I—"

She broke off as she glimpsed Connor watching her from across the lawn. She didn't have a chance to read his expression because suddenly Cynthia Rotham was bearing down on her.

"Well, well, well," Cynthia practically cooed with glee, "if it isn't the Last Good Girl in America."

Brittney's panic hardened into resolve. She refused to be cowed by Cynthia Rotham. "You know, I'm really starting to hate that title."

"Don't worry, darling, you've already lost it." The veil of kindness dropped from Cynthia's face as she leaned forward. "I'm surprised you had the guts to show your face today. You always struck me as such a spineless creature, not good for much but looking demure in pictures. Yet here you are. I can't decide if it's admirable or stupid."

Cynthia's arrogance was almost too much to bear.

Vanessa tried to wedge herself between Brittney and Cynthia like a human shield. "Why don't you go spew your venom on someone else?"

Cynthia glared at Vanessa. "Ah, Vanessa. Are you two friends all of a sudden? Do we have your influence to thank for Brittney's new loose morals?"

Brittney wasn't about to let Cynthia verbally knock Vanessa around. "I make my own decisions and my own mistakes. So back off."

"This was more than a mistake." She let loose a cackling laugh. "Little Miss Prim and Proper was caught with a man she barely knows. The backlash will do wonders for your father's career."

Brittney swayed. Hearing her worst fears voiced aloud made her light-headed. But before she could voice a rebuttal, she felt a hand on her elbow. She knew in an instant who it was.

Connor.

At the soothing stroke of his hand on her arm and the faint whiff of his scent—woodsy and masculine—something inside of her relaxed.

He extended a hand to Cynthia. "I don't think we've met. Brittney hasn't had time to introduce me to all of her friends yet."

Cynthia narrowed her gaze suspiciously. And didn't take his hand.

He left his hand in midair, all but forcing Cynthia to extend her own.

As he shook her hand, he added, "I'm Connor Stone. Brittney's fiancé."

Beside him, Connor felt Brittney tense. She might have been turned to stone. He could only hope her larynx was frozen as well. If he was going to throw himself under the bus to save her, he damn well didn't want her blocking his dive.

He talked fast, not giving the women a chance to speak. "Boy, we got caught, didn't we? Here we were, trying to hide our relationship just a little bit longer, and we goofed." He squeezed Brittney's shoulder. "Brit, why don't you introduce me to your friends?"

He recognized Vanessa Hughes, of course. Since she was standing shoulder to shoulder with Brittney, he assumed they were friends. The older woman, on the other hand, was clearly little more than a vulture come to feast on a scandal.

Brittney recovered first. "Connor, this is Cynthia

Rotham." Then she cleared her throat. "*Congresswoman* Rotham, that is."

Ah. That explained her obvious panic as well as the woman's rapacious expression. From what he understood, Congresswoman Rotham was one of Brittney's father's most vocal opponents.

He squeezed Brittney's shoulder while giving Cynthia his best smile. "I think people will forgive us for kissing in public, once they see how in love we are."

Cynthia scoffed. "Kissing? Is that what it was?"

Connor leveled his gaze at the older woman. "A man's still allowed to kiss his fiancée in public, isn't he?"

She ignored the quiet warning in his tone. "If you really are engaged."

Brittney opened her mouth to speak but Connor didn't give her the chance. "If it were up to me, we'd be married already."

Vanessa's lips twitched in an effort to suppress laughter.

Connor smiled broadly and said, "Now, if you'll excuse us, Brittney promised to introduce me to all the movers and shakers here."

As he took Brittney's arm and led her away, he thought he heard the congresswoman gasp at the implication that she wasn't important enough to count as one of those movers and shakers.

As soon as they were out of earshot, Brittney whispered, "Fiancé? What were you thinking, claiming to be my fiancé?"

She seemed unaware of the eyes still following them. He gave her arm a squeeze. He'd been squeezing a lot of her body parts this evening, and none of the good ones.

"Smile," he muttered under his breath. "The congresswoman isn't watching just now, but a lot of other people are."

She didn't miss a beat, quickly fixing a pleasant expression on her face. But her tone betrayed her arrogance. "What the hell are you doing?"

Man, she was good. Years of living in the public eye had apparently honed her ability to hide her true emotions.

He cut straight to the chase. "That picture was a disaster. For you, not me. I'm barely visible in the photo, and other than my elderly grandmother who will probably rip me a new one, no one cares what I do or who I sleep with."

"That's a nice image. Thanks for that."

"You, on the other hand, are easily recognizable. And correct me if I'm wrong, but isn't it an election year for your father? Which means that photo—"

"You don't have to tell me what it means," she snapped. They'd reached the edge of the lawn. In the dusk, lights strung along the tents glistened off the water, casting the harbor in a glow of warm light. She was obviously in no mood to enjoy any of it.

Keenly aware they were still the objects of curious stares, he settled his hand at the small of her back, knowing onlookers would interpret their actions as lovers seeking a moment for private conversation.

But that simple touch only served to remind him of what he'd touched the previous afternoon. Of the exquisite thrill of burying himself inside her heat. Of the way she gasped out her pleasure as he entered her.

He could think of about a hundred things he wanted to do with her right now. Enjoying a view of the harbor while being gawked at was at about a hundred and thirty-two. Talking about that damn photo was probably fifty slots lower.

What he should really be doing—finding a way to extricate himself from this relationship—was even lower than that. Of course, that was out the question now. Even he wasn't enough of an idiot to dump her under these circumstances.

But that did not explain why he'd rushed to her defense

by introducing himself as her fiancé. That was completely unexplainable. All he knew was that the second he'd seen Cynthia Rotham closing in for the kill, every protective instinct he had leaped to life. He'd spoken with no plan other than distracting Rotham.

Now that they were relatively alone, he said, "Neither of us could have anticipated this. What happened between us yesterday…" He stopped just shy of calling it a mistake. When he'd walked her to her car, she'd clearly been under the impression that sex up against the barn was going to lead to some kind of relationship. "Look, I should have stopped things before they got out of hand. I take full responsibility."

"*You* take full responsibility?" she sounded offended. "Why on earth would you be responsible for my actions? I'm an adult."

"Obviously. If you weren't, what happened yesterday would be illegal. Not to mention creepy." He flashed her a smile, hoping to lighten the mood. She didn't take the hint.

"I'm not joking." She stared him down with a hard gaze. All signs of the charmingly befuddled woman she'd been yesterday were now gone. "I don't blame you. It's not your mistake to take responsibility for."

"But I have more experience," he countered. "I should have—"

She tugged her arm from his grasp, still smiling cheerfully for anyone who might be watching as she said, "Yes, but I have more morals. If anyone should have stopped us, it's me."

The beginnings of a headache inched across his forehead. He rubbed his thumb across his brow to deaden the pain. "Morals aren't the issue here," he said under his breath.

"I just got caught—on film—mere minutes after having sex in public. With a stranger. I think morals are most definitely the issue."

"The picture looks worse than it was," he countered.

She glared at him from beneath her lashes. "We had sex up against the side of a barn. In full view of anyone who happened by." She threw up her hands as if pleading for mercy from some higher force. "The photo actually looks *better* than it was."

"True. But if they had a more incriminating picture, they would have used it. No one but us knows what actually happened."

The image of exactly what had happened between them played through his mind, unspooling in vivid and unforgettable detail. It was an effort, but he shut down his imagination. The last thing this conversation needed was him getting a hard-on. Or worse, coming on to her again.

Yeah, that would work great. *Hey, having sex with me just royally screwed up your life, but is there any chance you want to have another go at it?*

Unaware of his thoughts, she seemed to be considering his words, probably looking for the flaw in his logic. Finally, her shoulders seemed to relax. Only then did he realize how tensely she'd been holding herself. "Perhaps you're right. Maybe the photo they printed was the worst one they had." But she shook her head. "I still should have known better."

"You made one mistake."

The look she gave him was one of annoyance mingled with arrogance. "I didn't make just one mistake. I made the one mistake that could ruin my father's career."

"Don't you think that's overstating it a bit?"

"No. I don't. My actions reflect not just on me, but on him as well. The headline proved that." She shook her head, a faint glistening of tears in her eyes. "My mistake has stirred up all that old gossip about my mother. It's a disaster."

"Hey, whatever happened between your parents is their mistake, not yours. If your father blames you for that, then—"

She spun on him, her eyes alight with defensive fervor. "My father may not be the best father, but he's a great politician. He does amazing things for the good of this country. All he's ever asked of me is that I let him do his job. And now I've messed that up. Even if Cynthia Rotham bought your explanation, she's just one person. Everyone here has seen those pictures. Everyone who goes to that Web site will see those photos. For all I know, they're running the story on TMZ right this minute."

"What, you think I was just stepping in to defend you against Rotham?"

"I think you made a rash decision. You kept Cynthia from breathing down my neck. But she's far from the only one I'm worried about."

Before he could reply, her handbag buzzed loudly. She reached inside and pulled out her iPhone. "Great. A text from my father's senior staffer."

Grumbling under her breath, she stepped aside to respond.

The truth was, when he first spoke, he hadn't thought any further than the immediate crisis. He hadn't considered that the story might reach an audience broader than the gossips here in the Hamptons.

When she looked up, he said, "Okay. You're right. I didn't think this through. You'll have to excuse me. You're the first senator's daughter I've dated." At his use of the word "dated," she quirked an eyebrow. He ignored her silent commentary and pushed on. "I'm not used to life in the limelight. What do you suggest we do from here?"

She eyed him suspiciously. She held her phone in her hands, moving it between her thumb and forefinger like a string of rosary beads. After a moment, she shook her head. "I won't ask you to fix this for me."

"I don't leave my messes for other people to clean up."

She blanched as if he'd slapped her, and he instantly regretted his words.

"I am not your mess!" she snarled, turning on her heel and vanishing into the crowd.

So much for convincing the onlookers that they were blissfully engaged and planning a wedding.

She was right, of course. She wasn't his mess. She wasn't his anything. Nevertheless, he was to blame for this. He'd pursued her.

Knowing where she stood on the subject of casual sex, he'd pushed at her boundaries. He manipulated her into giving in to him. He'd created circumstances he'd known she wouldn't be able to resist.

And why had he done all of that? Because he was scared of how vulnerable she made him feel. Her own motives were so much purer. She talked about the good of the country and her father's career. Compared with her, he felt like a selfish jerk.

He prided himself on always getting what he went after. Now, that single-minded determination had gotten them both into serious trouble. And it was up to him to fix it.

Five

She didn't expect him to follow her.

If her behavior drove him to storm off, it would be a fitting end to her nightmare of a day. She made her way to the catering tent with the shortest line. One of the local Asian restaurants was offering up small takeout boxes brimming with stir-fried noodles and veggies. Brightly colored chopsticks stuck out of the boxes at an angle.

She snagged a box and a napkin, then made her way to one of the tables under a sprawling walnut. She stabbed the chopsticks into the box, digging around for a spear of broccoli. Pretending to eat without noticing the curious stares took all her concentration.

After a moment, Connor pulled out the chair beside her and sat down with his own box of noodles. Even without looking up, she felt his presence beside her.

Her emotions were still careening wildly out of control

and she couldn't muster the strength to offer the apology she knew he deserved.

"I never meant—" he began.

"I know." It was bad enough that she hadn't started with an apology. She couldn't sit here and listen to him apologize to her. She shifted to look at him. "You're right. This is a bad situation. Blaming one another certainly won't help. But I just can't ask you to sacrifice yourself for my mistake."

"*Our* mistake," he pointed out.

"No," she shook her head, "my mistake. You're the ladies' man. You're the charming smooth talker whom no woman can resist." His expression seemed to be hardening as she spoke, but she kept going. "I should have been stronger. I can't fault you for making me forget my standards. They're mine. If I don't stand by them, I have no one to blame but myself."

He tossed his chopsticks onto the table beside his takeout box, then leaned back in his chair. "So what you're saying," he spoke slowly and clearly, as if wanting to guarantee that she understood, "is that you don't blame me because I'm an amoral jerk. You, on the other hand, are to blame for even associating with me. And you should have known better."

"That is not what I said!"

He cocked his head to the side, his gaze steady and assessing. "Then what did you mean?"

"Just that—" But she broke off, because she couldn't think when he was watching her so closely. He muddled her mind. And she'd learned the hard way how easily he could trap her with his logic. "What I meant was, I knew what was at stake. True, I had no way of knowing we'd be caught, but I've lived my whole life in the public eye. I know better than most that every mistake you make comes back to haunt you. I should have known better."

His expression softened a little, as if her words were getting through to him. He ducked his head slightly, giving his expression a rueful puppy-dog quality. "True, you may have more experience with the press, but I have more experience with sex. I should have put a stop to things. I should have known they were getting out of hand. I just…"

He let his words trail off with a wry twist of a smile.

The implication hung there in the air between them. He hadn't stopped for the same reason she hadn't thought about the press. Their passion had gotten out of hand. Not because they were careless, but because this thing between them was more powerful than either of them expected.

In that instant, all of her doubts and self-recriminations vanished. She was back beside the barn, watching his expression as he looked at her near-naked body for the first time. Once again, she was flooded with that feeling of power, that sense that this passion between them was right. As if it was what she was born to do. As if her body had been created solely for the purpose of enticing him, just as his was made purely to bring her pleasure.

It was a heady feeling, this power she had over him, this passion that bloomed between them. It was stronger than anything she'd ever faced before. It was such a shame that she'd never get to experience it again.

He was a dangerous man. He'd already tempted her beyond anything she'd thought possible. She'd have to be even more careful around him.

He opened his mouth but she cut him off with a wave of her chopsticks. She didn't think she could stand any more confessions from him. "Let's just say we're both to blame and leave it at that."

He nodded, apparently willing to let that discussion go. "The question is, how do we fix it?"

"I don't know that we can."

"Trust me," he grinned. "I can fix this. I can fix anything."

He popped a bit of pork into his mouth. As he chewed, his smile held that touch of arrogance she found so exasperating. And yet somehow endearing, too. Gazing into his eyes, something caught inside her. She simultaneously wanted to cuddle against his chest and strip off her clothes. The urge to rest her head on his chest scared her more.

She forced herself to roll her eyes. "Fix it? Like your lie to Congresswoman Rotham? That didn't fix anything. Even if she believed you—"

"How much do you know about what I do?" he asked, cutting her off.

She stilled, a noodle midway to her mouth, surprised by the sudden shift in topic. "I know you're a hedge-fund manager, but I don't know more than that."

"Being a hedge-fund manager is a confidence game. I talk people into trusting me with huge amounts of money. For me to do that, they have to have absolute faith in me."

She could imagine. That smile of his alone—half self-deprecating, half charm—was pure confidence. If the job required him to win people over, he must be a natural at it. You just *wanted* to trust him.

Trusting him had created this problem. Falling for his charm had gotten her into this mess. Despite that, when he said, "Trust me," she wanted to.

"I came from nothing," he continued. "When I first started in this business, all I had was a good education, a hell of a lot of determination and my own belief I could succeed. On that alone, I convinced those first few people to hand over their fortunes. If I can do that, I can convince people that we're engaged."

She could imagine him charming people out of their money. Not because he intended to steal it out from under them but because he knew he could make them more, and he had the guts to go after his dream. She'd been subject to his persuasive tactics herself. She knew how convincing he could be.

Yet even now, she couldn't blame him for seducing her. No, his seduction had worked because he spoke to something inside of her, something no one else had tapped into. The experience had rocked her to her very soul. It shattered every belief she'd had about herself.

Which was precisely why she couldn't find it in her heart to wish she hadn't experienced it. Put simply, having sex with Connor was one of the best experiences of her entire life. Now that she'd had it, she couldn't wish it away any more than she could her own DNA. It was a part of her. Now she just had to learn to live with the repercussions.

Even if their fake engagement worked and her reputation stayed intact, she'd never again be the person she was before she met Connor Stone.

Connor couldn't read Brittney's emotions. She'd been silent while he spoke. Trying to gauge her reaction, his heart started pounding. What was up with that?

After all the clients he'd wooed, all the deals he'd put together, all the hundreds of millions of dollars he'd made— through all of that, he'd been as relaxed as a debutant getting her nails done. But *this* made him nervous?

All he could figure was for the first time, he actually cared about the gamble he was taking. With every other risk he'd taken, he'd always known something else was right around the corner. If he lost a client, he'd find another. If a deal fell through, he'd put together another one. If he lost money, he'd just make more. He never once doubted that he'd make it work one way or another. But with Brittney...well, there was only one of her. If he screwed this up, there'd be no second chance.

"What do you say? Do you trust me?" he prodded.

She searched his face, her eyes wide as she bit down on her lip. Finally she nodded. "I do."

All too aware of their surroundings, he set down his chopsticks and cupped her jaw with his palm. He ran his thumb across her cheek, entranced by how smooth her skin was. She blushed in response to his touch, her breath coming in a delicate tremble. The pink in her cheeks made her look unexpectedly vulnerable, and once again, the usually unflappable Brittney looked charmingly disheveled.

"Connor, really—"

He cut off her protest by kissing her. For an instant, she stiffened. Then, he ran his tongue along the seam of her lips, the gentlest of requests. Her mouth opened beneath his.

He deepened the kiss, his tongue moving against hers in a subtle imitation of the intimate act they'd performed just the day before. She lost herself in the kiss almost immediately, as if she'd been waiting all day for this moment, though she hadn't given him the slightest indication she had. Her hands clutched at his shoulders, and he felt her tension seep out of her.

His blood surged in response, but this time he didn't let his desire get the better of him. He kept one hand on her face, the other on her shoulder, focusing all his attention on just kissing her. Slowly, sensuously. Like a man content to spend all day doing only that.

And then, just as he'd planned, flashes went off. The paparazzi had arrived.

The burst of camera flashes snapped Brittney back to the present so quickly it made her head spin. One minute, Connor was kissing her with such soul-wrenching thoroughness she could barely remember her own name. The next she was the target of half a dozen flashing cameras.

Her mind reeled, only a single coherent thought tumbling through it: how the hell had this happened to her again?

She struggled to her feet, with Connor rising beside her. His hand was steady and sure at her back. He did not look nearly as surprised as she felt. Before she could wonder why, a reporter from one of the cable gossip shows shoved a microphone in her direction.

"This is the second time in two days you've been caught in a compromising position, Ms. Hannon. Would you care to comment?"

A second, less polite reporter pushed her microphone forward. "Any truth to the rumours about an engagement?"

"That 'good girl' comment must have really pissed you off, huh? Guess you have more of your mother in you than you've been letting on," a third reporter asked.

Brittney blinked as her confusion washed away in the wake of her anger. She was basically a peaceful person, but everyone had a breaking point. She reached out a hand, ready to grab the microphone and shove it somewhere creative.

Connor, it seemed, had not lost control of his faculties the way she had. He grabbed her hand and clutched it to his chest in a gesture that seemed cuddly rather than preventative. Then, to her amazement, he chuckled.

"You caught us again." He bumped his forehead against hers in show of playful affection. Then he turned the force of his charming smile on the reporters. "I just can't keep my hands off her. Can you blame me?"

She'd thought he'd worked a miracle with Cynthia Rotham, but that was nothing compared with how he handled the press. In the next fifteen minutes, he transformed the pack of microphone-wielding vicious paparazzi into a group about as bloodthirsty as papillon puppies.

By the time the reporters left, they were all smiling and chuckling. He'd convinced every one of them that she and

Connor were head over heels in love and—most importantly—that the photos from the day before were of innocent canoodling. Connor had one guy sharing tips on how to deal with meddling in-laws. Someone else had promised to e-mail him the name of a wedding caterer. She half expected Connor to toss them dog treats as they walked away.

Instead, he just smiled cheerfully and waved at them. Throughout the ordeal, he kept one arm firmly around her shoulder, glued to her as if he expected her to bolt.

Her own smile, she was sure, looked considerably less natural than his. "That was…" She shook her head. "I can't even think of words to describe what that was."

"Clever," he supplied easily. "Brilliant. Inspired."

She looked at him sideways. Dang it, but he was good-looking, with his easy smile and rakish black hair. "Do you always manage to get people to do exactly what you want?"

The look he gave her was surprisingly serious. "Only when it's really important."

"And this," she gestured to where the reporters had been. "Convincing these reporters that we're in love and that that photo yesterday was innocent—that's really important to you?"

As bizarre as it seemed, that was the only explanation that made sense.

"Is that so hard for you to believe?" he asked.

"Yes." She studied him again. She was used to his easy charm. It was the serious expressions she had trouble reading. "I just wonder what's in it for you."

He removed his arm from around her shoulder and shoved his hands deep in his pockets. "I clean up my messes."

And there it was again. The second time he'd referred to her as a mess. Something to be cleaned up and taken care of. Why was she destined to be people's mistakes? She'd known her whole life that her father saw her as an inconvenience at best, a political scandal waiting to re-erupt at worst. It was bad enough her own father saw her as a burden—she couldn't stand for Connor to see her that way, too.

She'd worked so hard to maintain her independence. She took care of herself. She never made mistakes, because it was the only way to guarantee that no one would ever have to rescue her.

Yet she was Connor's big mess. Once again a man she admired more than she wanted to saw her as little more than an inconvenience.

"We've gone over this already. It's my mess," she insisted. "Not yours."

"That's where you're wrong. If I hadn't been bent on seducing you, this never would have happened."

"Why? Because you're so irresistible?" As soon as she said the words, she regretted them. He *was* irresistible. Hadn't he proved that over and over again? Before he could answer, she snapped, "Get that smug expression off your face."

He shrugged innocently. "I didn't say anything."

"Yeah, but you were about to," she accused.

As if she needed to hear more on that subject. Yes, he was irresistible. Yes, every time he touched her she lost all sense of herself. Blah, blah, blah. Enough already.

This man had turned her life upside down in just a few days. A lifetime of perfect behavior, and she threw it out the window just because he's a good kisser? She'd had enough of this crap. She was taking control again. Starting now.

"Here's the deal." She rounded on him and poked a finger in his chest. "From here on out, I'm calling the shots."

He raised his eyebrows but said nothing.

True, so far, he'd handled things brilliantly. He was a genius at manipulating the press—as well as Cynthia Rotham. But she couldn't afford to let him manipulate her, as well. She was already far more drawn to him than was healthy. If they were going to spend the summer pretending to be in love, she'd have to find a way to put some emotional distance between them.

"If you really feel so bad about this," she said, "then you'll follow my lead and keep your mouth shut."

His lips quirked, as if the idea of following anyone's lead greatly amused him.

"Obviously you're good at handling the press, so you can be in charge of them. But when we're alone, I'm in charge. Do you think you can do that or not? Because if you can't—"

He pulled her to him and planted a firm kiss on her lips.

She wedged her hands against his chest and pushed, creating some room between them. "And no more kissing! And definitely no more sex! From here on out, it's strictly platonic."

"Of course," he agreed in a voice that didn't wholly convince her. It might have helped if he weren't still holding her body tightly to his.

"I mean it. We'll be engaged in public, but in private there'll be no canoodling, innocent or otherwise."

"And how long exactly am I supposed to live like a monk?"

She thought for a moment. "At least until the end of the polo season. After we return to the city, we'll be out of the spotlight and we can break things off."

She half expected him to protest. The end of the season was five weeks away.

But he just nodded. "Okay."

"Okay? You can really go that long—"

"Yes," he said, looking a little chagrined. "I can wait that long."

"Fine. Then you should start by letting me go."

"I would. But there's another reporter hiding behind the tent pole with his camera. It wouldn't do for us to be seen fighting in public."

She didn't have a chance to look over her shoulder and verify the reporter behind the pole, because the arrogant jerk leaned down and kissed her again.

Six

Just as they both hoped, the news about their relationship quickly overshadowed the gossip about the photo. Their engagement made the headlines and disappeared from the papers almost without her father's notice. There were several communications via his staff, but not so much as an e-mail from him personally. She was determined to view his lack of concern as faith in her ability to choose well.

After all, her father's interest in her love life had begun and ended with her brief stint dating Phillip. Their relationship had ended two years ago, and her father still met Phillip for golf every Saturday morning.

Given her tenuous relationship with her father, she was glad he didn't come out for the polo season anymore. She stayed at his house on Long Pond because she had enough flexibility in her schedule to work from home. Though she had the house and grounds to herself, she stayed in the guest quarters out by the pool, having converted one of the cottage's two bedrooms into an office. She spent her weekdays ensconced there, neck deep in Java code. Normally when she summered at her father's house, she got a tremendous amount of work done. But this year, her social calendar filled up faster than she could turn things down.

By lunch each Friday, Connor was back. The first two weekends, he'd stayed at a local hotel. But when she found out where he was staying, she insisted he take one of the bedrooms in her father's sprawling mansion.

"It's ten thousand square feet with no one in it except for the staff. My father never comes anymore, so there's no reason you shouldn't stay there," she told him the second Sunday of the polo season as they sat in the bleachers, watching a match.

"I can afford a hotel." His tone was terse—not unpleasant, but not the easy relaxed baritone she'd grown used to in such a short period of time.

She pulled her gaze from the match she was barely paying attention to and slanted a look at him. He was hard to read, his expression inscrutable. Charm came so easily to him, she hardly knew what to make of the tension she read in his shoulders or the curtness of his words.

She wanted to ask what was wrong. But that seemed like such a girlfriend thing to do. There could be a hundred things bothering him.

It could be work. She'd lived her whole life under the political microscope, but that was nothing compared with juggling billions of dollars in investments.

It could be something with his family. From comments he'd made, she gathered he had a large extended family, most of whom he wasn't close to but still kept in touch with. Her own family tree was tall but narrow. Only her grandmother, father and she remained from a line that stretched all the way back to the Pilgrims. Yet sometimes keeping just her father and grandmother happy was difficult enough. She couldn't imagine trying to negotiate the needs of three siblings, plus parents, aunts, uncles, cousins, etc. Surely that would be reason enough for him to be tense.

And of course, she realized with a thudding heart, it could be someone else. After all, what did she really know about his personal life, or about him? Yes, he'd come on to her, quite persuasively and persistently. But that didn't mean he didn't have someone else in the wings.

Before she could stop herself, she asked, "Is it someone else?"

"What?"

His baffled look made her instantly regret her question.

She forced her gaze back to the polo field where the horses and black-clad riders of the Black Wolves zipped by in a blur. "You seemed upset. I thought maybe…" She let her words trail off, unsure how to phrase the question that now seemed both presumptuous and ridiculous.

But he wouldn't let her get away with it. "You thought what?"

"I don't know, that maybe there was someone back in New York who was unhappy about this…" Again she trailed off, unable to put into words the complicated tangle of lies they'd fallen into.

"Someone like a girlfriend?"

If she'd thought his tone was tense before, it was nothing compared with the blunt force of his words now.

"Yes," she admitted defensively. "Like a girlfriend."

"You thought I had a girlfriend. In New York. That I didn't bother to mention."

"It didn't seem impossible," she hedged. Other men had done that kind of thing before. Phillip, for example.

"You don't think it would have come up before now?"

"Well, it's not like our engagement was something we had time to plan."

"True," he drew the word out. "But it was something I came up with. I wouldn't have suggested it if I had girlfriend in the city." Then he shook his head as if unable to believe he was even having this conversation. "Hell, if I had a girlfriend in the city, I wouldn't have slept with you in the first place. What kind of guy do you think I am?"

She tried not to cringe. "Look, I'm sorry. Obviously I offended—"

"Damn straight you offended me."

"You wouldn't be the first guy in the world to cheat and get caught."

"No, but I also wouldn't be the first guy in the world to make a mistake and do the honorable thing."

Good point. One she wished she'd thought of before opening her mouth.

He sat forward, ostensibly to watch the action at the far end of the field. But she couldn't help noticing the movement angled his back toward her. His shoulders, even tenser than before, were like a wall of unspoken accusations between them.

All she could do now was apologize. "I guess I don't know that many honorable guys." She raised her hand to hover just above his shoulder. "I'm sorry."

Her hand hung there for a moment in awkward indecision before she lowered it to his back. The muscles of his shoulder jumped under her hand, solid and unyielding. Instantly she wished she hadn't touched him. Then he straightened. He took her hand and wove his fingers through hers.

"Stop comparing me with other men you've known."

His hand was warm against hers, reassuring somehow, his gaze steady and confident. There was nothing sexual about the way he looked at her, but still, she felt a shiver of something heated and dark go through her.

Yes, she should definitely stop comparing him with other

men. The other men would always come up short. And she had the uncanny sensation that would always be true. That for the rest of her life, no man she ever met would measure up.

One summer with Connor Stone had ruined her for other men.

Brittney's delicate hand felt good in his. And for an instant, he nearly forgot that he didn't really have the right to hold it. If they weren't in public, she might not even allow him to touch her.

He took comfort in the fact that she'd obviously forgotten, too. Her expression shifted from one of doubt to delightfully befuddled confusion. She looked slightly shell-shocked. Well, good. He liked her off balance, and he thought it probably did her a world of good to have someone in her life who didn't do exactly what she expected.

She half-heartedly attempted to pull her hand from his, but he didn't let go, and she quickly gave in. Whether because her resistance was weak or because she didn't want to cause a scene, he didn't know.

It only bothered him a little that he didn't *want* to know. That he wanted to pretend it was because she wanted to hold his hand. To distract them both, he asked, "What brought this on anyway?"

"You seem tense," she answered after a minute. "Angry, almost. I thought maybe you were mad about having to keep up the facade for so long."

"I knew what I was getting into when I agreed to this."

She was certainly perceptive. Which wasn't surprising, given her experience in politics. He'd always thought of himself as being good at hiding his emotions. But you probably had to be pretty good at reading people to work on a political campaign.

"If you don't want to tell me what's wrong, it's fine," she said.

But her hand had tensed in his and he knew it wasn't really fine. Saying nothing would widen the gap between them.

He wasn't the kind of guy who opened up and shared his feelings very often—bonding just wasn't his thing. Maybe it was his solidly stoic, middle-American background. To his way of thinking, if you couldn't say it with a sports analogy or show it with car care, it wasn't worth saying. But as far as he knew, Brittney had a full-time driver in the city who took damn good care of her car and she didn't watch football.

He stared at the polo players galloping across the field, their horses gleaming and massive, their movements a ballet of aggressive grace, their strikes at the ball borderline violent. Yet the sport oozed elegance. Wealth and privilege. It was a world he worked and flirted with. But it wasn't the world he was born to. He'd been reminded of that spending these last few weeks with Brittney.

His blue-collar upbringing didn't bother him. But apparently it bothered her. Why else would she balk at introducing him to her father, the senator? And that *did* bother him. He didn't care what ninety-nine percent of the world thought of him. But her opinion mattered.

How the hell could he put that into words?

He tried. "I'm football and you're polo."

"You don't like watching polo?" She frowned, her forehead furrowing in that cute, confused way. "If you don't like it, you don't have to come out for every match."

"No. That's not it. It's a great sport. But I didn't grow up watching it. I was probably twenty before I knew it was sport, not just a logo on T-shirts."

"Oh," she nodded in understanding. Then she leaned forward. "Okay, look at that player on the sorrel pony. That horse is Maximo. He's ridden by Nicolas Valera. He's—"

He laughed, cutting her off. "No, I get the sport. I understand what they're doing."

"Then what's the problem?" Again she was frowning.

Man, she did not let things go.

"We're from different worlds. And it shouldn't be an issue. But—" He rolled his shoulders trying to release some of the tension that had taken up residence there. When had this gotten so complicated? "Look, I know why you'd be hesitant, but people will start wondering what's going on if I don't at least meet your father."

She twisted sharply in her seat to stare at him. "What? Meet my...what are you talking about?"

"Your father? The senator? The guy whose house you invited me to stay in because there's no way he'll come out to the Hamptons this season? That guy. That ring any bells for you?"

After another moment of doe-eyed gaping during which he wondered if he would have to spell it out for her more clearly, she grinned.

"That's what this is about? You think I'm embarrassed of you?"

He turned his attention back to the polo field. "I didn't say that."

"Oh, no. You didn't, did you?" She laughed. "Sheesh. Men." She faked a deep voice. "I'm football, you're polo. I don't have conversations about my feelings, so I'll just use a sports analogy. Maybe if I go long, she'll be able to hit a home run."

He wanted to be annoyed by her teasing. Really he did— and, damn it, how did she see right through him?—but he couldn't resist chuckling at her fumbled analogy. "Are you talking about football or baseball?"

"You know, you haven't exactly invited me to meet your family, either."

"Good point." He nodded. "Any time you want to experience the torture of driving out to Pennsylvania so my mom can throw a barbecue and introduce you to my brothers, their families, a dozen aunts and uncles and probably thirty or so cousins—plus neighbors—you just tell me and I'll set that up."

She looked baffled, like she'd been doing his family math in her head and had crossed over into the triple digits. "I..."

"I'm joking. I already called my mom and told her the truth. Don't worry, I swore her to secrecy and she'd drink hemlock before betraying the trust of one of her kids."

"I'm not worried," she reassured him.

"I didn't want her to get too excited. She generally ignores social gossip, but she salivates at the thought of grandchildren."

"Oh." Her tone sounded almost wistful. "No, I don't need to meet your family. But they sound nice."

He did a double take. "Nice? Crazy and overwhelming is how they sound." He studied her face, taking in the way her attempt at a smile didn't quite reach her eyes. "Why? What did your father say?"

"Oh, all the normal things you'd expect. He couldn't wait to welcome you to the family personally. He's impressed by you and thinks you're a shining example of how hard work and education can help the ambitious rise above their humble beginnings." Her lips twisted into a wry smile. "Didn't you watch his press conference?"

"Actually, I did. My secretary sent me the link on Hulu." He noticed that Brittney hadn't mentioned anything her father hadn't covered in the press conference. "You did actually talk to your father, didn't you?"

Brittney didn't meet his gaze but stared out at the polo field as if engrossed. "He's been very busy."

Connor did a quick scan of the field. Nope, none of the

players had sprouted wings. "You just got engaged. Didn't he call to ask a few questions? Doesn't he want to know anything about me, the man who is supposed to marry his little girl?"

"I've talked to his senior staffer a lot. Of course we talk almost every day anyway. She forwarded me your file."

"My file?" he asked.

She cringed. "You probably don't want to know more than that. I don't ask where he gets his information. Sorry." She softened the news with a rueful smile. "If it makes you feel any better, there was a Post-It note with the words, 'Seems like a good choice' on it."

"Yeah. That's much better."

"I'm sorry about the file thing. I probably shouldn't have mentioned it."

"Forget it," he said gently, taking her hand again.

What was *she* apologizing for? Her father was total jerk and *she* was sorry?

He felt like he was the one who should apologize. His family actually cared about him. Her father couldn't find the time to pick up the phone and call. What an idiot.

Connor gave her hand a squeeze. "Does he know what a great daughter he has?"

"I'm a valuable asset to his political team. I hear that all the time." But did she hear it from her father or from his staff? And did it matter? Being a valuable asset was not the same thing as being loved.

He was about to comment on exactly that when she changed the subject. "So, will you come stay at my father's place? I know money isn't an object for you—" she held up a hand as if to ward off his protests "—but I'd feel better knowing you're not in a hotel room every weekend. Besides, I live in the guest cottage so the main house is empty. Surely you'd be more comfortable having a place of your own instead of hauling things back and forth. And—"

She broke off, seeming hesitant.

"What is it?" he asked.

"Zoe, dad's staffer, has been talking about wanting him to throw us an engagement party at the end of the season. But don't worry. I'll convince her to call it off."

"Don't." Connor had trouble keeping his dislike from his voice, but he tried, for her. "Let your dad do his worst. It's only money, right? Just don't let him serve those little wieners on sticks. Make him pay for fancy appetizers."

She grinned. "Okay. I'll let Zoe know."

"I will come stay at the house. If it'll make you feel better."

"It will," she reassured him. "This whole thing has been enough of a mess as it is. I hate the thought of being even more of an inconvenience to you."

She made the comment in an offhand manner, turning her attention to the playing field as she said it. This time she really was watching the game, relaxing into the match.

Yet her words stuck with him. He could read between the lines. Because of the circumstances of her birth, she had been inconvenient to Senator Hannon's career. But instead of finding a way to look past that, it had affected his relationship with his daughter. Instead of seeing Brittney for the bright and wonderful woman she was, he saw her as a burden, despite the fact that she'd lived her whole life seeking his approval. By her own admission, she'd done a little boundary pushing in high school. But apparently she'd quickly realized that the affections of high school boys didn't make up for a father's love—thank God for that. Some women never made that intellectual leap. Since then, she'd been a model daughter. Every decision—personal and professional—had benefited her father's career. And the man was too much of a jerk to see it or appreciate it.

In that moment, Connor hoped he never did meet Senator Hannon. He just might punch the man.

He didn't think of himself as a violent person, but here he was, ready to coldcock someone for hurting Brittney. Again. First he'd been ready to trample some reporter, and now her father.

Where had these protective instincts come from? And what was it about her that stirred them up so easily?

Seven

The few remaining weeks of the polo season passed in a blur of social events. Even though she'd spent every summer in the Hamptons since she was a child, she'd never before been so busy. Connor was by her side the whole time, but she was rarely alone with him. And though he flirted outrageously with her, he never again pressed her to revisit the physical side of their relationship. But she knew she was in trouble. She was starting to fall for him. Her only consolation was in knowing that the summer would soon be over and her life would return to normal.

Before she knew it, the date of her engagement party had arrived. Decorators and caterers hired by her father's staff descended on the house three days before the party. During what would be the last few days of their relationship, she barely saw Connor at all. Which was probably for the best. What could come of it? Either she'd break down and beg him to make love to her one last time, or she'd do something really stupid like tell him she was falling in love with him.

On the night of the party, Brittney moved through the crowd with practiced ease. A lifetime of experience pretending to be the perfect senator's daughter was serving her well. No one watching her would sense how conflicted she felt.

From the first awkward introduction to her father and onward, Connor was by her side throughout the first part of the evening. If Connor felt any apprehension about meeting him, he didn't show it. His presence alleviated the strain between her and her father, those quiet, clumsy moments when neither of them knew what to say to the other. Connor's hand was warm and strong at her back.

And once her father left to talk to people he thought more important, Connor stayed by her side as she chatted with other guests, his charm smoothing over awkward silences, his wit providing answers to questions she couldn't anticipate.

Under other circumstances, she might have been unnerved by how easily he lied, but for now she was just grateful.

"Where did you meet?" people inevitably asked.

"Standing in line, waiting to pick up takeout at Brit's favourite Thai place. What's the name of the place, honey?"

"Topaz Thai," she'd mumble awkwardly.

"How long have you been together?" other people prodded.

"Almost three months now," he lied smoothly. "At first it was tough keeping our relationship secret. But I didn't want Brit to worry about the stress of dating in the public eye. So we managed it." Then he smiled ruefully, giving her shoulder a subtle squeeze. "Until we got caught."

Eventually, someone was bold enough to look pointedly at the bare ring finger of her left hand. "I do hope you're not going to be one of those modern couples who don't bother to have a ceremony in a church or even wear rings."

Connor just smiled at the nosy old biddy who made that comment. "No, ma'am," he said. "I'm having a ring made. I wanted Brit to wear my grandmother's ring. But I'm from a simple, working-class family. I knew Brit would love any ring I gave her, but I wanted her to be proud to wear it." He gave her shoulder a squeeze for effect. "So I'm having a small diamond and lapis stones taken out and replaced with a larger diamond and sapphires."

By the time he finished describing the ring, the old lady had tears in her eyes. She wasn't the only one. Brittney had to excuse herself before she welled up like an idiot.

Alone, with her back propped against the bathroom door, she wiped furiously at her tears. Why was she crying over a ring she wasn't ever going to get? The ring wasn't real. It was just a story meant to placate curious busybodies. That guy who had carefully designed and crafted that ring to give to his fiancée? He wasn't any more real than the ring.

Oh, but more and more she wished he were. She wished Connor were not just handsome and charming, but sincere as well. What would it be like to be loved by that man, and not just seduced by the playboy?

Connor was probably the first fiancé in the history of the world to hope for a if-you-hurt-my-little-girl-I'll-kill-you speech. When Senator Hannon angled to talk to Connor alone for a few minutes midway through the party, Connor actually hoped that's what he was in for. Until now, the senator had been blasé about their engagement. Connor knew her father's disinterest hurt Brittney's feelings. Why couldn't the guy at least feign concern?

But when the senator lead Connor from the party to the relative quiet of his study, Connor quickly realized that this meeting wasn't going to involve any protective speeches.

Senator Hannon poured Connor a Scotch and handed it

over, saying, "As you've probably realized, my daughter can be a bit strong-willed."

Connor said nothing but clenched the tumbler of Scotch in his hand. The senator's asinine opinions weren't Connor's problem to deal with. In a few short days, they'd be back in the city. A few weeks after that, as he and Brittney had agreed, they'd quietly end their engagement. He'd never have to see Senator Hannon again.

The fact that he'd never see Brittney again either was a matter he'd been studiously not thinking about.

"I suppose," the senator continued as he sat down behind the desk, "her intentions are good enough, but she has a tendency get the press riled up." He chuckled. "As I'm sure you've seen."

Connor nodded noncommittally, resisting the urge to point out that if it hadn't been for the senator's own indiscretions years ago, no one would care what Brittney did.

The senator cleared his throat. "The point is, it's an election year and I'd appreciate it if you would do what you can to keep her from making any more social gaffes in the next couple of months."

Connor was torn between wanting to laugh at the irony and wanting to beat the guy to a pulp. He settled for plunking the untouched glass of Scotch down on the senator's desk, propping his hands on the blotter and leaning forward.

"With all due respect, Senator, you're an idiot. If you cared half as much about your daughter as she does about your career, you'd be a better man. But since you don't, let me tell you a few things about her. She would never consciously do anything to hurt your career." He leaned ever closer, so the senator had to rock back in his chair. "And when we're married, I'd appreciate it if you'd do what you can to stay out of our lives."

And with that, Connor turned and walked away, leaving

the senator alone in stunned silence. It wasn't until he was back in the bustle of the party that he realized what he'd done. He'd spoken to Brittney's father as if they really were getting married. For a few minutes, he'd completely forgotten that their relationship was a lie. And that their ruse was about to come to an end.

After hours of mingling, smiling and bearing the painful congratulations of strangers, Brittney grabbed a glass of wine and found a quiet corner of the patio where she could recuperate.

She spotted Vanessa and Nicolas sneaking back toward the party from the formal gardens. There were spots throughout the gardens where an amorous couple could seize a few moments alone. It looked as though maybe Vanessa and Nicolas had done just that. Brittney had suspected they might be involved again several weeks ago, but his recent declaration at the polo match left no one in doubt of their relationship. The normally cool and reserved Nicolas had ridden up to Vanessa on his favorite horse, Maximo, and announced before God and everyone that he loved her. The act was all the more romantic because he was normally so cool and reserved. His grand gesture had melted the heart of every female there.

Until that moment, Brittney had doubted that the vivacious Vanessa could find happiness with such a man, but his actions that day had removed all of Brittney's doubts. And Vanessa's too, it seemed.

Brittney was thrilled for Vanessa's obvious contentment. But a little jealous, as well. It seemed as though everyone was destined to find love this summer, except Brittney.

Though, if she were honest with herself, that was not entirely true. She had found love. It just hadn't found her.

As Vanessa and Nicolas approached her hiding place, they paused. Nicolas bent down as Vanessa rose onto her toes.

At first Brittney feared she'd caught them about to kiss. But after a moment, she realized they were whispering. Nicolas reached up to twirl a lock of Vanessa's hair around his finger. Somehow the gesture was even more intimate than a kiss would have been.

Her cheeks burning, Brittney turned away and crept back to the house. They were too involved in one another to notice.

She snuck back into the party, painfully aware of her heated cheeks and thundering heart. The intimacy between Vanessa and Nicolas had unnerved her. It was true intimacy, of spirit and heart, not just body. The whispered moment between them was packed with more emotion than any passionate embrace.

Pressing the back of her hand to her cheek, she scanned the perimeter of the room for a tray where she could drop her empty glass. She barely noticed the man in front of her before she nearly walked into him.

"Hey, if it isn't the lucky lady herself." The man gave her arm a jovial, "'atta-girl" slap.

Try as she might, she couldn't suppress her cringe. He didn't notice anyway. Giving her arm a quick rub to take the sting out, she appraised him. Mid-thirties, manufactured smile, designer suit, hair meticulously styled to disguise the fact that it was thinning. He looked familiar, but if she had to guess, it was because he looked like half the men in New York, not because she actually knew him.

"Excuse me for asking, but have we met?" she asked as politely as she could.

"No," he slurred. "But I know you. In fact, I take credit for all of this." He waved a hand at the party taking place.

"Oh, then you must be John from the catering company." She extended her hand.

As the man shook her hand, he leaned in close. "No, I'm not a caterer." He laughed like the idea was hysterical. Then, still holding her hand, he winked and gave her a little toast with his glass. "For you and Connor."

"I'm sorry." She tugged at her hand, trying to get him to release it. "I don't understand."

"That night at the bar. You two never would have met if I hadn't bet Connor he couldn't get you into bed."

Connor watched from across a sea of people as Tim struck up a conversation with Brittney. Even from this distance, he could tell Tim had been drinking too much. Tim always got chummy when he was soused, slapping people on the arm and laughing with glee. His mouth sometimes got him into trouble when he was sober. Put a couple of drinks in him, and it was a disaster.

This was not a guy Connor wanted talking to Brittney.

He quickly excused himself from the conversation on trade restrictions he'd gotten suckered into with a colleague of Brittney's father. As he wended his way through the crowd, he kept an eye on her. Her expression drifted from confused to offended. She had the grace and good breeding to hide her feelings generally—Tim must have said something bad for offense to register on her face.

Connor picked up the pace as he elbowed past a giggling socialite. He walked up behind Brittney just in time to hear Tim saying, "You two never would have met if I hadn't bet Connor he couldn't get you into bed."

Before Tim even finished the sentence, Connor put his hand on Brittney's back. She flinched at his touch, jerking back to look up him. Her brow was furrowed as she looked from Connor to Tim and back again.

"Is he…" she began, but seemed unable to finish the sentence.

Connor managed a smile and said, "Tim, what kind of lies are you telling my fiancée about me?"

He reached out to shake Tim's hand in greeting while keeping his other hand firmly and possessively on Brittney's back, hoping that she'd read his sincerity in his touch.

"No, man," Tim said, giving Connor's hand an overly firm shake. "No lies. That was what, six or seven weeks ago, right? We were all at that jazz bar. You hit on Brittney."

Tim's voice started to rise with his insistence, and people nearby were turning to look as they couldn't help but overhear his drunken words. Connor could feel the tension growing in Brittney. Under his hand, her muscles had turned to rock and her posture was stick straight.

"She shot you down," Tim continued. "I tried to tell you she was out of your league, but you were determined to try again. Remember? I told you about the profile in that magazine. What's the name of that thing? The Profiler or something, right? That's when you bet me you'd get her into bed before the end of summer."

Tim paused to smile lewdly at Brittney. "So see, if it weren't for me, you two never would have gotten engaged." Tim gave Connor a whack on the arm. "Who knew this hound dog would ever settle down. Am I right?"

Connor forced another smile. "You're mistaken, buddy," he said to Tim in a voice just loud enough for others to overhear. He pulled Brittney tight against his side and dropped a kiss onto her forehead. "Six weeks ago, Brittney and I had already been dating for a couple of months. But we were still keeping our relationship a secret. I pretended to hit on her to have an excuse to say hello." Connor looked down at Brittney. Her expression was fixed, like she was trying to process too much information too quickly. "Isn't that right, honey?"

He gave her arm another squeeze, and after a second she nodded and smiled like the experienced navigator of social gaffes that she was. "Absolutely."

Tim looked first at Connor and then at Brittney. He was far

too slow to keep up. He looked like he wanted to argue, but Connor didn't give him a chance. Instead he gently steered the conversation around to Tim's work before making their excuses and maneuvering Brittney away.

Connor may have talked his way around Tim's confusion, but Brittney wouldn't be nearly so easy to manage. He could practically hear her thinking, figuring her way through the nonsense of Tim's rambling to the truth of that fateful conversation back at the beginning of the summer.

You wouldn't know it to look at her, though. As they moved through the crowd, she smiled with the ease that seemed second nature to her. And that made Connor very nervous.

She had the ability to conceal her distress so thoroughly that you could barely see any sign of it. But it was the defense mechanism she used when she was the most upset.

He'd rarely seen her this poised and smooth.

When he spotted the door to the butler's pantry, he steered her toward it. He didn't want her to have time to let Tim's words sink in and simmer.

The second the door closed behind them and they were alone, she shrugged off his touch.

"Brittney—" he began, but she held up a hand warding off his entreaty.

The butler's pantry was a long and narrow room connecting the main room to the kitchen. Glass-front cabinets lined both walls. Bottles of wine and empty glasses littered the soapstone countertops. Obviously the staff had been using the butler's pantry for its intended purpose, as a staging ground for the waiters distributing drinks and appetizers to the crowd. Which meant he wouldn't have long to explain before they were interrupted. He'd have to talk fast.

"I don't want to hear any more lies." She shivered, as if she was shedding something unpleasant. When she turned to face him, she had her arms wrapped around her waist.

"It's not how Tim made it sound."

"What, it's not like you saw me in a bar and decided to pick me up? It's not like you followed me out to the Hamptons to seduce me?" Her voice was tinged with bitterness. "Because, actually, it is like that. And I even knew it."

"Brittney," he reached a hand out to her, but even in the tight quarters, she managed to dodge his touch. "Tim made it sound like it was all just a bet. It wasn't."

"Yeah, well, it wasn't like you made it sound either. Like he was the ignorant rube in our little lover's game." She rolled her eyes. "God, you're so good at that."

"At what?"

"At making people believe what you want them to." Finally she met his gaze. "That's what makes you so dangerous."

The resolve he saw in her eyes sent a splash of icy dread over him. "You can't let what Tim said upset you. He's drunk and, well, kind of an idiot under the best of circumstances. And he's not remembering the way things really happened."

She let loose a bark of laughter. "Whatever gaps there may be in his memory, I can guarantee his version of that night is closer to the truth than the lies you just spun. That charming story about how we were keeping our relationship a secret? The way you only pretended to hit on me just to say hello?" She nodded in mock appreciation. "That's good stuff. Let's be sure to save that story for our grandchildren."

"Brittney—"

"Oh, wait. We're not going to have grandchildren. Because we're not really engaged. Nor are we really in love."

Connor heard a waiter reaching for the door behind him. With one hand, he grabbed the doorknob, holding the door shut. He reached for her again and caught her hand in his. Her fingers felt unnaturally cold, as if she were going into shock.

"Let's talk about this," he said. "Let me explain."

"What is there to explain? I know what happened. Don't get me wrong, I like the fairy tale, but I don't believe in it."

She gave her hand a tug, but he wouldn't let her go. Behind him, he could feel the waiter on the other side of the door struggling, but Connor kept his hand firmly on the knob, unwilling to have their conversation interrupted.

"You're upset. I'm not letting you leave like this."

She met his gaze again, slowly shaking her head. "It's okay. Really, it is." Again she tugged on her hand. Again he didn't loosen his hold on her. "The thing is, Connor, I—" Her voice broke and she swallowed back tears before continuing. "I think I really was starting to fall in love with you. I'd gotten so caught up in playing the role, I forgot it wasn't real. But the truth is, I hardly know you. All I know is this fantasy you've created, this persona of the perfect fiancé you've been playing for the past six weeks. Tim didn't tell me anything I didn't know. He just reminded me of reality."

Her gaze was so raw and pained, Connor could hardly stand to look her in the eyes. But he made himself. He'd done this to her. As proud as she was, as strong, as resilient—after all the things he'd done to try to protect her this summer—here he was, the one to break her.

"I know we agreed to break things off once we returned to the city, but I don't think I can wait that long. I can't pretend anymore. And I don't want to risk forgetting again."

Behind him, the waiter called out, "Hey, is there someone in there? I don't think anyone's supposed to be back there."

"Give us a minute," Connor ordered.

"No, it's okay," Brittney said quietly. "We're done here."

The waiter gave the knob one last violent turn, wrenching the door open. Brittney pulled her hand free and left through the door on the far side of the pantry.

She'd slipped right through his fingers.

Eight

Brittney received an unprecedented number of calls and e-mails during the days following her return to the city. Most were from people she hadn't had a chance to talk to during the party, wishing her congratulations. Some were from people who had noticed her early disappearance and who wanted to make sure she was all right—or to cash in on the gossip if she wasn't. A few were from people who seemed to be genuinely concerned. The only call she returned was Vanessa's. But she didn't have the heart to tell her friend what had happened, finding she couldn't put into words how quickly her well-ordered life had fallen apart.

The one person whom she hoped might call was Connor. For six weeks he'd been constantly by her side, defending her any time someone so much as spoke to her in a suggestive tone. But now, when she could use a shoulder to cry on, he was gone. Of course, he couldn't protect her from himself.

She stayed at home, working long hours on her father's Web

site, catching up on the work that hadn't gotten done over the summer. Almost an entire week went by without her seeing anyone other than the delivery guy from Topaz Thai. Finally, the Monday after she returned to the city, Vanessa came by and dragged her out for a lunch. While it was good to be in the company of another person, she hated how careful Vanessa seemed.

Brittney never thought of herself as a frail person. She didn't need coddling. Maybe it was being in the company of Vanessa—or maybe she simply felt more vulnerable than normal—but she found herself opening up and telling her the truth.

The two women sat across from each other in a little café just down the street from Brittney's condo, drinking coffee. Brittney poked morosely at the bright pink topping of her raspberry yogurt parfait.

"I should look on the bright side," she finally said. "I only fell a little bit in love with him."

Brittney nibbled on the tip of the spoon. She looked across the table at Vanessa only when she realized Vanessa had said nothing in response. She had an odd expression on her face— half wince, half cringe.

"What?" Brittney asked.

"Nothing," Vanessa said too quickly.

"No, it's not nothing. You looked like you wanted to say something."

"It's just—" Vanessa set down her spoon and leaned forward "—I don't think you can fall only a little bit in love."

"Of course you can fall only a little bit in love. My roommate in college did it all the time."

"Yes, of course *people* can. I meant I'm not sure *you* can."

"What are you saying? You think I'm defective?"

"No." Vanessa patted Brittney on the back of the hand. "I

just think maybe you're an all-or-nothing kind of girl." Then she paused and tilted her head to the side, considering. "What you said, about Connor doing all of this just because he felt guilty about that stupid bet? I don't buy it."

"Vanessa, he—"

"Because I swear, the way he looks at you sometimes, it reminds me of…" Vanessa shook her head, her expression pensive.

"Of what?"

"Well, of the way Nicolas looks at me."

Brittney nearly snorted with disbelief. "I've seen the way Nicolas looks at you. It's steamy, with intense possessiveness."

"Exactly!" Vanessa pointed her spoon at Brittney emphatically.

"I think new love is coloring your perspective. What you're imagining is love on Connor's part is merely…I don't know, indigestion or something." She smiled at the look on Vanessa's face. "But thank you for imagining he could be in love with me. You're a good friend."

Vanessa gave Brittney a wink. "I am, aren't I?"

Brittney couldn't help but laugh. She left their lunch feeling better.

On her way home, she thought about what Vanessa had said about her not being able to fall in love only a little bit. What if Vanessa were right? What if she'd fallen in love with a man who could never love her back? Being with Connor had unleashed a passionate side she'd always kept under tight control. What would happen to that part of her now that Connor wasn't in her life? Would she ever find another man with whom she felt so comfortable? And who stirred her emotions and her senses?

Later that night, she was contemplating that very depressing possibility while she waited for her takeout to be delivered.

Her bell rang and she buzzed the delivery guy in, ready for another night of Topaz Thai. But when she opened her door, she didn't find a guy with coconut soup.

Instead, she found Connor.

His appearance startled her. He'd never been less than impeccably dressed, even when dressed casually for the matches. Today he wore faded jeans and a plain white oxford shirt left untucked. He stood with his shoulder propped against the wall and his hands shoved deep into his pockets. His hair was messy, his face lined with exhaustion. He looked as if he hadn't slept in a week. In short, he looked as exhausted as she felt.

He didn't greet her, pushing his way into her apartment before she could protest. "I'm not giving you up," he announced.

She blinked. "You're what?"

"Not giving you up." With each word, he stalked a step closer to her. It wasn't long before he'd closed the distance between them. He wrapped a hand around her upper arm, keeping her from retreating. "I know this started out as just a ruse, but we're good together." His thumb circled the skin on the inside of her arm.

He did that kind of thing all the time, touching her so casually. It drove her to distraction, and she'd always assumed that was his intention. Now, watching him, she wondered if perhaps instead of a calculated enticement, the habit was more of a compulsion, as if he couldn't keep his hands off her, just as he'd told the reporters.

The idea that he might simply need to touch her was a tempting one. Too tempting. She couldn't let herself fall into that trap.

Pulling her arm away from his touch, she put some distance between them. "I'm sorry, Connor. I don't care how good we are in bed. I can't base a relationship on a single sexual experience. Sure, we could draw out this fake engagement for another six months or a year, but eventually, this will end. And no matter how or when that happens, it's going to be bad for me. At least if I end it now, I have some hope of getting over you."

He studied her features, his expression intense. Serious, in a way she'd never seen before. "What if it doesn't end? What if I don't want you to get over me?"

Her breath caught in her chest. "What are saying?"

"We make it real. We stay together. We make it work."

She backed up a step, sinking onto her sofa when it bumped against her legs. Her heart pounded as she considered his proposal.

That's what it was—a proposal. Probably the least romantic proposal she'd ever heard, but a proposal nevertheless. Funny, the complete lack of artifice almost won her over. Normally he was so smooth, so charming. Did this bare-bones proposal stem from genuine emotion?

And then she remembered what the last six weeks had been like. Watching him charm everyone he came in contact with. Listening to him tell lies so smoothly. Never knowing which Connor was the real Connor. Could she live like that for the rest of her life?

Shaking her head, she said, "No. I can't do it. Vanessa told me she thought I was an all-or-nothing kind of girl. That once I fell in love, it would be forever. I think she's probably right. I don't want to be in love with you forever."

He flinched as if she'd hauled back and punched him in the gut. Then, in an instant, his expression settled into quiet resolve, his jaw clenched. He turned to leave. "Okay."

If she hadn't been watching so closely, she would have missed the flash of pain completely. But she had seen it on his face, and she couldn't let him go without explaining.

She leaped to her feet and grabbed his arm before he made it to the door. "Let me explain."

He studied her, his expression cold and distant. "You were very succinct. No explanation is necessary."

"Connor, it's not that I don't *want* to love you. It's that I'm afraid to." She searched his face for understanding. When she didn't see any, she kept talking. "I've watched you this summer. You're a total chameleon, capable of being anything to anybody. I'd never know how you really felt about me."

"That's all?" he asked. "You're afraid I don't love you?"

She pulled her hand away. "Trust me. That's enough. I've spent my whole life never knowing whether or not my father loves me or if I was just a mistake he had to twist to his political advantage. I don't think I could stand not knowing if you—"

He wrapped his arms around her and cut off her explanation with a kiss. It was a breath-stealing, soul-searing kiss she felt down to her very bones, like he was pouring a lifetime's worth of reassurances into that one gesture.

When he pulled back, he said, "If you want to know how I feel about you, all you have to do is ask. You make me crazy. You terrify me. You make me do things I never thought I'd do."

"Is this bad or good?" she asked hesitantly.

"Good." He laughed an all-out laugh. "I've never felt this way about anyone else. There's no one else who knows me the way you do. And I have never lied to you."

"The bet—"

"Forget the bet. It was never about that for me. I would have pursued you hard, no matter what. Do you want to know why?"

She could only nod.

"I knew from the minute I met you that I was in serious trouble. I kept telling myself if I spent enough time with you,

I'd get over it. That I'd get over *you*. I didn't realize until the engagement party that I didn't want to get over you."

She frowned. "The engagement party? Then why—"

"Did I take so long to come talk to you? Because I wanted to do it right. I was having this made." He reached into his back pocket and pulled out a small black jewelry box.

Flipping it open with his thumb, he went down on one knee. "Brittney Hannon, will you marry me?"

Brittney gasped. It was the ring he'd described to the older woman. A platinum filigree ring, with a single large diamond in the center and tiny sapphires on each side.

"I'm tired of doing things halfway, Brit. If you're an all-or-nothing girl, then I want to be your all-or-nothing guy." He stood and reached for her, cupping her face in his hands, his thumbs resting along her cheeks. "You said that you were already a little in love with me. Well, then you're slower than I am, because I'm more than a little in love with you. But I'm not worried. I figure a little in love is a start. And I'm not going anywhere. If I stick around long enough, you're bound to fall even more in love with me. I can wait."

As he spoke, something tightened deep in her chest, making her feel like she couldn't breath. Like his words were wrapping themselves around her very heart and giving it a squeeze.

All her life, she'd never had anyone who was always there for her. She'd never had anyone whose love she could count one. Not her mother who'd so quickly abandoned her. Not even her father, who'd always been there, but not there. And now there was Connor, promising her a lifetime.

"Do you mean that?"

He leaned down and kissed her. Slowly, gently. When he finally lifted his head, all her doubts were gone. Of course, he'd always been a persuasive kisser.

Just in case his kiss alone wasn't enough to convince her, he said, "I do mean that. I'm not going anywhere. I'm going to be right here beside you until you believe me or fall so in love with me that you don't care."

The smile she could no longer contain broke across her face. "Are you really going to make me wait that long? Because I'm ready now."

He took her in his arms and kissed her deeply. Unlike his earlier gentle kisses, this one was tinged with the heat that had marked their first kisses. There was nothing soul-soothing or careful about him. Instead it was fierce and possessive, hungry and joyful all at the same time.

Before she knew it, his fingers had worked free the buttons of her blouse and his mouth had nudged it off her shoulder. "Thank goodness," he muttered against her skin. "Feels like I've been waiting forever to touch you again." His hands reached down to cup her bottom. He lifted her against him, and she instinctively wrapped her legs around his waist. "Please tell me I'm not going to have to debate abstinence for another hour before you'll let me touch you."

She threw her head back and laughed. "Let's talk about it in the bedroom."

With one arm supporting her weight and the other across her back, he had carried her a few steps towards her bedroom when the doorbell rang.

He quirked his eyebrow.

"Takeout, from Topaz Thai."

Connor nodded. "He can wait. I can't."

Which was just fine with Brittney. She'd been waiting for Connor her whole life.

Epilogue

Brittney Stone walked into the VIP tent of the 2011 Clearwater Media Polo tournament with her husband's hand possessively resting on the small of her back. Though her father had pushed for a big summer wedding, she and Connor had decided to have a quiet ceremony in the early spring, right on the shore of Long Pond, surrounded by the crocus blooms. Their wedding was everything she could have hoped for. Small, unpretentious and lacking the drama and scandal that had marked their early courtship. It had been a day filled with happiness and laughter.

Since returning from their honeymoon to Costa Rica, they'd been living quietly in the city. This was their first big social event as a married couple.

In the tent, she caught Vanessa's and Nicolas's eyes. The married couple waved them over enthusiastically. Brittney smiled at the sight of tiny baby Gabriella propped on Vanessa's hip. Vanessa and Nicolas had married at the end of the previous year's polo season. As they approached their first anniversary, they looked as happy as ever.

Vanessa gave Brittney a quick buss on the cheek. "Marriage must agree with you. You look fabulous."

"You, too." Brittney leaned back to give her friend an assessing stare while Nicolas greeted Connor. Nicolas and Vanessa had been traveling so much following the polo circuit, it seemed ages since Brittney had seen them. Now, she could only chuckle. "How you manage to still wear your signature white while carrying around a baby, I'll never know."

Vanessa laughed, then leaned forward and whispered, "The baby is actually the trick. She's so cute no one notices me."

"May I?" Brittney asked, with a nod toward Gabriella.

"Sure." Vanessa carefully handed the baby over to Brittney.

Holding her sturdy little body close to her chest, Brittney felt something inside her melt into goo. Gabriella swung out a chubby fist to grab a lock of Brittney's hair. Gabriella had her father's soulful eyes and her mother's sassy smile. In short, she was perfect. Even better, she was obviously surrounded by a loving family.

On the way into the tent, Brittney and Connor had run into the other members of the Hughes family. Christian, who was now semiretired and well on the road to recovery, had been holding his other grandchild, Christian Fitzgerald Hughes, showing him the polo ponies. Julia and Sebastian, who were hosting the event again this season, were near the entrance mingling with guests. Julia was clearly flourishing as the new VP of PR for Clearwater, and the expression on Sebastian's face showed just how proud he was of his wife. It was obvious to anyone who saw them that although they worked together, there was nothing businesslike about their relationship.

The Hugheses stood talking to Sheikh Adham and Sabrina, who had returned to the Hamptons to celebrate their first anniversary. Brittney had heard through the grapevine about the success of Grant Vineyards and Winery and of Adham's horse farm. More than just their businesses were flourishing. Sabrina all but glowed as she ran a hand along the top of her heavy belly. Though she looked ready to give birth any day now, it obviously hadn't slowed her down.

Since Adham's mother, younger sister and older brother had accompanied them to the States to attend the birth of the latest addition to their royal family, Sabrina was surrounded by the love of a close-knit family. Even the king pledged he'd fly over the moment she went into labor. It was obvious to anyone watching the couple together that the love affair that had blossomed between Sabrina and her desert prince during the previous season was blazing brighter every day. They were regularly providing the polo community and the paparazzi with more sensational instances of spontaneous passion.

The sheikh's family wasn't the only royalty in attendance, since the VIP tent held its share of Hollywood royalty as well. Matthew and Carmen Birmingham returned to the Hamptons this summer with their three-month-old twin sons. Everyone was convinced the little darlings were conceived the year before at the Hamptons since the couple spent a lot of time behind closed doors, and when they were seen at a polo match you could clearly see the love shining between them. Even though it was only summer and awards season was months away, Hollywood gossip was already touting the Birminghams' documentary film on the history of the Statue of Liberty as shoo-in for an Academy Award for Best Documentary Feature.

As Vanessa and Nicolas and Gabriella moved on to greet the Birminghams—and no doubt compare baby stories—Connor led Brittney over to Richard Wells and Catherine Lawson. Connor knew Richard from the city, and they'd run into the other couple socially a few times. The men immediately launched into a discussion about the polo team's season. Brittany gave Catherine a brief hug.

"You got our RSVP for the wedding, right?" she asked.

Catherine nodded. "They've been flooding in, but I definitely remember seeing yours."

Richard and Catherine had planned their wedding for the end of the season. Catherine had confided that she and Richard had both wanted to take the time to get to know each other better before the wedding. It was certainly an approach Brittney could appreciate, though it was obvious how much they adored each other.

"How's the riding school going?" Brittney asked.

Catherine's face split into a grin. "Huge success! We have plenty of students and we're making real gains with the underprivileged kids who are being sponsored to attend on weekends. Spring camp was a success, and the summer camp looks to be even better. Thanks for sponsoring some of the kids."

"It's the least I can do," Brittney said. "Just let us know when we can help again."

Catherine positively beamed. "I'm so blessed to have friends like you to support the school. In less than a year, I've gone from just dreams to a reality that's better than I could have imagined."

But Brittney knew, watching Catherine's expression, that the real blessing was Richard, whose financial guidance at the school was just the tip of the iceberg.

Richard had also succeeded in tracking down the polo team owner/patron who set Catherine's father up in a horse-doping scandal thirteen years ago. The patron's assets and horses had been seized, and he was being held in custody while under further investigation by the authorities. He looked to be facing a long time in jail for that and other illegal activities. None of that would bring Catherine's father back, but she seemed to feel he had been vindicated and his name had been publicly cleared of all scandal. Now, Brittney couldn't help noticing how happy Catherine looked. She was obviously looking forward to the next stage in her life with a light and happy heart and knew that with Richard by her side she could do and achieve anything.

After chatting a few minutes longer, Brittney and Connor headed out to the bleachers in hopes of catching a little of the match. Besides, although the social scene was fun, Brittney really just wanted to be alone with her husband.

Now, just a few months into their marriage, all her initial doubts about Connor had faded. Their love no longer felt fragile and new. He'd been true to his word. He'd shown her how much he loved her every day, in a million tiny ways. And in many not-so-little ways, she thought with a grin as her hand drifted over her belly.

She didn't know if she was pregnant—it was too soon for that—but she had hopes, and she had a husband who would be by her side no matter what. What more could a woman ask for?

* * * * *

Book of the Month

MODERN

MAISEY YATES
The Highest Price to Pay

BOOK
OF THE
MONTH

We love this book because...

Maisey Yates has an incredible talent for writing intense, emotional romance with a sexy, sassy edge. In *The Highest Price to Pay*, she creates a world of high fashion and even higher stakes!

On sale 15th July

MILLS & BOON

Visit us Online

Find out more at
www.millsandboon.co.uk/BOTM

0711/BOTM

Special Offers

Every month we put together collections and longer reads written by your favourite authors.

Here are some of next month's highlights— don't miss our fabulous discount online!

On sale 15th July   On sale 15th July   On sale 5th August

 *Save 20% on all Special Releases*

Find out more at
www.millsandboon.co.uk/specialreleases

 Visit us Online

0711/ST/MB346

New Voices is back!

New Voices
returns on
13th September 2011!

For sneak previews and exclusives:

 Like us on facebook.com/romancehq

Follow us on twitter.com/MillsandBoonUK

Last year your votes helped Leah Ashton win New Voices 2010 with her fabulous story *Secrets & Speed Dating*!

Who will you be voting for this year?

Visit us Online | Find out more at
www.romanceisnotdead.com

NEW_VOICES

Special Offers
Bestselling Stars Collection

A stunning collection of passion and glamour from your favourite bestselling authors of international romance

Lynne Graham
Passion

On sale 20th May

Sandra Marton
Pleasure

On sale 17th June

Miranda Lee
Seduction

On sale 15th July

Carole Mortimer
Fascination

On sale 19th August

Sharon Kendrick
Satisfaction

On sale 16th September

Carol Marinelli
Celebration

On sale 21st October

Save 20% on Special Releases Collections

Find out more at
www.millsandboon.co.uk/specialreleases

Visit us
Online

0611/10/MB342

BAD BLOOD

A POWERFUL
DYNASTY,
WHERE SECRETS
AND SCANDAL
NEVER SLEEP!

VOLUME 1 – 15th April 2011
TORTURED RAKE
by Sarah Morgan

VOLUME 2 – 6th May 2011
SHAMELESS PLAYBOY
by Caitlin Crews

VOLUME 3 – 20th May 2011
RESTLESS BILLIONAIRE
by Abby Green

VOLUME 4 – 3rd June 2011
FEARLESS MAVERICK
by Robyn Grady

8 VOLUMES IN ALL TO COLLECT!

MILLS & BOON

www.millsandboon.co.uk

BAD BLOOD

A POWERFUL
DYNASTY,
WHERE SECRETS
AND SCANDAL
NEVER SLEEP!

VOLUME 5 – 17th June 2011
HEARTLESS REBEL
by Lynn Raye Harris

VOLUME 6 – 1st July 2011
ILLEGITIMATE TYCOON
by Janette Kenny

VOLUME 7 – 15th July 2011
FORGOTTEN DAUGHTER
by Jennie Lucas

VOLUME 8 – 5th August 2011
LONE WOLFE
by Kate Hewitt

8 VOLUMES IN ALL TO COLLECT!

www.millsandboon.co.uk

0711/06

There's Something About a Rebel...
by Anne Oliver

Why does sexy, brooding Blake Everett have to come back into Lissa's life when she's at a low point? Yet there's something about this rebel—he's irresistible!

The Crown Affair
by Lucy King

Laura spent an amazing night with the gorgeous stranger next door before starting a job on a Mediterranean island. But the island's new king is Laura's guy-next-door! Crown affairs have never been so hot...

Swept Off Her Stilettos
by Fiona Harper

Coreen Fraser's film-star style gives her any man she wants! Adam is the only man who knows the girl underneath the skyscraper heels. Is she brave enough to go barefoot?

Mr Right There All Along
by Jackie Braun

Chloe McDaniels has always depended on Simon Ford, even while he makes her heart flutter! But now Simon plans to show Chloe that love is worth the risk...

On sale from 5th August 2011
Don't miss out!

*Available at WHSmith, Tesco, ASDA, Eason
and all good bookshops*

www.millsandboon.co.uk

WEB/M&B/RTL3

Discover Pure Reading Pleasure with

MILLS &
BOON

**Visit the Mills & Boon website for all
the latest in romance**

Buy all the latest
releases, backlist
and eBooks

Find out more
about our authors
and their books

Join our community
and chat to authors
and other readers

Free online reads
from your favourite
authors

Win with our
fantastic online
competitions

Sign up for our
free monthly
eNewsletter

Tell us what you
think by signing up to
our reader panel

Rate and review
books with our star
system

www.millsandboon.co.uk

 Follow us at twitter.com/millsandboonuk

 Become a fan at facebook.com/romancehq